FINDING PLUCK

by

Peter Difatta

Finding Pluck

Pembroke Publications
1031 First St. S. 804
Jacksonville Beach, FL

PembrokePublicationsLLC@gmail.com

This book has been laid out for the printed version and the ebook version using Apple Pages. Type fonts used are Iowan Old Style, Mona Lisa Solid ITC TT, Underwood Champion created by Vic Fieger and Underwood Champion created by Richard Polt.

Book cover based on photo of Polk Place at the University of North Carolina at Chapel Hill. Permission of use granted by the North Carolina Collection, University of North Carolina at Chapel Hill Library.

Cover artwork and design by Marlene S. Piskin

ISBN-13: 978-0692375235

Chapter 1

Congratulations

"Taylor," his dad shouted from the kitchen, "go get your mother. Let's eat!"

Taylor Hanes was watching television, a mindless show reporting on the latest activities of pop stars. And he didn't want to be bothered. It wasn't so much that he was reluctant to leave the television; it was more that he didn't want to have to deal with his mother.

In 1989, as Taylor was starting middle school, his mother began a mental downward spiral, and Taylor was pained to see it happen. His mother was one of the rare people to develop early-onset Alzheimer's disease; she had been diagnosed at the age of thirty-four. She had deteriorated steadily and was continuing to do so.

Taylor reluctantly clicked off the television and dragged himself to her bedroom. He stopped at the doorway and looked in. She was sitting straight up in a chair, looking serenely out the window. The sun was setting; streams of light filtered through the trees and cast shadows against one wall. Taylor stared at her, looking at the remnants of his mother, once a vibrant, active, cheerful woman, now just a stiff, lifeless image. The only movement in the room was from small dust particles floating in the streaks of sunlight. The calmness of the scene unnerved Taylor. It reminded him of Tartan, his small hometown where he was living and going to school, a place he thought was backward and stuck in the Dark Ages with nothing going on and nothing to do. And it reminded him how badly he wanted to get away.

As he looked in, she seemed so much older now than when he had last noticed. When he compared his dad, who was only a few months younger, to his mom, there seemed a significant difference. His dad was trim and athletic, with a lot of energy, and looked younger than his age of forty. He owned a car repair business; between his daily activities at work and running occasionally on weekends, he managed to stay in shape. Previously, he had pursued many outside interests, including bowling, hiking, and fishing. Now, however, because of his wife's advancing illness, he was forced to assume more household duties, including cooking, cleaning, and laundry, all of which Taylor shared. His mother, on the other hand, was headed in the opposite direction; she had already lost interest in anything physical and spent most of her recent days looking at television or staring out the window.

"Mom, Dad wants you to come for dinner." Taylor knew that at this point in her illness, most of the time she would understand what he said to her, but he also knew that could soon change. So, whenever he tried to communicate with her and she responded, inside he felt a small sense of relief.

She answered without looking toward him. "I'll be right there."

There was a pause as he waited to see if she would get up.

Then she added, "Those animals with the fluffy tails; what are they called?"

"Squirrels," he replied.

"Squirrels, yes. They are so cute, running up and down the trees." She then looked over at him. "I'm so hungry. When will lunch be ready?"

"It's dinner, Mom. It's ready right now, so let's go."

He noticed a slight moment of surprise on her face. But then she immediately got up and followed Taylor into the kitchen. His dad had just finished placing all the food on the table, and they sat down and began to eat.

After a few minutes, Taylor's dad spoke. "Have you talked to Mrs. Anderson yet about scholarship money?"

Taylor had been accepted to Carolina. However, his mother had been forced to quit teaching, and there were mounting medical bills, so his father's income alone couldn't pay for college. Disability payments and Medicare were helping greatly, but he and his dad knew that as his mom's illness progressed, there would be even bigger expenses. Additionally, his dad would have to take off increasingly more time from work to care for her, and less work meant less income.

"Yeah, at this point, Mrs. Anderson wasn't too positive," Taylor responded. "She said that, first of all, there are less scholarships based on need going around, and that with the economy, there are more people competing for them."

"Are there other kids from your school that got scholarships?" his father asked as he cut a piece of cube steak.

Taylor knew where this was going. He could have made better grades if he had pushed himself, something his dad had often mentioned. But that was the past, and now he had to live with the consequences, and there was no use talking about it.

"Sada Bertram got a four-year merit scholarship. She's the smartest in the school. I don't know of anyone else."

Mr. Hanes pressed his lips together and looked down. "Is that it, or is Mrs. Anderson still working on it?"

"She said she was still going to try to find something."

Mr. Hanes sighed. "All right. Let's hope for the best. I suppose you could go to the community college here, at least for a couple years." He looked at his wife Kathryn, who was just staring straight ahead, apparently not following the conversation.

Taylor didn't respond to his dad's mention of the community college. He wanted to go to a university and was elated at being accepted to Carolina. He wanted to exhaust all possibilities for that first.

"Mrs. Anderson did suggest that I contact one of the student aid counselors at Carolina and talk to them because they are aware of lots of other ways to get scholarships."

"Oh, yeah?" his dad responded.

"She suggested setting something up the Monday after next since it's a teachers' workday and school will be closed. I could drive up there and see what they have. She's given me the counselor's phone number to make an appointment." Taylor waited for a reaction; his dad nodded and shrugged. Taylor continued, "So, it's okay to go?"

"Sure, why not? Sounds like a good idea." Then after a pause, he added, "You don't need me to go along, do you?"

"No, no. I can handle it."

The following day, Taylor had no problem setting up an appointment. As the day of the appointment approached, he had many discussions with his dad about what to wear. Taylor wanted to go casual, but his dad thought he should "put his best foot forward" and wear a suit. Taylor thought that was too serious. They settled on khakis and a sport coat.

❀ ❀ ❀

It was the day of the meeting. In preparation, Taylor had washed his 1985 Ford Fairlane, which his father had bought, repaired, and given to him last year. Taylor arrived on campus on time, dressed in khakis and a sport coat as he and his dad had agreed. He had been coached by Mrs. Anderson on how to conduct himself. She had told him that the counselors had a lot of influence over who would be selected for scholarships, so it was important to make a good impression. After waiting fifteen minutes outside the counselor's office, the receptionist showed him in.

As Taylor entered, a tall, thin, slightly balding, fortyish man stood up from behind his desk and extended his hand, which Taylor shook.

"I'm Ed Branston."

"Taylor Hanes. Good to meet you."

"Good to meet you too. Have a seat."

Taylor and Ed both sat down as Ed reached around to grab a file. After a moment of looking at the first page, Ed spoke.

"Okay. You are here to see if we can get you some money to go to school."

"Yes, sir."

"As you know, it won't be a merit scholarship, even though your grades are not that bad." He looked through some handwritten notes and then continued. "Oh, yes, we've already reviewed your family's financial records, and—"

"Mrs. Anderson," Taylor interrupted, "wanted me to point out that some of our finances have changed and may not show up in that information."

"Who is Mrs. Anderson? Your guidance counselor?"

"Yes."

Mr. Branston shuffled some papers. "Oh, yes, here's a letter from her." There was a pause as he scanned it. "Oh, your mother is seriously ill."

"Yes, early-onset Alzheimer's. It's pretty rare."

Mr. Branston looked up at Taylor. "I'm so sorry about all of this. I can identify with you. My mother developed Alzheimer's, but she was in her seventies. This must be really hard on you and your family."

Taylor nodded. Mr. Branston then closed the file and set it down. "However, I think we should take another approach. Money for need scholarships has pretty much been used up, or it has dried up. However, there is this whole giant database of legacy scholarships that is available."

"Legacy? What's that?" Taylor asked.

"Legacy scholarships are scholarships that are developed by people or foundations to further the ideals of those organizations and to recognize the families of former members of those organizations." Taylor was frowning, and it was obvious he didn't understand. Mr. Branston continued, "Well, it can be an organization like the Elks Club that gives away scholarships, but in that case, you have to be a child or grandchild of someone who is an Elks member. Is your dad an Elk?"

"No, but I'm sure he would join."

"Usually, they have a certain time period restriction on the membership. Usually, they have to have been a member for three years or so. But there are many others, families for instance, that have bequeathed huge amounts of money to go toward scholarships. Often they have some restriction that you had to grow up and graduate in a certain city or county." He lifted a stack of papers from his desk and began reading from them. "For instance, here is one, that if your surname is McTavish and you are of Scottish descent, you would qualify for this scholarship."

"I'll change my name," Taylor suggested.

Mr. Branston chuckled. "Afraid not; they would check. We have several binders that deal with scholarships, which I will set you up with, and you'll have to go through them on your own. Also, we have a computer database that we can use. Hopefully, we can find you something. Here's another related to a country. Are you or your relatives from the Federal Islamic Republic of the Comoros Islands?" Mr. Branston looked up for a reaction.

"Where?"

"It's a very obscure African country. Are you black? No. You're not a female with a clubfoot. Are you the son or daughter of any person who has died while climbing a Himalayan mountain?" At this point, Mr. Branston was just naming scholarships as a bit of humor and to illustrate the variety available.

"No."

"Do you have congenital scoliosis and are planning a career in medicine?" Taylor smiled and shook his head no.

Mr. Branston read aloud a list of five diseases, none of which Taylor recognized. Mr. Branston chuckled and added, "Sorry, just some inside humor. I really have to apologize. Right before you came in, I had some really, really good news, and I'm kind of whacky over that. But some of these scholarships are pretty bizarre stuff."

Even though Taylor found his joking somewhat amusing, it also made him feel he would not qualify for any scholarship, and he was beginning to get discouraged.

"Oh, wait; here are several scholarships for gays and lesbians."

Taylor immediately thought of Amanda Trolley in his class. Amanda was large and very athletic. She hardly ever talked to guys, had never been seen on a date, and could probably take down any guy in school except maybe Buck Truitt, the biggest, meanest guy on the football team. *Still, that doesn't make her a lesbian,* he thought. *Maybe she will marry and have kids and be a grandmother eventually. Who knows what her sex life is except her and the person she sleeps with. Actually, how does anybody know if you're gay?*

Mr. Branston continued reading; then he exclaimed, "Wow! This is a generous scholarship. It's from a well-funded trust. It covers everything: room, board, tuition, extracurricular activity funds. In fact, the man who funded it has a few campus buildings named after him. That's right! I remember now. We awarded a scholarship two years ago to a young lady on campus. I think she's a tuba player. One of the few female tuba players around. Anyway, that's a possibility . . ." He paused and looked up at Taylor; then he continued, "that is, if you are gay."

Taylor sat there, just blankly staring ahead, thinking about a full scholarship.

"Well, anyway, you can apply for any that you want. I'm going to set you up in the next room. As I mentioned, there are binders and a computer terminal that accesses our database of scholarships. Also, there is a printer and a copy machine, and you can copy information for any that you choose."

Then Taylor asked haltingly, "What—what would someone have to do if they had this scholarship?"

"The one for gay students? Let's see what the other requirements are." There was a short pause as Mr. Branston looked through the document. He then continued, "Well, according to the description, Bernard Pembroke was the benefactor who started the trust." Mr. Branston looked up to give Taylor some additional information. "Bernard Pembroke was a huge benefactor of this campus, and as stated in his will, his entire estate went to a foundation for scholarships. Most are called The Bernard Pembroke Teaching Scholarship, the Bernard Pembroke Engineering Scholarship, et cetera. This one's called— I thought it strange—the Pluck Gay and Lesbian Equality Scholarship. Don't know what that 'Pluck' is all about and why it's not set up with his name like the rest." He looked down and continued perusing the information while speaking. "Anyway, it is aimed at giving a distinct advantage to gay and lesbian students who may have been discriminated against and who are encouraged to make positive changes in the world." He shrugged; then he continued, "And most likely, you would have to get involved in school or community organizations that work against discrimination and such against gay people. Hmm. It doesn't really say, specifically. There appears to be an administrator of the trust who the student has to answer to. Probably a lawyer. And the usual contact and information on how to apply."

"Well," Taylor said after a brief pause, "well, let's throw that in, too."

Mr. Branston stopped for a moment, looked at Taylor suspiciously, and asked, "So—so you're gay?"

"Me, gay?" Taylor responded.

"Yes, you know. Are you a homosexual?"

After a short pause, Taylor responded softly, almost so softly that Mr. Branston could barely hear. "Well, yes. Yes, I'm gay."

Mr. Branston looked at him; then he asked again. "Are you sure you're gay? It took you a long time to answer."

Taylor squirmed in his chair. "I—I was—I'm reluctant to let anybody know. Because, you know. Other people might—"

"I understand," Mr. Branston interrupted. "Other people might treat you differently. Discriminate against you." There was a short pause as Mr. Branston shrugged and started to get up.

"Okay. I'll give you a copy of this and then set you up at a table with all this other information. There may be a scholarship that is more suitable for you."

Taylor followed him to a room with a table and a computer. After showing Taylor how to reference the database and giving him a short explanation of the printed scholarship guides, he left the room and shut the door.

In no time, Taylor had developed a system to browse the hundreds of scholarships in the database. Some were categorized, which helped him eliminate large blocks at one time. Others required reading the first line, which identified the main purpose of the scholarship. After forty-five minutes, Taylor was done with the database, and he began to browse the printed books. These were indexed, which made things much easier. In two-and-a-half hours, he was through. In all this time, his mind kept wandering back to the gay scholarship. It paid everything and then some. The only other scholarships that he had found and briefly considered were small scholarships in science and several for students from his county of Horton. But those required pursuing a teaching degree and then teaching in the county for three years. While he was making copies of the ones he had selected, Mr. Branston opened the door.

"Well, how's it going? I just came in to check on you."

"Fine, I got through them all. There weren't many more that applied to me. I'm going to go for these four."

"Oh! So, you're going after the Pembroke gay scholarship? Well, talk it over with your folks and get back with me on what you decide. We don't have too much time, so don't wait on this." Mr. Branston led Taylor to the outer office; then he paused and said, "Mrs. Brown has many of the applications here on file. Just tell her which ones, and she'll see if she can locate them."

Taylor thanked Mr. Branston and handed Mrs. Brown the sheets he was holding. She smiled, got up, went to the file cabinets, and pulled out packets for three of them. Then she turned to him and said, "This one, we don't have on file. You'll have to write for an application." He looked down at the paper. It was one of the science scholarships, which paid only a few thousand. He thanked her and left.

On the drive back, Taylor mentally debated his lying about being gay. He felt that he rarely lied. But the scholarship equated to a lot of money, and he needed it. It was unclear what he would be required to do as a scholarship holder. He thought, *Who can I talk to about this? Was it wrong to lie about being gay? After all, is it fair that I would be discriminated against and denied this scholarship because I'm not gay? Is your sex life anybody's business except your own? And it is a full scholarship.*

After much mental argument, he determined that he would apply for the Pembroke gay scholarship and deal with the consequences if he should be caught. But, just in case he didn't get that one, he would also apply for the other three.

When Taylor got home, it was still early afternoon. He sat down and began to fill out the paperwork, starting with the application for the Pembroke scholarship. Once he got beyond the general information questions about his name, age, place of birth, and hometown address, the questions got more personal. The Activities section asked if he had been involved in any clubs or organizations whose goals were to further equality and fairness. His first instinct was to make something up. However, he decided that not only was the big lie furthering additional lies but whatever he said or made up could be checked too. He ended up saying that because Tartan was a small town, there were no clubs that fit that description, but if there had been, he would have joined.

Finally, the application asked him to write a five-hundred-word essay about himself and what he personally had done to discourage prejudice against gays and lesbians. Upon reading about this essay, he almost gave up, throwing the pencil down in anger and getting up and walking through the house. Then he went into the kitchen to get something to drink. He saw a note on the refrigerator door from his dad, saying he hoped the interview went well and telling him to pull out some chicken breasts from the freezer. Taylor pulled out the frozen meat and put it in the sink. Then it occurred to him that his dad never discriminated against anyone and had always taught him to be kind and welcoming to everyone he encountered. He remembered his dad telling him never to gang up on someone, physically or verbally, and not to participate if people were saying bad things about others. He thought, *Yeah, I will write this as my dad would and as he taught me.* As he began to write, he thought of and included examples from school in which some of the guys and even girls had tried to bully others. Each time, he had tried to stop it by changing the subject or saying something nice about the person instead. He thoughtfully included several examples of this nobility, even if his altruism was exaggerated.

After a few hours, he had composed the five hundred words, and he was happy with what he had written. He edited it and neatly typed it. He was done with that one, and he sealed it in its self-addressed envelope, ready for mailing. Before he could even read any of the other applications, he heard his father's truck pull into the driveway. He looked out the living room window to see his dad helping his mom out of the cab. His father had taken his mom to the adult care center for the day and had just picked her up on his way home from work.

That evening, at the dinner table, Taylor's father asked him about the interview. He told his father only that he and the university counselor were working on some possibilities and he would be applying for four scholarships. He said he had completed one of the applications, and his father offered to take it to the post office the following morning. Then the subject was dropped.

By the end of next week, Taylor had mailed off the other applications. He also thought it would be a good time to follow up with Mr. Branston about other possibilities for financing his education, such as working his way through school. He attempted to reach Mr. Branson by phone after school, but he was in a meeting, and his secretary said he would call him back. Taylor hung up, a little angry because he didn't want to wait around all afternoon for the call, which might not even occur that day. Within a few minutes, however, the phone rang. It was Mr. Branston. After a short chat, Mr. Branston revealed to Taylor that an attorney for the Pembroke scholarship had already phoned him, and he had given the attorney a very strong recommendation to award the scholarship to Taylor. Surprised at this, Taylor nevertheless was able to stutter a weak, "Thank you."

"You're welcome, Taylor. I—I hope—rather, I trust you will live up to the expectations of the scholarship. To be honest, it was a crazy, busy week. A lot was going on, and I was given word that I am being promoted to a higher position in the School of Medicine. Similar responsibilities but really a promotion, and I was so excited about that, so I really, uh . . . pushed your recommendation. But I think you have the potential to be an excellent Pembroke scholar . . . so I don't regret it. Recommending you was one of my last duties in this position, and I wanted everything, I guess, to end on a happy note. So I'm excited for you, too."

Taylor, not sure what to say, replied, "Well, uh, then congratulations to you!"

Mr. Branston told Taylor not to be concerned about his leaving. Jeff Black, an attorney and the administrator of the scholarship, had all the paperwork, and he would be handling everything from now on. Mr. Branston said that Taylor could ask Mr. Black any question pertaining to the specifics of the scholarship, and Mr. Black would likely be calling him within a few days.

On Wednesday the following week, Taylor received a phone call from Mr. Black. Taylor thought this would probably be a phone interview to see if he qualified for the scholarship, but instead, Mr. Black spoke to Taylor as if he had already been awarded the scholarship. He said things such as, "You will be living in Emerson Hall, and you will be required to keep records of all monies spent on books, tuition, and activities. You will be given a quarterly stipend and will need a local bank account." The real clincher was when he asked for Taylor's Social Security number, which he promptly gave. He then asked if Taylor could come to Chapel Hill to sign the scholarship agreement. Would he be available this Thursday, around four o'clock? Taylor had school but knew that Mrs. Anderson would allow him to skip afternoon classes for this. He swallowed and gulped out a barely audible, "Yes."

"Great," Mr. Black said. Then he added, "Oh yes, and congratulations! I know you will prove to be a positive example of this scholarship."

Apparently it's a done deal, Taylor thought. Finally, just as they were about to hang up, Taylor remembered to ask what responsibilities he had to fulfill as a recipient of the scholarship. Mr. Black answered that he would be encouraged to join and be active in any gay and lesbian support groups at the university and within the community. And he should report in writing each month on his activities in those groups. To Taylor, even though he was facing unknown demands of college life, that didn't seem too bad. Plus, Mr. Black had said "encouraged to join," not "required to join," so he was wondering how much flexibility he had. Taylor responded without hesitation, "Okay. That sounds good."

The final words from Mr. Black before they hung up were, "Great. I'll see you this Thursday; and again, congratulations!"

Chapter 2

I Feel Guilty

After I hung up speaking to Mr. Black, I was elated. But then I began feeling like when I was a little kid and I insisted that my parents let me ride the roller coaster at the state fair in Raleigh. Once I got on and we reached the first hill, I wanted to get off, but it was too late. I was scared, but I'm older now, so I'm not scared but worried, and I'm also feeling guilty. I had deceived Mr. Branston, the counselor, and now the attorney too. What sort of trouble would this get me into? Would I have to prove I was gay? How would I prove it? Would I feel uncomfortable being in these gay groups? Could I handle it?

Sure, why not? I don't have any bad feelings about gay people. Their attraction to each other is weird and not for me, but hey, I believe in letting people live the way they want. I think Dad feels that way too. And Dad . . . What if Dad found out about my deceptions? How would he react if I said I was gay? Which is easier to tell him, . . . that I'm gay or that I lied to get a scholarship? If I say I lied, he will make me give it back, so if I want to keep the scholarship, I'll have to say I'm gay. And my girlfriend, Christine? Her family is very religious and probably wouldn't approve. No, they definitely wouldn't approve. Of the lying or being gay.

And also, I feel guilty leaving Dad to contend with Mom and going off to Carolina. He has enough on his plate just paying the bills. And now as time goes on, with Mom getting progressively worse, he has that much more. He has to work, trying to provide for us, pay the mortgage, put food on the table, pay medical bills. Now he also has to spend time shopping for groceries, cooking, taking Mom to the doctors, seeing she takes her medicine, making sure she eats and gets bathed, and helping her dress. How does he manage to do all that? And he wants me to not worry about it but spend my time studying instead. I can only study so much; then I can't take it any longer. My mind will only absorb so much; then I've got to do something else.

Dad did let me take over doing the laundry—but even that he helps with—and occasionally doing the shopping. And of course, I do the yard. But with the shopping, he says it's just as easy for him to do it than to have to write it down, because he never knows what he's going to fix. I've learned to cook some things, but Dad is so much better.

But I do feel guilty going off to school. Then even Dad won't be able to depend on me to run errands or sit with Mom. It's gotten to the point that she needs attention twenty-four hours a day. It's possible she could just wander off. And it's going to get worse, and it will happen fairly quickly, according to the doctor. I especially feel guilty about this because I really don't want to be here seeing it happen, seeing her decline more, seeing her become less and less of what was my mom. Having to face the possibility of changing her diaper. I couldn't do that for my mom. Dad says, I wouldn't have to, that if it comes to that, he's only five minutes from work and he'll come home. He also says he really wants to make sure nothing stops me from getting a college education and is afraid that if I take a year off, it will never happen. So he really wants me to go.

Thinking back, I remember what were probably the first signs. I was in the sixth grade and overheard some high school students talking about Mom. They referred to her as "old lady Hanes" and said how she couldn't remember from one day to the next if she had taught a lesson or not. It was in the cafeteria, and they didn't know I was her son. Even before that, for years, I had dreaded getting into Mom's English Literature class. She was the school librarian and also taught Literature to every student who went through high school. I didn't want her to be my teacher because if I did well, everyone would say she was giving me preferential treatment, and if I did badly, she and Dad would be angry at me and I would be angry at myself. I hoped that, by some miracle, they would have enough funding in the school system to hire someone else and just let Mom be the librarian. But when I was in middle school, she had to go on disability, so I didn't have to worry. Selfish me. I was relieved that she couldn't teach anymore.

The doctor said she is now in the intermediate-to-advanced stage of the disease. I've had trouble with Mom when she'd get confused and angry because she didn't understand something and we'd holler at each other. How does Dad manage it? He remains so calm and smooths everything over, and she seems to respond to this. Later, the doctor says, she'll have trouble swallowing and become incontinent, and eventually all bodily functions will cease. That will most likely happen sometime when I'm in college, and Dad will have to deal with it all . . . alone.

Yes, I feel guilty.

Chapter 3

It's Been a Weird Day

That evening, after five minutes of silence at the dinner table, Taylor spoke up. "Apparently," Taylor began; then he hesitated for a few seconds. "I may have gotten a scholarship."

His dad stopped eating, smiled and looked over at him. "Really, from those applications you mailed off?"

"Yeah, it's called a legacy scholarship and is funded by some dead guy named Bernard Pembroke and . . . and anyway, the counselor is recommending me for it."

"How much will it pay?"

"Well, pretty sure it's tuition and some other stuff."

"What? Well, that's great. But you know tuition is only part of the cost. In fact, a relatively small part."

Taylor looked over at his mom, who was sitting quietly, picking at her food. "Yeah, yeah, I know. Books, room and food. It may pay for more. I'm willing to work my way through college."

There were a few seconds of silence, and then his father spoke. "And I want you to go. More than anything. I've been hearing about student loans. I guess we could look into that."

"There's an administrator," Taylor continued, "who will, I guess, be the one who makes the final decision. He made it sound pretty positive. He wants to meet me next Thursday and sign some papers."

"Thursday? That's fast. I thought these things take a lot more time. Humph! Well, that sounds promising. So, what about school?"

"It's in the late afternoon, so I'm going to talk to Mrs. Anderson and see if I can get her to give me permission to skip the last class or last two classes."

"Okay. Do you need a note from me or anything?"

"I'll talk to her and let you know."

When Thursday arrived, Taylor could hardly hold himself back. Mrs. Anderson encouraged him to take two classes off so that he would have plenty of time. He arrived in Chapel Hill and located the law office of Sheffield and Sheffield, one block off the main street, with more than a half hour to spare. After parking his car, he took a few minutes to explore Franklin Street, the main street in town.

Hundreds of students were walking up and down the street in the late afternoon sunshine. Some were carrying backpacks, others were carrying a few books under their arms, and some were carrying nothing. Most of the male and female students were dressed as they had in high school, a kind of grungy jeans-and-sweatshirt look, with the guys wearing caps turned backward. But there were a significant number of men and some women who had a dressier look, with khakis and button-down shirts for the men and skirts and sweaters for the women.

Chapel Hill was so different from Tartan, where you would find only a handful of people on the street and hardly any stores that weren't empty or boarded up. Only a hardware store, a bridal shop, and a florist remained.

Tartan had lost its main economic driver when textile jobs were shipped overseas. These remaining stores had managed to survive in Tartan because almost everyone needed the hardware store to fix things, they needed the bridal shop because almost everybody in Tartan got married at least once, and they needed the florist for the weddings and for the funerals when everybody eventually died. Dealing in death was a good business, and the town was able to support two very prosperous-looking funeral homes. There used to be a baby store, a clothing store, a fabric store, and a grocery store, but all those closed when a Walmart opened outside the edge of town.

As Taylor walked down the street, he saw a restaurant bar, a cafeteria, a bookstore, a gift shop, a men's clothing store, a Greek restaurant, a drug store, a real estate office, a florist, and then a Thai restaurant and a Mexican restaurant. On the other side of the street were shops that looked even more interesting. After looking in various windows, he went into the bookstore and entertained himself until a few minutes before his appointment.

Upon entering the attorney's office, the receptionist greeted him. "Hello, you must be Taylor Hanes."

"Hey. Yes, how are you?"

"I'm fine. Mr. Black is expecting you and will be out in a few minutes. Have a seat."

Before he could sit down, a tall, dark-haired man carrying a green file folder came into the waiting room and extended his hand. "Taylor, I'm Jeff Black." They shook hands. "And if you haven't introduced yourself, this is Marlene Hanover. You'll be having to make contact with her from time to time. Come on back." Taylor smiled and nodded to Marlene; then Jeff directed Taylor to an office in the back with a large conference table.

"Have a seat anywhere. We just have some papers for you to read and a few documents to sign."

Taylor took the first seat at the table to the left of the doorway. Jeff sat down to the right of him.

"I guess this is an exciting time in your life, going off to school."

"Actually, it is. It'll be the first time I'll ever have been away from home longer than a few days."

"Where are you from?"

"Tartan."

"Tartan; that used to be a textile town, right?"

"Yes, sir. It got its name because early mills would copy the Scottish patterns for clothing and stuff and sell them all over the world."

"Are there any mills still operating?"

"No, sir, the last one was a coat factory. It closed in 1990. The economy there is hurting."

"Yeah. Outsourcing of jobs really hurt. That's tough for a small town."

"Yes, sir."

"Well, college will be one of the best experiences in your entire life. It's such a rewarding experience, so take every opportunity to make the best of it."

"I'm just hoping to be able to go."

"What do you mean?" Jeff asked, looking at him questioningly.

"Well," Taylor replied, "I'm hoping that my family—my dad —will have enough money to send me."

"Oh," Jeff chuckled. "Maybe I didn't explain. But this scholarship will pay for everything." He paused a moment and then repeated it with emphasis. "Everything! It'll be tuition, books, room, meals, laundry, just about anything you need while in college. And it gives you an additional five hundred dollars a month for miscellaneous expenses. That's the only part you won't have to account for. All the others will require you to keep receipts."

Taylor didn't reply but simply sat there with a blank look on his face and his mouth open. The idea of not having to pay for any of it and having spending money too was something he couldn't fathom. He immediately thought of possibly sending some of the extra money back to his dad to help care for his mom.

"You probably haven't had a chance to open a checking account."

"Actually, I already have one with Wachovia Bank, and I noticed they have a branch here in town."

"Perfect. We'll need the checking account number. Did you bring your checkbook?"

"No . . . wait. I carry a blank check in my wallet."

"Okay, great. Let me have that, and I'll get Marlene to copy it. What we'll do, in a month or so, is first feed you some money upfront into your checking account. This will allow you to prepay tuition, room, and any bills that come in before you start school. Then after that, whenever you have school expenses, you will need to send us those receipts. Every month, we'll take those receipts and tally them and reimburse you for your expenses. Pretty neat, huh?"

"Yeah, wow! I can't believe this."

"And if there are any questions, just call this office, and the receptionist will be able to answer just about anything. There may be a time when something unexpected will come up and we'll have to fund you more money out of the trust fund. Like, for instance, do you have a computer?"

"Yes, I've got a Mac."

"How old is it?"

"We got it secondhand, so I guess it's about four years old."

"Well, you'll probably find the need to upgrade it in the near future. They tell me all students will be on the Internet in the next few years, and you would want a computer capable of that. So, when the need comes up, just let us know and we can discuss. Okay?"

Taylor nervously swallowed and replied, "Sure."

"Okay. Well," Jeff began as he opened the file folder and lifted the first packet of pages, "this really explains in detail the procedure . . . what you can spend money on, or not. So you will need to read this and sign at the end. Basically, you're acknowledging you understand the rules." He lifted the second document. "And here is everything concerning the scholarship. It explains some things about the benefactor, what the intention of the scholarship is, and the requirements for maintaining the scholarship."

Taylor leaned toward the document, trying to read it, and asked, "So, what are some of the requirements?"

"Well, let's see. I've never administered this scholarship." He scanned the document quickly and then stopped. "Okay. It pretty much encourages you to get involved in activities that further equality for gay people. Now, as an administrator, I would encourage you to join any organizations that have that as part of their goal. There is something on campus called the Gay, Lesbian, uh, Bisexual and Straight Alliance or something like that. So, organizations like that would be okay. Now, just showing up at a gay bar once a week won't hack it." Jeff laughed as he said this.

Taylor smiled and asked, "So, do I report back to you?"

"Exactly. You can mail in a report on activity once a month or drop it by the office. Keep in mind, if there is an opportunity in your school work . . . what's your major, by the way?"

"I think it's going to be math."

"Well, this probably wouldn't apply, but maybe in your first couple of years of prerequisites, you might . . . if you choose to write a paper, for instance, about gay issues, that would qualify. Or even if you wrote letters to the editor of the newspaper, taking a stance against discrimination, that would qualify. Really, there is no limit. But you should demonstrate some activity. So, I think, to make sure this is above board, you need to send in to us something that demonstrates your involvement. For instance, if you wrote a letter to the paper, send that in, or if you attended a meeting, send in something that tells us what the meeting was about. And really, we're looking for once a month. So, if you attend a local chapter meeting of a gay equality or support group, that would count."

"Oh, okay. I think I can handle that."

"All right. Well then, the lawyer in me says you should be aware of what you sign. I want you to take some time and read through all of this. Then you sign here and here. And that's it. Just bring it all up to the front when you're done. I'll give this check to the receptionist to get the account numbers."

Mr. Black got up from his chair and extended his hand, which Taylor shook. Then Mr. Black added, "Take as much time as you need, and really, good luck on your educational pursuits. You can call and discuss anytime you need, if you have questions."

As Mr. Black was closing the door, Taylor said, "Thank you."

Taylor sat silently. Then he let out a huge sigh. There wasn't any interview to determine if he qualified. In fact, there weren't any questions at all. Taylor was relieved but also excited about the extent of the scholarship and, at the same time, feeling guilty for the deception. He immediately concentrated on going through the documents.

The first packet dealt with the procedure for spending and getting reimbursed, with explanations of what expenses would qualify. This was all pretty much what Mr. Black had told him. He immediately signed and dated that document. Then he began reading the second document. First, it explained that Bernard Pembroke had been a builder who had constructed many private and government buildings throughout the state, including several at Carolina. Next, it explained that the goal of the scholarship was to further the educational pursuits of gays and lesbians by providing financial support, so that they would be well prepared upon graduation to take leadership positions in furthering equality. That was followed by a short paragraph that encouraged involvement in activities that furthered society's acceptance of gays and lesbians. The last paragraph was written in the form of a pledge in boldfaced type. It read, "I pledge, as a gay or lesbian, to promote and further equality through school activities and involvement in organizations that support equality and improve acceptance among people."

Taylor reread this several times and paused; the guilt of deception kept coming back to him. He sat there, nervously flicking the pen in his hand, trying to decide what to do. Then he laid the pen down. The scholarship was right in his hands, only a few ink drops away. He thought about getting a degree with all its prestige and hopes for a meaningful career. Then his mind went to the beautiful campus with all the happy students on the street. He thought of ball games, theater productions, music, films, and other activities on campus he had heard about. He thought of all the female students and dating and sex. And he thought of his mom with a shortened life, his dad struggling to take care of her, and Tartan, a bleak, gray, dreary little town with a broken back. He immediately grabbed the pen and quickly signed and dated the document.

At that moment, he was startled as if he had felt the presence of someone in the room. He looked all around. The door was still closed. He looked straight ahead and could see out the window to the top of another building, but inside, there was no one else in the room. Then, in a quick flash, he saw a shadow standing in the corner, an impression of a tall, dark figure, which instantly disappeared. He swiftly collected the papers together, put them in the folder, and headed to the receptionist's office.

On the hour-and-a-half drive back home, Taylor's mind flicked from one unbelievable thing to the next about what had just happened to him. The first was the lawyer assuring him that everything would be paid for in school; the second was the image or shadow that he had seen or imagined in the room after he had signed the document. Then there was the weight of his lying, something he rarely ever did, something that to him was unbelievable. These thoughts kept going around in his mind, from elation to fright to guilt. He fumbled through the glove compartment, looking for a cassette tape to put in the car player. He pulled out a Johnny Cash tape and stuck it in the player, and "Ring of Fire" began playing. He turned up the volume very loud, trying to get the thoughts out of his mind, but they were still there. He started to sing along; only momentarily could he forget.

He looked in his rearview mirror and saw a state trooper following him. Their eyes met; then Taylor looked down and saw that he was going sixty-two in a fifty-five miles per hour speed limit zone. He applied the brakes, and the trooper smirked and proceeded to pass him. An image flashed before his mind of having to tell his dad that he had gotten a ticket, but now he felt immensely lucky that it didn't happen. To prevent further speeding, he put the cruise control on and continued singing. By the time he got home, he had played and sung the entire tape twice.

Once inside his house, he heard the phone ring and answered it. It was Trad. "Hey, Trad. You won't believe what I . . ." He hesitated. He was at once happy about the scholarship, ready to shout it from the rooftops. At the same time, however, he was embarrassed that he had lied to get it and embarrassed to have to tell anyone, even his best friend, that it was a gay scholarship. "Uh-uh, I'll tell you later. It's a long story. What's up with you?"

Trad was one of Taylor's closest friends. Living in the same neighborhood, he must have seen Taylor pull into his driveway. Trad lived only six houses down and across the street. Growing up together, they had formed a strong bond, which endured to the present day.

Trad's family had a similar economic background, but his mother and father had divorced about five years ago. His parents had decided that Trad and his sister, who was three years older, would live with his father and his mother would move out. Trad's dad owned a struggling nightclub in town called the Cosmic Jungle, which was usually slow on weeknights but attracted a sizable crowd of twenty- to thirty-year-olds on weekends.

Trad spoke with a slow Southern drawl, different from Taylor's speech, which was faster and had intonations which resembled those of his parents, who had moved here from Pennsylvania. "My ol' man's going to be out of town this weekend. He's taking his new girlfriend to the beach."

"So, a party at your house?" Taylor kidded.

"Even better than that," Trad continued. "We're going to the Cosmic Jungle tomorrow night if you're not busy. Dad's hired some new barkeeps that won't know what's going on, so I figure we can get all the free beer we want."

"Serious? Cool, no problem. I'm in." Then he added, "I need that!"

"Great, I've called Ben, and he's game, and maybe Gordon will come too."

After Taylor had hung up, he thought seriously about telling Trad about the scholarship. He was sure that if he explained why he was taking the scholarship, Trad would understand. Ben and

Gordon were other good friends, who lived in a neighborhood a couple miles away. They all had done many things together, having gone to the same middle and high schools. But Taylor was still a lot closer to Trad, and if Taylor had to confide anything in anyone, he would feel more comfortable doing so with Trad. Maybe tomorrow night, he would have the opportunity.

Taylor didn't sleep well that night because of thoughts going through his head about lying and people learning he had been awarded a gay scholarship and seeing the strange image when he had signed the paper. He went to school that morning as usual, but throughout the day, he felt the burden of these thoughts with no one to tell them to. He thought of dropping in to see Mrs. Anderson since she had aided him with the scholarship, but he couldn't even bring himself to do that. When he saw his friends Ben and Trad out on the lawn, he didn't try to get their attention and instead continued down the hall. His classes seemed endless as he sought to concentrate on what the instructors were teaching while his mind kept wandering off. He very quickly ate lunch alone and then retreated to an empty classroom as he waited for his next class. His late afternoon physical education class was canceled because the coach was sick, so he quickly left school, got in his car and headed home. *Maybe*, he thought, *by going out with friends tonight, I can get past this.*

That night, Trad had borrowed his sister's car since she was on a date and her boyfriend was picking her up. Trad picked up Taylor, and Ben and Gordon a few minutes later.

"Okay, guys," Trad said as they approached the edge of town, "these barkeeps are new, and they have met me but don't technically know I'm underage. But that's not a problem. I have access to the beer cases in the back, and I'll get you all the beer you want."

Ben spoke up. "Are we gonna have to drink in the back?"

"Oh, no, no," Trad reassured. "We'll get a table. A booth would be better. One barkeep will think the other carded you and it was okay, and vice versa. Besides, they're new, and it will be pretty busy, so they won't even think about it."

Gordon spoke up. "I can't drink at all. My mom smells my breath every time I go out."

"Is she still doing that?" Trad asked.

"Oh, yeah. Nothing's changed."

"Sticks her nose in your face when you come home?" Trad asked.

"Yep," Gordon snapped.

"Oh, well," Trad continued, "I can drink more, and you can drive us back."

Taylor followed all the various conversations in the car but didn't feel compelled to add to them.

After arriving, they settled into a booth in the back, and Trad went into the back room and got each of them a bottle of Bud Light. It wasn't long before they were talking about the girls in school. Taylor had been dating Christine for six months. She was a cute girl on the cheerleading squad who had previously dated other guys, but for both of them, it was a relationship of convenience more than anything else. Everybody knew she came from a conservative religious family, so they didn't ask Taylor about her, and Taylor still didn't feel like talking much.

Trad never seemed to want to stick to any one girl and played the field the most. Because of this, he was the first one to score with a girl in his freshman year, or so he had said. Because he dated a lot, this was usually the primary topic of their conversation.

Ben and Gordon were both laid back and only dated on special occasions like homecoming and the prom. Soon, on their second beer, they got hungry and ordered a pizza from the takeout next door. While they waited for the pizza, they went on to their third beer, and the talk turned to college. While the beer was beginning to calm Taylor, the talk of college caught his attention.

Gordon had done well in the sciences and won a local competition in a science fair, which had helped him get a partial scholarship to NC State. His parents were able to pay for the rest of his college.

Ben was going to East Carolina University to major in communications and was able to get some financial help.

Trad, on the other hand, always got passing but not good grades, and his dad had never emphasized trying to get him into college. As a result, Trad expected to go to the local community college at the edge of the county while working part-time helping his dad at the bar.

All of Taylor's friends knew that Taylor had been accepted to Carolina. But they also knew that his mother was ill, making it difficult or even impossible for him to go to college unless there was some assistance from somewhere. As a result, no one at the table asked him any direct questions about college.

"Just think, guys, in four or five years," Trad said while gesturing to Ben and Gordon, "you guys will be graduating from college, and me and . . ." He paused a moment, looking for a reaction from Taylor, who seemed to have a buzzed-out smile, and then continued, "and Taylor will still be here, holding this godforsaken town together."

Taylor smiled, the alcohol having totally relaxed him. He decided this moment was too good to pass up and he would tell all of them about his scholarship. He quickly glanced around the crowded, noisy bar and said, "Not so fast. I've . . . I've got an announcement to make. You all need to raise your bottle for a toast to me."

"Why, what's happened?" Gordon asked.

"Well, today, . . ." Taylor felt himself trembling, his mind spinning. *I shouldn't tell them—It's too late—I can't not tell them now.* So he continued, "this very day, I signed papers that gave me a . . ." He paused momentarily for dramatic effect. "Da, da, da, da . . . a full scholarship to Carolina!"

The table was quiet for a few seconds. Then Gordon said, "Yeah, right."

"No, it's true," Taylor shot back.

"Really?" Ben asked.

"Yep!" Taylor replied, nodding his head.

Suddenly, after a slight pause, there was a round of high-fives and whoops as they all congratulated him. Trad appeared happy too and participated in the jubilation, but Taylor noticed a little concern in Trad's face and tried to downplay any more excitement.

"Look, it's no big deal. It will make things so much easier for my mom and dad."

"Was this a need-based scholarship?" Gordon asked.

"No, it wasn't need-based . . . although I really needed it."

Gordon continued, "Well, I know it wasn't an athletic scholarship or based on academics."

"No, it's what they call an endowed scholarship."

"Hey, I know they don't give it for that," Ben quipped. They all laughed. "Besides, you wouldn't qualify." They laughed some more.

As the laughter died, Trad and Ben looked at him with dazed interest while Gordon stared intently, all expecting an explanation to follow.

Taylor spoke. "Apparently, this rich dude set up this trust for this full scholarship that they give every year. The money just sits there accumulating interest for these scholarships."

"Wow!" Ben and Trad exclaimed.

"Yeah! It even pays for books and housing, and I have a monthly spending allowance."

"No way," Ben replied.

"How do I apply?" Gordon asked.

"You have to be a minority," Taylor snapped.

Everyone froze.

"A minority?" Gordon questioned.

There was a small pause while Taylor gathered his thoughts. Lowering his voice, he spoke. "Look, guys. I . . . I, uh, pulled a fast one."

"What? You told them you were black and they believed you?" Ben quipped.

"No, no," Taylor replied while laughing. "I . . . I got this scholarship where I have to work toward . . . for further acceptance and rights for gays and lesbians."

"You got a gay scholarship?" Trad asked.

"Did you have to blow someone?" Ben asked.

"I didn't know you were gay," Gordon commented. "Are you?"

"Look, no, no. You got to promise to keep this quiet."

"I do remember," Gordon continued while chuckling, "that camping trip when we were in the Scouts."

Just as Ben said, "Will you be my date tonight?" a girl delivering the pizza arrived at the table. The conversation quickly turned toward splitting up the bill and tip. As soon as she left, it started back.

"Are you going to have to display a rainbow flag in your dorm room?" Gordon asked.

"Does Christine know about this?" Trad asked.

"Hold on. Hold on," Taylor responded, slightly annoyed at the jokes. "Let me out; I gotta take a leak. Then I'll answer all your questions."

As he was moving away, Ben shouted, "If you take too long and your knees are wet when you come back, we'll know what's been happening." They all howled.

Taylor rushed back to the table and leaned into them with a pointed finger. "Look, guys. I hate fags as much as the rest of you!"

They continued laughing as Taylor swung around and headed for the restroom. He turned a corner and proceeded down a long, poorly lit hallway. Just before he reached the restroom door, a man dressed in a leather coat and flat-brimmed leather hat materialized before him. The man grabbed him by the shirt and slammed him against the wall, raising him several inches off the floor with his clenched fist under Taylor's chin.

"So, you hate fags, and just t-today, you signed a d-document that you would support the furtherance of g-gay equality." There was a pause as the man stared menacingly into Taylor's face. His eyes were dark and moist with anger. Taylor stared back in shock. The man's ice-cold fist was cutting into his throat, and Taylor feared for his life. Then the man added, "You're pathetic!" He let Taylor slide down, released him, turned, and disappeared into vapor.

A few minutes later, after nervously relieving himself, Taylor returned to the table as the guys were busily eating. His shirt was still pulled out of his pants and was bunched under one arm. They all paused from their pizza and looked up at him. His face held a cold, blank, tortured stare.

"My God!" Ben exclaimed. "What the hell!" Trad moved over to make room as Taylor sat down.

"God, what happened?" Trad asked.

"I—I—I don't know!" Taylor said softly.

"Did you pass out?" Trad asked.

"No, no. I didn't fall. Or pass out. I saw something."

"Action in the bathroom?" Ben asked.

Taylor spoke slowly and haltingly. "No. It was nothing. Let's finish up and get out of here."

"Damn," Ben said. "I wanted to have at least another beer."

"Come on," Trad insisted, "tell us what happened."

After a pause, Taylor began. "This guy—this big guy just lifted me and threw me against the wall."

"What did he look like?" Trad asked, looking toward the bathroom. "We can all take him down."

"We can?" Ben quipped.

"No!" Taylor replied. "He's long gone. Let's just get out of here."

They all finished quickly and left. In the car, they were quiet until Ben finally spoke up. "So, come on. Tell us about this guy attacking you."

Taylor didn't say anything for about ten seconds; then he said, almost shouting, "I don't want to talk about it. It's been a weird day."

Chapter 4

What It Is

I just don't want to talk about it; I . . . it's just that . . . I'm considered calm and laid back like my dad, and that's how I want to come across. And I'm worried that maybe I'm going nuts. They tried to explain to me about my mom and her Alzheimer's. There is one kind called familial where a gene is passed down, and what if I have that? They said research was being done on it, and it is very inconclusive at this time and not to worry about it. But my mom is dying and, half the time, doesn't know what is going on, . . . and now I'm seeing a ghost. Maybe it's happening to me. This scares me, and being attacked scares me, but I won't let anyone know I'm scared. I won't even talk about it.

I've got to get it out of my mind. I know I'm not insane. I'm a very logical person that relies on empirical evidence and mathematical precision. I like the way that formulae are balanced and everything works out logically. But I know I saw something, and then it . . . it picked me up. If it was a spirit or ghost, it had the ability to physically move me and hurt me. Logically, if that is the case, then I should be able to move it and maybe even hurt it if I fight back. Makes sense. Or, what if it's an evil force, maybe even the devil, like in that old movie I saw on TV, The Exorcist. Oh, crap, that's just Hollywood! That kind of thing is fun, but I'm better than that. I'm logical. I can figure this out. There is an explanation. I will find out what it is.

Chapter 5

Things Just Wouldn't Be the Same

On Saturday morning, Taylor awoke with the sun shining through the window directly in his face. The image of the man was still with him. Even awake, he couldn't get it out of his mind.

He looked around the house and found it empty. Apparently, his father had gotten up earlier, helped his mom dress and eat, taken her to the assisted living center, and gone to work.

After gathering up a load of laundry and starting the washer, Taylor ate breakfast. He then got on the phone, called Trad, and asked him if he wanted to take a bike ride to the top of Gunther Hill at the edge of town. It was a pleasant, clear day at a comfortable temperature, and Taylor wanted to get some exercise and try to forget that guy or thing that had attacked him last night.

Trad was all for it, and soon Taylor was over at Trad's house, ringing his doorbell. Trad's road bike was standing by the stoop.

Immediately, Trad bounced out the front door, bike helmet in hand.

His sister yelled from inside, "Dad wants you to cut the lawn!"

"Yeah, I know! I'll do it later," he yelled back, and turned to Taylor. "Damn, a year and a half older, and she thinks she runs the place!"

"So, is Gunther Hill okay with you?"

"Yeah, it's a good ride if we do the whole park and the hill, but I'm up to it." Trad adjusted his helmet and put it on. He asked, "So, last night, just what happened to you when you went into the bathroom?"

Taylor acted as if he were annoyed to be asked, but he tried to give some sort of sensible answer. "Well, this guy . . . this guy came . . . came out of nowhere and slammed me up against the wall and started yelling at me. He was big; a lot bigger than me. Then . . . then he was gone."

"Wow!" Trad exclaimed. "What did he say?"

"He—he was yelling something about fags. Maybe he overheard our conversation at the table and got pissed off about it. Anyway, it scared me to death. I thought he was going to kill me."

"What did he look like?"

"He had this black leather sport coat and a black leather hat with a brim, almost like a cowboy hat, but it was flat."

"Weird," Trad said. "I didn't see anyone in the bar dressed like that."

Taylor thought for a moment; then he added, "He could have come in through the back door."

Trad quickly replied, "Usually that door is locked, but sometimes it does get left open when the bar guys carry out boxes and trash. Which way did he leave?"

Taylor hesitated. For a moment, he pondered telling Trad, his best friend for years, about the man just vaporizing, but then he decided not to. Getting on his bike and moving forward slightly, Taylor said, "I'm trying to forget about it. No physical harm was done. We got big tests this month, and I've got a lot on my mind."

Trad got on his bike and followed, replying, "Okay, let's go." They both began to pedal harder down the street.

They followed the road through the neighborhood to the main highway, which took them to the edge of town, past some farms and to the entrance of Gunther Park. In the park, there were miles of roads as well as many hiking trails. Traveling for about six miles, they went past a small lake with a parking lot and picnic tables and then past a camping area. Shifting into lower gears, they began to climb the two-and-a-half mile ascent up Gunther Hill. It was slow going in some areas because of a steep incline, which leveled off for about a half mile before becoming another steep slope. At the top was a large, flat parking area with restroom facilities and a few picnic tables. By the time they had reached the top, they were panting heavily and ready for a break. They got off their bikes, took off their helmets, and drank some water. Each had some energy bars, so they sat down on one of the picnic tables and began to eat. Below them lay the town. The air was very clear, and they could make out most of the layout of the town. From here, Taylor could see the tiny speck of his dad's garage where his dad was probably repairing someone's car, and also the tiny speck of the assisted living center where his mother was.

Trad spoke first. "So, how's Christine reacting to you going to a different school?"

"Well, first of all, she could have gone to Carolina, too. Her grades were good enough to get in, but her parents had a big influence on her, so she's going to Wingate University, at least for the first two years."

"Where the hell is Wingate University?"

"It's somewhere south of Charlotte. She said her mom and pop wanted her to go there because it's supported by the Baptist Church or some connection and it's the alma mater of Jesse Helms."

"Jesse Helms! You mean that old senator guy?"

"Yeah, him. We'll be about three hours away, so I guess we can see each other on some weekends. I think we can work it out." There was a pause as Trad nodded. Then Taylor asked, "What about Nancy? Is she going to college? Wait, no, you were dating that junior. What was her name . . . Sharon?"

"That was several weeks ago. I'm now dating a girl who works at the drug store in Elma." Elma was the next small town over and an occasional football rival.

"What's she like?"

"Oh . . ." Trad paused momentarily, searching for words. "Loose."

Taylor chuckled. "Well, that could be good."

After a moment, Trad spoke up. "You know, I'm really jealous of you going off to college, learning a career. You'll never be back here. You'll be gone. You'll be off in the world."

Taylor smiled and nodded. "Yeah."

"And I," Trad continued, "will forever be stuck in this fuckin' town, probably working my old man's bar for the rest of my life."

Taylor smiled. "Hey, that could be a good life. All the beer and women you could ever want!"

They both laughed; then they got on their bikes and headed back.

❧ ❧ ❧

Three months later, on a Friday morning, it was graduation day at Tartan High. The class consisted of ninety-eight students, and they were dressed in dark gray caps and gowns. Their families and friends, who had come to watch the ceremony, were already seated in the auditorium. Mr. Hanes had considered bringing his wife, but at the last moment, it became apparent she was having a bad day and would have been confused and disoriented in the unfamiliar surroundings of the graduation ceremony. Dressed in his dark blue, rarely worn suit, he had driven Taylor to the school and had already gotten a seat in the auditorium.

The future graduates were lined up on the sidewalk in front of the auditorium in two groups of forty-nine facing each other. They were arranged by height with the shortest in front. By tradition, the honor classmates, the valedictorian and the salutatorian, led the class into the auditorium. Sada Bertram, the valedictorian, was one of the shortest students in the class, so her position fit in with the height arrangement. Also, by tradition, to honor the valedictorian, Sada wore a large stole with the school's tartan pattern draped over her shoulders. The salutatorian, who was much taller, stood right behind Sada and wore a more modest tartan stole. Taylor was about three-quarters back in one line, and Trad was about three-quarters back in the other line.

At 10:25 a.m., at the appropriate signal, the two lines of the senior class were directed to proceed up the steps of the auditorium and into the lobby through separate front doors. Inside, a half-dozen teachers were standing. The teachers were then instructed to proceed down the aisle and sit in the first row to the right of the aisle. The two graduating lines were then instructed to stop at the doorways at both ends of the lobby, which led to the side aisles of the auditorium. "Pomp and Circumstance" began playing over the PA system, and as the audience rose, the students proceeded slowly down each aisle. They were directed to fill the first six rows of seats, which had been reserved for them. As soon as the students were in place standing in front of their seats, a recording of "The Star-Spangled Banner" began playing. Next, the principal of the school, Lee Howard, a tall, sturdy man with a constant frown on his face, moved to the podium. Speaking into the microphone, he said, "Now we will all turn to our flag for the Pledge of Allegiance."

After the Pledge was recited, the principal told everyone to be seated. He welcomed everyone to the graduation ceremony and introduced the class president, a tall, affable student. The class president welcomed everyone, too, and joked that the hardest thing he had done in his four years of high school was run for president. He introduced the salutatorian, who gave a speech thanking the entire faculty, naming just about everyone and stating that they did their best to prepare the graduating class for the world outside of Tartan High. Next, she turned to a discussion of hope, hope that the world would become a better place in the face of many troubling events. She referenced the Kobe, Japan earthquake killing over 6,400 people, the Baring Bank collapse because of unscrupulous trading, and the Oklahoma City bombing, which had taken place only about a month earlier. At that point, she asked everyone to please pause with heads bowed and pray for the people of Oklahoma City. She concluded by noting that through their high school education, they had received the strength of wisdom and knowledge, which they would continue to build on. And equipped with that wisdom, as part of a bigger body of graduates, they could make a better world. Everyone applauded. Then the principal introduced Sada Bertram, the valedictorian.

The entire audience stared with anticipation at Sada as she approached the stage and the podium, not because of how she looked but because no one could recall ever hearing her speak. Everyone remembered seeing her in class and knew she was smart because of grade postings, but no one ever remembered her saying anything except perhaps when directly asked a question by the teacher. And even then, her answers, though always correct, were soft-spoken and barely heard at all.

But now she was giving a speech. Her quite short stature posed a problem at the podium. No one had thought of giving her something extra to stand on, so at the podium, hardly anyone could see her face, certainly not those in the first twenty rows. She began to speak; as expected, even with the microphone amplification, she was soft-spoken. The topic was entitled "Challenges," which most people heard. But soon she droned on barely audibly, and even with the microphone amplification, most people zoned out. After about ten excruciatingly long minutes, she was finished and people applauded, which was followed by much noise of everyone repositioning themselves and shuffling their feet.

At this time, Mrs. Jane Anderson, the guidance counselor, approached the podium and began to speak. She was young, always smiling, and very positive about everything and was well liked by the students.

"I want to take this opportunity to congratulate all of our graduates today, the class of nineteen ninety-five. This is your first big step out into the world. This is where each of you head in new directions, and I want to encourage you all to hitch your wagon to a star. Go out and take your life as far as it possibly will go, and I wish you the best of luck."

She paused for a moment and locked her eyes with several students; then she continued. "Now, it is with great pleasure that I want to pass on to you some of the additional honors that have been bestowed on members of our graduating class. When I call your name, please stand up."

Mrs. Anderson went on to name each scholarship winner and describe the scholarship he or she had received. She did this with five students, including Sada Bertram. Then she named Buck Truitt, and as he got up, Taylor realized that Buck was directly behind him. Buck was a tall, brutish guy with significant athletic skills, particularly in football. In the past, he had bullied numerous guys in the class, including Taylor. It made Taylor's skin crawl to realize Buck was right behind him.

With great fanfare, Mrs. Anderson announced that Buck had been awarded a full four-year athletic scholarship to North Carolina State. There was much applause.

Next, something happened that Taylor had not expected. Mrs. Anderson called out Taylor's name. He froze. Mrs. Anderson didn't see anyone standing; she scanned the audience while saying, "Taylor, please stand up."

Reluctantly and slowly, Taylor stood, his face now reddened. She explained the details of his scholarship, which would cover tuition, room and board, books, and incidental spending money. People throughout the audience were softly expressing words of amazement. Most people knew Taylor and knew that he was a smart guy, but not that smart. He was getting a scholarship that covered more things than any other graduate's scholarship did, even more than Sada's and Buck's, which contributed to the astonishment. Taylor looked down embarrassed and then over at Trad, who sat in the next row in front of him, about seven seats down. As Taylor caught Trad's eyes, Trad grimaced, jokingly hid his face with his hand, and looked away. Mrs. Anderson continued, and then she spoke the words "The Pluck Gay and Lesbian Equality Scholarship." Taylor was bright red at this moment and just fell back into his seat as everyone applauded.

Additional expressions of astonishment resounded through the audience, peppered with laughter. Then, from behind him, Buck leaned toward his neck and spoke so forcefully that Taylor could feel the heat and moisture of his breath. "I knew you were a fag!" More chuckles sounded. Then, mimicking the sound of a chicken, he added, "Pluck, pluck, pluck." There was more laughter.

Immediately, Mrs. Anderson spoke loudly. "Ladies and gentlemen, let's act like ladies and gentlemen. You are graduating today." This seemed to do little to calm people down, and remarks were being spoken throughout until Mrs. Anderson reintroduced the principal, Lee Howard, who got up in front of the podium. His stern look scanning the audience seemed to make everyone forget what had just gone on, and all became quiet.

Mr. Howard was a no-nonsense disciplinarian and manager, and since the ceremony was well choreographed, he immediately went into the final phase of the graduation. He instructed the graduates to proceed through a side door and up onto the stage, where he would call out their names as they walked across the stage and received their diplomas. This seemed like a slow, tedious process. Taylor felt oppressed with Buck sitting directly behind him and other people staring at him, and he wanted to get it out of the way quickly.

Occasionally, a student's parents or friends showed extra support by applauding loudly or shouting a few words of enthusiasm as their daughter or son received their diploma. Then Taylor's feeling of oppression would break, but only momentarily.

Trad's row stood up and went onto the stage, and Trad got some applause and cheering since he had a broad range of friends. Taylor applauded enthusiastically. Finally, Taylor's row was instructed to stand. As he got up, he looked briefly at Buck, who was pursing his lips and making kissing motions. Taylor was angry and wanted to give him the finger but feared retribution, so he just ignored him.

Soon, Taylor was on stage with one person in front of him. Taylor was tense, angry, and embarrassed. At the same time, he was mentally going through the motions as the grads had been instructed: Shake with your right hand while extending your left on top to receive your diploma.

Taylor was now up. He proceeded to the center of the stage, shook Mr. Howard's hand while forcing a smile, and grabbed the certificate. "Faggot!" a loud voice bellowed. It was Buck, shouting as he stood to walk onto the stage. People laughed as Mr. Howard and Taylor stared at Buck. Taylor couldn't believe he was going through this and wanted to disappear through some imagined trap door in the floor.

Taylor looked up at Mr. Howard and noticed a slight smile, which he quickly dropped from his face. Then Mr. Howard held out his arm, pointing to Buck. "I can hold back your diploma!"

Taylor rushed off the stage. For a moment, he wanted to dart out the back of the auditorium, but instead he kept moving with the other students funneling into the seats. Just before he was to file back into his row, he realized Buck would still be sitting behind him. Unable to deal with that, he continued walking toward the front door. In a moment, he spotted his father, apparently agitated, in the audience at the end of a row, and their eyes met. Taylor looked down and rushed out the door as his father followed.

Outside, Taylor stopped and leaned against the wall of the building, moisture welling up in his eyes. His father approached and spoke softly. "Taylor, what's this all about?"

Taylor just stood there with his head lowered; then he started to walk down the steps, followed by his father. At this moment, he wanted to tell his father that he was not gay and that he was really straight, but he knew his father would be furious to hear that he had lied on the application for the scholarship. His father would probably make him give it up, and then he wouldn't be able to go to college.

As they walked a few steps along the sidewalk, his father added, "Look, we've always been able to talk about everything."

Taylor was still silent; then he stopped walking and turned toward his father, his eyes still downcast.

Mr. Hanes added, "Son, I know with your mom's illness and everything going on, I . . . I haven't been very available to you. But if you needed to talk, damn, I would have found time. I— I . . . just don't understand." Mr. Hanes lowered his voice to a barely audible level. "You seemed to be interested in girls. What about Christine? And—and . . . where did this all come from?" Then he raised his voice to a normal level. "On the other hand, I'm just amazed; I mean I'm really proud you took the initiative to get this scholarship. It blew my mind. This is all too much information coming at me at one time."

Taylor looked directly at his father. "Look, Dad. I, um, I've got a lot going on right now that I, uh, have to sort out. So—so could we talk about this later?"

There was a long pause; then Mr. Hanes softly responded, "Sure, Taylor. We have plenty of time. Whenever you're ready, we'll talk. Okay?" Taylor nodded in agreement.

Taylor proceeded back up the stairs, followed by his father. As they reached the top, the processional music began playing. Taylor and his dad stood flanking the doorway and watched as the graduates began exiting the building. Some of them yelped and threw their caps into the air. There was much laughing and smiling, yet Taylor noticed some classmates looking at him strangely. Christine came out of the building, flicked a brief smile in his direction, and moved on down the stairs. When Trad came out, he raised his open hand, on which Taylor slapped a high five. Trad yelled, "We did it!" Taylor noticed his father eyeing Trad without expression. Taylor realized that his father must be thinking that since Trad was his best friend and they spent a lot of time together, Trad was gay too, and they were having sex. Taylor laughed to himself, amused that such a thing was the furthest thing from his mind, but at the same time somewhat frightened that his lie was growing out of control. Now everyone at school, teachers included, thought he was gay, and his father suspected that his best friend was also gay.

But Christine won't think I'm gay, he thought. He searched for her to go speak to her, but by this time, her parents had led her down the sidewalk, and they were climbing into their car. She would know he wasn't gay, but what about her parents? They seemed very judgmental. What would they think?

Wanting to clear his mind of all these thoughts, he turned to his father and Trad and said, "I'm hungry. Let's get out of here and have some lunch."

Mr. Hanes spoke up. "Good idea. Congratulations to you, Trad. Is your dad here?"

"No, Mr. Hanes. He couldn't make it. He was . . . he had other things to do."

"Well," Mr. Hanes continued, "sorry he couldn't make it. I'm sure he is very proud of you. So, come along, Trad. I'm buying. Where would you boys like to have lunch?"

As they turned to walk down the steps, Taylor noticed his dad raising his hand to place it on Taylor's shoulder as he had done many times before, only to stop as he continued walking. Taylor knew that from this point on, his father would react to him differently and they would have an entirely different relationship. In fact, everyone in town would react to him differently. Things just wouldn't be the same.

Chapter 6

A Clean Break

Long ago, Taylor had decided that when summer arrived, he would use every bit of free time to earn as much money as possible for college. So, months ago, he had called Hal Brockten, who owned Hal's, a local eatery. Taylor had worked there the last two summers, and he asked Hal if he could use his help again this year. Hal liked Taylor because he worked hard. With Taylor and Angela, the server, Hal could take entire days off to go fishing, so Hal told Taylor to start whenever he liked. Taylor started the day after graduation.

Hal's was located a few blocks from the center of town, easily walkable from the courthouse or any of the businesses in town. It was surrounded by a large, hard-packed dirt parking area, so no one had any trouble finding a spot to park.

The building was a rectangular structure with a flat roof and large glass windows in front. It had a small dining room with seven gray Formica-topped tables, a luncheon bar with the same

Formica, a jukebox off in one corner, and the kitchen in the back. The whole place showed a lot of wear, from the peeling paint on the red and gray outdoor sign that read HAL'S to the worn vinyl gray and white tiles on the floor. But despite its appearance, the restaurant usually had every seat filled for breakfast and lunch. This was because Hal's served good food, the usual luncheon fare of burgers, hot dogs, barbecue, and French fries. However, Hal's real claim to fame, was the coleslaw that his wife Emily made, which was served in generous portions on all the sandwiches.

Taylor had tried working at his dad's garage, but the schedule was irregular, which Taylor didn't like. He liked to know in advance when to go in and when to leave. That didn't always work with the garage; sometimes there was a lot of work, and sometimes there was none, and his dad only paid him when he was needed.

The garage and hamburger jobs were both messy and greasy. One coated you with dirty grease and the other with smelly grease, and Taylor hated that about both jobs. With either job, Taylor couldn't wait to get home, strip off all his clothes, put them in the washer, and then jump in the shower. The good things about the restaurant job were the steady hours and all the different people who were always coming in. Through the open window to the counter, he could talk with them briefly when business was slow. And sometimes, if the kitchen wasn't busy, he would stand behind the counter and talk with the customers.

It was shortly after the lunch rush on Saturday, the day after graduation, when Taylor noticed Christine coming in. She was expressionless and paused briefly after entering the front door. Taylor looked through the window, caught her eye, smiled, and waved. She did not smile back but gave only a halfhearted wave; then she approached the counter, which was now empty except for a man at the end reading the newspaper and finishing his coffee. Hal had gone to the store to get supplies for the following week.

Taylor quickly untied his apron and went through the swinging doors toward her.

"Hey, what's up? You look sad."

She looked him in the eyes briefly, and then looked down. Finally, she spoke. "So, what's all this stuff with Buck Truitt calling you a faggot?"

Taylor looked over to see if the man at the end had heard her. He waved her farther down the counter away from him.

His voice went softer. "You know Buck; he's just an asshole."

"Yeah, he's just a jerk, but what about this scholarship, this gay scholarship?"

Taylor shrugged, annoyed at her question. "It's to work for equality for gay people because they're discriminated against. That doesn't mean that I have to be . . . that I'm gay. Besides, you should know better than anyone else. It's just a scholarship, and it will pay for everything!"

There was a pause as she looked up at him. "So, you will be working toward supporting the gay lifestyle?" Taylor looked at her questioningly. Christine continued more hurriedly. "You know, my parents were at the graduation and—and last night, they were all over my case. Don't you feel that this— this . . ." She was looking for the right words but seemed only able to curl her upper lip in revulsion. "Aren't you . . . aren't you, by doing this—"

"What?" Taylor interrupted. "Enabling them? I don't know. I don't really approve of the gay lifestyle myself, but you know, it's a lot of money. If—if they're foolish enough to take me, I—I can play along with it."

Taylor looked up. Standing in front of the window and looking in was the man in the leather jacket and leather hat. He was staring directly at Taylor with a severe frown. Taylor jumped, startled by this menacing figure, and exclaimed, "What the . . ."

Christine turned to look at what Taylor was reacting to but saw nothing. "What is the matter with you?"

Taylor hurried outside as he said, "I've got to find out what this—this—this guy wants." Once outside, though, he saw no one close by. Taylor looked up and down the street and saw no one except an old woman with a cane a block away. He stood there with his heart racing, momentarily bewildered; then he went back inside.

"What was that all about?" Christine asked.

"I—I saw someone looking in the window. Didn't you see him? He was right there where you looked. But—but now he's gone."

There was a long pause as Taylor tried to calm down and Christine studied Taylor's unusual agitation.

Finally, Taylor asked, "What—what were we talking about?"

Christine looked down again and began to speak slowly. "Well, anyway, even before this gay scholarship thing, I had already been thinking. With you going to Carolina and me at Wingate, we're a good three hours away. It might be a good opportunity for us to meet other people."

Taylor looked surprised. This was a kiss-off. "Oh, I see," he said. "This is a split up." She looked up directly into his eyes. He added, "Well, I'd been thinking the same thing." He felt comfortable saying this because when he had first learned he had been accepted to Carolina, he immediately thought about all the new girls he might get to meet. He then added, "Okay, we can do this if you want. I'm okay with it."

The conversation ended quickly with a few halfhearted words about keeping in touch through phone calls and letters and seeing each other during holidays. But first, there would be the summer. He certainly would see her around town or at the diner. And he would be bothered, of course, especially if she were with another guy.

❀ ❀ ❀

For the rest of the summer, Taylor tried to forget Christine by concentrating on his work, making lists of supplies and clothes to take to college, shopping for missing items, and enjoying the people who entered the diner, sometimes engaging them in long conversations about almost anything. He began to really know people who came in on a regular basis, especially the ones who came in before or after the lunch rush. There was Fran, about fifty years old, who worked in the wedding shop down the street. They talked about her mother, who had died from Alzheimer's, and they compared notes. There was Edgar, the elderly attorney, who worked in the courthouse. He ordered the same meal every day Monday through Friday. It consisted of a hamburger, pink on the inside, with cheese, pickle and mustard only and a large order of French fries. Edgar knew everybody in town and talked to everybody. He had gone to undergraduate and law school at Carolina years ago, and he and Taylor compared notes. There was Jessie, the twenty-year-old who worked at his dad's garage and had a late lunch there every day. They mostly talked about work at the garage and sometimes about Taylor's dad, who Jessie thought was really a great boss.

There was Alan, who also had a late lunch and had graduated several years ago and now worked at Hatcher's florist shop. In high school, he had always been surrounded by girls. He was tall, reasonably attractive, always well dressed, and seemed to have a harem. But there was something different about him. He was not a jock type, but he was also not effeminate. *What's the story with that?* Taylor thought. Now he came to the restaurant regularly to talk to Taylor but without his harem, who probably had all gotten married.

Taylor always chitchatted politely with him but felt uncomfortable about what to talk about. In July, one such awkward conversation was taking place when Pastor Robbins entered the restaurant. Taylor and his family had occasionally gone to the Methodist church where Pastor Robbins was the minister, and they were on speaking terms with him. When their eyes met, Taylor smiled and nodded hello. As he did so, Alan turned around to see who came in. The minister leered at them both, turned around and left.

"What was that all about?" Taylor asked. "He didn't even say hello."

Alan shrugged. "Guess he learned about your change in status."

Taylor blinked and thought, *Change in status? Alan heard about the scholarship. My God, Alan is gay. Everyone suspected. It must be true, and he heard about the scholarship.* Then a rush of thoughts came over him. *Pastor Robbins thinks I'm gay, and he's angry. Also, no girls are coming in the diner to talk to me. They all think I'm gay. The only young people who talk to me are Alan and—and wait, Jessie, who works at the garage. Jessie, gay? Could this be true? Would Dad know? Of course, I couldn't ask him.*

That night, he decided to call Trad and see what he knew. When Taylor told him what had happened, Trad started laughing hysterically.

After he had gotten control of himself, Trad said, "Yeah, of course Alan's gay. And Jessie too!"

"How do you know all this? Do you have gaydar?"

"Look, when you work at a bar, you learn a lot of stuff. People drink and get loose lips, and people go home with people. You learn a lot about people."

"Well, what about me? How far has this scholarship thing gone?"

Trad laughed again. "It was in the newspaper a month ago, right after graduation. My dad's girlfriend brought it to my attention."

"You're kidding!" Taylor didn't know if he was telling the truth or not, but the very idea sent a flush of heat throughout his body.

"Not kidding. She even said, 'Your boyfriend's in the paper.'" Trad said this in a mockingly high-pitched Southern voice. "Then she threw the paper down in front of me. She's okay. She likes to tease me."

"*The Tartan Gazette*? It was in *The Tartan Gazette*? Why was it in *The Tartan Gazette*?"

"You know, small town, they report on everything, and getting a scholarship is big news."

Taylor cringed. "God, everyone knows! Everyone knows!"

At this moment, Taylor wanted to just disappear. Now he couldn't wait to leave this town. He just wanted to put all this behind him and move to Chapel Hill where Carolina was located, where he would arrive as an unknown among thousands of other students and could just be himself. He knew his last month working at the restaurant would seem like six months. But he liked interacting with people, and even though time passed slowly, he still enjoyed talking to Fran and Edgar and even to Alan and Jessie.

In fact, the more he got to know Alan and Jessie, the more relaxed he became with them and the more he got to like them. He was actually learning things from them. Jessie taught him things about engines that he previously hadn't understood. When Jessie explained things to him, they made more sense than when his father had tried to teach him. From Alan, he learned about choosing quality clothing and dressing well. Alan had several friends in college throughout the state and had visited them occasionally on weekends. He advised Taylor on what kinds of clothing guys were wearing now and told him about sales going on in nearby towns. By the time Taylor was about to go to college for orientation, he felt that he could handle most minor car problems and he had a more than adequate wardrobe for school. These guys were okay; he was surprised, but he really liked them.

In his last week at work before going off to school, they were both kidding him about how much fun he was going to have with football games, concerts, and drinking beer. He almost invited them to join him on some weekends, but then he stopped short of asking. He had not even asked his best friend Trad, so why should he have asked them, two guys he liked but did not consider close friends? He wondered why he hadn't asked Trad, but then he realized the truth. What he really wanted, at least at this point, was to make a clean break.

Chapter 7

All Promising

Only a few more days, and Dad will be driving me to Chapel Hill. It will be like a whole new chapter in my life. I'm really stoked. I'll meet new people, be exposed to new things, and who knows where it will go from there.

Mom continues to decline, but fortunately, Dad's working out some details to get some help on a regular basis. Between her school insurance and Medicare, it will cover most of it, but with everything else, it's still going to be hard on Dad. I know I'm selfish, but Dad doesn't agree, and he's fine with it.

I really want to leave this town. It's really dried up and suffering, and the people are small-minded and depressing. There is no future here. No jobs. No entertainment. There's so much of the world out there. I've broken up with Christine. The preacher thinks I'm destined for hell, not that what he thinks bothers me. The whole town thinks I'm a pervert, and I get these funny looks and feel people are talking about me. As time goes on, that's bothering me less and less, and then there is this ghost thing here that's been harassing me. Hope he stays here.

So, I'm looking at getting away. It's like starting a new life. I see it as all promising.

Chapter 8

His New Life

To Taylor, the summer had seemed endless because of his longing to leave Tartan. Now it was the middle of August, and his dad had driven him to the Carolina campus in his dad's pickup, loaded with almost all of Taylor's personal possessions in the bed of the truck. University rules didn't allow freshmen to have cars, so Taylor's dad had advertised his Fairlane, and it had sold in two days because his dad had kept it in such great condition. Taylor was all right with this, figuring that his dad needed the extra money and could find him something as good or better when he became a sophomore.

They stopped at the Residence Office and picked up Taylor's dorm key and a campus map. Then they wound their way past several dorms busy with incoming freshmen and their parents and through an alleyway, ending up in the parking lot assigned to his residence, Emerson Hall. Mr. Hanes pulled into the parking spot that was closest to a sign reading EMERSON HALL, and they both got out.

"I don't see any students moving in," his dad said. "Are you sure this is the right place?" They looked at the unusually built structure. It was concrete and actually stair-stepped like bleachers, and the front door of the building defined by a sign overhead was on the side of the bleachers.

"Oh, I remember reading now," Taylor said. "This was originally the old stadium that became too small for their sporting events, and the campus continued to grow up around the stadium. Guess the other side was torn down and they converted this into a dorm."

"Wow," Mr. Hanes said, "it's not much to look at. Couldn't you have gotten into one of the regular dorms with windows and a roof?"

"Nah, for the first year, they assign your dorm to you. Then after that, you can choose where you want to live. They also have this system where they try to group you with people who are in the same curriculum. I guess they figure you're going to get along better with people who have similar interests."

"You mean like all the chemistry majors together?"

"Yeah."

"That makes sense. Well, let's check it out."

They decided to carry some things in with them. Taylor grabbed several garment bags and threw them over his shoulder, and Taylor's dad grabbed a TV in one hand and a suitcase in the other. Entering the dark, curving hallway, they ran into a young female student who was heading out the door. They greeted each other with a smile and a quick hi; then Taylor began to look for room 12, key in hand.

"Coed dorms?" Mr. Hanes asked.

Just ahead, a bathroom door swung open, and a tall, muscular student with only a towel around his waist started to walk toward them. He smiled, and his eyes locked onto Taylor's dad as he said, "Well, hello, handsome." Mr. Hanes looked back speechless but managed to break a smile. They proceeded ahead silently. After reaching room 12, they both stopped and turned around to see the student staring at Mr. Hanes's butt. Taylor quickly unlocked the door, and both entered, chuckling.

"What was that all about?" Mr. Hanes whispered.

"Dad, you just got cruised by that guy. He also was checking out your butt."

"Nah, he could have been looking at you."

"I'm carrying garment bags. There is nothing to see. Besides, he was staring at you." After they had set things down, Taylor continued, "This dorm houses a lot of dramatic arts students. He's probably a dancer or actor."

"Oh," Mr. Hanes replied. "You know, Taylor, you may want to take up running or at least hit the gym a little more. That guy was quite buff." Taylor just stood there, surprised at what he was hearing. His dad continued, "You should have gotten a haircut before we came up. Maybe shorter on the sides. That seems to be in now."

Taylor laughed. "Look, Dad, I'm quite comfortable with my body image." As he said that, he thought, *Well, not completely. I would like to be a few inches taller, a little bigger in the chest, and a couple inches thinner in the waist. And besides, Dad is in such good shape because he does physical labor all day and runs on weekends.*

"No, no," Mr. Hanes continued. "You look good. You're—you're just fine the way you are. And besides, you're here to get an education."

Suddenly the air was shattered with the loud banter of a young girl almost shrieking. The door across the hall swung open, and the girl hurried out into the hall, shouting, "You are absolutely fucked up! You are so fucking weird! This is it! I'm getting out of here!" Then she turned and quickly scurried down the hall. From the darkened room she had just left, Taylor and his dad could hear another woman in deep laughter. They looked at each other as the laughter seemed to rise in volume and then subside.

Curious, they stepped toward the doorway and noticed that the room was dimly lit but spotted with specks of rotating points of light, apparently from a disco ball. They moved closer to the open door and saw a female student in a black robe kneeling in front of a pentagram on the floor, with candles lit on the end of each point. She was in the process of blowing out the candles and still chuckling.

As they approached, their shadows from the hall light crossed over the pentagram, and she looked up.

"Oh, hello!" she said cheerfully. She blew out the rest of the candles, got up and turned on a lamp. "Please come in." In the light, they could see she was an attractive girl, a little overweight for her frame, wearing dark, heavy makeup. She stretched out her hand to Taylor. "You must be a new dorm member. I'm Marcia Templeton. I'm a witch."

Taylor responded. "I'm Taylor Hanes, across the hall, just moving in."

She then turned to Taylor's dad. "And a parent, helping."

Taylor's dad shook her hand. "Yes, Ben Hanes, Taylor's dad."

"Great." Then turning back to Taylor, she asked, "Your first year?"

"Yep. What about you?"

"I'm a junior but may stay for grad school." There was a pause as Taylor and his dad looked down at the pentagram. Finally, Mr. Hanes spoke up while grimacing and scratching his head.

"Is there a degree in witchcraft?"

Marcia broke out in laughter, followed by Taylor and then by Taylor's dad. "No, no, no. You'll have to excuse all this." Her voice got softer as if she did not want to be heard outside the room. "This is the third dorm room I've gotten at this university, and I really love it. Look . . ." She pointed to the number 13 on the door. "It even has my lucky number: 13! So I do not want to ever move until I'm through with this university. And they had assigned me this tightass, blonde squeak from the Bible Belt. God, I had to get rid of her really quick."

"You just didn't get along?" Mr. Hanes asked.

"Well, I knew it was going to be a disaster. She's ultra-conservative. And I wanted the room all to myself, so I concocted this devil-worship crap. I've gotten rid of other roommates this way, but this bitch was so easy. Oops! Guess I shouldn't be cursing in front of your dad."

"That's okay. He works in a garage."

"Anyway, she scared really easy. It was so funny. But I actually am a witch," she continued. "But we don't use this sort of stuff unless we wanted to raise the devil, and why would we want to do that?"

"Oh, okay!" Mr. Hanes replied. Then he said , "Taylor, we got a whole truckload that needs to be carried in."

"Right!" Taylor responded. "Well, guess I'll be seeing you around."

"Yeah. Wait! You don't seem like the other guys in this dorm. What's your major going to be?"

"Right now it's math."

"I'm in Dramatic Arts. Math? Huh! Okay, see you later." They walked into Taylor's room as she shut her door.

For a moment, they stood silently and looked around the room. The room was just below the stair-stepped bleachers, and the stairsteps could be seen above. In the risers between the steps of one row, there were three narrow slits to allow for natural light.

Mr. Hanes said, "There is no real window in this place, so it's kind of dark."

"Well, I've been told that, most of the time, I'll be in classes or the library and won't be here until after dark to study and sleep. And it'll keep me from getting distracted. It seems pretty quiet. I think it will be okay."

"I guess your roommate hasn't arrived yet. Will he be a freshman too?"

"I'm going to have the room all to myself."

"Really. How did that happen?"

"I didn't want a lot of distractions, you know, with a roommate, so I contacted the Residence Office to get a single room. The scholarship had extra funding to do that."

Mr. Hanes looked at him, surprised. "Really? That's great! You'll have more privacy and be able to study better."

"Yeah, exactly what I'm hoping to achieve."

"Tell me something," Mr. Hanes said. "That guy in the hall. You said he was probably an actor or dancer and—and Marcia, she's in dramatic arts. So how did you get grouped with them if you are a math major?"

Taylor sighed and sat down on the bed. "Well, I guess just about everybody here is in dramatic arts or dance or other arts, and evidently they placed me here because of my scholarship." His dad just stared at him; then Taylor added, "But I'll move next year."

Mr. Hanes still appeared confused, but he brushed it aside and shrugged. "Okay, it's probably best you did that. And you can change next year, right?"

"Sure, at least I think so. We'll see how it goes."

"And besides, look," Mr. Hanes said, "you've already made a friend across the hall—Marcia. There's something about her I like."

Taylor smiled and said, "Yeah, she's all right. And Dad, stick around a while, and maybe you can be friends with that buff guy down the hall! There's something about you he also likes."

Mr. Hanes sneered. "All right, let's get that truck unloaded."

Taylor's dad stayed late into the afternoon, unloading the truck and helping Taylor organize his room. It had been a long time since Taylor and his dad had done anything together, and Taylor was enjoying it. Likewise, Taylor's dad seemed to be appreciating the whole college experience. He kept asking for details on how many classes Taylor would be taking and what activities were available. Taylor had done quite a bit of reading about the campus and could talk about it extensively, and his dad was amazed at all the things that were available.

It was after four o'clock when Mr. Hanes realized he'd have to leave to get back to Tartan to pick up Kathryn, his wife, from the Council on Aging where she was being supervised. Taylor walked his dad to the truck, and they both hugged, and then his dad got into the truck and left. A swell of loneliness swept over Taylor as he walked back down the hall and into his room. He closed the door, fell onto the bed, and looked up at the ceiling. He thought, *Now what?* He hadn't gotten any books, nothing was going on around campus, and he didn't know anybody. Then he thought of Trad, who was probably at his father's bar. He immediately called the bar. Trad answered.

"What's up, Trad?"

"I'm cleaning the bathrooms here at my dad's place. He wanted me to work today. Are you in your new dorm room?"

"Yeah, it's all set up. Kind of dark and dreary, but for the most part, it's okay."

There was a long pause; then Trad asked, "So, when do classes start?"

"Next Monday. This week is all orientation. We go to some lectures. We meet with our counselor and get class assignments, buy books, check out different stuff on campus."

"Neat," Trad replied. There was another long pause.

"So," Taylor asked, "who did you date last night? And how'd that go?"

"Cécile, from the grocery store. She's okay. Nothing to report." There was another pause; then Trad continued. "So, was there a reason you called?"

Taylor was bothered by this question. In the past, they would talk for no reason at all, but now he realized that things would be different. Trad was at work cleaning bathrooms, and Taylor was in college, starting a new chapter in his life. Their friendship would no longer be the same. Trad knew it, and now Taylor did, too. And this bothered Taylor.

Taylor edged out a sentence, "I—I, uh, guess I just wanted to talk. I was feeling sort of lonely."

Trad responded almost gruffly, "Haven't you met anyone?"

"Well, no. I just moved into the dorm. I saw people in the hall, but . . . oh, yeah! This girl across the hall. I met her this afternoon. She's somewhat attractive and kind of edgy, but—"

"There you are," Trad interrupted. "Get to know her better. You know how to meet people. Better than me."

"Yeah, yeah. Guess you're right."

"Well, Dad's eyeing me. I got to finish this."

Taylor wanted to talk more, but they said goodbye and hung up. Taylor lay there, looking up with lips pressed tight. Then he jumped up, opened his door, and knocked on Marcia's door. She quickly answered.

"Hi," Taylor said. "So, where do you get food around this place?"

"Food . . . You mean snacks, or are you talking dinner?"

"Well, it is getting late. No, wait. It's barely five. Are you up for dinner?"

Marcia thought for a moment. "Sure, I missed lunch, so I'm hungry. Also, I can point out some places to eat."

They headed out, and Taylor asked Marcia to point out any buildings he might need to know. Once out of the alley that led to their dorm, they crossed the street, where she pointed out the student union. They went in, looked at the campus snack bar, briefly looked at the menu, and then left. She pointed out the undergraduate and graduate library and then turned toward

Lenoir Hall, the cafeteria that was centrally located. They went in and looked around but decided to head into town, which would be a ten-minute walk.

Marcia asked Taylor about his hometown, and he began a long explanation about how Tartan used to be a thriving textile town but was now suffering. He went into detail about which businesses had folded and what was left and how he could never see himself going back. Marcia said that she thoroughly understood how he must feel. After Marcia had pointed out a few other buildings and some campus history and legends, they found themselves on Franklin Street, at the edge of the campus. They crossed the street and entered a place called Mac's Pizza where, according to Marcia, they served good food and a variety of beers. They found a booth toward the rear.

"Do you drink beer?" Marcia asked.

"Yeah, but they check IDs, don't they?"

"I got one. I'll place the order at the bar. Is a veggie pizza okay?"

"Sounds great."

After a few minutes, Marcia returned with a pitcher of beer and two glasses.

"So, are you twenty-one?" Taylor asked.

"No, twenty. But I've got a fake ID. We make them in the theatrical art department. I'll get one made for you."

"Could you?"

"Sure. Just don't report me to the school or to your parents."

"Dad doesn't mind if I drink, if I do it responsibly. He says when he was my age, he was allowed to drink beer at eighteen, and it didn't hurt him. I've never seen him with a drink of any kind, wine or beer or anything."

"Yeah, this 'twenty-one' nonsense only started like ten years ago."

"So, are you a vegetarian? You ordered a veggie pizza."

"I am. I don't like slaughtering animals for food. What about you?"

"I've given it a lot of thought, but right now, I'm still eating meat. There weren't many places where I'm from that you could get a vegetarian meal."

Marcia laughed. "Yeah, the town with nothing there. That could be your chamber of commerce's motto."

After more discussion about Tartan, Taylor asked Marcia about her hometown. They laughed when Marcia explained that she was from Wichita, Kansas, claiming it was purely a coincidence. Taylor took the opportunity to broach the subject he was eager to ask about.

"So, tell me, what's all this stuff about being a witch?"

"Well, what do you mean?"

"Is this something you really believe," he prodded, "or were you just playing with your roommate to get her to leave?"

Marcia answered slowly without any expression. "We are all born witches. It is then up to the individual. If you desire to promote change in your life or the lives of others to do positive things in the world, then you need to study more about witchcraft. Some of this includes meditation and various other ways to focus your mind, which will strengthen it, all in order to elevate the level of consciousness. I believe it is very powerful and that it is a science where one can control the secret forces of nature."

Taylor looked at Marcia straight in the eye, wanting to laugh or make fun of her, yet he felt she was serious and didn't want to offend her. "So," he asked, "do you do magic and that sort of thing?"

Marcia nodded. "Magic is all part of the law of nature, although not fully understood, but it's not something that's supernatural. Instead, it is part of the powers that reside in the self, inside all of us."

At this point, their meal was brought, and after rearranging the plates, they began to eat.

"So, do you do spells?" Taylor asked.

"Well, yeah, it's all part of the magic we use," Marcia replied. "But I have to point out that it should only be used for good purposes."

"So if you misuse this magic to hurt someone, what happens? You're thrown in hell for eternity?"

Marcia smiled and said, "First of all, there is no head witch, like we don't have a pope, so beliefs are all over the board about afterlife and that sort of thing. Some believe in reincarnation where you come back as another human being . . . hopefully, to continually advance spiritually. Others believe in reincarnation of the soul through different species. Some believe that the soul rests for a while in a place called the Otherworld. Many witches believe that souls can be reached through spirit mediums. In fact, my Aunt Zena does this all the time."

There were a few moments of silence as Taylor thought about the figure in the black hat, no doubt a spirit from the Otherworld, which had appeared to him several times. And the name Zena seemed familiar to him. "Zena . . . Zena . . ." Taylor said aloud. "I remember! There was a fortune-teller outside of town. I saw it as we were coming to campus."

"That's her. She works from her house and tells fortunes and communicates with the dead." Then Marcia added with emphasis, "Now, she's a witch!"

Taylor laughed. "What do you mean?"

"Well, she's studied for years and years. And she can communicate with the Otherworld at the drop of a hat."

There was more silence; then Taylor added, "She sounds interesting. I would love to meet her sometime."

"And she would love to meet you. I go there all the time, especially on weekends. We'll have to set something up."

"That would be great! Okay, the next question . . ."

Marcia looked directly into Taylor's eyes and smiled. "Yeah?"

"So, when you're not being a witch, what are you?" Marcia tilted her head as if not understanding the question. Taylor continued, "You know, what do you do as a Dramatic Arts major?"

"Well, I'm in my junior year. And that's when the course work gets more interesting."

"How so?"

"Well, the first two years are pretty much core courses, a lot of the same stuff you probably will be taking. But this year, it will be more specialized, and I'll study contemporary theater and speech courses and acting methods. But the best thing is we get to take a two-part course that spans both semesters, called Stage Productions. And in this, we'll be trying out for actual productions that will be produced and staged this semester and next, so we'll actually be acting on the stage. And then we can also take some television and motion picture courses."

"Wow, that sounds really exciting."

"Yeah, I think it will be. I'm looking forward to it."

Following their meal, Marcia suggested walking down Franklin Street so she could point out more good places to eat or get a beer. After doing that, they headed back to campus. As they passed by the Player's Theatre, an old building that resembled a Grecian temple, she related some of the history of the building. They passed through the Courtyard, a wide, paved brick area interspersed with trees and grassy areas. She related that it was used as a public forum and gathering place and was a venue for small concerts. From there, they headed back to Emerson Hall.

They both entered the building and headed down the curving hallway.

"So, do you like this dorm?" Taylor asked. "It's pretty dark and depressing."

Marcia laughed. "Only on your side."

"What?" Taylor chuckled. "You think I'm an agent of the devil or something?"

"No, come look," she said as they approached her room. She unlocked the door and flicked on the light. Her room had two beds like his and two desks, but because it was larger, there was enough space for a love seat in front of a television. She walked over to a large window that was covered with heavy drapes and yanked the drapes open to reveal the large, multi-paned window.

"See, I get a lot of light in here, especially when it's bright daylight."

"Wow!" Taylor responded. "And your room is huge. I guess it's because of the pie-shaped arrangement of the rooms in this building."

"Yeah, I love it. I've been in most of the dorms on campus, and with one or two exceptions, these are the best rooms."

"Not my room," Taylor reacted. "Have you been across the hall?" As he said this, he gestured through her open door to his door and noticed an envelope wedged between the door and doorframe. "Huh. Someone left me a note." He grabbed it off the door, opened it, and began to read what looked like a formal invitation.

Marcia continued talking as she followed Taylor to the door. "Oh, sure, I know they are kind of dark, but I even like them. They are bigger than most rooms."

While Taylor continued reading the invitation, he reached in his pocket for keys, unlocked his door, and flipped on the light. Marcia followed him into the room.

"Wow! A party invite!" Taylor said.

"Party!" Marcia reacted with surprise. "Where?"

"Well, not exactly a party. It's really a reception. Put on by the university. Are you busy this Thursday at six o'clock?"

"I don't know. Some of these university receptions are pretty stuffy. What's it for?"

"All students who received certain scholarships are invited to it. I can bring a friend or a date."

"You have a scholarship? That's impressive. Is it at the president's house?"

"It's not a *merit* scholarship," Taylor responded. "It's at someplace called Castlewood, and they gave directions."

"You're kidding!" Marcia exclaimed. "And yes, I'll go! I've been wanting to get in that place forever—well, ever since I've been a student here."

Taylor looked at her, smiling at her enthusiastic reaction. "Why, what's it like?"

"It is so cool. Well, first of all, it is truly a castle, like from the Middle Ages, only with more Gothic overtones. It is truly creepy and wonderful. But the best thing is that it's reputed to be haunted. And I mean *really* haunted, not just chamber-of-commerce-stuff-to-get-you-to-come-to-town haunted but really, *really* haunted."

Taylor was unfazed and softly responded, "Cool. Also says IDs required if consuming alcohol. Must be serving beer or wine."

"Even better. I'm looking forward to it."

"It's a dress-up affair," Taylor said. "Cocktail attire."

"I've got a black cocktail dress," Marcia added. "All my clothes are black."

Taylor was silent for a moment; then he said, "Oh, the witch theme. Will you be arriving on a broom?"

Marcia smiled. "Actually, black is slimming. And it makes it easier to coordinate things." She looked around the room. Taylor's bed was made with a brown and white striped bedspread. There were several books neatly arranged on the bookshelf above his desk. A jar of natural peanut butter and a box of saltines were sitting in a bin on the top of his small refrigerator. She added, "You've really got this set up nicely. Look at this! A bowl of fruit!"

"It's Dad. He really likes things neat and organized. And he believes in healthy eating. I just hope I've inherited some of this from him."

"I go through phases. If I have time, I become highly organized. But then it all breaks down when, in the middle of the semester or toward exam times, I run out of time. Then my room looks like the aftermath of a hurricane."

"I can identify with that."

"Hey, I have a couple of cold beers. Do you want a brew and maybe watch the tube?"

Taylor thought for a moment. He had really enjoyed getting to know Marcia and was happy to make a friend, so he didn't want to sound like he was putting her off. He answered, "You know, that sounds like fun, but tomorrow is the first day of orientation, and there is an initial meeting at nine o'clock, and I've got some other loose ends to handle before I turn in. So, what about a rain check?"

"Fine. Yeah, it's only your first day here. Well, if you have any questions or need some help, you know where to find me." She moved toward her room.

"But," Taylor added quickly, "we're on for Thursday, right?"

"Definitely; I wouldn't miss it. And look, I have a car. Be glad to drive."

"Oh, okay."

"See you later." She closed her door.

Taylor shut his door and smiled. He thought about the fact that this was day one at Carolina and there would be many more days after this. He wanted to do really well in school; it would require lots of discipline and hard work, but he was willing to put in the necessary time. He thought about his mom and dad and being away from Tartan and missed them a little. He thought about Christine, whose detachment didn't seem to bother him for some reason, and he thought about Trad, who probably would be stuck at his father's bar for the rest of his life. But then he thought about all the interesting coursework he would experience, expanding his mind with new concepts and ideas and preparing himself for some career. And he thought about Marcia and meeting other new people and making new friendships. All of this really was what he wanted, and he welcomed his new life.

Chapter 9

What's He After?

It was Thursday evening, and the temperature was perfect, so Taylor called Marcia and asked her if she would be open to walking instead of driving to Castlewood for the party. Marcia said she liked the idea and wanted the exercise but she was planning to wear heels, and since it was about a twenty-minute walk, she would rather not. However, fifteen minutes before their appointed time, she knocked on Taylor's door, dressed in a knee-length cocktail dress, holding a black handbag and wearing flats. Dressed in his dark suit, he opened the door and just stared at her. Her hair was perfect and glistened from the overhead hall light, and her face was made up beautifully for an evening out. She was wearing small diamond earrings that matched a small pendant necklace, and both caught the light, too.

"You look . . . wow, great!" Taylor said.

"And you clean up pretty nicely yourself."

They both laughed; then Marcia added, "Okay, I decided we'll walk. The flats are more comfortable anyway, and like you said, it's beautiful outside."

"Okay, so are you ready? We'll have to leave now to get there on time."

"I'm all set."

Marcia knew where the castle was located and directed them as they went. As they walked through the campus and the residential area that led to Castlewood, Marcia described some other haunted buildings and places in the area, including The Carolina Inn, Memorial Hall, New East, The Players Theatre, and the cemetery. However, Taylor was so distracted by how attractive she was, he could barely concentrate on what she was saying. At every opportunity, he would turn his head toward her to get another look. The girls in Tartan he had dated had just never seemed this well put together. Because of her theater training, Taylor thought, *Marcia must really know how to put on makeup and dress the part.*

Soon they were on a residential street, where they passed a Catholic church. Then the road just seemed to dead-end in front of towering, open gates held up by massive stone columns.

"This is it," Marcia said as they proceeded through and continued walking along a winding driveway. At the first point where their view was unobstructed by trees, they stopped in amazement.

"Look at this place," Marcia expressed in a hushed voice.

It was much larger than either of them had expected. It was constructed of large stone blocks. The center section appeared to be three stories tall, with numerous other wings fanning off, and an immense porte-cochere off the front where the driveway passed through. There were several turrets and elaborate decorative leaded glass windows throughout. As they continued closer, they were able to note many interesting and unusual gargoyles under the eaves, on the chimneys, and on the peaks of the roofs.

"Someone had lots of money," Taylor commented. "Who built this place?"

"I'm not sure," Marcia replied, "but I think it was a family member of Bernard Pembroke, and he was a benefactor of—"

"Bernard Pembroke?" Taylor interrupted. "He's the one who sponsored my scholarship."

"Yeah? Oh, really?" Marcia continued. "He's given a lot to this university, and there's this huge foundation for scholarships and other projects."

As they approached the front door, it opened, held by a young man in a sport jacket and tie, apparently a volunteer student. He welcomed them and instructed them to write their names and either "Student" or their university title on name tags and put them on. He then pointed them to the inner room, where the reception was already underway with about thirty other scholarship recipients. Additionally, there were about ten older people, who looked like professors or administrators.

This large central room had a very high ceiling and was flanked by smaller reception rooms, which were accessed through immense doorways. Further back on one side was a massive staircase with intricately carved handrails. It led to a second-floor landing that joined a long balcony against the rear wall that led to other rooms. Underneath the balcony, a series of long banquet tables had been set up with food, and in both corners were cocktail bars attended by servers in black jackets.

Additional wait staff moved through the room, bringing in more food and removing used dishes and glasses.

Marcia and Taylor stood motionless and surveyed the room in awe. The gargoyle theme continued inside, under the balcony and on decorative arches and doorways. Directly above was a gigantic chandelier made entirely of buckhorn and holding at least sixty individual electric candle lights.

Marcia leaned into Taylor and whispered, "This place is haunted. Just like I heard."

"How do you know?"

"When studying witchcraft, you are taught to be aware of your feelings and to interpret them. I feel a ghostly presence here. I wonder if Aunt Zena knows anything about this place."

At that moment, they felt that they were being watched and approached by someone from their right. It was an elderly woman, who was smiling at them. She was probably less than five feet tall and was walking ever so slowly with the aid of a walker. They smiled in return, and because of how slowly she was inching toward them, they felt compelled to respond and moved toward her. She stopped and put out her right hand.

"Welcome! I'm Delores Delany. You may call me Deedee."

Marcia and Taylor introduced themselves.

Deedee continued, "I'm the longest-standing docent for Castlewood. I've been a docent here for almost forty years, ever since it was turned over to the university." Looking at Taylor's name tag, she added, "I see, Taylor, you are a student. What year?"

"Yes, ma'am. I'm a freshman," Taylor replied.

"Well, welcome to Carolina, and welcome to Castlewood." Then looking at Marcia's name tag, she said, "And you, Marcia, are a witch. Well, this is a liberal arts college, and we accept all kinds." They all laughed as Taylor looked over at Marcia's name tag and blushed.

Taylor quickly said, "Actually, I'm the scholarship recipient, and Marcia is my guest, who—who is also a student, with a sense of humor." They all chuckled again.

Deedee said, "Well, there is plenty of food and drink, so please help yourself and make yourself at home."

They thanked her and slowly moved away toward the food tables and the bar. Marcia managed to get two mixed drinks on her ID and brought one to Taylor. After sampling a few items on the food tables, Marcia spoke. "Let's go upstairs. I want to see this place."

"Look," Taylor said, "we're guests. We can't just be wandering around this place."

"Uh!" Marcia responded. "It belongs to the university, and it's a state university, so it belongs to me as much as it does to anybody else here. Besides, she said to make ourselves at home. Let's check out this hallway, and if anybody asks, we'll just say we're looking for a bathroom."

By now, the room was filled with fifty or sixty people, so they felt more comfortable about moving down the hallway unseen. As they proceeded, Marcia said, "It would have been too obvious to go up the main staircases, but usually these old mansions have a back stairway."

As they continued down the hallway, they noticed offices that appeared locked, a bathroom that they passed by, and then a back staircase.

"Bingo," Marcia whispered as she started to climb it.

After they reached the top, they continued down a hallway, and Marcia tried a few doors, all of which were locked. Taylor stiffened each time she reached for a knob and then relaxed when it didn't open. Then they reached a room with double doors, and when Marcia tried the knob, they opened. The light was on in the room, and they peeked inside. They didn't see anyone, so they entered the room. It was a large library, with shelves up to the ceiling that were filled with books. On both sides of the room, there were sliding wooden steps designed to allow people to reach the upper shelves. Leather chairs with adjacent tables were placed around the room. Off to one side was a large antique desk. On the far wall was a large fireplace with carved stone gargoyles, and above the mantel was a large painting.

When Taylor's eyes fell on the painting, he froze and softly said, "Oh my God!"

Marcia looked too. The painting was a full-length portrait of a man who appeared to be forty-five to fifty years old, standing next to a horse. The man was fully dressed in dark clothing with a flat-brimmed leather hat.

"That—that's him!" Taylor stammered.

Just as Marcia was about to ask him for an explanation, they were interrupted by a voice from behind. "Can I help you find something?" They quickly spun around to see Deedee standing there, holding on to her walker.

"Uh, we came up looking for a bathroom," Marcia said quickly.

Taylor was still speechless and kept shifting his gaze between Deedee and the portrait.

"Relax," Deedee added. "Intelligent students have a natural curiosity to learn and to explore. And that's a good thing. And I will be glad to answer any questions or show you around anytime."

"Oh, uh," Taylor stammered. "Thanks, I—I do have a question. Who is that dude, that guy in the picture?"

Deedee chuckled slightly and answered, "That's a portrait of Bernard Pembroke, of course, and his favorite horse at the time, no doubt. He owned and lived in this house. That is, this was his primary residence. He had other homes in Spain and Argentina."

"Oh, he's the one who funded my scholarship."

"Most likely," she replied, "or the trust that he set up."

"So," Taylor inquired, "he's not still alive?"

"Oh, no," Deedee responded. "He died at the age of fifty-nine, almost thirty years ago. A heart problem. I first got to meet him when he passed this place on to the university about ten years prior to his death, and I got to know him quite well during the transition."

"Deedee," Marcia said, "you've been around this house a long time. Have you ever noticed some unusual occurrences, you know, unexplainable things that have happened?"

"You mean ghosts?" she chuckled. "We'll have to leave that for another evening. But we should be getting back to the party for now."

As they turned to walk out, Marcia continued, "And you, how did you . . . I just saw you downstairs. How did you get up here so fast?"

"An elevator across the hall. I'll show you."

"Oh," Marcia laughed. "I was just about to nickname you Speedy Deedee."

They all laughed. "By the way," Deedee added, "all recipients of Pembroke scholarships have the right of access anytime to this building and to use this library. It was stipulated in Mr. Pembroke's will."

"Really," Taylor responded. "I could use the library?"

"And guests of recipients?" Marcia asked.

"Well, maybe that could be arranged," Deedee responded. "When we get downstairs, I'll give you my card. It has all the contact information for scheduling and that sort of thing. The library is well stocked with rare and unusual books and manuscripts. Mr. Pembroke wanted this information to be easily accessible to all scholarship recipients and for this to be a place of study for them."

After they had gotten downstairs, Marcia and Taylor got the card from Deedee and decided to stay for another drink and some more food.

"You know," Taylor said to Marcia, "I find this guy Pembroke and his house really intriguing."

"Yeah, I agree with that too."

"If you don't mind," Taylor continued, "I'd like for us to circulate for a while and get to know some of these people. Maybe I can find out some more information about this Pembroke guy and his funding of these scholarships."

"That's a great idea," Marcia agreed. "Go on. I'll follow your lead."

Taylor immediately went up to a man who looked like a faculty member and introduced himself. The man turned out to be a chemistry professor. Taylor felt he couldn't really relate to him, so after explaining that he was a freshman trying to learn the ropes, he ended the conversation and moved on to a student.

He and Marcia talked to the student about their majors and their scholarships; then he ended that conversation too and moved on to other students.

Taylor introduced himself and Marcia to a blonde female student, who said her name was Brenda Evans and indicated that she too was a Bernard Pembroke Scholarship recipient. Taylor asked her what her field of study was.

"Music. I'm studying tuba."

"What?" Taylor said. "Are you on the Pluck Scholarship?"

"Yes," the girl answered. "How did you know?"

"Oh, when I was applying for this scholarship, I remembered the university counselor had mentioned that a female tuba player had received the scholarship a couple of years ago, so really, I was just guessing."

"Oh, I see," she replied. "So, you've just gotten yours? You're a freshman?"

"I am," he replied. "And listen, I was wondering if I could talk to you sometime—not now, of course—but that I could call you and ask you some questions that have cropped up. Mainly about requirements expected of the scholarship holders and stuff like that."

"Of course," she replied. "Yeah, I understand. Not everything is clearly defined. Let me give you my phone number."

Marcia had a pen and some paper in her handbag and gave them to the girl to write down her phone number. After that, Taylor and Marcia noticed other people leaving and decided it was time to go.

After walking in silence toward the campus for about ten minutes, Marcia spoke up. "You really looked like you saw a ghost." Taylor didn't respond, and Marcia added, "When you looked at that painting."

"Well, yes. I think I did see a ghost. Last fall. That guy in the painting appeared to me and threatened me."

"Uh-oh!" Marcia softly responded.

Taylor continued. "Then later this summer, he showed up again at the restaurant I was working at."

"Are you sure it was him?"

"No question in my mind: The same clothes, the same hat, in both instances. Not too many people wear that hat. His face even looked the same."

"Was he right in the restaurant?"

"No, I saw him outside looking in at us, and when I went out, he was gone. Like a ghost."

"This probably means he's a troubled soul. He's not ready to move to the other side for some reason or another. When I was in the house, I did feel an Otherworld type of spirit." After walking in silence for a while, Marcia continued, "He may be evil. Some evil souls are still here to exact revenge. However, I didn't feel anything ominous. I didn't feel threatened in the house. What about you? Did you feel anything?"

Taylor shrugged. "No, I—I felt really good in the house. You know, sort of like I was welcomed. I guess that could be the alcohol." They both chuckled; then Taylor added, "Also, that he would open his house to the scholarship recipients was really a neat gesture. And to be able to use that library."

"Yeah," Marcia said. "Some of those books looked really old." After a pause, she added, "We might need to see Aunt Zena. She has a lot more experience than I could ever imagine. She can help you sort this out."

"Maybe that's a good idea. You know, starting college, I'm not sure I need to be dealing with all of this too."

"You've got to face it. You can't walk away from it. This is kind of strange, though. The man who has funded your scholarship is coming back and threatening you. That certainly raises some questions."

Taylor was silent as he thought through all this. After a few moments, he said, "It does raise some questions. What's he after?"

Chapter 10

I'm Positive It Was

That was a nice evening at Castlewood. I enjoyed everything about it. I liked that it felt like a fancy party, and I had a smoking date. And I even liked the castle, even though it turns out that it was originally the home of the ghost that has been harassing me. Nevertheless, I felt welcome there and probably will look into the offer of that nice lady, Deedee, to use the library for research and study.

Marcia looked so hot, unlike that first day in the dorm when Dad was helping me move in, when she had on all this Goth makeup. She looked creepy then, but she is quite pretty. And I enjoyed being with her that night. She's a little funky and adventuresome, but I like that about her. You can tell she's super smart. The witch thing is somewhat strange, but then, hey, I'm seeing ghosts, and she's a witch. And when I told her all about it, she didn't freak out but understood the whole situation and tried to help.

I called the blonde student, Brenda Evans, the one who plays the tuba, who is on a Pluck scholarship, and she said to come over to her dorm so we could talk. It turns out she was pretty cool. She had decided to become involved in B–GLAD, a student organization whose name stands for Bisexual, Gay, Lesbian and Allies for Diversity. They have about thirty or forty students in their organization and put out a newsletter when they can and supplement it with a flyer to keep people updated on gay and lesbian issues on campus and around town. The student government is always trying to defund the organization, so it's an uphill battle. She gave me several back issues of the newsletters. She's never written anything for the newsletters but just attends their monthly meetings and reports that back, and that satisfies her scholarship requirement. She says she feels guilty for not doing more and really does want to. She did go on a trip last summer with some other women to New York City to celebrate Stonewall 25. They carried their UNC B–GLAD flag, and some of the women marched topless with a bunch of other women in the parade. That must have been wild.

She then pointed out that in early October, it's National Coming Out Day and that last year, some of the others convinced her to come out to her parents and to wear a coming-out sweatshirt around campus and to class, all of which she did. Her parents said they knew long ago and were cool about it. She then encouraged me to come out this October. I chuckled, hemmed and hawed, probably turned red and finally said I'd think about it. I added that I was just a freshman and had a lot on my plate and might not want to take that on just yet.

I then asked her if, after taking the scholarship, she had ever felt the presence of some other spirit-like thing anytime. She looked at me curiously; then her face lit up, and she said something like, "Yeah! Sometimes when I'm working on Lambda stuff and even some other schoolwork, I do feel like there is a presence with me." She said it felt like someone was there who was guiding her and helping her. I asked her if that bothered her, and she said no, it actually was sort of comforting.

As I was getting ready to leave, she remembered that when she was a freshman, a senior who was on the same scholarship had talked to her and mentioned to her that he had felt a presence. She then asked me if I thought it could be the spirit of the benefactor, Bernard Pembroke. I smiled as I left and said I'm positive it was.

Chapter 11

I'd Like That

It was the middle of August 1927, and the harshness of the hot summer had barely abated. The university was reawakening from the summer break and being filled with activity. There were summer school classes, of course, as there had been for years. But the tempo of those months was reminiscent of a slow, lazy ballad while the fall and spring semesters were more upbeat, with a faster rhythm and a more energetic step to everything that was going on. This activity on campus was increased further because 1927 was the peak of the Roaring Twenties, particularly in the United States, and it was a frenetic time by any standard. Change seemed to be going on in all areas.

This was the first decade after a war in which women had been employed in factories, and their new independence had fueled enactment of a constitutional amendment giving them the right to vote. More women now worked, and more began going to universities, although the percentages were still in the single digits at Carolina. As expressions of their freedom, women patronized illegal speakeasies, bobbed their hair, smoked cigarettes, and wore short, revealing dresses. Young people in college and elsewhere craved social situations and participated in dances, parties, wild fads, and sexual experimentation.

The cultural landscape changed in almost all areas, as artists broke from romantic rural themes and turned more toward an urban characterization of America. Musicians reflected this with quick tempos representing the sounds of the city, and writers wrote about everyday people, many of their works dealing with city life. F. Scott Fitzgerald published his second successful novel, *The Great Gatsby*, depicting greed, status, and prosperity in the flapper-era Jazz Age. Movies continued to influence the populace and were now promising an even bigger impact with the soon-to-come talkies everyone was anticipating. Many students had Victrolas and looked forward to new recordings, and a few had radios, although in North Carolina, stations were few and signals were weak.

The country was being reborn with prosperity, and new accomplishments were revealed daily with the publishing of each newspaper. Lindbergh's flying solo across the Atlantic, the first air-conditioned theater, the first demonstration of city-to-city television, all were hailed in the mid-1920s, and young people embraced everything that was new.

Electric irons, mixers, and vacuum cleaners were common, along with many other products and the availability of installment purchasing to pay for them. The self-contained home refrigerator was growing in popularity, and the pop-up electric toaster came into being in 1926.

In science, new discoveries were being made in physics, astronomy, molecular theory, electronics, and medicine. Diphtheria became controllable; diabetics were helped with insulin injections. The discovery of Tutankhamen's tomb only a few years earlier had flamed a popular interest in Egyptian art and history.

It was a time of enthusiasm, confidence, prosperity, and optimism. It truly was an exciting time to be alive. Even more so, at a university.

On the campus of the University of North Carolina, the trees were still full of summer foliage. Young men and women were freely enjoying the last few days before classes began by playing croquet in the courtyards between the dorms. Other groups of men were tossing footballs or pitching softballs while many others were just sitting around talking and smoking cigarettes. The dress was still quite casual, a holdover from summer break and summer school classes, during which professors had eased off from the usual requirement of suits for men and dark dresses for women. Even this unwritten dress code was slowly falling by the wayside as students were becoming more aware of the casual fashions of the Twenties from newspapers, magazines, and movies. Music, mostly jazz, from Victrolas could be heard drifting out of open dorm windows.

This week was freshman orientation. Bernard Pembroke, now a sophomore, was already situated in his dorm, ready to start the semester. He was a member of the Order of the Pantheon, a service organization, and so was there a week early to welcome and guide incoming freshmen. Because of his shyness and tendency to stutter, Bernard didn't particularly want to interact with new students—or with any students. But his father insisted that he be involved in at least one service organization, one athletic team, and one academic organization. He also insisted that his son participate in the student government association and pledge a fraternity, of course, one of several of which his father approved. According to Bernard Pembroke Senior, it was all about meeting the right people, making the right contacts, and developing your interpersonal skills. His father also looked down on participating in the concert band, the choir, the orchestra, the theatre, or any dance club or dance organization. He deemed those activities frivolous, useless entertainment, and populated by people of questionable background and direction.

Because of his father's dictum, Bernard had chosen to be in the Order of the Pantheon, the Rowing Club, the History Club, and the Political Awareness Club as a member of the finance committee. However, he was yet to pledge a fraternity. He was most concerned about having to join a fraternity because it would require him to be social.

Everyone on campus who knew Bernard considered him a "good chap" because he was intelligent and dressed appropriately in the three-piece suit and tie that almost every male student wore. Still, in his first year of school, he had not developed any real friendships, primarily because he was quiet and withdrawn. Additionally, he wore round, dark-rimmed glasses that made him appear "bookish," so people left him alone, regarding him as too serious. In spite of this, he was graciously given the nickname "Fitz," derived from his middle name Fitzpatrick, since it was a fad for all students to have nicknames. Even though he didn't like it at first, he grew to accept it. But because of his isolation, when others were going into town or doing things outside of the college, he was never invited to join and instead kept himself busy reading and dreaming of lands and activities far away.

The Order of the Pantheon had hung a large banner on the side of South Building, reading WELCOME CLASS OF 1931. Rows of tables manned by members of the organization were set up in the shade of the building. Bernard was dressed in a three-piece dark suit, as were most of his fellow Pantheon brothers. Each table had signs indicating organizations about which you could find information. Bernard was stuck with University Chorus, Theatre Club, and Band only because everyone else had already chosen all the other clubs and effectively forced Bernard to take these.

Bernard really didn't know anything about the chorus, theater or band other than what building they used to meet and practice. He concluded that all he could do was give the freshmen direction on how to get to that building. There, a representative of the organization would have a table set up with all the necessary information and a form for joining.

As he sat there, two female freshmen approached his table, and one asked him when and where the chorus practiced. Hardly looking up, he circled a building on a college map and handed it to them, saying, "G-g-go there!" They were momentarily shocked at his behavior; then they turned and went to another table. A male freshman approached, inquiring about the band, and Bernard dispatched him in a similar fashion. This went on for more than an hour, after which there was a lull in activity, apparently the result of a break in the university's scheduled orientation events. Many of those staffing the tables took this opportunity to get up and stretch, smoke a cigarette and walk around before a new batch of students came along. Bernard looked up to see one of his Pantheon brothers, Charles Goodman, nicknamed Chappie, approaching his table. Chappie's father was a successful industrialist from Boston who belonged to several exclusive men's clubs. Chappie spoke with a typical Boston accent.

Chappie extended his hand to Bernard. "Fitz, how are you doing?"

Bernard stood and answered as they shook hands, "Ch–Chappie, things are moving along well."

"Well, another year. How was your summer?"

"Stayed here at home with f–father." Bernard especially stuttered when first talking to people, especially anyone he did not know well. Once he relaxed, it wasn't so pronounced. "It's b–been hot. And you?"

"Summered in Connecticut with my parents. They also have a place at the shore. It was swell. And lots of Shebas up there. Did you meet any women down here for the summer?"

"No, I—I stayed close to home and helped father with his b–business."

"Well, that certainly put a damper on your fun. Oh, speaking of fun: See that skirt over there?"

Bernard sat down and eyed a female student two tables over. She was talking to two men, her body weight on one leg with her opposite arm holding a lit cigarette dangling from her fingertips. She wasn't wearing dark stockings or baggy clothes like the other women. Her hair was bobbed in the latest style, and her dress hung limply and closely around her trim body. Her makeup was heavier than other women's in school, more like what could be seen in movie magazines.

"Yeah, what about her?"

"Name's Maisey. Quite a chassis, right?"

"Yeah, quite a looker."

"Well, she's been asking about you."

"Me. Why me?"

"She's a gold digger. Not here to get an education but to find a doctor or lawyer for a husband."

Bernard was quiet for a moment as they both watched her chatting to the fellows at the table. Then he spoke. "Well, I'm a c-commerce major, and I'll be running my father's c-construction company."

"I know, but quite a successful construction company. You've done many public works and several buildings on this campus, including part of the new stadium. Uh-oh, here she comes." As Chappie moved away, he said in a low voice, "Might be good for a roll in the hay."

Bernard shook his head as the young woman approached. She reached his table, extended her right hand, and said, "Hello, I'm Maisey Denton."

Bernard stood up and shook her hand. "B-Bernard Pembroke."

"Oh, I'm not a freshman looking for information," she related. "In case you didn't realize that."

There was a pause as Bernard searched for something to say; then he asked, "So, why are you here this week?"

"I needed to get some things done and to have some fun. You know, once classes start, it ain't easy."

"Yeah, c-classes can be demanding," Bernard replied.

"So this gives me time to go out and get to know people and have some fun." After another pause, she added with a sly smile, "You look like someone who knows how to have fun."

"N–not really," he quickly answered. "I n–never g–go out. I, uh, really stay b–busy with schoolwork. You know, n–nose to the grindstone."

She stood there with a surprised look on her face. He added, "If you'll excuse me, I've run out of c–campus maps, and I need to g–get more from one of the other tables." He moved toward Chappie's table as she stood there frowning; then she turned and walked off.

"That was quick," Chappie said.

"Oh, she j–just had a question. Do you have any more school maps? I almost ran out." Chappie looked at a box behind his seat, grabbed a large handful, and handed them to Bernard.

Just then, their attention was drawn to the nearby street where a convertible sports car had pulled up. A young man wearing knickers and a V–neck sweater with a bow tie hopped out of the passenger seat.

Eyeing the sleek convertible, Chappie commented, "Look at that breezer. That's certainly the cat's meow."

All the other young men at the tables stopped what they were doing and admired the car, discussing what they knew of that model. The young man went around to the driver's side, shook his hand, and waved him goodbye as the car sped away.

"And look at that fella in the knickers!" Chappie added.

"It's become the style up n–north. C–c–crossed over to the Ivy League schools from England."

"Yeah?" Chappie replied. "I've seen them in ads. I like it. It's the bee's knees. Guess I'll be out shopping."

As the young man moved across the lawn toward the row of tables, Bernard noticed that his hair was not slicked down, shiny and darkened by the usual pomades that all the other guys used. It was light brown, full, shiny, and parted at the sides, and it bounced when he walked. The sweater had an argyle pattern that matched his socks.

"Must be a fish," Chappie quipped, a term used for freshmen. "He's heading our way."

Bernard turned and began walking off. "Well, back to my station."

The young man reached the tables at the far end of the line and made some comments to a few people, but he quickly moved past the tables, reading the signs as he went.

When he got to Bernard's table, he said, "Oh, here we go. Yes, the chorus and the theater club. Yes, I want to join both of those."

Bernard grabbed a map and looked up to see the man smiling at him. The man extended his hand, and they shook. "I'm Damien Holdrich."

"I'm B–B–Bernard Pembroke."

"Bubba Bernard, is that really your name? I like that."

"N–n–no, it's Bernard or Fitz. People here call me Fitz from my middle name, Fitzpatrick."

"Oh, too bad! Bubba Bernard is really hip. I wish that were your name. But, well, I'll call you Fitz if that's what you prefer. Or do you prefer Bernard?"

"Bernard," he confirmed.

"Then that shall it be. Well, so about these clubs, what information do you have?"

Bernard circled a building on a map and said, "G–go to this b–building, and there will be someone there to help you with b–both those clubs."

"Oh, I see. Uh, also, do you have any recommendations?" Bernard just stared upward through his round, dark-rimmed glasses as the young man continued smiling and talking. "I'm interested in singing and theater and dance, so I see clubs for that. But I figured I'd try something athletic too, but I'm not good at much. I grew up in New York City, and there wasn't much opportunity to play ball of any sort."

"I—I'm not athletic either, but here you c–can learn and have fun."

"Perfect, Bernard. Well, I will get plenty of exercise for my legs with dancing, but I was thinking I needed something for my upper body."

"Rowing!"

"Rowing?"

"Yes, it's a collegiate sport where a nine-man c–c–crew race on the river. Very exhausting. But it works your entire torso. I belong to the rowing club."

"You do? I remember seeing long boats rowing on the Hudson. It looks like such great fun. Swell! Where do I sign up?"

"Over there. Third t–table. We're called the Skimmers."

Grabbing the map and rapidly moving away, he answered, "Thanks, Bernard. See you around."

"Hold on! Come back here!" Damien skidded to a stop and came back. "T–two things I may as well tell you now. Knickers are not permitted in any c–classroom or auditorium. Only outside."

"Righto, my good man. I've heard. In Oxford, they wear baggies over their knickers." Baggies were long-cuffed trousers with very loose-fitting legs.

Bernard bowed his head in agreement and said, "Yes, but p–probably too hot for the South."

"Well, true. And what was the other thing?"

"You do know how to swim, d–d–don't you?"

"Well, no. No one swims in New York."

"It's a requirement to be on the rowing team. They will t–test you."

"Aw, applesauce!" Damien seemed crestfallen.

"I'm sorry," Bernard continued, "but those are the rules. Safety, you know."

"I'll learn! How hard can it be?"

"Some people never learn. The crew selection is September fifteenth. That's not too far away."

"I can do it. Could you teach me?"

There was a long pause as Bernard stared back at Damien through his rimmed glasses, amazed at his forwardness. "W–why would I, who h–have only met you m–minutes ago, agree to t–teach you—assuming I c–could even do so—how to swim?"

"Well, first of all, you would be helping in gaining a new member of your rowing team. Secondly, you are a member of this university, whose code requires you to aid and assist your fellow students. And you are a member of this service organization, which I assume conveys additional responsibility of aiding your fellow students. And you are on the Orientation Committee, whose purpose is to assist incoming freshmen, of whom I am one. And finally, *finally*, above all, I believe, you are a gentleman, who would be willing to assist me because it is . . . a gentlemanly thing to do."

Bernard's look of astonishment suddenly broke; looking directly at Damien, he cracked a slight smile and slowly spoke. "All—all of this is true."

"So, you will do it?"

Bernard shrugged his shoulders and answered, "You're a very persuasive fella. Maybe you should be on the d–debating t–t–team. And yes, I will do it."

"Wonderful! And I," Damien gestured with a swipe of a finger, "will do something for you. I will get rid of your stuttering."

Suddenly, the slight smile dropped from Bernard's face as he rose from his chair, and with a deepened voice, he slowly blurted out, "You sir, are a b–bastard!"

"I apologize. I did not mean to offend. Please forgive me."

Several seconds passed as they looked each other in the eye; then Damien extended his hand for a handshake. Bernard scowled at him defiantly, reached to meet Damien's hand, shook it, and nodded in affirmation.

There they stood for a few seconds, hands together, eyes locked, until Damien finally said softly, "Thank you." Releasing his grip, Damien began to turn; then he stopped. "Oh, I need to know your dorm room." Bernard stared at him questioningly. "To be able to contact you about the swim lessons."

"201 New West."

"201 New West. I'll be in touch."

❊ ❊ ❊

Damien didn't waste any time. He had them meet the following day at the indoor pool, wearing bathing suits.

"Good God, man," Damien expressed in surprise upon seeing Bernard's torso, "under that three-piece suit, you look like an athlete."

"It's the rowing! If you're accepted, it'll happen t–to you. Jump in."

After they had jumped in the water, Bernard asked, "You're not at all afraid of the water?"

"No, not when I can see the bottom. Now the river in New York, that's different."

"Well, today, everything will be in the shallow end so you c–can always touch bottom."

"Good."

"B–by the way, why is it you d–don't have a New York accent like that fellow that was in my class last year?"

"Yoo wan me to tawlk like a New Yawkah?" Damien mimicked in a strong accent.

Bernard chuckled, "That's very good."

"I grew up around a lot of stage actors and actresses, and I've studied accents a bit. My mother was from Savannah, Georgia, and I was exposed to lots of different accents. You don't have a Southern accent. Why is that?"

"M–my mother's influence. She was from up north . . . Pennsylvania."

"I see. Boy, some of these guys down here have some strong Southern accents. I can barely understand them."

"Yep."

"That one guy from tobacco country, Johnston County, I think, talks so slow, that when he starts a sentence, first I have difficulty understanding what he's saying. And by the time he ends it, it had been so long ago, I'd forgotten what the beginning of the sentence was about."

Bernard laughed. "So true, I g–guess. I grew up here, so I hardly notice. Why d–did you decide to go to school here in North C–Carolina instead of up north?"

"It was my mother. New York can be a rough life, with all the mobsters and crime. She wanted me to be exposed to a safer, gentler life, away from the big city."

Bernard smiled and nodded. Then he said, "All right. First, let's get used to being in the water."

Bernard instructed Damien to hold his breath and go underwater. Damien followed, with both of them doing this several times.

"Now, you must learn to float. You will have to t–trust me with this."

Damien nodded, and Bernard demonstrated how to float on his back. Then he asked Damien to do this and placed his hand gently under Damien's back to support him.

"My feet are sinking."

"That's normal. Just relax."

Next, Bernard showed him how to flutter kick with his shoulders and arms resting on the edge of the pool. From there, he instructed him to combine both floating on his back and the flutter kick. When Damien did so, he glided easily from the shallow side of one end of the pool to the other.

"You are swimming. You are a fast learner. But now you need to learn the crawl."

Bernard demonstrated how to float facedown while holding his breath, and Damien did quite well with his feet only sinking a little. From there, Bernard had Damien flutter kick with his hands touching the edge of the pool. Bernard complimented him on each step. Then he had him combine floating face down and flutter kicking from one side of the shallow end to the other for as long as he could hold his breath. Damien did this, stopping twice to breathe.

Afterward, Damien was excited. "This is wonderful. It's a bit like choreography. Adding step by step. I feel like I'm halfway there."

"You are. Now for the arms and the b–breathing."

Bernard showed Damien the arm motions for the crawl followed by the turning of the head to catch a breath with each stroke. Damien practiced this while standing for a few minutes; then he tried it in the water. He completed this task, going from one end of the pool to the other, only stopping to stand once. Then he tried it again and swam the entire length nonstop.

"Congratulations. You're a really fast learner. Your sense of rhythm should be g–good for rowing, as well."

"Thanks, I guess dancing helps. I want to try to the deep end."

Bernard was surprised. "Are you sure you are ready?"

"Well, there's only one way to find out." With that, he turned toward the deep end and started paddling. In a few minutes, he had successfully crossed and was hanging on the opposite side.

"Congratulations!" Bernard shouted.

After a brief rest, he was swimming back to Bernard. In another few minutes, he had made it, coughing from inhaled water and panting heavily.

"You did amazingly well," Bernard said. "I'm astounded."

Damien, breathless, could barely speak but managed to reply, "Thanks, but I'm exhausted. This is so tiring."

"No, you're just not relaxed yet. You need to come b–back every day and swim. It gets easier and easier each time. Trust me."

Damien did come back every day that week; soon he was swimming a quarter mile without stopping.

❀ ❀ ❀

As the sun set on Friday afternoon, Damien, carrying a shoulder bag, went to Bernard's room and tapped on his door. From inside, he heard Bernard call, "Come in."

He opened the door and looked around. There was no one in there except Bernard, sitting in an overstuffed chair, a book in his hand.

"You have this room all to yourself?"

"Yep. Have a seat."

Damien sat on the bed. "I share with two other chaps."

"Freshmen don't get it as nice. Plus, Father agreed to p–pay extra for a private room."

"Nifty."

"So, how's the swimming going?"

"That's why I'm here. Today, I crossed the pool nonstop eighteen times. I believe that's a quarter mile."

"Congratulations! You've exceeded my wildest expectations."

"So, I've invited myself over to invite you to celebrate this achievement of mine, which is a result of your excellent teaching skills, which we need to celebrate also."

Bernard sat there smiling for a moment; then he said, "All right. What do you want to do to celebrate?"

Damien reached into his shoulder bag and pulled out a bottle of clear liquid. "Hooch! Do you drink?"

"Where did you g–get that?"

"A speakeasy in town."

"Sir, this c–country p–prohibits the m–manufacture, p–purchase and c–consumption of alcohol."

Damien laughed deeply, reeling at the statement. "I'll have to remember that sentence. But look, Prohibition is a bunch of hooey. It's phonus balonus. It has caused more damage to this country than good."

"Yes, many agree. B–but we also have a university rule against liquor on c–campus."

"So Orientation has instructed me. But I've only been here a week, and almost every night, huge groups of students come from town ossified, barely able to walk, men and women. And already I've seen dorm parties almost as wild as juice joints."

"True, the administration generally doesn't b–bother you . . . if you don't damage p–property . . . or be too loud. And they're even much laxer on weekends."

"And it's the weekend, so . . ."

"So let's celebrate!" Bernard agreed, closing his book and slamming it down on the table.

Damien reached into his bag and pulled out two small glasses. "Borrowed this from the cafeteria. Juice glasses. We'll be drinking juice." He opened the bottle, poured the drinks, and handed one to Bernard. They raised their glasses. "Here's to my learning to swim."

Bernard took a sip and coughed. "It's been a—a while." He took another sip. "Mmm, not bad. D–did you get it at Clancy's?"

"Yeah!"

"Heard they had good stuff. That's where my father gets his."

"One more toast! Here's to a great swim instructor."

"Th-thank you, Damien." They drained their glasses.

Damien grabbed the bottle, held it over Bernard's glass, and asked, "More?"

"What the hell. It—it's Friday." Bernard took a sip and just stared straight ahead. "You, my fellow man, are going to make an excellent c–crew."

"You think so?"

"Yes, you have natural rhythm. You'll be an asset to the c–crew."

"Thank you, but you talk like I'll be admitted to the crew." Bernard smiled without speaking. Damien continued, "So, tell me all about the whole process of joining."

Bernard went through a slow explanation, noting that almost everyone was accepted into a crew if he could swim, because it was still a relatively new sport at the school. First, the new recruits would take the swimming test, which was about an eighth of a mile in the lake. After that, there were two or three classroom sessions in which the coach went over the equipment, basic techniques, and rules for racing. Recruits were then assigned to a boat, sent out into the water, and given instruction on how to paddle. Later, after their ability was evaluated, they were assigned to a particular boat based on skill sets. Bernard went over practice times: Getting up early at the crack of dawn to crew for about an hour and forty-five minutes and afternoon practices when preparing for a race with other schools.

By this time, they had finished their second glass, and Damien poured a third.

"So," Bernard asked, "do you think you're able to put in that much time?"

"Absolutely; at least I'll try."

"Good!"

"Getting up so early in the morning will be the tough part."

"It is difficult, but it really wakes you up, especially in the cold months. And then you're all set for class."

A few moments passed as they sat there, feeling the lightheadedness from the alcohol. Then Bernard spoke again, this time in a softer, more serious tone. "Damien, were you serious when you said you c–could keep me from stuttering?"

Damien smiled, and their eyes met. "Absolutely! Now do as I say. Take another sip." Bernard complied. Damien continued, "I was raised in a speakeasy."

"Really?"

"Yes, my mother was—is an entertainer in a speakeasy near Tin Pan Alley in New York."

"You're not putting me on?"

"No. Absolutely the truth."

"Well," Bernard said softly and slowly with lowered eyes, "B–be glad you have a mother. Mine d–died when I was ten years old."

"Oh, I'm sorry. I love my mother so much. What happened to her?"

"The Spanish flu. Many people died here; all over, really. Even President Graham of the university."

"The president. That's awful," Damien responded. "It was quite an epidemic in New York too. Many people wore masks, and many houses were quarantined. I was afraid to cough or sneeze in school because I was afraid I would be separated from my mother and sent to the hospital. Eventually, she kept me at home for about a month. I couldn't go out and play or nothing. The city even closed theaters and required that work schedules be staggered. But, as a result, the city did quite well. New York had a lot of experience with disease."

For a few moments, no one said anything; then Damien continued. "So, what were we talking about? Oh yeah, stuttering. Well, anyway, I grew up in the city in this joint and would see men and women of all sorts come in there, many with broken lives. Especially those men who had been lucky enough to make it back from the war in one piece, some not whole, with missing limbs, but more often than not, not right in the head. You would see all kinds. Then there were a couple like you, who stuttered. And everyone noted that when these guys drank a little bit, they stopped stuttering."

"Horsefeathers!"

"No, it's true!"

"Bullshit!"

"Okay, hold on now. Let's do an experiment. Now that you've had a few glasses of juice, I want you to say something."

Bernard was frowning, angry at the direction of this conversation. "What?" he grunted.

"When I came in and showed you the hooch, you said, 'Sir, this country prohibits the manufacture, purchase and consumption of alcohol.' Now I want you to say it again, and say it, giving it your best try."

Bernard sat there frowning; then he quickly burst out, "S–sir, this country prohibits the manufacture, purchase and consumption of alcohol." He sat there, wide-eyed in amazement. He repeated in a softer voice, "Sir, this country prohibits the manufacture, purchase and consumption of alcohol! My God, I did it!"

"Yes. Proves my point."

"What point? I certainly can't go around zozzled all the time."

"No, but it shows you have potential to conquer this. And I think there are other ways to get you past this."

"Believe me," Bernard angrily said, "my father had me go to numerous speech correctionists, and very little was accomplished."

"Well, hell! I just said that I c–could get you to stop stuttering, and I did. I didn't p–promise I would do it without you g–getting d–drunk. Oh, crap. You're cured, and now I'm stuttering!"

They both broke into laughter and continued chuckling for a few moments, giddy from the alcohol. After their laughter had subsided, Damien said, "I'm hungry. Where can we get something to eat?"

"Me too," Bernard said, looking at his wristwatch. "Better hurry. The cafeteria's open for another forty-five minutes." They got up, but Bernard stopped, adding, "Hold on, I don't know if I should be seen with you!"

"Why's that?"

"Rumors that you might be an Ethel."

"Ethel? You mean a fag?" Walking out the door, they both laughed; then Damien added, "Only a week, and they figured me out?" They laughed again; then Damien asked more seriously, "So, does that really bother you?"

"No, not much. Especially after a few drinks, less so. None of these damn guys are my friends anyway. They ignore me. So we can be friends."

"I'd like that. Yeah, I really would."

"Me too," Bernard agreed. "I'd like that."

Chapter 12

Things Were Going Well

Taylor dove head-on into his first semester. He was taking the usual prerequisites of Modern Civilization, English Literature, Physical Education, a math course, and the first semester of French. Taylor placed high in mathematics on the entrance exam, so he was able to take Calculus. He had room for one elective, and he chose a sociology course.

Modern Civilization was Taylor's most demanding course because his high school history classes had been taught by the gym coach, who had also served as the football coach and track coach. He hadn't expected much knowledge of history from his students. Also, Modern Civilization required a tremendous amount of reading from numerous books, not just the assigned text.

He found these long reading assignments from other books exasperating since the needed books were often already checked out of the library. Then there was also the pain of carting these large volumes around with his other books. Taylor soon discovered that the library at Castlewood contained not only all his course texts but also most of the required supplemental reading texts. Consequently, he made it a habit to spend several days a week reading in that library. Additionally, it was so much quieter than the main library that Taylor found it the perfect place to write any research paper that was due. A desktop computer was also available for his use, and he was allowed to store work on it.

At first, Taylor felt uncomfortable sitting under a painting of the ghost that had attacked him, and he would only study at a table that was away from the stare of the man in the painting. However, it was only a painting, he told himself, and as time went on, he became more comfortable with the room and felt he could sit anywhere.

Deedee Delaney, the older woman with the walker, was there on most days. Soon Taylor and Deedee became friends and would engage in short conversations and join each other for coffee downstairs. It wasn't long before Deedee had given Taylor a key to the building so that he could access it anytime he chose, even after their regular business hours.

Taylor and Marcia's friendship continued to develop, and when Marcia wasn't in a night workshop, they would often have dinner together at Lenoir Hall or the Student Union. Occasionally, they would also meet for lunch. When Taylor wasn't at Castlewood, he was either in class, at the library, at the gym, or studying in his room.

It was now mid-October, and Taylor had just completed a six-page paper in his room and was printing it out when he heard a loud scream coming from the hallway. He got up and went out.

There was the muscular student who lived down the hall, holding Marcia horizontally above his head. She was giggling, and then he let her down.

"Wow, what's going on?" Taylor asked.

Both Marcia and the muscular guy were now laughing.

"Hey!" a female voice echoed from down the hall. "Will you keep it down! People do study!"

The three turned to see a blonde girl leaning out of her opened door at the far end of the hall. She was the same girl that Marcia had scared out of her room at the beginning of the semester.

"Sorry," Alex yelled back.

"Yeah, sorry," Taylor repeated. Marcia frowned. Taylor lowered his voice to a whisper. "Is she still in this dorm?"

"Yeah," Marcia sneered and spoke softly. "There was an opening, and she took it."

"Oh," Taylor said. "Well, what's all this acrobatics about?"

"We were practicing," Marcia said.

"For what, the cheerleading squad?" Taylor asked.

"No," Marcia continued. "We both got roles in Shakespeare's *The Taming of The Shrew*."

"Oh, well, congratulations!"

"I'm going to be Kate, and Alex . . . you know Alex, don't you?"

"Uh, we've run into each other in the hall," he replied as they shook hands. "Taylor Hanes. Good to meet you."

"Alex will be Petruchio. It's going to be produced in an exaggerated commedia dell'arte style, so there's going to be a lot of physical activity in our scenes. You have to be familiar with the play, but Alex will be lifting me and throwing me around his shoulders."

"Yeah," Alex added, "and I guess I'll have to be hitting heavier weights with my bench press."

"Thanks, bitch," Marcia sneered as she glared at Alex.

"Oops, sorry," Alex responded. "Wait; you could use witchcraft and just levitate."

The blonde girl came out into the hall again and stared at them.

"Sorry again," Taylor said.

"Put some headphones on, bitch," Marcia whispered.

Alex said in an excited whisper, "Hey, let's all go out and celebrate. What about you, Taylor?"

"Hey, great! I just finished a paper, and no classes tomorrow."

Everybody agreed to meet outside in ten minutes. But when Taylor walked into his room, the phone rang. It was Jeff Black, the lawyer and the administrator of his scholarship. After an exchange of pleasantries, Mr. Black began to restate Taylor's responsibilities as a scholarship recipient.

"Your scholarship agreement is pretty explicit that you were to report on a monthly basis on your involvement in gay and lesbian support groups. We have been receiving disbursement requests for books and other things but nothing on your activities. And it is my fiscal responsibility to the trust to ensure that the parameters of the trust will be carried out."

Taylor froze, not knowing what to say. He was still getting used to the workload of college, and he hadn't joined any groups or even attended any meetings. He was doing nothing except attending classes and studying. *Well,* he thought, *I did go out once with Marcia to see a movie on campus, but I really needed that.*

Finally, he spoke, voice cracking. "I thought it was phrased that I was strongly . . . encouraged to get involved with these groups. I didn't really—"

The lawyer interrupted him. "It's true that the documents might have been phrased that way. However, the intent of the trust was that you would get involved and would do your part in support of these groups. I'm quite sure I made that clear."

"Oh, sure. I understood that," Taylor said. Taylor immediately feared he could lose the scholarship and didn't want that to happen. "Okay, I . . . I'll see what I can do."

Then suddenly, the lawyer's tone changed. "Look, you just started college. It's your first semester. There's a huge learning curve getting adjusted. It's going to take some time to know what you want to get involved in, so don't worry about it too much. We want you to succeed in school first and foremost. I know you're going to be under a lot of pressure with your classes, so just take this semester and start some investigation. Start looking at some of the organizations on campus and around town. Attend some meetings to scope them out, and when you do, make a note of it and send it along with your disbursement requests. That's all."

After they had spoken a little while longer, Taylor realized that Marcia and Alex were probably waiting for him, so he hastened the end of the call with many promises to pursue what was asked of him. That seemed to satisfy Mr. Black, and after hanging up, he headed out.

When he met them standing outside, it was apparent that Alex and Marcia had completely changed their clothing.

"Oops! Look at me. In the same clothes. Just where are we going?"

"Don't worry," Marcia said. "We're dramatic arts students who always want to dress up. We don't know where we're going." They all laughed; then she held out a card to him. "And here, I got you a fake ID. Now you're legal."

Taylor looked at it and asked, "So why did you change my home address to Wichita, Kansas?"

"It's because everybody here knows what a North Carolina driver's license looks like but they don't know anything about the Kansas license. It's identical to mine, so it works."

As they walked through campus to the edge of town, Alex and Marcia kept talking about *The Taming of the Shrew* and all the other people who had gotten parts. Taylor was quiet, and Marcia seemed to notice. They ended up in a booth at Harry's. As soon as they walked in, Alex broke away and was all over the restaurant, talking to different people at the bar and sitting in the booths.

After a few minutes, the server came to their table, and Alex rushed back over to place his order. Marcia and Taylor each ordered a beer while Alex ordered a Cosmo. Taylor showed his new ID, which was readily accepted. They kidded Alex about ordering the Cosmo, saying that he must be planning to make a night of it.

The drinks arrived soon, and the conversation again turned to Alex and his Cosmo.

"So, how many beers do you think that is equivalent to?" Taylor asked.

Alex sipped and then said, "I can handle it. I know I've had five of these and was still able to walk a straight line."

Taylor asked, "So, are you two in many classes together?"

Marcia and Alex looked at each other, thinking; then Marcia said, "Just Advanced Stage Productions. We were in a class together last year. Voice and Accents."

"Yeah, that was a bitch," Alex added. "But I managed a B+." Then he looked at Taylor and said, "And you're a freshman, right?"

"Yep! Am I that obvious?"

"No, it's just that I figured as much when the semester began; you were an early arrival . . . and a new person in the dorm."

"Oh, Orientation Week."

"Yeah, Marcia and I came early to get organized . . . and to get away from home."

Marcia laughed and said, "True. I'm surprised that you two didn't know each other."

"Why's that?" Alex asked.

"Nothing. Just you two being gay . . . I thought you'd see each other around at a gay bar or something."

"You're gay?" Alex asked. "I didn't know you were gay."

Taylor sat in silence, feeling a little embarrassed.

Marcia laughed. "Alex, you better get your gaydar checked."

Taylor chuckled and said, "Actually, he seems to prefer older men. When I was moving into the dorm, Alex tried to hit on my dad."

"That was your dad! Man, he's hot!" They all laughed. "I guess I should have known. Thought it was your older brother or something. Now I feel embarrassed."

"Don't be," Taylor responded. "I think he was secretly flattered."

Then Alex noticed someone in another booth. "Be back in a minute. I've got to catch someone."

After Alex had left, Taylor became expressionless and stared at his beer in front of him while slowly fingering the droplets of moisture on the glass.

"Is something bothering you?" Marcia asked.

"Oh, because I was sort of quiet? I just got a call from the administrator of the scholarship. He . . . reminded me that I was responsible to perform some duties as required by the trust of my scholarship and . . . I haven't done anything yet."

"What kind of duties?"

"Just join some organizations or attend meetings of gay and lesbian support groups."

"Okay."

"And I've been so involved in school, I hadn't even thought about it. I really don't even know where to begin."

"I've seen things on campus bulletin boards, but that's about all I know. On campus, there is so much going on. You could spend your entire day going to things." She then noticed Alex coming back to the table. "Ask Alex. He knows everybody."

"Ask me what?" Alex said as he sat down.

Taylor then told him about the requirements of his scholarship. Alex said, "Wow! I just have to put on some tights and dance and sing for my scholarship." They all laughed; then Alex got more serious as he began to think. "Well, to be honest, the only groups I belong to dealing with gays and lesbians are the two gay bars in town . . . and I do see postings on their bulletin boards occasionally, about things going on. But now that you asked, I'll keep it on my radar and see what I come up with. And I really should be more involved in stuff like that."

"Thanks," Taylor responded. "I appreciate that. I was also thinking maybe my guidance counselor could give me some direction too. Except there are long lines to see him. He appears overworked and probably couldn't help me much."

"And speaking of gay bars," Alex broke in, "I'm going to be joining some of my friends over there at Tingle's later. Do you all want to come along?" Marcia and Taylor looked at each other and shrugged. "You can decide later, but what about another drink?"

They all had another round of drinks; then Alex was ready to leave.

"So," Marcia said, turning to Taylor, "you heading to the bar?"

"Well, uh, what are you going to do?"

"I've picked up this tape of an early televised version of *The Taming of The Shrew*. It was really good. I saw it quite a while ago, so I thought I'd review that. It would be good preparation for the play."

"Can I watch it with you?" Taylor said.

"Well, sure, if you want to. I'd thought you'd want to go to the bar."

"Nah. Since you're going to be in this big production, I need to see what this is all about."

"Well, all right. Let's pick up some beer at the grocery store and take it back with us."

At the grocery store, they also picked up ingredients for a salad and a spaghetti dinner. Back at the dorm, Marcia put on the tape, and they began watching while she boiled the pasta on a hotplate and heated the jarred sauce in the microwave. Taylor prepared two salads in small bowls. Marcia put a tablecloth on the trunk, which served as a coffee table, and placed paper napkins and forks on top.

Taylor had read *Hamlet* in high school and liked it quite a bit, but with *The Taming of the Shrew*, he was particularly fascinated by the humor as the play went on. They paused the tape while they filled their plates with dinner and sat back on the love seat. In the big scene in which Petruchio meets Kate and tosses her around the stage, the dialogue was so fast and intense that Taylor asked to replay the scene twice. Even after viewing it for the second and third time, they often broke into laughter.

After that scene, Taylor grabbed the remote, paused the tape and said, "I'm amazed at how bawdy this is."

"Yeah," Marcia responded. "Very little has been said that Shakespeare hadn't already said."

"And," Taylor continued, "how does an actor learn all that dialogue? It's so complicated and goes so quickly."

"That is a problem. Now these actors are experts. We'll try to get up to that speed, but it's not going to hurt if it's slowed down somewhat. I mean, your average audience will have difficulty understanding it if it is too fast, like you did. So slowing it a bit won't hurt and might help. This is really one of the most difficult and fast scenes because it involves fast dialogue and very quick repartee. Fortunately, Alex and I have already practiced some of it for the audition, and we're both in the same dorm so we can get together to practice a lot more easily. It's still going to be a challenge, though, but after you've been acting a while, you learn the ability to memorize lines and physical movements."

"Well," Taylor said, "if there is any way I could help by reading the other part, just ask, and if I have the time, I'll be glad to help."

Marcia thanked him and said she would keep that in mind. By the end of the play, they were finishing their second beer at dinner. The small love seat was sagging in the middle and bringing them very close together.

Marcia clicked off the television. Smiling, she turned toward Taylor. "So, what now? Do you want to watch some more TV?"

Smiling back, he looked at her. Their heads moved closer, and they kissed. In a few minutes, they were on the bed, and he was undressing her while she was undressing him. After a few minutes of caressing and kissing, he reached over and turned off the light.

"It's too dark now," Marcia whispered. "Open the drapes. There's a street light in the alley which will give us light." Taylor got up and opened the drapes, which were over the bed. This allowed a soft, almost moonlight glow to flow into the room. After several more minutes of lovemaking, Marcia grabbed Taylor and started to guide him toward her.

Suddenly, something blocked the light from the window. Taylor looked up and stopped with a gasp.

"What's the matter?" Marcia asked. Then she looked out the window, too. There was the man in the black clothing. She grabbed a pillow to cover herself and screamed.

They both jumped off the bed and closed the drapes.

"It's him!" Marcia said. "The guy in the picture!"

"You saw him too! I'm . . . I'm not insane!"

"No, no! It was definitely there. He must be a ghost! He must be bothered with you or wants to make contact with you. I guess I can see him because I'm a witch and have developed a sensitivity to Otherworld spirits. It's the first ghost I've ever seen, but I did see it."

They got dressed. Shook up and now completely sober, they decided to have another beer. Taylor decided it was time to tell Marcia the whole story. Taylor sat on the trunk, facing Marcia, who sat on the sofa. While occasionally glancing at the window, he carefully described the details, including his thought process and his lying when he had applied for the scholarship.

After he had finished, Marcia sat quietly for a few moments. "So, you aren't gay?" Marcia asked with a little irritation in her voice.

"No, it was just to get the scholarship. Why do you seem bothered? You know, I don't like to lie, but it was—"

"No, I feel you were deceiving me to get me in bed. You know, pretending to be gay like you wouldn't have ever had any interest in sleeping with a woman, and—and that I was being used."

"What?" he replied in a raised voice. "I felt like you were using me as an object or a conquest of some sort. That you were trying to convert me to being straight!"

They were silent for a few seconds as they stared at each other, frowning and thinking about what they had just said; then they burst into laughter. They raised their beers, clicked them together and took a swig.

"It wasn't bad being used," Taylor said. He leaned over and kissed her on the lips. "But I don't think I'm up to it now."

"Me either. Will you stay here with me tonight? I'm kind of creeped out by that thing."

"Sure."

"Wait," she continued. "Let's sleep in your bed. This window's going to bother me for a while."

They moved across the hall. Taylor got up on a chair and taped paper over the small window above his bed. Soon they were fast asleep in each other's arms. In the morning, they awoke feeling surprisingly good in spite of the beers, and within an hour, they had completed what they had started the night before.

Afterward, Taylor and Marcia both lay in bed, silently cuddling. For a moment, Taylor was at peace, but then he began thinking of the ghost, a supernatural being who was haunting him, and of some upcoming tests and research papers. And he thought about the pressure he was under to get involved in some gay support groups or else possibly lose his scholarship and be forced to drop out of school. Thoughts of Tartan and the greasy work at the auto shop, Hal's, the greasy kitchen where he had worked, and the depressing life of that small town flashed through his mind. Then he thought of his mom and dad and all that they were going through. The more he thought about all this, the tenser he became. But then he recalled his dad's advice: When things seem bad, focus on the good things in your life. So Taylor focused on the fact that he was at Carolina, he was enjoying most classes and finding them stimulating, he was enjoying on-campus and off-campus activities, and now he had Marcia, someone he could relate to. In those respects, things were actually going well.

Chapter 13

So Far, So Good

I've been in school several months now, I guess. I've been so busy and enjoying it so much, I can't keep track. I mark down when assignments are due, then immediately get to them the moment there is some free time. So far, even though it's demanding, I've been able to keep up.

It's October, and the leaves are beginning to change. They say it will be beautiful here, so that will be one more thing that makes it even greater. Football here is always a fun day, and I've gone to several games with Marcia. My classes are great. The math is easy. The literature class is fun. I'm in a super interesting Sociology class, my one elective. Modern Civilization is difficult, but it's nevertheless interesting. French is a bear, but at least the professor makes it interesting, and I'm keeping up with it. And even PE is fun. Fortunately, I passed the basic physical requirement, including swimming, and was able to elect to take whatever sport I wanted. So I've done racquetball, and now I'm in fencing. Next semester, I'll do archery and scuba diving. Whoever heard of someone in Tartan doing this stuff? For me, this is great, since I was never very good at football or baseball. I've eaten new foods, like sushi and Thai and Greek, and even some Indian food. So far, I've liked it all. It's good that I have the stipend that allows me the luxury of eating in town occasionally, and I even help pay for Marcia.

I'm in a very quiet dorm compared to other dorms, and I've grown to really like it, even though I've found out it is known by most people as the gay dorm. At first, this bothered me, but now I think it's ironic since I've clicked with Marcia. I'm with Marcia an awful lot. We really hit it off. Now we sleep together most nights, go on campus and have breakfast, and have lunch together on Monday, Wednesday, and Friday. There's a class conflict on Tuesdays and Thursdays. We often have dinner together if she's not involved in some production. Then on weekends, if I don't catch the bus home, we are usually together the whole time. But I've only been home a couple of times.

So, I see everything going really, really well except for two things. I have to fulfill the requirement for the scholarship, and then there's the ghost. But the good thing is, I'm not imagining it. Marcia has seen it, too, and wants to help find out what it's after. She says that's part of her responsibility as a witch. But after those two things, so far, so good.

Chapter 14

You're All Right

The Skimmers Rowing Club contacted Damien by a note under his dorm room door. All seven candidates were ordered to assemble by the lake at sunrise to take their swimming test. The nighttime air temperature had fallen only slightly, and the water in the lake was still warm. However, the club chose to force the candidates to jump into the lake early in the morning instead of using the warmer indoor pool, solely to test the mettle of the candidates.

The university rowing coach, a tall, muscular man in his thirties, introduced himself and instructed the candidates on how the test would play out. The coach, along with some members of the team, would row out into the lake approximately one-eighth of a mile. At the appropriate white flag signal, all the candidates would swim to the boat, circle it, and head back to shore.

As the boat was rowed out to the required point, the candidates took off their bathrobes and other clothing that had been keeping them warm. They were all discussing whether or not it would be better to just jump in at the signal or wade in now and try to adjust to the water. Before they could decide, the white flag was down, and they were being yelled at by other club members and the coach to start swimming. All jumped in, yelling and screaming from the shock of the water, but soon everyone was heading to the boat.

Damien, still new to swimming, was lagging behind the rest. However, in a few minutes, two of the swimmers began to slow down from exhaustion, and Damien overtook them just as they were circling the boat. Two excellent swimmers were far ahead and completed the loop in less than ten minutes. Next, two more came to shore breathing heavily, followed by Damien, who didn't seem to be winded at all. Finally, the last two arrived, one barely able to pull himself on shore, falling to his knees several times.

While all this was going on, some of the rest of the club members were arriving, including the club president and Bernard, and they all applauded and shook the candidates' hands.

As they dressed, the coach arrived back at the dock. The president of the club, a thin, muscular fellow with a deep Southern drawl, introduced himself. He congratulated all the candidates and told them that with their current openings, all the candidates were accepted into the rowing club and they were now officially members of the Skimmers. He further explained that it was a new club, still in development, and it had been in existence only three years but had come a long way. The president then briefly explained when and where they were to meet for their first rowing lessons and turned it over to the coach. The coach said a few words, welcoming them, and briefly summarized upcoming in-class training followed by row training on the lake. Then they were dismissed.

As the group began breaking up, Bernard approached Damien and shook his hand again. "You were amazing! G–good show! And you were not even b–breathing heavily."

"Thanks. Once again, you were a good teacher!"

"Have you eaten b–breakfast?"

"No, I'm hungry. Should have enough time before class."

They stopped by Damien's dorm to drop off his wet swimsuit and change into dry clothes, and then they rushed to the cafeteria. As they sat down with their trays and started to eat, Bernard leaned forward and began to speak in a soft voice.

"I've g–got to warn you about something. This c–club has started this stupid tr–tradition of hazing."

"Oh, I've heard that fraternities do that a lot. What will it be?"

"I'm not supposed to t–tell, but . . ." There was a long pause as he scanned the room and searched for the rest of what he was going to say. "I helped g–get you into this." Damien just kept eating and looking at Bernard. "Stupid stuff. Sometimes requiring you to d–dress up as women around c–campus, singing stupid songs."

"Singing, I might like that. Dressing as a woman . . . haven't done that before, but I'd be up to it."

"But the worst is, they lead you around c–campus blindfolded and hands t–tied behind your b–back for forty-five minutes; seems like d–days. All the while they are t–telling you that this is to teach you t–trust in your crew members. Then they lead you up onto the pier and p–push you over the side."

"With your hands tied?"

"Yes, b–but they have some club m–members quietly wade in. They let you struggle awhile; then they bring you t–to shore."

"And this is to make you trust them?"

Bernard shrugged, raised his arms, and said, "Stupid!"

"Well, I'm not sure which I dread more! The shock of the cold water or having my hands tied!"

The following afternoon, there was banging on Damien's door and a loud voice shouting, "Damien Holdrich!" By this time of day, most classes were over except for labs for upperclassmen. Damien was lying on his bed, reading. His two roommates were out. As he got up to open the door, a tall student whom he recognized from the rowing club pushed open the door.

"Get your swimsuit on and your gym shoes," he barked. "We're going boating." When Damien started to object, the guy shouted, "You do want to be on the team, don't you?"

Damien reluctantly put on his swimsuit, which was still damp from yesterday, and tied his gym shoes while the guy kept shouting for him to hurry it up. As they ran downstairs and out the door, Damien saw five men in their bathing suits, running in place in the Courtyard with a crewing boat upside down over their heads. Several students, including two women, were standing around, looking and laughing at this spectacle.

The tall guy yelled to Damien, "You take the front of the shell. Hinkler, you are relieved." Everyone shifted back as Damien took the position in the front.

"All right, gentlemen," the tall guy yelled, "let's hear the song."

In unison, the men began singing, "Row, row, row your boat, gently down the stream . . ." Damien obligingly chimed in with a strong tenor voice.

Then the tall guy shouted, "Forward!" and the team of five ran forward, circling the Courtyard four times while singing. Then they veered off and passed several buildings until they reached the next new team member's dorm. When they found he was absent, they took off around the edges of the campus, back through the Courtyard, and then down to the lake. There they returned the boat to its boathouse, placing it into its cradle.

The tall guy then introduced himself individually to each one, shaking his hand and welcoming him to the club. As the guys walked back to their dorm, they laughed at the whole experience and speculated on what would be next. It wasn't long before they found out. On Friday night, they were left a note to assemble in front of Swain Hall at noon on Saturday.

Damien was really annoyed because the weather was going to be nice on Saturday and he had been planning to spend some time reading on the grass. Nevertheless, he met the rest of the group as instructed, but one student had already dropped out of the club for some reason.

Approximately twenty men, including Bernard, the rest presumably club members, gathered along with the six remaining inductees. The president of the club began to speak. He first asked each of the new inductees to introduce himself. Then he explained that what they were going to do next was a test of their trust and that, as crew novices, it was important that they learn to trust the skills and experience of their teammates. At that point, black cloths were brought out, and each of the inductees was blindfolded. Then their hands were bound behind their backs. After that, each inductee was spun around several times, instructed not to say a word, and led off by a small group of three or four club members. Bernard chose to follow the group that was leading Damien.

Damien, confident of what was going to happen, went along without worry wherever they pushed him. In about thirty minutes, even though he could only see a little light out of the bottom of the blindfold, he realized there were many other people around him, presumably the other inductees and their guides. From the sound of everyone's footsteps shuffling on the floorboards, he realized that they were now stepping onto the dock. Then he was pushed into the water along with all the other inductees.

Fortunately for some of the inductees, their blindfolds came off with the force of the water, but they still had to contend with treading water with only their legs. The others had to do this with their eyes still covered.

Damien was nowhere to be seen. Bernard was the first to notice and began to panic. After a few seconds, the other men who had waded into the water grabbed the inductees and pulled them to shore with most of the novices falling on the grass, some coughing up water. Their hands were then untied, and any remaining blindfolds were removed.

The rest of the group that had overseen Damien were panicking. He had not surfaced. Bernard began to shout, "Damien! Where's Damien? He didn't come up!" All the other men dove into the water and began frantically searching with their hands, some diving under the water with their eyes open.

Damien calmly moved from under the dock and walked up onto the edge of the shore. People searching in the water didn't see him, and he heard someone on the pier say, "Oh, my God. He's drowned!"

Damien flopped down on the grass as the other inductees laughed and stared ahead. Finally, one yelled, "Hey, no one drowned. We're all here!" One by one, the men in the water looked toward the shore at the inductees sitting on the grass and realized that six were sitting there and everybody was all right.

They hurriedly rushed to shore, and one angrily asked, "Which one of them was it?"

Another one shouted as he pointed. "It was that Damien!"

Then another shouted, "Let's show him!" Six guys, including Bernard, descended on Damien, grabbed each of his arms and legs and held him high from underneath as they carried him back to the dock.

Damien was kicking and yelling, "No, no!" Then the guys counted to three and threw him in. They all laughed, and as Damien surfaced, he was laughing too.

As they all headed back to their dorms, several team members patted Damien on the back and welcomed him to the club.

Later that evening, Bernard knocked on Damien's door. It opened, and Damien peeked out.

"Your roommates out?"

"Yeah, out on the town."

"So, how d–did you d–do it?"

Just as Damien was about to speak, Bernard interrupted. "Look, I got some food in my room and some gin from Dad, so you got plans?"

"I do now. Let me get my coat."

Once they were in Bernard's room and had the food spread out and drinks poured, Damien began to explain. "It was simple, really. First, I had already been practicing holding my breath in the pool and swimming the entire length underwater. Guess, ever since the Titanic sinking and other boats during the war, I thought it might be good to be able to hold your breath in case of an emergency. Then you warned me about the blindfolds and the hands being tied. I just prepared, and before they tied my hands, I reached in my pocket for my pocketknife and held it where they couldn't see it. Then as we got close to the pier, I cut a few of the ropes, and they popped off when I went in."

"D–damn, you had me scared." He paused for a few moments as he looked at Damien smiling back, and added, "I'm glad you're all right."

Chapter 15

End Up Trapped

It was Tuesday afternoon, classes were over for the day, and Taylor trudged down the hall toward his room, carrying a backpack full of books over his shoulder and a large Coke in one hand. As he pulled his keys from his pocket, he stopped in front of his door, which had numerous multicolored flyers and notes wedged between the door and doorframe. Knowing that they might fly everywhere when he opened the door, he put the edge of his cup in his mouth to free his left hand and grabbed all the papers as he unlocked his door.

Taylor assumed these were the usual flyers for deals on pizza deliveries, the local deli, or a computerized dating service and was about to toss them in the trash. Then he noticed one folded sheet inscribed with large cursive script. Setting his backpack down, he read the note: "Saw this at the bar last Saturday night. I'll go if you go! Alex." He opened it up and quickly read it.

It was a flyer advertising a talk the following Friday by Lieutenant Colonel Ralph Johnson, a former Air Force officer described as a "war hero" and "superstar" by his commanders. Johnson had been subsequently discharged for revealing he was gay. The program was being put on by the campus chapter of the Force Against Inequality (FAI), and there would be a "Meet the Speaker" with refreshments afterward.

Taylor thought this would definitely fulfill one of the requirements for his scholarship. And Friday night was good for him. Then he thought of Marcia, with whom he likely would have spent Friday evening. *Maybe she'll go too*, Taylor thought. *Alex won't think this is a date, will he? With her, that will solve the problem. Or will it? No big deal. Play it as it goes.* He decided to tell Alex that he would go and ask Marcia to come along.

Taylor went to the bathroom, relieved himself, and rinsed his face. Then he went to the end of the hall to retrieve his mail and took it back to his room. All the mail went into the trash except for a postcard from his dad. It was always a picture postcard, which his dad had probably picked up at the grocery store or drugstore, and it usually had a nature scene of a mountain or a lake or farmland. He never called or wrote a letter.

The message on the back was always short: "Went fishing on Sat. Love, Dad." Sometimes it was cryptic: "Mom failed PET. Love, Dad." And sometimes it was bittersweet: "Last night, Mom and I danced. Love, Dad." But Taylor knew it was his dad's way of showing interest in him and was thankful for the almost weekly correspondence, as brief as it was. Taylor opened his desk drawer and placed the card on the stack of the other postcards from his dad. Then he went down the hall to Alex's room and knocked on the door. From inside he heard Alex's muffled panting voice, "Come . . . in . . . it's . . . unlocked."

Apprehensive because of the panting, Taylor responded, "I can come back later!"

"No . . . come in . . . now!"

Taylor turned the knob and slowly pushed the door open. He was relieved to see Alex was alone. Shirtless and wearing gym shorts, he was on a mat on the floor, doing sit-ups.

Taylor laughed as he slumped down in a chair. "I heard this panting inside, and I thought that . . . I thought that—"

"I wish," Alex interrupted. Then he counted off the last sit-ups: "Ninety-four, ninety-five, ninety-six, ninety-seven, ninety-eight, ninety-nine, one hundred." He let out a huge sigh as he fell back on the floor.

"Wow!" Taylor exclaimed. "You do a hundred sit-ups?"

"Sometimes twice a day."

As Alex got up and wiped himself with a T-shirt, Taylor commented, "Well, it's really given you a six-pack."

"Thanks," Alex responded. "Yeah, it definitely works."

"Got your note."

"Yeah?"

"I think I'll go."

"Good. Then I'll go too."

"Is it okay to invite Marcia?"

"Sure, if she wants to go. Do you think she would want to go?"

There was a pause as the question sank in; then Taylor responded. "Well, I don't know. I'll ask."

As Taylor got up to leave, Alex remembered something. "Oh, wait . . . wait. I want to show you something." He directed

Taylor to his desk, where he picked up a *Daily Tar Heel* and flipped through it, finding an article.

"This is the guy who's giving the talk." Taylor looked and saw a picture of a fortyish pilot in a flight suit with one foot propped up on a large object on the tarmac. "He's hot," Alex continued. "We don't want to miss this."

Taylor smiled and read the headline aloud, "'Hero Discharged after 20 Years of Service.' That's right. You like older men."

Alex shrugged. "So, we all set?"

"Yup. Friday. I'll be back from class around four-thirty or five. It starts at seven-thirty. I'll also ask Marcia."

❉ ❉ ❉

As it turned out, Marcia did want to go. On Friday, after convening at the dorm, the three went to Lenoir Hall, had a quick dinner, and went to the student union's second floor, where there were two small auditoriums. They looked at two posted billboards: One was an inter-fraternity meeting, and the other was the talk with Lieutenant Colonel Ralph Johnson. They proceeded in and sat midway in the theater.

After a short introduction by the president of the Force Against Inequality, Lt. Col. Johnson stood up and positioned himself behind the podium. He began speaking.

"I want to say first that I love my country. I loved being in the Air Force, and I embraced all the duties that were required by the Air Force. I found the life of an Air Force officer very fulfilling, and I was willing to do everything necessary in defense of my country."

He retraced his record of 75 combat missions, 1,900 flying hours, over 1,000 fighter hours and 405 combat missions. Along with these missions was the awarding of eight air medals, including two for heroism.

He stated he was one-and-a-half years short of retirement with full military pension; nevertheless, he had intended to re-enlist with the desire to reach a higher military rank. But that did not happen. He was exposed as a homosexual and eventually removed from service and stripped of his pension.

Before he began giving the details of this, he went back in time to relate his early life. His father had been a career military officer and had instilled in him the ideals of serving one's country. Later, he had gone to military school and graduated as a commissioned officer. At this point, he made reference to several detailed accomplishments and to his daily life.

Johnson was an engaging speaker, relating how he had evolved from someone considered a military hero to someone ostracized and finally removed from the organization around which he had built his life. The attention of the small audience of about thirty-five people seemed fixed on his every word. Taylor in particular tried to put himself in Johnson's shoes.

For nearly twenty years, he had hid his sexual orientation from everyone except a few close friends. Some of these friends were in the military and some were not, and together they would occasionally go to a local gay bar off base. One evening, he met someone at the bar, and they exchanged telephone numbers. A growing friendship developed, which resulted in the divulging of increasingly more personal information.

"Then the person threatened to blackmail me about my sexual orientation, and I realized it had all been a setup. When I tried to disregard these threats, the blackmailer made assault accusations to my commanding officer. My commanding officer asked me directly about my sexual orientation, and I answered with the truth. My only other choice was to lie and have more misinformation swirling around me. When I came clean, discharge proceedings began."

After much investigation by the local authorities, all the accusations of assault were dropped and the blackmailer was deemed an unreliable source. But the damage was already done.

"I was documented as a homosexual, and according to the military, I was not compatible with their goals of high morale, good order, discipline, and unit cohesion. I was removed, just a year and a half before retiring with dignity and receiving a full retirement pension."

Taylor sat there amazed at what he was hearing. Someone could be discharged just because of whom they had slept with. If it had been a man and woman, the matter would have been immediately dropped.

Lt. Col. Johnson concluded his talk, and everyone applauded. Taylor leaned over toward Marcia and said, "I never realized any of this was going on."

Alex, who was sitting on the other side of Marcia, responded, "That 'Don't Ask, Don't Tell' has made it worse. Twenty years, and then to lose it all."

The president then thanked Lt. Col. Johnson and invited everyone on stage for refreshments and an opportunity to meet the speaker.

"Here's your chance," Taylor kidded to Alex.

"Watch me in operation," Alex answered.

About twenty people, including Marcia, Taylor, and Alex, went up onto the stage. Alex immediately moved toward Lt. Col. Johnson but had to wait since two other students had gotten to him first. Marcia and Taylor nibbled on some chips and dip with cups of soda; then they walked over to a table on which were numerous pamphlets about the organization. They both began perusing the literature.

"I had never paid any attention to this organization before," Marcia said, "but it appears they do a lot of good things. And it's not only about gay rights. They've gotten involved in some local issues in town dealing with prayers in public school and some race issues."

"Yeah," Taylor chuckled, "but I don't see anything in here about working for discriminated witches."

Marcia smiled, adding, "Well, maybe it's just not yet our time."

For the next fifteen minutes, people talked with each other while Marcia and Taylor read most of the literature. Taylor grabbed a half-page application and told Marcia that he was planning to join the organization and was wondering if he should introduce himself to the president. The stage was clearing out, but the president was still occupied talking to a female student who seemed to have a lot to discuss. The president noticed Taylor standing nearby and would occasionally look over at him, but the student apparently didn't get the signal and continued talking. Alex had corralled Lt. Col. Johnson alone, and they were exchanging some written information.

Taylor stuffed the application and literature into his pocket. "Looks like she is going to take some time. I can send this in. I think we should go."

"Yeah, I agree. Looks like Alex might be tied up."

Taylor tried to signal Alex that they were leaving, and Alex hollered for them to wait for him. Taylor gestured at the lobby, indicating they would be out there. Taylor and Marcia moved up the aisle and exited the auditorium. The meeting across the hall was ending, and people were leaving that auditorium as well.

Marcia and Taylor stood there looking at two guys, obviously fraternity brothers, who were leaving. The guys paused; then they looked at the billboard announcing Lt. Col. Johnson's speech. They approached it and began to read the poster.

"Look, some fag Air Force guy is whining about getting kicked out of the service!" They both laughed. Immediately, a hand grabbed the shoulder of the guy who had spoken and spun him around. It was Alex, who had just happened upon the conversation.

"Look, I don't know who the hell you think you are, but that guy, a war hero, was protecting your life while you were having your beer-busting frat parties! He's more of a man than you'll ever be!"

The guy was shocked, and they both drew back.

"I'm—I'm sorry. It was just a . . . just a stupid comment."

Alex turned to Marcia and Taylor and said, "Let's go."

When they had gotten outside, they felt some relief from the coolness of the fall air after having been in the stuffy auditorium and having witnessed the tense encounter. They walked toward the dorm for several minutes in silence. Then Marcia asked, "Did you get a date? We saw you exchanging numbers."

"Nah, he was just giving me the title of a book that had interviews from a bunch of men and women who had been kicked out of the service. It talks about all the stuff they are going through in fighting this."

"You've got to feel for him," Taylor said. "All that he worked for in his career, just down the drain. And he seemed like a likable guy."

"Yeah, he did," Marcia added. "He had a good personality. Alex, you should pursue this."

After a moment of thought, Alex replied, "I don't think that a military war hero like that would be interested in a . . . a . . . dancer."

"Don't sell yourself short," Marcia replied. "You're a tall, good looking guy."

"With an awesome physique," Taylor added. "And you were great standing up to those assholes in the lobby."

"Yeah," Marcia continued. "You were impressive!"

Alex drooped his head, feigning embarrassment, and softly said, "That's all true."

They all laughed.

"Hey, guys," Taylor interjected. "What are we doing going back to the dorm? It's Friday night. Shouldn't we be doing something?"

Both Alex and Marcia appeared interested.

Taylor continued. "I don't have any classes tomorrow. What about you?"

Marcia and Alex looked at each other; then Marcia spoke. "We both have rehearsals for *The Taming of the Shrew*."

"But that's not until one o'clock," Alex added.

They talked about it for a few minutes and decided that all they really needed was about an hour to prepare in the morning, and they would be okay. Going out tonight sounded like a great idea, so they turned around toward town.

"Besides," Marcia added, looking at Taylor, "I wanted to talk to you about Aunt Zena."

"Yeah? What about?"

"Well, it's about that ghost. Aunt Zena was concerned . . . well, after I saw it too, I called Aunt Zena to talk about it." She looked up at Taylor to get his reaction.

"Oh, that's okay. What did she say?"

"Well, we talked a while; then a customer came in for a palm reading, so she didn't finish much. She said she really wants us to sit down with her and go over it."

While this conversation was going on, Alex was listening with great curiosity. Finally, he asked, "Okay. You both saw a ghost? What's this all about?"

Marcia looked at Taylor, "You don't mind me telling Alex, do you?"

"No, it's fine. I think I could use him for protection anyway."

They briefly told Alex how, earlier in the year, Taylor had been attacked by a ghost in a black leather hat and had also seen him at the restaurant where he worked. Then they told him that the ghost was Bernard Pembroke of University fame and that they had seen his picture in Castlewood. Alex recognized the name and said that the bell tower and another building on campus had been named after him. Then Marcia related that she had seen Pembroke, too.

"I've always felt," Alex responded, "there was more out there than what we normally see on a day-to-day basis. I've even had situations where I swear there was a presence around me that couldn't be seen."

"Well, my Aunt Zena," Marcia continued, "wanted us to come over and talk about it. I'm going to suggest that she conduct a seance and see if we can contact this guy."

"Really!" Alex blurted out. "I would really love to go to a seance."

"I guess it would be all right for you to come along. What do you think, Taylor?"

"I'm all for it. How can it hurt? Maybe, if the ghost gets violent again, Alex can take him on. When are we talking about?"

"Well, that is a problem," Marcia sighed. "With classes, it's kind of hard for us during the week. Seances work best at night. And Aunt Zena does most of her business on weekends."

"We could do it one evening in the week," Taylor added.

"Next Wednesday," Alex said. "We don't have rehearsals. How's that for you, Marcia?"

"Good for me," Taylor said.

"Great," Marcia answered. "I'll set it up with Aunt Zena."

They ended up at Harry's again. After ordering drinks, their conversation once again turned to Lt. Col. Johnson.

"This whole thing sucks for gay people in the military," Marcia said. "I have a gay cousin; she's a girl in the Army, and she said lots of the women are lesbian . . . and it's like, no questions asked."

"But are they open about it?" Alex asked.

"Probably not. Especially with the 'Don't Ask, Don't Tell' thing."

"I think," Taylor said, "it'd be worse for guys though. Can you imagine? Working for twenty years in a career you really love, and you have to live a life under the radar screen. You can't be who you really are. Eventually, you come to the point and ask yourself, 'What am I doing here?' But it may be too late to change careers. People end up trapped."

Chapter 16

Good at This

Damien and Bernard, like many of the other men in the rowing club, had classes that began at 9:00 a.m. every weekday. Rowing practice was from 6:00 a.m. to 7:45 a.m., so they had an hour and fifteen minutes to shower, change their clothes, eat breakfast, and get to class, which was doable if they rushed. An additional long practice was on Saturday from 8 a.m. until noon.

The day after acceptance into the rowing club, the new members were required to meet with the coach for two mornings of basic rowing instructions prior to training with the experienced rowers. The first day was classroom instructions, during which they were given a rowing manual to read and were taught basic information, including terminology of the boat, proper commands used by the coxswain, and general guidelines on racing. This was followed by one morning in the gym with a demonstration on the rowing machines to learn rowing techniques. The new members, including Damien, were then given some time to practice on the machines, with the coach paying individual attention to their progress.

On Saturday, as instructed, the entire club gathered in front of the boathouse, dressed in athletic short-sleeved shirts, shorts, socks and canvas shoes. Thirty-one men now belonged to the Skimmers, which worked out well for the club's three boats. Each boat held a crew of eight plus a coxswain. That left four club members who rotated in positions of Marshals, including the Starter, who started the boats when racing, the Timer, who operated the stopwatch, and the Clerk, who recorded the times. One person each day was left with no duties. But there were numerous circumstances such as illnesses, family emergencies, or failing to get up in time, that could cause at least one person to miss practice. The club discouraged missing practice because if too many people from a boat were absent, the boat would be rowing without a complete team, a definite disadvantage. This would result in berating of the offenders by their teammates; repeated absences could result in their expulsion from the club.

Additionally, besides the coach, there was a faculty volunteer, Dr. David Smith, a professor from the Commerce Department, who assisted with coaching and stood in as a marshal when needed.

The club was divided into three crews based on skill levels, each with an assigned nickname. The best rowers, usually upperclassmen, were in the Bullfrog Crew. The next most proficient were in the Froglet Crew. And the novices, usually made up of freshmen and sophomores, were in the Tadpole Crew.

This was the first day of the season that the club was meeting to be on the water. The coach got their attention and explained that he wanted to get the new members performing adequately by mixing them in with the more experienced teams. He grouped them by the years that they had been on a crewing team. Then he integrated the novices with the more experienced crew members and assigned them to boats.

Bernard was a strong rower, but since he was only in his second year of rowing, he knew he would likely end up in the Froglet Crew. In this first day of integrating the novices with the experienced rowers, Damien and two other novices ended up in the same boat as Bernard and four more experienced upperclassmen. After a short explanation of the proper way to pick up a boat from its cradle and place it in the water, the coach asked one crew to demonstrate the procedure. Hamilton Conners, the most experienced coxswain in the club, shouted the various commands to lift the boat and then gave the orders to place it in the water. All of the crew boarded the boat. Then the next crew launched their boat with the faculty volunteer serving as the coxswain and shouting the commands. Finally, Bernard and Damien's crew completed their launch with the coach serving as coxswain.

Each cox secured his megaphone in place on his head. Then the coach gave initial instructions, shouting loudly through his megaphone to all the boats. "For the beginning part of today, your cox will be your coach. I want you to take your boats to different parts of the lake. I want you to just learn the process of following the stroke. For those people who didn't read your manual or weren't paying attention in class, that's seat eight, or the rower who is closest to the stern. Follow the stroke. He is one of the most experienced members of your crew, so learn from him."

After this, the coach directed one boat to the far end of the lake and one toward the middle and left his boat closest to the boathouse.

In Damien and Bernard's boat, an experienced rower was seated in the bow seat. Damien was seated in the second seat, followed by another novice in the third seat. In the fourth seat was an experienced rower, followed by Bernard, two novices, and an experienced rower in the stroke position. The coach, in the position of the cox, faced the crew.

Bernard turned around, caught Damien's eyes and waved, and Damien smiled and waved back.

For the next two hours, the coach gave the crew instructions on proper stroke technique and techniques for turning, slowing and stopping, and he familiarized them with the cox's commands. Then he made them practice this. After that, they spent an hour on the open water rowing at a moderate speed. By this time, Damien and the other novices were exhausted, while the other crew members who had not rowed the entire summer were also quite tired. However, the coach then made them go through an exercise in which they would speed up for about three minutes and then slow down for an equal amount of time. This practice lasted for another hour; then the coach gave them the order that they were through for the day and could take their boats back to the dock. When they were given the command to lift the boat out of the water, there were many wobbly crew members, and the coach assisted them in their efforts. Each boat was carried to the boathouse and carefully placed on a rack.

"Listen up," the coach said, getting everyone's attention. "That was a good workout. We have a great team, and I can see we have some great new team members. You are really going to do well this year, and more importantly, you will come out of this a stronger, more confident man. So, keep that in mind. Now, get some rest, and we'll see you Monday morning, bright and early. Oh, by the way, I'll be posting your boat and your position in the crew Monday morning at the front of the boathouse. See you then." At that, everyone began dispersing.

Bernard came over to Damien, and they looked at each other directly. Both were weary-eyed and red-faced with tousled hair. Damien was weaving slightly but managed to grunt out, "What the hell did you get me into?"

Bernard chuckled, "It gets easier. B–believe me." They both turned and headed up the hill.

"God," Damien moaned, "that was unbelievably hard. Coach Barnes is hard-boiled."

"Absolutely," Bernard replied, "b–but he gets the b–best out of you. You're in good shape. You'll recover quickly. And remember, 'S–stronger and a more c–confident man!'"

"I—I don't know. Right now, I just need to lie down. But I have so much reading to do."

"Welcome to c–college life. I suggest resting, maybe t–taking a nap. Then read some. We can meet for d–dinner; then go to the l–library for several hours."

"Yeah," Damien replied. "That sounds reasonable. Six o'clock at the cafeteria? No, I forgot. Tonight I'm going to the Welcome Back Hop."

"Oh, the monthly d–dance is tonight?"

"Yeah, I told one of the birds from Lit class that I would dance with her. You should come along."

Bernard was quiet for awhile; then he said, "I don't . . . I should s–study."

"Bull. Come to the dance."

"N–no," Bernard answered, shaking his head.

"Then at least we can still meet for dinner. You have to eat."

"All right. S–six o'clock." They split up and headed for their respective dorms.

Later that evening, they did meet for dinner. Damien had napped and seemed back to his energetic self. He effused over the rowing club and how he had enjoyed skimming over the water and how all the men in the club seemed friendly and a good bunch of guys. Bernard just nodded and smiled. Their dinner was over within an hour, and Damien went back to dress for the dance, which would start at eight.

Bernard headed to the library to do some reading. Most of the library windows were open, and around eight o'clock, Bernard's attention was drawn to jazzy music that had started playing. The sound was drifting up the hill from the Tin Can, a large metallic building that housed the courts for basketball and other indoor sports; it also was the place where dances were held. He tried to ignore it and concentrate on his reading, but he kept getting distracted as each new tune began. After about forty-five minutes, Bernard got up from the table to stretch. He looked all around and noticed that there was no one else in the room. He looked at his wristwatch. It was fifteen minutes before the library closed, so he gathered up his books, dropped them off at his dorm, and walked over to the Tin Can.

As he approached, the music, a rapid rendition of "Sweet Georgia Brown," grew louder, and he noticed the overhead lights in the building were ramped up to full brightness. The front doors of the building were thrown open for ventilation, and he continued in through the lobby and onto the main floor. It was filled with several hundred people around the edge of the room, with about thirty people in the middle dancing rapidly to the loud music being played by a ten-piece band in the corner on his right. All the men were dressed in sport coats, some of which had been draped over chairs around the room. The women, most of whom had been bused in from the North Carolina College for Women, were spiffed up, many with beads and jewelry that sparkled in the bright light from above. Bernard's eyes fell on Damien, moving quickly across the floor with a pretty female student as they danced rapidly to the energetic music. After a few minutes, many of the other couples stopped their dancing and moved aside to look at Damien and his partner as they apparently broke into unfamiliar dance steps that everyone seemed to admire. Bernard continued to watch with everyone else. As the music ended, several people applauded not only the band but also Damien and his partner's dancing. Bernard's eyes followed Damien as he moved into the crowd at the side, acknowledging some men, exchanging a few words, hugging a few girls and then disappearing to the refreshment table.

"That fella is quite a floor flusher!" said a male voice behind Bernard. He turned to see that it was Chappie, holding a cigarette.

"G–good evening, Chappie. Yes, he c–can certainly dance. Music sounded great, t–too."

"One of our own from Rocky Mount. Graduated last year. James Kyser. Just took the name Kay Kyser. He's good." After a pause, Chappie continued. "About that dancer: Heard from one of the coeds, he's an odd bird, a three-letter man."

Bernard paused, looking at Chappie questioningly. "A three-letter man?"

"Oh, you know," Chappie continued as he casually blew a large puff of smoke. "A man's man. Someone who enjoys a man's company over a woman's."

Bernard frowned at Chappie, seething for a moment. He said, "My God, Ch-Chappie, I guess that explains why there are so many g-gentlemen's clubs in B-Boston from where you hail." He slowly turned and walked toward the exit.

❀ ❀ ❀

Monday morning, at five minutes to six, Bernard saw Damien ahead of him, walking slowly toward the boathouse. "Hey, Damien! You're moving at a s-snail's pace!"

Damien looked up at him with a wry smile. "I'm in so much pain, I could barely get out of bed or even walk. And look at my blistered hands!"

"Me too!" Bernard added. "B-but better this morning."

"The good thing," Damien continued, "is that all I could do Sunday was lie around and read, so I got everything caught up and even read additional chapters."

"Wonderful!"

"Did I see you at the dance on Saturday night?"

Bernard smiled. "C-came for a moment. Saw you d-dancing. Must not be hurting too b-bad."

"The soreness didn't set in until the next day."

As they approached the boathouse, they noticed a bunch of the guys looking at a posting on the front.

"G-get in line," Bernard said. "We'll see where we've been placed."

When Bernard reached the posting, he immediately noticed his name. "F-Froglet crew . . . to be expected!"

Then Damien raised his voice. "What the devil! They made me cox in the Tadpole Crew. I wanted to row. Ah, horsefeathers! This rowing thing's just not working out." He quickly turned, pushed by some others gathered around the billboard, and headed to the side of the boathouse. Bernard followed, looking at him sympathetically. Damien flopped down on a bench and stared at the blank side of the structure.

"This is good news!" Bernard said, trying to be enthusiastic.

"No, I wanted upper body strength. I should have known, with my size and all. Darn, now all I'll be doing is sitting in a boat, yelling at the guys."

"Whoa!" Bernard quickly interrupted. "F–first of all, you will get upper body strength since we'll be working on weights in the gym t–twice a week. B–but what is more important, this is one of the m–most important p–positions in the whole c–crew."

"Yeah? How's that?"

"The cox is a p–position of leadership. You stand in when the c–coach is not there. You encourage and m–motivate the crew. A good cox can d–determine whether you are a winning team or not. He sets the p–pace, gives encouragement, and guides the boat."

Damien stood looking at Bernard, thinking about what he had said.

Bernard continued, "I think the c–coach saw something in you . . . the way you were f–friendly with the other guys and joked with them and got to know them . . . and th–they responded in a p–positive way. That's all-important in a team's spirit, and—"

Just then, they heard someone shout loudly, "Ah, shit! Missed the cox position! Damien got it."

"Hear that?" Bernard asked, gesturing over his back with a thumb. "It's a d–desirable position. Well, not everyone c–can be happy. I hope the c–coach didn't hear that cursing."

Damien smiled and said, "Yeah, yeah. What you said makes sense. This could be quite nifty. You know . . . you know, I think I could be good at this!"

Chapter 17

Dig Deeper

Late Wednesday afternoon, Marcia, Taylor, and Alex walked from their dorm through the parking lot to Marcia's beat-up 1990 black two-door Chevy Lumina.

"Looks like a witch's car," Alex commented.

As she was getting in, she said, "Hope this thing cranks. I don't use it every week, and it's been sitting here for a while."

"Since you're a witch, you can always use magic," Taylor joked.

Alex laughed as he got into the rear seat while Marcia rolled her eyes, put the key in the ignition, and turned it. The car groaned, turning over slowly for a few seconds. She released the key and sat back. "What are we going to do now?"

Taylor said, "Sounds like your battery. It's run down."

"Use some of your magic like Taylor said," Alex quipped.

"Let me see," Marcia pondered. "There are the usual love spells, spells to find lost items, spells to get money, really a bunch of spells, but I can't recall one to get your car to start. Most of them require candles and other objects." She paused, thinking for a moment as Taylor looked at her incredulously.

"Wait," she said as she reached over to the glove compartment and opened it. "I have a lighter in here. Here it is. Maybe it's just the fire." She paused a moment to concentrate with her eyes shut. "Okay! This is really for healing people, but maybe it'll work on the car." She lit the lighter and said, "In the divine name of the . . . goddess who breathes life into us all, I consecrate and charge this candle—er, lighter as a magical tool for healing." She held the lighter to the dashboard and said, "Magic mend and lighter burn, sickness end, good health return." She turned the key, and the engine slowly turned, then started.

Everyone laughed. "Good job!" Taylor shouted.

"That's amazing!" Alex added.

Marcia shrugged. As she started backing out, she said, "I'll have to remember that when the toilet gets stopped up."

In twenty minutes, they were slowing down and turning in to Aunt Zena's house, a 1960s white clapboard ranch set back from the highway. It was twilight, and as the sun dipped down to a dried cornfield across the road, it gave the front of the house a red hue. As they stopped and got out of the car, the front door of the house opened, and a woman in an orangey-red dress with long, curly, bright red hair moved out onto the stoop. She raised her hand to shield her eyes from the sun's glare. Her face and hands were also washed with the same red glow. Long earrings of flat metal dangled from her ears, and a long, knotted clear glass necklace both caught the setting sun and reflected it back to the group in pinpoints of sparkling light.

"Aunt Zena!" Marcia called out as they climbed the steps. With arms outstretched, Aunt Zena embraced Marcia.

"It's been a while," Zena stated.

"You know, school." Marcia introduced Taylor and Alex, and Zena welcomed them into her home.

What would normally have been the living room appeared to be a waiting room with about ten armless chairs made of various materials, some made of wood, some of metal, and others of molded resin.

"Come this way," Zena said as she led them down a small hallway into a comfortable den with bookshelves, a love seat, several overstuffed chairs, and a table draped in a white tablecloth.

Zena and Alex sat in two of the larger chairs, and Marcia and Taylor sat on the love seat. After a brief conversation about school and the classes they were taking, Marcia became serious.

"Aunt Zena, thanks so much for seeing us. All of us are at the point in the semester with tests and papers, so I want to get right to our reason for our visit. It's about that ghost that I talked to you about."

Zena looked at Alex. "It's you who the ghost is bothering? He's probably angry because you stole his girlfriend."

"No, it's Taylor who's seen the ghost. And I'm gay, so no worries about girlfriends."

"Maybe I have a spell to fix that," Zena quickly responded.

"No, I'm quite fine with who I am."

"Well, okay. You are right. You are fine." Turning to Taylor, she said, "It's you who has seen the ghost."

"That's right," Taylor responded. "And now, Marcia."

Zena looked directly at Marcia. "That's right. You said you saw the ghost! Are you sure?"

Marcia answered. "Yes, Aunt Zena. I saw him too."

Zena looked at Marcia sternly and said, "This is significant. You are absolutely sure you saw the ghost, and it's just not a matter of the power of suggestion or you were taking something and imagined it."

"Well," Marcia chuckled, "we had numerous beers, but I knew what was going on. What's the big deal? I thought witches had the capability of seeing ghosts?"

Zena paused for a moment as if searching for the right answer; then she spoke. "That's true. Witches do have the ability to see ghosts . . . when they choose to make their appearance to other people."

"It appears to be," Marcia continued, "something with Taylor. The ghost is angry with Taylor."

Everyone looked over at Taylor, who sighed and spoke. "Look, here's what I think. This all started when I applied for a scholarship. You see, nothing was available for me, and I really wanted to go to college. I had been accepted to Carolina, but my family . . . my father couldn't afford to send me. So, the counselor found this Pembroke scholarship for gay students. You had to be gay . . . and you had to demonstrate that you were working toward equality for gay people. So I lied and said I was gay."

"I was right," Alex spoke up. "I didn't think you were gay."

"No, I'm not. Anyway, when I signed the scholarship agreement was when I first felt something strange."

"What do you mean something strange?" Zena asked.

"Well, it's hard to describe. But it was like the room had become filled with this . . . presence . . . someone else's presence, and I looked up and saw a shadow that quickly disappeared. Then several days later, I was accosted by this ghost when I was out with some friends. And I had said some things against gays."

After Taylor had said this, he looked over at Alex, who sat still, intently following every word. Then Taylor added, "It was . . . The only reason I said anything was because my friends were kidding around and ribbing me about taking a gay scholarship. But this time, when I went to the restroom, the ghost literally picked me up and slammed me against the wall. I was really shook up and feared for my life. Then, a month or so later, during the summer, at my job at a restaurant, he appeared outside of the restaurant. This time, he just appeared when I was talking with my . . . with a friend, and when I went outside to confront him, he was gone."

A few seconds went by as everyone absorbed what Taylor had just said. Then Zena asked, "Then what?"

"Well, first, Marcia and I were at his mansion, and we saw his portrait. That's when I realized the ghost must be Bernard Pembroke."

"Castlewood!" Zena interrupted. "I heard it was haunted."

"The next time he appeared, I was with Marcia."

Zena looked at Marcia. "And that's when you saw him too?"

"Yes," Marcia answered. "So, I was thinking that if we could communicate with this ghost, we might be able to figure out what he wants."

Zena asked, "When did this man die, and what were the circumstances?"

Marcia answered, "Well, according to a lady who works there at the castle, Pembroke died almost thirty years ago. It was a heart problem. We didn't learn of any unusual circumstances surrounding his death."

Zena was quiet for a moment; then she spoke. "Well, it's obvious that this man Pembroke is a troubled soul, and for some reason, his spirit does not want to move on. It could be he is angry with you taking the scholarship using deceit, but that wouldn't be the complete reason since he's been hanging around for thirty years, long before you were even born. It's got to be something else."

"Makes sense," Taylor responded. "Also makes me feel better."

Zena continued, "So, you were thinking that maybe we could communicate through a seance?"

"Yeah," Marcia replied.

"Well, I don't know."

"Aunt Zena, it's worth a try."

"I suppose. Okay, we'll give it a try. Grab two more chairs and put them around the table."

Zena lit four candles on the table and lowered the lights as Taylor and Alex sat down opposite each other. Marcia sat in between.

"It is important to relax to get into the mood, so I'm going to put on some soft music as we all relax."

After turning on soft music from a tape player on the shelf, Zena came back and sat down with the rest. "Now it is important to open your mind and remove any negative feelings you may have. Whatever you feel, see, or experience with this seance, please make a mental note because we will want you to relate it to the rest of us after it is over. Now concentrate. If you feel any strong negative feelings, try to deflect it by concentrating on white light. Now it is agreed we are here to attempt to make contact with—what's his full name?"

"Bernard Pembroke," Taylor answered.

"Bernard Pembroke," Zena continued. "With deceased persons, we generally send love vibrations because these are souls we care about. In this case, it is a person who has been threatening, and they may not want to communicate with us. Usually, in cases like this, we seek the help of spirit guides to contact these troubled souls. So what we will be doing is sending the love vibrations to an unknown spirit who we will ask to be an intermediary with Bernard Pembroke. So now, just relax and focus on pleasant thoughts, people you enjoy or things you enjoy doing, and after a few minutes, we will begin."

Zena closed her eyes and then Marcia did too. Alex and Taylor followed suit.

They remained this way for a few minutes; then Zena lowered the music until it was off and spoke up. "Now join hands as we contact the Otherworld, but please keep your eyes closed momentarily. Please continue to concentrate on pleasant thoughts."

When Taylor and Marcia's hands made contact, Taylor gave her hand an additional squeeze, which Marcia gently returned.

Zena spoke in a soft, slow manner. "We are seeking a helping spirit of the Otherworld. Come, Otherworld Spirit. You are welcome to our table. Come speak to us and guide us."

Zena waited a short while and then intoned again. "Guiding Spirit of the Otherworld, come help us. Help us find answers to our questions. Come speak to us."

Then, from Marcia's direction, a weak, trembling voice emanated as if from a very old woman. "What answers are you seeking?"

Everyone opened their eyes and looked over at Marcia; her eyes were closed, and her mouth was gaping.

"Are you faking this?" Taylor asked.

Zena grabbed both Taylor's and Alex's hands tightly and whispered firmly, "No, leave her alone. The spirit is channeling through her. We actually did it." Then Zena said, "O Guiding Spirit of the Otherworld, what is your name?"

"Ariel," the shaky voice responded.

"Ariel . . . Thank you for your help. I am Zena. To my right is Alex. To my left is Taylor. The person you are speaking through, in front of me, is Marcia." Zena paused as if waiting for a response, but after a few seconds, she continued. "A spirit of the Otherworld has made his presence known to Taylor and Marcia. He has frightened them both and even attacked Taylor. We are seeking to learn why he is doing this and what he wants. His name is Bernard Pembroke."

Ariel replied. "I am familiar with the spirit of Bernard Pembroke. He has not gone over to the Otherworld. He is a troubled spirit who senses he was wronged in his earthly life."

There was a pause; then Zena asked, "Can you help us with these answers?"

The voice seemed strained as it said, "I've said too much. I can't help. I must go."

Then Marcia let out a moan and started to collapse onto the table, but Taylor quickly grabbed her. Her eyes opened, and she gasped. Zena hurriedly got out of her chair and moved toward her.

"Are you all right?" Taylor asked.

"He was there," Marcia replied. "And he was angry."

"You sensed him. What else?" Zena asked.

"Ariel . . . Ariel the helping spirit was afraid, and she left. I sensed her fear."

"Were you in danger?" Zena asked. "Did you feel in danger?"

Marcia thought for a moment; then she said, "No. No, not at all. It was as if Pembroke was keeping his distance from me."

"I thought so," Zena replied quietly.

"What—what do you mean?" Marcia asked.

"I'll tell you later. But first, Taylor, did you see or hear anything else?"

"No, nothing other than that. The spirit Ariel was familiar with Pembroke and appeared frightened and left."

Zena turned toward Alex. "And you, Alex?"

"Well, actually, I did."

"What?" Zena asked.

"Well, it's kind of weird, but when you were talking to the spirit and you mentioned Bernard Pembroke, I immediately felt like there was someone else in the room. But it wasn't a threatening entity. It was one who felt friendly. I don't know. I just felt comfortable with it."

"Interesting," Zena replied. "We need to contact Pembroke directly. For some reason, it's not going to work with a guide medium. He's preventing it. We'll have to see if he will talk to us directly. You mentioned you were in his house, Castlewood."

"Yeah," Marcia answered.

"Can you get back in there?"

"Definitely. I have a door key," Taylor responded.

"You do?" Zena replied.

"Yeah, as a result of my scholarship, I get to use the library there."

"I've heard about that library. Supposedly, there are some very old and very rare books dealing with the spiritual world."

"I believe there are," replied Taylor. "There is even a side room that is climate-controlled, with old religious texts and this occult collection from the Middle Ages. That Pembroke guy apparently collected a lot of ancient books and had an interest in the supernatural."

"I would love to see them," Zena said. "In fact, when you try to reach a particular dead person, it is best to do it in a location which they are most familiar with, like their place of work or their home. We need to do a seance in that house. There are a lot of questions which need answering."

Taylor paused a moment as everyone looked at him. "Well, I'm told he grew up there and lived there for many years. Yeah, why not? I want answers. When can we do it?"

Zena replied, "Next Saturday night?"

Marcia asked, "But what about your loss of business?"

"This is more important. Much more important. I'll just put a sign out that I'm out of town. It's also close to Halloween. Souls are always more receptive to communicating with the living on days surrounding Halloween. So, is everyone okay with next Saturday?"

Everyone nodded as Alex said, "We're on. Let's plan to dig deeper."

Chapter 18

I Believe in You

Bernard began the rowing season in the Froglet Crew, a team in the intermediate category. Damien was assigned to cox the Tadpoles, a team in the novice category. His crew consisted of all of the inexperienced rowers from the freshman and sophomore classes and one experienced rower who, because of previous illnesses, was considered the weakest of the experienced rowers.

Damien set about getting to know each of the crew. By this time, except for Damien, all the rowers had gotten nicknames, which were usually shortened versions of their actual names or references to their physical appearance. The stroke was Dune for Duncan Fester. In seat seven was Flem for Robert Fleming Bryan. In seats six, five, four, and three were sturdy-framed, muscular fellows nicknamed Red, Bull, Speedy, and Chunk. The crew was rounded out by Jenks for Jenkins in seat two and Legal for Frederick Law in seat one.

During a rest period, a discussion arose about getting a nickname for Damien. Dame was discarded for obvious reasons. Dam was considered but ultimately rejected because several Baptists thought it sounded like a curse word. Cox was considered, but because of the sexual connotation and the fact that his position could change, it too was rejected. They considered Rich or Hold but rejected those also. Unable to reach a consensus, they continued calling him Damien.

The coach and his volunteer assistant, Dr. Smith, each had a single scull and would row out to each of the crew, coaching them or timing them in trials. During the first week of practice, Coach Barnes spent as much time coaching the Tadpoles as he did the other crews. However, since the first race of the season in mid-October against Duke University was fast approaching, both coaches started spending more and more time with the Froglets and the Bullfrogs. It was highly important to Coach Barnes that they do well in the intermediate and advanced categories. The novices could wait.

Damien and the whole crew of eight had noticed this by the second week. While on the water during a Saturday practice break, a discussion about it arose.

"For crying out loud," Legal groused, "Coach Barnes is practically ignoring us."

"I'll say!" Dune added. "We could be sitting all morning dead in the water, and Coach wouldn't care."

There were a few other grumblings; then Damien shouted at them. "Wait up a minute! Wait a minute! They're all part of our team. We want to beat Duke, and Coach is doing what he thinks is proper. But that shouldn't stop us. We've got the rowing technique down. All we need to do now is get stronger and faster, and we can do that on our own. Bull's already there. He's like a big six. We can be better than them. I'll put my dough on it!"

Chunk then shouted, "Damien's right! I'd bet on it too. Let's just row. Let's just practice. That's what we're here for. We can beat them."

For the next forty-five minutes, Damien used his basic commands. Most of them were "push," "stroke," "kick," and "squeeze," followed by "lean" or "lay" or "now," interspersing them with "power ten" commands. With a power ten, Damien would take the crew up to full force, making them give it everything they had for ten strokes.

After they had almost lost sight of the coaches and the other crews, Damien stopped them and said, "I want to try something new. I noticed that sometimes we're slightly out of step with each other. You know, this is all rhythm. Everything we're doing is rhythm."

"And you're doing a great job," Red shouted. Several others shouted agreement.

"Thanks," Damien said. "But I want to try something new." There was a pause as they all looked up, interested. "We all love music. Music helps us get through the pain. I'm going to be singing and throwing in some commands. What do you think?"

"Let's do it!" Chunk shouted.

With that, they turned the boat around and headed back. Once they got to full speed, Damien began to sing the song, "If You Knew Susie." Everyone was familiar with this tune, which had been recorded several years earlier and was popular on the radio and dance floors. It had catchy lyrics with a solid cadence.

Damien sang it with made-up lyrics that came to mind, occasionally interspersing them with rowing commands:

"We are the Skimmers, all of us winners
Stroke! Stroke! Boy, what a team!
We're nine so hopeful
We won't be boastful!
Stroke! Stroke! Yes sir baby! We'll be forceful!
On to winning; give all we got!
All the medals
We're so sure to get a lot
We are the Skimmers; all of us winners
Stroke! Stroke! What a team!"

When everybody seemed to tire of this song or when Damien wanted to up the speed, he would switch to other songs such as "Yes Sir, That's My Baby" or "Five Foot Two, Eyes of Blue." The crew liked what they were doing. Damien had an excellent, strong tenor voice, the others enjoyed hearing him sing, and because of the music, the time seemed to pass quickly.

Damien used this method to get everyone in sync for about a half hour; he then directed them toward the opposite side of the lake where the other crews were.

As they got closer, Law exclaimed to the others, "Oh, God! What is Coach gonna think of this!"

Damien yelled, "Let's give him our best speed!" and began to sing "If You Knew Susie" again.

The coach had the other crews grouped together getting instructions. As the Tadpoles approached with Damien singing, everyone looked their way, and Coach Barnes exclaimed, "What the hell?" He watched for a moment; then he said, "Oh, sorry, gentlemen, no cursing." Then he leaned over to Dr. Smith and said, "You know, they seem to be going at a good pace! Let's do some time trials."

Coach Barnes waved them in and instructed Dr. Smith to row down the lake about five hundred yards and position himself with the stopwatch. He then told the crews that as the last exercise of the day, each crew would race in a time trial. He instructed them to position themselves about twenty yards back for a running start, and once they passed his boat, he would yell "Go!" and Dr. Smith would begin timing their distance.

First up was the Bullfrog crew, and when the coach gave the signal, they raced ahead. Next, the coach sent the Froglet crew to the starting position and got them racing. Then he shouted, "Tadpoles! You looked fast out there. I want to see everything you've got! Cox, I want you to do it exactly like before, with the singing." There was a moment of silence; then the whole crew laughed. He continued, "I mean it. With the singing. All right, crew. Get in position!"

Damien gave them the command to start rowing, and once he passed the coach's boat and the coach shouted, "Go!" Damien began singing. As they got about one-third of the way to Dr. Smith, Damien made them do a power ten and then he resumed singing. Within a hundred yards of Dr. Smith's boat, he made them do another power ten; finally, they crossed the finish line. Dr. Smith recorded the times on a notepad and rode back toward Coach Barnes.

❊ ❊ ❊

On Monday morning, Damien was reassigned to cox the Froglets. The Tadpoles had beat the Froglets' time and come really close to the Bullfrogs'. After Damien had consulted with Coach Barnes, the coach did some time trials with Red, Bull, Chunk, and Dune and repositioned Bull and Chunk in the Froglet crew.

After practice was over and Bernard and Damien were having their breakfast, Bernard said, "I'm unbelievably impressed. The way you motivated your c-crew and moved up to Froglet."

"It's really all about the team working together. There's a lot of great guys on that crew."

"Evidently. When the c-coach started replacing some of the Froglets with your c-crew, I was concerned he might move me back to T-Tadpole."

Damien stopped smiling; he looked down and became serious. "Actually, the coach mentioned putting you with the Tadpoles." Then he looked up and smiled. "But I told him you were too good for that. You were to be in my crew. And he went along."

Bernard stared at him in silence. Then he said, "You d-did? Why?"

After a pause, Damien answered, "Because I believe in you."

Chapter 19

You Saw It Too?

Castlewood usually closed at 5:00 p.m., sometimes sooner. It all depended on the particular date of the academic year and whether there would be faculty and students on campus. Castlewood and its administrative staff existed for no other purpose than as a monument to the late Bernard Pembroke. To keep the memory of the man alive, it housed his furniture, books, paintings, and collections from his worldly travels. It had always been funded by the enormous trust set up before his death and would be maintained in perpetuity, similar to the scholarships he had set up to keep his name alive.

The castle was not open to the public but was often used for formal college functions that were arranged through the university president's office. Prior to the start of each semester, a reception would be given there welcoming all of the new faculty. This would start with a tour of the house, highlighting Pembroke's contributions to the university. These tours were always conducted by Deedee Delaney or one of the other two docents.

Castlewood was at the end of a cul-de-sac. Deedee lived only three houses from the Castlewood property; even at her slow speed, she could walk to the castle in about ten minutes.

On Saturday, Deedee had conducted two tours. The first was for a new faculty member who had missed the reception at the start of the semester. The other was conducted after a catered reception for a group of visiting Japanese scientists who were being entertained by the Chemistry Department.

All of the staff had left around five o'clock, and Deedee, the last one to leave, set the alarm system, locked up the castle, and departed. She was home in her kitchen by five-thirty.

Shortly thereafter, Taylor, driving Marcia's car, entered the front gates of Castlewood. Marcia was sitting in the front seat with him, and Aunt Zena and Alex were in the back seat.

The sun was setting, and streaks of light filtered through the trees, casting eerie shadows on the stone walls of Castlewood. As the car approached the building, Alex remarked, "Reminds me of some old horror movie. I love it."

Everyone else was silent as Taylor pulled over under the porte cochere, and everyone got out. Taylor unlocked the front door, and they entered. He disengaged the pinging security pad and flicked on more lights.

"Wow," Alex gasped. "This is wonderful. It looks like a movie set." Zena was wide-eyed as she gazed all around the main hall.

"The library's upstairs," Taylor said as he led the group toward the large staircase.

As they climbed the stairs, Alex spotted crossed fencing swords on the wall and reached for one, but Taylor ordered, "Leave the swords, Alex."

Undaunted, Alex pretended to grab a sword off the wall. With vocal metallic and swishing sounds, he lunged up the staircase as if he were recreating a fight scene from a swashbuckling movie. Upon reaching the top, he plunged the sword deep into his make-believe assailant and yelled, "Take that, you beastly cur!" The rest of the group chuckled as they reached the top.

"This way," Taylor said as he led them to the doors of the library. He swung one of the doors open. "Hold on, let me get the light." With the lights on, the others went in.

"Nice," Alex said. "Perfect place for a murder mystery." Then looking up at the painting, he asked, "Is this the guy?"

"Yeah, that's him," Marcia replied.

"Cute," Alex said. "But ninety years is even too old for me." Taylor shook his head.

Zena spoke while eyeing the contents of the room. "He must have traveled all over the world. He has such unusual stuff."

"Evidently loved to travel," Taylor said. "And he collected many things."

Alex spotted a human skull on a shelf. He grabbed it in one hand, held it high, and said in an overly bombastic voice, "Alas, poor Yorick! I knew him, Horatio, a fellow of inf—"

"Alex!" Taylor shouted. "Put the skull down!"

Zena began looking at bindings on one of the shelves. "Where's his occult collection?"

"This way," Taylor responded as he led them to a side room with a glass door. "I was told it was okay to go in but to be careful in handling anything. Some of this stuff is over four hundred years old." They went in and closed the door. The room was about fifteen by twenty feet. In the center of the room was a large solid wooden table with two lamps on top. On all four sides were shelves with old, leather-bound books.

Zena immediately went to the shelves as if looking for something. Her eyes zigzagged across the backs of the bindings as she moved from one section to another. "Many of these are in German and French. Old German and French. I don't speak those languages."

"What are you looking for, Aunt Zena?" Marcia asked.

Zena didn't reply. Finally, she said, "Wait, there is this section in English." She hurriedly looked further; then she stopped as if astonished. She held her hands back as if finding a holy relic. "Here . . . here it is! I knew he would have one!"

"What?" Taylor asked as they all rushed to it.

"I've always heard these existed: *A Compendium of Witch Genealogy*." She gently pulled it off the shelf and laid it on the table. "I need more light. This book was printed in 1838 and attempts to trace the genealogy of witches."

Alex turned on both table lamps as Zena began to flip through the pages. Her finger pointed to a page, and she said, "Look how many witches were executed. And it tells how: mostly by burning." Everyone looked briefly at the page of unusual names. Then she continued, turning more pages—and suddenly halted with a gasp. Her finger hurried down the page and then stopped. "Yes, I was right. This is my grandmother, Eliza Schnitzel. She was a gypsy from Rumania."

Everyone leaned over to gaze at the print. "So that's my great-grandmother then?" Marcia asked.

"Yes, and we can see that this woman, Dagmar Shunt, was arrested for witchcraft in 1802 and jailed, but by that time, execution of witches was outlawed. She was probably a true witch. You see, a true witch occurs every seventh generation. I'm sixth generation. If Dagmar Shunt was a true witch, it would mean that if I had a child, she would be a true witch. And it also means, Marcia, that you, being seventh generation, are a true witch."

"Wait a minute," Marcia interrupted. "You're going too fast! I'm not following. I thought you were a witch."

"No, no, no. Not really. I embrace witchcraft and all that the sisterhood stands for, and in that regard, I am a witch. But only with every seventh generation is there a true witch. A true witch has special powers, powers that connect you with otherworldly spirits. That's why you were able to see the ghost! And that's why, this week, you were the one channeling the seance, not me. You are connected to the Otherworld."

Marcia appeared shocked. "I thought you had special powers!"

"No, not really. I just fake it. I'm really a fake, like most fortunetellers. Fake spells, fake seances, fake fortunes, fake name, fake eyelashes, fake boobs! They're all fake."

Alex laughed, "Hey, make-believe can be good!"

"So what does this mean?" Marcia asked.

"Well, honey, it means you have a wonderful power at your disposal and you should cherish and cultivate it."

Taylor spoke up. "This witchcraft thing bothers me. Most of the time, we associate it with doing evil things. I know there are good witches too, but—"

"It's all fear of the unknown," Zena interrupted. "This has caused great discrimination against witches. Thousands and thousands were burned alive or executed in some other way. Just look in this book! Many witches, including many from our family, were executed until the late seventeenth century. But the truth is that, historically, many saints recognized by the Catholic Church were witches. The Church just chose to look at them differently and use them to their advantage. After all, what is the difference between performing a miracle as the saints have done and casting a spell? They both manage to accomplish something that is supernatural. Joan of Arc is a prime example of a person who was a religious mystic, but then the church accused her of being a witch and had her burned, only later to declare her a saint. There were many, many other examples."

"Is that true," Taylor asked, "that the church burned witches alive?"

"The most accurate estimate is that 30,000 women, all believed to be witches, were burned alive. Some were even burned here in America."

"Burning was preferred by the Church," Alex added. "And don't forget that thousands of gay people were burned alive, many in the public square of Verona, Italy."

"Yes, I read that too," Zena added. "More gay people were executed there than anywhere else in Europe; that is, until the Holocaust."

"Wait a minute, Aunt Zena. Why is it that Taylor could see the ghost, yet he's not a witch—or is he?"

Taylor raised his eyebrows and shrugged.

"No, no, dear. The ghost chose to make himself visible to Taylor to threaten him. They have the ability to materialize in various degrees to anybody they wish. They can be a shadow, or they can be fully visible and even carry weight and physically move people as Pembroke has done with Taylor. But a ghost cannot hide from a true witch. A true witch has the power to see a ghost whenever he chooses to materialize to someone else, and a true witch can sense a ghost even when they don't materialize."

"So, Aunt Zena," Marcia said, "although I'm having difficulty assimilating all this you told me, I gather you think I would be best conducting the seance."

"That's right, honey. I think that we would make better progress if you did. You were actually the one conducting it last time, although you didn't know it. This way, you will be in control. Are you up to it?" Marcia thought for a while as Zena added, "I will be here, and I will help."

Marcia was quiet for a few moments as she absorbed all this. She looked at Taylor as if seeking some guidance.

"Only you can decide this," Taylor said.

"Well, all right. Let's do it."

They walked back into the main library, and all eyes immediately fell on the round, leather-topped mahogany table that stood below the portrait of Bernard Pembroke.

"Let's have it here," Zena said. Six chairs were presently around the table, and Alex and Taylor each removed one. "Do we have any candles? Why didn't we think of the candles?"

"I got one," Marcia said as she pulled it from her purse. "This is the one I now carry in my purse."

Taylor chuckled. "Oh, is this your substitute for the AAA?"

"Good girl," Zena said. "A few more would be better. We really need more . . . although a dimly lit lamp will do."

"Wait," Taylor said, "I think I saw some down in the kitchen. Yeah, I know there are some little candles they have when they have catered affairs. I'll go check it out. Be back in a second."

Three houses down the road, Deedee had just finished a light dinner and was rinsing her dinner plate when she looked out her kitchen window and noticed lights shining through the trees from Castlewood. She thought this was nothing unusual, figuring it was probably Taylor or a couple of students using the library for research. She dried her dish and fork and went into the living room to resume reading her book.

In a few minutes, Taylor returned with a box of tea candles and some matches. Zena took the candles and placed several around the room and four in the middle of the table. Alex began to light them.

Marcia was already seated in the chair facing the portrait. She was very nervous; Taylor noticed it and leaned close to her. "Are you all right?"

"Yeah, you know. Opening night jitters. But Aunt Zena pointed out that I have thousands of years of genetic history behind me and I should do all right."

"You know, you don't have to do this."

"No. I actually want to do it. It'd . . ." She paused, searching for what to say. "It'd be wrong not to use this power. Besides, it will be helping you. And maybe I can help this guy too." Taylor leaned over and gently kissed her on the lips.

"Well, break a leg."

Marcia smiled, relaxing a bit. "Thanks."

"All right," Zena said. "Let's get started." Zena took the chair to the left of Marcia. "I'll be here if you need me, and I can prompt you."

Taylor sat to her right. "And I'll be here for you too." Marcia smiled at them both. Alex sat across from Marcia.

"Turn off all the lights," Zena commanded. Taylor got up, flipped the switches, and sat back down. "Now everyone join hands."

"I can take it from here," Marcia quietly said. "Now everyone relax and close your eyes. Remove any negative feelings you may have. Once we reach spirits in the Otherworld, you may release your grip on the person next to you and open your eyes and ask questions as you wish."

They all closed their eyes and were silent for a few minutes. Then Marcia spoke in a slow, controlled manner. "We are here to reach a spirit in the Otherworld. Please come to this table and speak to us."

Immediately, there were swirls of air they could feel brushing against their skin. They all opened their eyes, startled to see streaks of light that seemed to dart all around them. Alex was wide-eyed with mouth agape.

"So quickly," Zena whispered.

Marcia continued. "We are here . . . to talk to Bernard Pembroke. Bernard Pembroke, are you here?"

The streaks of light and swirls of air intensified and were now accompanied by periodic flashes of light.

Zena softly spoke, "All this indicates a troubled soul."

Sitting at home and getting sleepy, Deedee happened to look up from her book toward the mantel clock. Through her window, she noticed that the light coming from Castlewood was now flickering. She immediately got up, grabbed her shawl, and went out the front door to investigate. *Students may be using Castlewood as a place to party,* she thought, *and that is not permitted.*

"Bernard Pembroke," Marcia intoned. "Are you there? We . . . need your help."

The swirling of air and the streaks and flashes of light intensified and were now accompanied by low groaning noises like the voices of thousands of tormented souls.

Marcia continued, "Speak to us, Bernard Pem—"

"What d–do you want?" a low, anguished voice interrupted. Then a specter, a semi-opaque, moving version of the figure in the painting, appeared behind Alex. It was Bernard Pembroke.

Marcia, Taylor, and Zena all reacted, and Alex jerked around to see what they were looking at.

Everyone at the table shot frightened looks at each other, not knowing what they had unleashed.

"Are you Bernard Pembroke?" Marcia nervously asked.

Slowly he answered, "I am B–Bernard Pembroke. What d–do you want?"

"We are . . . we are . . ." Marcia groped for what to ask. "We are seeking to know why you are troubled."

"Who are you . . ." he quickly shot back, "to ask me such a thing. What g–gives you the nerve to d–delve into my happenings?"

Taylor nervously responded, "You—you threatened me and—and scared Marcia. Why . . . why did you . . . what are you after?"

The swirling, the groaning, and the streaks and flashes of light intensified even more.

Deedee was now partway down the driveway of Castlewood and had a clear view of the flashing and streaking in the library window. Her slow pace grew faster as she hurried toward the building.

"You," Pembroke said while pointing to Taylor, "who are living a life of deceit, asks me this?" Then he pointed to Marcia and said, "And you, a witch, but a clueless witch?" Then he pointed to Zena. "And you, a cheap imitator?"

Zena bristled but held her tongue.

"Only one among you is w–worthy to hold your head high."

Marcia spoke. "We are not here to offend you. We are here to seek understanding and maybe . . . in some way, to resolve any conflict you may have been exposed to."

A few moments passed in silence. Then there was a slight decrease in the intensity of the lights and swirling noises, and Pembroke dissolved and reappeared, this time standing next to Zena.

Taylor said, "Are you angry because I took that scholarship? I will quit the scholarship and confess the whole thing, if that's what you want." Marcia looked over at Taylor.

The noise faded to a whisper, and the flashing and swirls of light disappeared. All that remained was the ghostly figure of Pembroke. "I was angry. You had lied about w–who you are. But it d–doesn't m–matter. You are more than capable of doing g–good with the scholarship."

"So . . . so . . ." Alex asked gently, "what is the reason for this chip on your shoulder?"

Pembroke smiled at Alex and looked at him with a faraway stare. Then after a moment, Pembroke said slowly, "The p–person who captured the d–depth of my soul was t–taken away when I was young—as you are today. D–Damien was a person p–pure of heart and mind. He was a m–man who was a shining spark who inspired p–people and made them happy, someone who c–could excite your soul and give you joy, but he d–disappeared . . ."

Marcia gently spoke, "We are deeply sorry to hear this."

Pembroke continued, "I searched for years and years . . . and eventually . . . g–gave up . . . assuming he had d–died. I worked to the b–best of my ability to improve the world I was living in and to leave it a b–better, wiser p–place." Then his countenance changed, and his voice became angry. "I expected that when I d–died, he would be waiting for me to help me cross over." There was a long pause as Pembroke seemed to be breaking down and couldn't speak. "B–But . . . b–but he . . . was not there. He was not here. He was not here."

At that moment, Deedee reached the outside of the library. Setting her walker down and bracing her left hand on it, she grabbed the doorknob and flung the door open.

Everyone looked around, and when Deedee saw Pembroke, she screamed and fainted, falling forward. Taylor, seeing this, jumped out of his chair and grabbed her, keeping her from hitting the floor. Pembroke dissolved into nothing. Zena steadied Marcia, who was slumping in her chair, and Alex jumped up and turned on the lights.

"It's Deedee!" Taylor cried out. "Oh my God!" They carried her to the couch. Alex felt her pulse as Deedee started to open her eyes.

"Deedee," Taylor said excitedly. "Are you all right? I'm . . . so sorry this happened to you. Are you all right?"

Her rapid breathing began to slow as she looked around the room. After a few moments, she smiled. "I'm fine . . . and I'm damn glad I saw that."

Taylor asked, "You saw it too?"

Chapter 20

I'm Learning

Although the whole seance thing was unnerving, in some small way, I've gotten some solace from it. Pembroke isn't around just because he's angry at me. He's looking for someone named Damien, a friend—Marcia says his lover—who went missing years ago. I've talked to Marcia quite a bit about it, and she says it's her responsibility to help him move to the Otherworld, and I also want to help him. I got the feeling that, with the seance and bringing in Aunt Zena and Marcia and, I suppose, even Alex, he is more accepting of me taking the scholarship because he senses we are trying to help him. Still, dealing with a supernatural being is disturbing, but Marcia has helped me feel more settled about it.

At the same time, I've been getting involved in FAI, reading up on the gay issues and doing research in the library about some of these issues, which I am using in a paper for my Sociology class. This paper can count toward one of the requirements for the scholarship. I'm not sure Pembroke is aware I'm doing this paper, but it doesn't really matter. I'm learning from it, and it's changing how I view things. It's really all affecting me. I *think a lot about Colonel Johnson being kicked out of the military and about all the other people who have been treated unfairly. There are a lot of issues that most people don't even know about. I didn't, but I'm learning.*

Chapter 21

Calling Him Pluck

It was Tuesday morning, and Bernard and Damien had just finished their morning rowing practice and were heading up the hill to their dorms. Damien turned toward Bernard and asked, "Are you going to be home with your dad to celebrate Thanksgiving?"

Bernard sneered and made a hissing sound, expressing disdain. "Dad's out of town in Atlanta and won't be back for several weeks."

"Perfect!" Damien exclaimed as Bernard reacted with surprise. "My mother sent me some scratch, ten bucks, and told me to take you to dinner for Thanksgiving. That's enough for multiple dinners and nights on the town."

"Really? You t-talked to her about me?"

"Absolutely! I told her what a great guy you were and how you got me to learn swimming and . . . and joining the rowing club."

"Thank you. And she sent money for a Thanksgiving dinner?"

"Well, she knew it was too expensive and time-consuming for me to take a train all the way back to New York, so as a gift, she sent me the money instead and told me to take you out."

"Well, that was really nice of her, b–but—"

"But I have a better idea. Instead of wasting this money on food, I want the both of us to do something exciting." Bernard smiled and shook his head as Damien continued. "I heard about this Scotsman who's set up this airfield north of town, off of 86, and he will take you up in his Jenny . . . for a fee, of course." Bernard just stopped and looked at him in amazement. Excited, Damien continued. "So, instead of buying you a turkey dinner with all the trimmings, I want to give you an exciting memory you'll never forget. So—so what do you think?"

"This is that b–barnstormer I've heard about, isn't it?"

Damien was silent for a moment; then he said, "Probably. Yes, I think he's done some stunts and worked with some wing walkers. That looks like so much fun. I saw several shows over Coney Island last sum—"

"And," Bernard interrupted, "d–dangerous. Two p–people were killed just this year."

"True," Damien conceded. "That was the wing walkers, but the pilots were okay."

"Even that is dangerous."

"No, no, no. These Jennies are a very stable and reliable aircraft. I've talked to several guys that were in the Air Service during the war, and they were trained in those, and they all swear by them."

Bernard looked away as if he didn't want anything to do with the thought. After a few seconds, Damien added, "I'll tell you what: I suggest we just go out there and look, and then we'll decide what we'll do. We can hitchhike out there. It will be fun. Maybe we'll see some planes in the air." Bernard relented, and instead of hitchhiking, he offered to get his father's car to drive to the airfield.

Thanksgiving break began when classes ended that afternoon. Bernard and Damien decided to drive there right away in case the man with the plane might be going somewhere for Thanksgiving.

After his last class, Bernard, still dressed in his three-piece suit, hurried home and got the car, a two-tone green convertible. It was sunny and mild, so he put the top down and headed back to campus. At a quarter past two, Bernard arrived in front of the Old Well and saw Damien standing by the curb, dressed in knickers and a Carolina sweatshirt with the letters NC on the front.

Upon seeing the convertible with the top down, Damien was delightedly surprised. He exclaimed, "Wow! This is a Star Six Roadster, isn't it?"

"Yes, it is. Get in."

Damien went around to the passenger side and got in. "This model is nifty. It is so sporty."

"D–Dad intended it for me, I think. Last year. G–guess he thought it would improve my image or s–something like that."

"Well, you look spiffy driving it." Bernard looked down at his suit and smiled. Damien added, "So, I take it you don't drive it much."

"Schoolwork. I d–don't have a need for a car. I can walk to my d–dad's in fifteen minutes. He was d–disappointed, I think, that I wasn't excited about it. Then I felt bad for d–disappointing him."

As they approached the edge of town, the landscape suddenly changed from homes to farm pastures. Damien spoke up. "Can I drive it? I've been trained, and have a driver's license."

Bernard pulled over and got out and went to the passenger side as Damien crawled over to the driver's side. Bernard said, "Good, I don't like to drive."

Damien pulled away quickly in a cloud of dust. When they were a quarter mile down the road, Bernard added, "They don't require driver's licenses in North Carolina yet. Living in the city, why do you have one for New York?"

"They've required them for several years there. My mother wanted me to have it in case I ever needed to take her somewhere. I kidded her about needing a getaway driver, but really, I think she wanted me to someday take her to Savannah to visit what's left of her family. But that never happened."

Soon they approached a field with several small buildings and a light tan, soiled and worn biplane. "I believe this is it," Damien said as he turned into the dusty road leading to the buildings. Slowing down, he pulled up to a building with dirty windows. The front door was ajar. Outside was a sign painted in crude letters that read THRILL RIDES, with smaller letters below that read CAPTAIN COLL MCKENZIE.

They both got out of the car and looked around. Damien said loudly, "Hello. Hello. Anyone here?" All was quiet, and he gingerly approached the door, pushing it open further. They both slowly went in and took a moment to let their eyes adjust. They were sure this had to be the place since it had several flight hats and goggles hanging from hooks, a large oil can on a table, several wrenches, and a large gasoline can. Then toward the rear, they noticed a sleeping man lying on his back on top of a desk, a partially wrapped, half-eaten sandwich sitting inches from his open hand and an empty pint of whiskey lying on its side near his head.

Bernard leaned toward Damien's ear and whispered, "Not g–good. Let's g–go."

Noticing a framed photograph behind the desk, Damien waved him aside and moved nearer to get a better look. He examined it closely. It was a man, apparently Captain McKenzie in military uniform, standing in front of a biplane. He then turned around to get Bernard to look at it and inadvertently stepped on a metal plate from a mess kit, which hit a leg of the desk with a loud clang. The sleeping man awoke with a start, looked up from the desk and eyed Damien suspiciously. Partially raising himself up, he looked around the room. Spotting Bernard, he got off the desk while stretching his arms and asked, in a heavy Scottish brogue, "Oyee, my good gentlemen, whit can I do fer ye lads?"

Bernard was about to speak up when Damien quickly responded, "Are you Captain McKenzie?"

McKenzie extended his hand and said, "Aye, that I ahm, my good fellow."

Damien shook his hand. "I'm Damien Holdrich." He pointed to Bernard. "And this is Bernard Pembroke."

McKenzie nodded to Bernard and said, "Hello to you both. So, you want to go up in the air, is it?"

"Yeah! Yes, if we can afford to, that is."

"It's three clams for thirty minutes."

Damien nodded and answered, "That's good!" Before Damien could say anything more, Captain McKenzie grabbed three sets of goggles, rushed toward the door and went out.

"This way, gentlemen." He led them to the airplane and looked at both of them. "So which of you lads wants to go furst?"

Damien spoke up. "We'd both like to go . . . at the same time."

"Oh no, no," Captain McKenzie replied. He pointed to the plane. "You see, there's only two cuckpits. I'll be flying in that a one an' you be flying in the other."

Damien looked at Bernard, who just shrugged and smiled, relieved that this would not work out. Then Damien asked, "Oh, what about if I rode on the wing?"

"What!" Bernard shouted.

For a while, Captain McKenzie didn't say anything but simply stood there with his mouth open. Finally, he spoke slowly. "Well, lad, people do this all the time for carnivals and sooch, bot they are professionals who git paiyed. You could slip and kill yerself."

"How hard could it be? I'm not going to do headstands and such."

Bernard was waving his hands back and forth, trying to get Damien to shut up.

Captain McKenzie said quickly, "It would still be six books for the two of ya."

Damien quickly reached into his wallet, handed him six dollars and said, "Then let's go! Can you take us over the campus?"

"Ah, that I ken."

Damien asked the captain what kind of engine the plane had, and the captain replied, "It's a V8 Curtiss OX-5." Then Damien asked if it had a lot of power, and the captain assured him that it did.

MacKenzie showed them how to climb on board, placing the right foot into an opening on the bottom of the fuselage and grabbing a strut with the left hand to lift oneself into the rear cockpit. For getting into the front cockpit, he showed them a metal strip that ran along the fuselage. "You cannae walk on the fabric, or your fut will go through. You moost walk on this tread." After demonstrating this, he added, "One of ya have to get ina cockpit to the rear to help me git it started. Then when I tell ya, you'll have to move to the other."

Bernard, following Damien's orders, got into the front cockpit and buckled himself in. Then Damien immediately got into the rear cockpit and looked around as the captain explained which switch Damien was to flip when instructed and how to control the throttle. "Here is the throttle. You cannae let the throttle roon too fast, lest yer gaun be flyin the plane yerself." Damien nodded, hoping he understood. Then the captain said, "Are ya lads ready for a thrrr–ill ride?"

Bernard shrugged and raised his arms in resignation as Damien said loudly, "Yeah! Okay, let's go!"

The captain went around to the front of the plane and turned the propeller several times. Then he shouted to Damien, "Turn it own!" Damien flipped the switch. The captain grabbed one end of the propeller, and with his right leg extended up, he swung his leg down while thrusting the propeller down. The propeller turned, but the engine did not start. He repeated the raised leg motion while swinging the prop down. This time, it started, sputtering at first, in a loud, irregular rhythm, and then it smoothed out. The captain quickly ran around and climbed up next to Damien. He yelled to him over the engine noise. "If you stand right there and hold on to this strut, you shudden fall off. Dinnae wok on the wing!"

Damien climbed over to where the captain was pointing, right next to Bernard; the captain nodded and climbed into the rear cockpit. Damien pointed to Bernard's goggles on top of his head and told him to put them on. Damien put his goggles on and waved to the captain while shouting, "Were you in the Air Service a long time?" Bernard turned around to look at the captain and noticed he was taking a swig out of a pint of whiskey.

The captain answered while putting the bottle back in his jacket, "Oooh no! The dirty bastarts booted me the furst yer!" With that, the captain raced the engine and the plane began moving forward.

As the plane proceeded, Bernard looked at Damien and shouted over the roar of the engine, "What the hell are we doing?"

Damien shouted back, "Too late now!"

As the plane began to gain speed, it lumbered across the field, which was spotted with irregular growths of grasses. The plane pitched and rolled as it went over these mounds. To hold on better, Damien repositioned his grip on the strut. As the speed increased, the irregular motion turned into more of a heavy vibration. As the plane went even faster, the motion gradually changed to quick vibrations, and it smoothed out entirely as the wheels of the plane lifted off the ground. Damien, exhilarated by the speed and sudden uplift, grinned from ear to ear, looked at Bernard and let out a loud, "Whooee!" Bernard, although nervous, grinned back with excitement.

After they had climbed over the trees, the plane began to sputter a little louder, which made Bernard nervous. They both looked over at the captain, who shouted to them, "Ah, not to worry!"

Damien shrugged to Bernard and laughed. The plane began a banking turn, and Damien shouted to Bernard, "He's taking us to the campus!"

It was a clear afternoon, and the plane flew smoothly even though the engine popped and occasionally backfired in an irregular fashion. They crossed several fields where crops had been harvested and which now lay barren and dry. Bernard and Damien looked back and saw the shed and the car that they had just left and watched as both grew smaller as they quickly moved away. Soon they were crossing over a forested area that was resplendent with red, yellow, and orange leaves, as well as some green. This was followed by more empty fields and more trees; then they spotted buildings on the outskirts of Chapel Hill. Damien looked at the captain, who now was taking another swig. Damien frowned, and Bernard quickly turned to see the captain with the bottle in hand. They were now over the town and could see several cars going down Franklin Street. Damien got the Captain's attention and pointed in the direction of the campus, shouting, "Go down low, down low!"

The captain nodded; while turning, he let the plane descend to a point safely above the large trees. From there, Damien and Bernard could almost make out the faces of other students walking on the campus. Some looked up. Damien waved wildly and shouted at some of them, "Woohoo! Woohoo!"

Bernard picked up the action and began to wave and yell along with Damien. They had crossed over Davey Poplar, the oldest tree on campus, and were just going over South Building to the Courtyard where many students were walking, having likely finished their last class of the day. Damien shouted, "Go lower, go lower!" Seeing the wide-open space, the captain dove the plane down to a few hundred feet and then throttled up to full engine speed to climb out of the dive.

All the while, Damien was shouting, "Woo, woo, woo!" while waving wildly. Bernard, a bit nervous about the dive, just waved. People below stopped and looked and pointed at them. Then Damien looked at the captain and made a circling motion, instructing him to do it again. The captain banked in a wide arc, proceeded again over South Building, and took another dive, this time even lower. More people had gathered down below and were waving back as both Damien and Bernard shouted, "Car-o-li-na, Car-o-li-na!"

As the dive continued even lower, both Damien and Bernard started to think they might not make it. But with full throttle, the Captain began to climb again, causing Damien to grab the strut tightly with both hands. This time the engine struggled and began to run with a loud cyclical roar. The plane barely made it over the top of a building under construction as the captain began to turn.

The cyclical, irregular noise from the engine grew louder, and the captain shouted, "Lost a cylinder!" The plane continued flying at a relatively low altitude as the repetitive oscillating roar continued.

Bernard looked frightened and shouted to Damien, "Oh my God!"

Damien replied, "Don't worry! We have seven more!"

The captain completed the turn and headed back to the field.

Twenty minutes later, they were in the car, waving goodbye to the captain, who repeatedly insisted they return and bring friends. After riding down the road awhile with slight grins on their faces, Bernard turned to Damien. Wide-eyed, he shouted as loud as he could, "This is crazy! You are crazy! What the hell did you just get us into?"

Damien just looked straight ahead and then burst into laughter. Then Bernard erupted in laughter too, saying, "It will no doubt be one of the greatest memories of my life!"

After traveling a few more miles without saying anything, Bernard got serious and said, "My G–God, we'll be in b–big trouble if they find out it was us."

Damien thought for a few moments; then he said, "You're right! I'm going to stop the car and turn my sweatshirt inside out. Nobody will recognize us because of the goggles, but if they see me driving up with this sweatshirt, they may make a connection."

On Monday morning, the Tar Heel ran a front-page story with the headline A LOT OF PLUCK! The article reported that the university president had been very upset by what had appeared to be a Carolina student buzzing the campus while standing on the wing of a biplane. He was quoted as saying, "Whoever it was had a lot of pluck and, if discovered, will be expelled because of the reckless danger he posed to the campus and students."

Bernard and Damien didn't tell anyone it was they. For many weeks afterward, there was much campus talk speculating about who had been on the plane. The administration never did find out, but suddenly the rowing club began treating Damien with even more respect and calling him Pluck.

Chapter 22

Winding Down

For weeks afterward, Taylor thought of the appearance of Bernard Pembroke at the seance, even while he was home visiting his mom and dad over Thanksgiving break. On numerous occasions, he discussed it with Marcia or Alex, and now Deedee was part of the mix too.

One afternoon, Taylor ran into Deedee at Castlewood, and they discussed Bernard Pembroke's presence there.

"When I started working here," Deedee began, "it was ten years before Bernard Pembroke's death. He had begun the process of turning over Castlewood to the university, but he had stipulated that he would remain living here until his death. He was in the process of setting up numerous foundations and trusts for scholarships and grants."

"Like the one I got," Taylor added.

"Exactly, so I was hired to help him out: typing the letters, doing some research, and just about anything that was necessary to get everything going. He was really good to work for, and I must confess I found him terribly attractive. I had been married once but lost my husband during the war, and in a way, I thought I might remarry someday. But I soon learned of Bernard's sexual orientation and knew there wouldn't be anything to our relationship other than strictly business. That was fine because I really liked to work for him, and I greatly respected him and the things he was trying to accomplish."

Deedee went on to explain that his wealth had come from Pembroke Construction, which his grandfather had started. The company had built numerous buildings on campus and around the state, particularly those that had connections to state funding. "It was really his father who had taken the company to its highest level and had built Castlewood in 1896. When his father died, Bernard was still a young man and didn't know what to do. He had little to no experience with running a construction company, and he told me he had even less of a desire to. He had just graduated from college, it was the height of the Depression, and state contracts were just not coming through."

"I can understand that," Taylor said, "especially during the Depression."

"Fortunately, his father's assistant, Charles Bowman, was quite knowledgeable about the business, and he made Charles an offer of twenty-five percent of the business if he would manage it. Evidently, they became a good team, with Bernard going out and generating business and Charles managing the day-to-day operations, and they were able to survive."

"Evidently," Taylor interjected, "he must have done quite well. He was able to travel a lot. He's got things here from all over the world."

"That is true," Deedee answered. "Bernard was a good pilot and had his own plane. He loved to fly. When not working, he was always elsewhere. He was always searching for something or exploring something. And he spent much time and money in trying to change the world. He got very involved with minority groups to help their cause, particularly speaking out on equal rights for gays and lesbians.

"He still had no interest in the business, and over time, Charles and his people were totally taking care of it. Then, by the time Charles was in his seventies and wanted to retire—I think it was in the late fifties—Bernard took the company public with new management out of Raleigh. He received cash and stock, which is still doing quite well to this day and helps contribute to the portfolio."

"So, is that when Mr. Pembroke turns this place over to the university?"

"Yes, you are correct. Bernard wanted this place to remain exactly the way it is, so he instituted the foundation for the preservation of this place. He gave it to the university with the stipulation that it would be used to help administer the various grants and scholarships."

"And," Taylor said, "that's when you come on board, and Mr. Pembroke dies ten years later, correct?"

"Yes, I was very disturbed when Bernard died. But when I looked back, I felt he knew that his life was coming to an end, and that's why he so carefully set up everything so that it would be transferred to the university and carefully monitored. And interestingly, I felt he didn't seem to mind knowing that his life would end soon. It was like he expected it and was . . . I don't know, okay with it. But now comes the strange part."

"What's that?" Taylor asked.

Deedee explained that strange things began happening at Castlewood shortly after Bernard Pembroke died. Chairs would be moved and books would be found on tables instead of on shelves when she opened up in the morning. Some people claimed they saw shadows dart across the room, and others often felt areas of profound cold. Deedee said that, at that time, she had suspected it was the ghost of Bernard Pembroke and wanted to communicate with him. She had felt that he was a disturbed spirit that had not yet settled some aspects of his life and she had felt sorry for him. Deedee said that she had tried to communicate with the ghost many times and had stayed at the castle late into the night talking to him, but he had never made his presence known. She eventually took that as a sign he wanted to be alone. Then those sightings had become less frequent, and she hadn't seen or heard anything for years, until now.

"Now, I know that his spirit is restless still and has unresolved issues and can't leave this earth. I want to help so that his soul will be at rest and find peace in his afterlife."

She showed Taylor that many of the Pembroke archives, both on Pembroke and his father, had been organized and filed and were in cabinets in the large library. But a vast amount of additional information that had not been gone through was stored in boxes. She said she would be willing to spend time researching whatever they needed, if it would help find some answers.

These discussions with Deedee and Alex and Marcia significantly reduced the anxiety Taylor had been feeling about the night that they had summoned the spirit of Pembroke.

Marcia and Alex said that by talking about it, they were becoming more accepting of the experience, too. But it also seemed to increase their desire to find out how they could help Pembroke.

However, there was also school. Fall was now giving way to cooler weather, and mornings and evenings had a nip in the air. Most of the student body was preparing for semester finals and getting ready to take their Christmas break.

It was Friday afternoon, and Taylor had just finished his last class. On his way to the gym, he passed through the large, open area on campus called the Courtyard. The Courtyard was about the size of a football field and covered with bricks, with islands of vegetation and trees. Distributed throughout the area were several eight-sided platforms surrounded by benches. These dated back to the early years of the university when one of the presidents of the university had encouraged public speaking to facilitate the exchange of ideas and had these platforms built. Since then, the Courtyard had been a venue for the dispensing of news during the two world wars, including deaths and victories; protests, especially in the 1960s; meeting spots for various organizations; and informal acts by drama groups. It was always considered an open forum that anyone was permitted to use. It was not unusual for someone from a church to be standing on a platform preaching his or her religion. The only time that free speech had been suppressed in the Courtyard was in 1963, during the height of the Cold War. The North Carolina legislature had rushed through a law forbidding Communists and other "subversives" from speaking on any of the University of North Carolina campuses. The law was later declared invalid because of its vagueness.

As Taylor passed through, his thoughts were mostly focused on the brown and yellow rustling leaves that were being blown in gusts, as if leading him forward. He noticed a group of about seven students looking up at someone standing on a platform and speaking. As he hurried by, he heard some of the words from the speaker: ". . . deviant, degenerate, and debauched America, having accepted the lie that it's okay to be homosexual, has consequently changed God's truth into a lie . . ."

Taylor immediately stopped and moved to hear better, catching the rest of the sentence: ". . . 'and worshipped and served the creature more than the Creator, who is blessed for ever. Amen.' Romans, one, twenty-five."

The person speaking was a thin, blonde young man in a light jacket and jeans. He had a deeply Southern drawl with extreme variations in pitch and volume. As he spoke, he gestured and looked directly at his audience with piercing, unblinking blue eyes. "'For this cause God gave them up unto vile affections: for even their women did change the natural use into that which is against nature: And likewise also the men, leaving the natural use of the woman, burned in their lust one toward another; men with men working that which is unseemly.' Romans, one, twenty-six through twenty-seven. 'Ye adulterers and adulteresses, know ye not that the friendship of the world is enmity with God? whosoever therefore will be a friend of the world is the enemy of God.' James, four, four. Abstain, you fools."

Taylor was tired from a long week of studying and papers. He was sure that what he was hearing was nonsense. Yet as he listened, he also felt that the slow, up-and-down vocalization was somewhat hypnotic and that he was being drawn into some kind of mesmeric state. Any moment now, he would have to force himself to break away.

But suddenly, someone to his right broke through his daze. "Hey, how have you been doing?" Taylor turned to face a male student holding a sign. "I saw you at the Force Against Inequality meeting."

Then Taylor recognized him. "Right, you're the chapter president. How are you?"

"Great," he replied, extending his hand. "Brad Turner."

"Taylor Hanes," Taylor said while shaking his hand. Then he looked up at the sign and read it aloud. "'Keep Your Religion Off My Civil Rights.' That's a good one. You know, I'm new to a lot of this. I didn't know there was this much hate, especially toward gay people."

"This church is the worst. It's been going on for years. And this guy is actually getting followers."

They listened for a few minutes. "'But the men of Sodom were wicked and sinners before the Lord exceedingly.' Genesis, thirteen, thirteen. 'Then the Lord rained upon Sodom and upon Gomorrah brimstone and fire from the Lord out of heaven; And he overthrew those cities, and all the plain, and all the inhabitants of the cities, and that which grew upon the ground.' Genesis, nineteen, twenty-four through twenty-five."

Then the speaker paused for a moment. While bending slightly at the knees and gesturing to the crowd in a slow-moving arch with an upward open hand, he said, "'Ye serpents, ye generation of vipers, how can ye escape the damnation of hell?' Matthew, twenty-three, thirty-three. 'As a dog returneth to his vomit, so a fool returneth to his folly.' Proverbs, twenty-six, eleven."

Staring intently at one pair of eyes and then at another, he continued. "'For without are dogs, and sorcerers, and whoremongers, and murderers, and idolaters, and whosoever loveth and maketh a lie.' Revelation, twenty-two, fifteen. 'But the fearful, and unbelieving, and the abominable, and murderers, and whoremongers, and sorcerers, and idolaters, and all liars, shall have their part in the lake which burneth with fire and brimstone: which is the second death.' Revelation, twenty-one, eight."

At this point, they both noticed that most of the people were walking away. Brad spoke up. "Let's go. Nothing worse than no one listening." As they moved away from the speaker, leaving him with only two listeners, Brad said, "Hey, you want to get some coffee or something?"

Taylor wanted to know a little more about the Force Against Inequality but wondered if this invitation was a come-on or something. Taylor had gotten to know some gay people, like Alex, and a few people from his hometown, like Jessie. And he felt comfortable with them. But at the same time, he didn't want to get into an uncomfortable situation. This guy was attractive, not at all effeminate. And he seemed to have a good personality, making eye contact when he spoke and seeming to want to get to know you. *Maybe that's what is making me cautious*, Taylor thought. But brushing all that aside, he made a quick decision and accepted.

"Sure. Where at?"

"I need to drop this sign off in my room. It's in the quad. Then there's a snack bar across from the quad. Were you going in that direction?"

"Yeah. Okay, that's not far. Just a short diversion."

As they walked toward the quad, Brad began to ask Taylor questions. "So, are you a freshman?"

"Yeah, I'm a freshman." There was a pause; then Taylor asked while chuckling, "Does it show that much?"

Brad laughed, "Oh, no. It's just that you said you're new to a lot of this. You know, the hatred of gay people. Did you come from a small town?"

From this, Taylor realized that Brad thought he was gay, no doubt because of his attending the Lt. Col. Johnson lecture and his recent comment about hatred toward gays. But he was living this lie, so he needed to go along with it.

"Yeah! Tartan. About ten thousand people. What about you?"

"I'm from Annville, Pennsylvania, another small town. Not far from Hershey."

"Oh, yeah."

"I know where you're coming from," Brad continued. "Narrow minds. Don't want to admit there are gay people and prefer that they remain in the dark or the closet. It's probably worse where you come from, here in the Bible Belt."

Taylor had heard the term "Bible Belt" but had never paid any attention to it. Now he suddenly knew what it meant.

"So, do your parents know?" Brad asked.

Taylor didn't respond readily. After struggling, he finally said, "My Dad and I, uh . . . talked about it. Mom's out of it. She's been sick."

"Oh, okay."

They were at Brad's dorm. "I'll be right back. You can come up if you want."

"I'll just wait here."

Taylor looked around wondering if Brad's dorm, too, was considered a gay dorm like Emerson Hall. There wasn't anyone in the quad. Apparently, people were off doing things on Friday afternoon. Then Taylor remembered he had been heading to the gym and looking forward to a good end-of-the-week workout. Well, tomorrow morning would do even though he wanted to study for finals then. And besides, Brad seemed like a nice guy even though he was gay.

Brad returned and spoke. "Okay, let's cross here. It's on the other side of the quad."

They crossed over the grassy area to the dorm on the other side and entered a small snack bar. After ordering coffees, Brad suggested they go outside. There they sat on the tops of some picnic tables.

Brad spoke. "So, anyway, it's a lot easier in college. You know, to be yourself. You're not dealing directly with your parents and your church and the small minds of a small town."

"Yeah, it's definitely a lot more open. And, I don't know, accepting of how other people live."

"You've met many gay people?"

"Well, no. Just one. Well, there were a couple back at my hometown. They were good guys. I liked them. And now you."

"Oh, no, well, I'm not gay. Most people think I am."

Taylor smiled, thinking he was kidding. Then he looked him in the eye.

Brad shook his head no. "You see, when—"

"Oh, I'm sorry," Taylor interrupted. "I just assumed . . ."

"First," Brad continued, "no need to apologize. There is going to be this natural assumption. Force Against Inequality was—well, actually is—an organization that tries to defend any group of people who are being discriminated against. It just so happens that our chapter has a lot of gay and lesbian members, and naturally we get involved in issues dealing with them. We do other things, too. I can identify with their concerns, however. You see, when I was growing up, I had this older cousin who I looked up to. He was a great guy. And his parents and teachers and everyone he knew were mean to him. I didn't understand it at the time, but he was gay, and everyone made his life miserable. His parents eventually threw him out of the house. He went somewhere, lived on the streets, and eventually died of AIDS."

"Oh, I'm sorry."

"It was all these people who destroyed his life because of their prejudices. So, I guess there was a part of me that wanted to fight that backwardness and . . . ignorance like that guy in the Courtyard. Anyway, most on the council are gay, except I think one of the women from town isn't. We don't ask, and we don't care."

There was a moment of silence as they sipped their coffee. Then Taylor began to chuckle. He suddenly realized that he had experienced homophobia, yet Brad wasn't coming on to him nor was he even gay.

"What's that about?" Brad asked. "What are you laughing about?"

"Oh, nothing. Hey, do you get hit on a lot by some of the gay guys?"

"Um! Occasionally. It doesn't bother me. Most of the people involved in these organizations are, you know, gentlemen and ladies. They're devoted to why they are club members and take it seriously. By the way, have you joined?"

"I've sent the paperwork in."

"Okay, great! Someone will deliver a packet to you, or maybe you'll get it in the mail. It'll get you up to speed on some of the issues and outline our program for the year."

Then Taylor asked Brad specific questions about the structure of the Force Against Inequality and mentioned that he had attended the last meeting in November but hadn't seen him there. Brad replied he had been out of town dealing with a family problem so he couldn't attend, but he read the minutes later.

Taylor mentioned he was taking a Sociology course that required a paper, and he was writing one dealing with discrimination against gays and lesbians. He was wondering if FAI would be a good resource for information. Brad said that it was indeed a good resource with lots of literature. He added that he would also be happy to read Taylor's paper and give him insight on possible directions the paper should go and even solicit inputs from other people if Taylor wanted. Taylor was impressed with his desire to help. They talked for several more minutes, and Brad answered all of Taylor's questions.

Then Brad looked at his watch. "Speaking of FAI, I need to run by our office at the student union to pick up some packets."

Replacing the lid on his cup, Taylor said, "I'll walk with you. My dorm's in that direction."

They had to backtrack somewhat, and when they reached the Courtyard, they noticed the preacher still on the platform, talking to a few students. They were about to head in two different directions, so they paused to continue their conversation.

Taylor asked, "So, what's the story on that guy?"

"He's there about every other week. His church dates from way back in this county. I think it was a branch of the Baptist Church, but I don't think even they want to have anything to do with it. It's really a small church, mainly just a bunch of the family members, but in the last couple of years, it has had some traction with new members. They take a real literal interpretation of the Bible and use religion to promote hatemongering. And it's not just gays they condemn. They attack Jews, Muslims, Catholics, just about everything outside of their realm of warped Christianity. They often do offensive protest. And we do counter-protest. If you stick with us, we'll get you involved. It can really be quite a lot of fun. Well, I better head on."

"Okay," Taylor replied. "Looking forward to it." Brad walked toward the Student Union, and Taylor began to walk toward his dorm. Then he paused, turned around, and looked at the preacher again. He was still talking, with only two students listening to him.

Taylor noticed that the sun had sunk toward the horizon, now with only a few specks of light showing between the trees, and he felt chilly and zipped up his jacket. The days were getting shorter and leaves were falling. Papers were due and finals were looming. The semester was winding down.

Chapter 23

Helping Out

Wow, Brad is such an uplifting guy. It's like he rushes by, and you are immediately sucked into his enthusiasm. He is so smart, and what is amazing is that he seems to really want to make meaningful change in this world. He is willing to spend so much time as the president of FAI to help promote important issues, even if it does not directly benefit himself. I admire that and realize that I am so self-centered and really, for the most part, only think about myself. But he is willing to step out of his own shoes and walk in someone else's to see how they live and to experience their injustices. All in all, I guess he figures that, in the long run, it will make a better world, and, therefore, he and everyone else will benefit. This sounds idealistic, but in some way, it's got to help.

And then there's those people, like that preacher interpreting the Bible the way he does. He does nothing but put people down and spew hatred in the name of God, which ends up hurting people like Brad's cousin who was rejected by his family. Even Bernard Pembroke's spirit must still be dealing with the anger and the injustice that he must have experienced in his lifetime. I guess I understand now why it was so important for him to bequeath these scholarships. I shouldn't have lied to get it, but then, as far as I know, nobody else had applied, and there is no gay student out there who missed out because of me, so why shouldn't I have it and contribute what I can. What Brad is doing is important. With whatever extra time I have, I should commit some of it to learning more and helping out.

Chapter 24

It Was Important

Taylor had taken only one elective in the first semester of his freshman year. He had chosen an introductory course in Sociology, which included a study of social structures and institutions, cultures, social change, individuals and populations, social psychology, differences and equality, and social interaction. If he were asked why he had chosen this, he would just say that he had a desire to learn more about what drives societies to be the way they are and how to study them and influence them. In addition, his mother had minored in Sociology, which had initially piqued his interest in the subject. Overall, he found the course to be extremely interesting and had no trouble following the material that was being taught.

His professor was Dr. Elizabeth Carrol, a large, intellectual-looking, middle-aged woman, who while speaking, always had a smile. She had done postdoctoral work studying the people in the village of Navala, a traditional native village in Viti Levu, the largest island in the then Dominion of Fiji (now the Republic of Fiji). Her classes were known to be stimulating though not demanding and motivated her students to learn more by studying on their own.

Early in the semester, Taylor had learned that one-fourth of his grade in the course would be a term paper, approximately five thousand words or about twelve to fifteen pages, due two weeks before the end of the semester. The assignment was to document, in as much detail as possible, social interaction between two separate groups or peoples in a society. The professor recommended staying as local as possible since direct personal observation was considered an accurate means of gathering data to support one's argument.

In addition to writing the paper, the professor wanted each student to give a ten-minute presentation on his or her paper, followed by an open discussion of the topic for up to ten minutes during the last two weeks of the semester.

A good part of the course dealt with social interaction, and some of it related to discrimination against certain segments of society. When Taylor learned this, it immediately occurred to him that if he wrote about gays and lesbians in America, he could use it to fulfill the November requirements for his scholarship. For this reason, he immediately began to do research for the paper.

Taylor had already learned a great deal about discrimination against gays in the armed forces from the lecture given by Lt. Col. Ralph Johnson. Taylor decided he would do more research in this area and include it in his paper. "Don't Ask, Don't Tell" had become the official policy for gays in the military only a few years before. It was still in the news, so having something current in the paper seemed like an asset.

Over dinner with Marcia in Lenoir Hall one evening, Taylor discussed the progress of the paper.

"It's going very well. I've done a lot of research in the library, and I talked to some people at FAI, and they gave me tons of stuff, so I have no shortage of information to include in it."

"You should do a paper about witchcraft and how witches have been discriminated against for ages."

Taylor looked at her, his face expressionless. Then he smiled. "Okay, perhaps in an advanced course in Sociology, if I take one. But I kind of think that I'm going to have a tough enough time with handling this gay issue paper."

"Aww, come on, nobody does anything for us witches."

"And besides, you couldn't find any recent legal discrimination or legal cases involving witchcraft like you can with the gay issue."

"It's illegal to practice witchcraft in several countries. South Africa, for one."

Taylor chuckled. "I'll keep that in mind. But there's a lot more material about discrimination against gays. Did you know that there is only a small percentage of countries in the world where consensual sex acts between a guy and a guy are legal? You could be thrown in jail and have it on your record for life. Even in the United States, there are about fifteen states where it is still illegal. North Carolina is one of them. And penalties include imprisonment for two to ten years and fines in the thousands of dollars."

"Wow! I did not know that. Kind of ironic that you got a scholarship from a state institution for supporting gay issues and being gay is against the law."

Taylor looked around to see if anyone was listening and lowered his voice to a whisper. "I know. I really became scared when I read that. I even called up the lawyer that administered the scholarship and talked with him about it. They have a document where I actually signed a paper that stated I was a homosexual."

They both sat silently, looking at each other and thinking about all this; then Marcia smiled and said, "And in prison, you could become some gangster's bitch!" They both broke out in loud laughter.

"Fortunately," Taylor said, "the lawyer reassured me that no one would have access to this information unless they were subpoenaed, and he couldn't imagine any reason for this to happen. Plus, more and more people are becoming accepting of gays and lesbians, and no one enforces these laws on the books. There are a bunch of laws still on the books that nobody even knows about. I bet there are laws concerning witchcraft too."

"I don't doubt it. Someone should really comb through these laws and eliminate ones that are outdated."

"There's a research paper for you!"

❊ ❊ ❊

The day after Thanksgiving break, Dr. Carrol made everyone draw a slip of paper at random from a bowl. The slips of paper indicated when each student would be required to give his or her ten-minute presentation. During the last two weeks of class, three people would be giving a talk at each session. Since the class met three times a week, this would exactly cover all eighteen students in the class.

Taylor looked at his piece of paper and was somewhat relieved that he would be first on the next to the last day of class for the semester. Carolina was a liberal university, and most students had a live-and-let-live attitude. Still, Taylor felt that there would be some pushback on his topic and he didn't want to interact with those people for very long. One more class after his talk, and the semester would be over, and the chance of having classes with those people again or even interacting with them again was pretty remote. Plus, this gave him a few extra days to prepare for the talk.

Taylor's Sociology paper ended up exceeding six thousand words. On the first Monday of the last two weeks of class, everyone had to turn in their papers.

The reports on the papers and the following discussions began immediately after that. The first talk was given by a student who had written about the social interaction of members of his intramural soccer team. It covered competition between players, team building, and team spirit. There was little discussion by the class afterward, and Dr. Carrol called for the next talk. The second was by a student who discussed social interaction among her sorority sisters. It covered interacting with people in the dining room during sorority parties and other gatherings and working on projects. A few other female students in the class raised questions. It was apparent they were only interested in joining a sorority and wanted some inside information. Then there was a report given by a student who had documented his encounters with people while standing in line in the cafeteria, at the movies, buying concert tickets, and even at the grocery store. Much of the class complimented him on his creative approach to the topic, but they added little to the discussion about his insights or conclusions. The class finished up early, and everyone was dismissed.

On Wednesday, three more people gave presentations. The first was by a tall, skinny guy who talked about the interaction of Carolina students at the local Baptist church with the rest of the congregation from the community. He emphasized that, in student groups at the church, there was a lot of discussion by church preachers as well as laymen about the permissive lifestyle of the Carolina student body. And they agreed that the students from the church should lead and set an example for the rest of the student body. Taylor shifted in his seat as he thought about the preacher back home who had seemed to disapprove of Taylor because he believed Taylor was gay. Taylor hoped this guy would not make a big deal of his own topic when it was time to give his discussion. There were no questions or discussion after this talk.

The next presentation was given by a student who had written about his part-time job working with employees at the computer lab and interacting with students and professors who used the lab. The final presentation was given by a student who had documented his interaction with various vendors who ran businesses in Chapel Hill, including a men's clothing store, a post office, the various restaurants, and the store where everyone bought their CDs.

Friday opened with a black student who presented a report on pickup basketball at the gym, in which he had participated on most afternoons. Next was a female student who presented a paper on the interaction between male and female students in her coed dorm. This generated several questions related to privacy issues. This was followed by a student who worked at the student-run radio station and reported on his interaction with the various other volunteers.

On Monday morning of the following week, there was a talk from a hefty guy who had documented the social interaction of the barkeeps with the servers at a local bar called The Watering Hole. For his research, he had chosen a seat at the far end of the bar, where the servers placed and picked up orders. There he was able to hear most of the conversations between the barkeeps and servers as well as some of the conversations among the servers as they waited for their orders. The class seemed to find this interesting, and one student questioned whether he had been drinking while he was collecting his research information. He admitted he had to drink to disguise the fact that he was gathering data on the participants.

His presentation was followed by one from a female art student who had written her paper on the interaction of students in the art lab, emphasizing the language they used with each other regarding subtle critiques of each other's work and perceived preferences of the art professor, based on his personal bias. And then there was a male singer in the local Presbyterian Church's choir who talked about how the choir interacted with the choir master and deacon to decide what music would be sung. Taylor was not sure how this guy would react to his topic either.

On Wednesday, there was more of the same: a fraternity guy documenting his interaction with his fraternity brothers, a girl talking about her interaction with friends at other schools, and then another student talking about the Catholic Student Union she belonged to and her interactions with them.

How did this happen? Taylor wondered. Three people who were connected to their churches had given talks related to their religion, and he would be talking about supporting efforts to grant gays and lesbians more rights. He sensed this could be a problem, but he couldn't do anything about it now. He tried briefly to think of ways he could revise his talk and make it sound strictly like a research project in which he was just a scientific observer rather than an observer with an opinion. But it was really too late. He had other commitments, so he didn't have the time to take his presentation in another direction. Besides, it followed his paper, and he liked the approach he had taken. He would leave it as it is.

On Monday morning, Taylor was first up. Upon getting the go-ahead from Dr. Carrol, Taylor got up from his desk and stood behind the podium. He had several pages of notes in front of him. He looked around the room and saw faces that appeared interested in what he was going to say. Then he began.

"I want to do this by starting out a little differently and not telling you what my topic is right off. But instead, I want to ask you some questions for you to think about. Here goes. What if you were in a long-term committed relationship and you were not able to be at the side of the person you loved when they were hospitalized, or you were not able to make a decision about their final resting place if they died? Or what if you were a war hero, who had defended your country, risking your own life, but because of someone you were seeing, you were relieved of duty without retirement benefits as a result of that? Or what if you were discriminated against by the IRS, and as a result, you were forced to pay thousands of dollars more in taxes than people in a similar situation? And what if there were hundreds of laws on the books that put you in a disadvantaged position over someone else, affecting your personal and financial well-being?

"Well, this is happening in this country as well as other countries. It is because of one group, which is the majority, imposing its beliefs and standards and rules on a minority. This minority group I'm talking about today is gays and lesbians. What this is called, and it's also the title of my paper, is 'Tyranny of the Majority.'"

While he spoke, Taylor kept his eyes moving from one person to another, and everyone seemed to be looking at him with interest. Then his eyes fell on the skinny Baptist student who was frowning back at him. Taylor continued, "So, that's what my paper is about. It is about a large majority socially interacting with a minority, gays and lesbians, and how this majority is exercising tyranny over this minority."

Then Taylor discussed actual cases of gays not being able to see a dying loved one in the hospital, Lt. Col. Johnson's discharge from the Air Force, and the amounts of money gays and lesbians lose each year because their partnership is treated differently from heterosexual marriage.

"Now, I want to take you back in this country to other minorities who were discriminated against and draw a parallel." Taylor asked everyone to forget about gays and lesbians and look at America's past history. Taylor outlined how laws, religion, and tradition had deprived other people of basic rights. He pointed out that from the earliest times in our country's history until recently, blacks had been denied basic rights. Slaves were once considered property and were thought to lack enough intelligence to learn very much. More significantly, educating them was generally discouraged.

Taylor pointed out that in 1740, North Carolina had passed the first law prohibiting slave education. It made it illegal to teach them to write. Its purpose was to suppress their ability to communicate with one another through the spread of abolitionist written and printed material. Slave owners in particular did not want the slaves to question their position in life, so educating slaves was banned. According to sources, Taylor added, slaves would be whipped for trying to learn to read.

He briefly mentioned that even after the Civil War and passage of the Fifteenth Amendment that gave blacks the right to vote, there still remained the Jim Crow laws, with new ones being enacted over the years. "These served to segregate public schools, public places, transportation, restrooms, restaurants, and drinking fountains as well as the U.S. military and prevent black people from participating in the voting process. They were supposed to be based on the concept of 'separate but equal,' but in reality, they led to conditions for blacks that were inferior to those of whites." Taylor's eyes momentarily met those of the black student in the class.

Then Taylor asked the class to consider the status of women in America. "For centuries, women were given little rights because they were thought to be inferior, second-class citizens. They had a great struggle, and eventually Congress passed the Nineteenth Amendment, which gave women the right to vote in 1920. And there have been many more struggles for the rights of women since then." As he said this, his eyes passed from one female student to another.

"Our country has come a long way, but," Taylor emphasized, "even today, there is one minority in the population that is still being discriminated against in the laws, and that is the gay and lesbian population. I will quickly add that the laws have come a long way for gays and lesbians too. For instance, only a few decades ago in certain states, being convicted of homosexuality allowed the state to classify you as a mental defective and gave the government justification to place you in a mental institution. In those institutions, there were recorded cases where people were treated with injections of massive doses of male hormones or administered electroshock or other aversion therapy, and some hospitals even performed prefrontal lobotomies on their patients."

Taylor paused to catch his breath and look around the room. Then he continued. "After World War II, there was a lot of concern about Communists, and Senator Joseph McCarthy was searching out homosexuals who were considered by some as dangerous as actual Communists. In 1950, the Truman administration investigated 382 civil servants for sexual perversion, many of whom were forced to resign."

Next, Taylor turned to discussing religion, stating that discriminatory laws had been put on the books and justified by reference to religious tenets; in particular, the Bible. "The Bible had been used to justify slavery and then Jim Crow laws and keeping women in secondary positions. It is still being used as a justification to deny gays certain rights and to keep discriminatory laws affecting gays on the books. The Bible says that God created Adam and Eve and that homosexuality is wrong and that this is the written word of God; therefore it is true. But," Taylor asked, "didn't Man write the Bible with his own interpretation? And what if you don't believe in the Bible? Does that mean you have lost certain rights?"

As Taylor paused again and looked around the room, he noticed that several people were expressionless, though blinking, but the Baptist student looked incensed. Taylor continued. "Wasn't the Constitution written for this country to guarantee freedom of religion and, by extension, freedom from religion? Didn't the Founding Fathers make a great effort to form a wall between church and state? Yes! Yet, because of religious prejudice, the laws were designed to conform to religious beliefs, to the detriment of blacks and women and, still to this day, gays and lesbians. The rights of the minority have always been in conflict with the views of the majority. However, our Constitution was created to protect the individual. For the government to discriminate against any person or group of people is wrong, yet that is what is still happening."

Then he talked about tradition. "By tradition—and we are discounting religion—men pair up with women. Yet we know homosexuals have existed since the beginning of time. Some societies embraced the concept of homosexuality. Our country does not. Take same-sex marriage. People look back on history and say that men always married women. We all have been indoctrinated to think only one way about marriage. It's tradition. But the truth is, the Constitution guarantees equal protection and equal access to civil benefits, as it should. So by that guiding document which we all follow, gays and lesbians should be given the right to marry." As he spoke this, Taylor saw several people flinch.

Taylor looked at his wristwatch and said, "I see that I've run out of time, so I want to end it with this. The laws, religions, and traditions of our society—and, I want to add, bias and ignorance—all form barriers that have harmed minorities in the past. Today, those barriers harm gays and lesbians, another segment of society, and this is simply wrong. One's personal beliefs and emotions should never dictate the laws of society."

As Taylor finished his last sentence, everyone seemed to be frozen absorbing his last words. After a moment, there was a loud shuffling of feet and the sound of people repositioning themselves in their seats.

Taylor gathered up his notes and moved toward his seat as Dr. Carrol rose to speak. "Thank you, Mr. Hanes." She moved toward the front of the class, but before she could say anything further, the tall, skinny Baptist student's hand shot up. "Yes, Mr. Kimbel?"

"I don't know what to say. I don't know where to begin. The idea of allowing two people, two people of the same sex, who—who participate in unnatural acts and who commit crimes against God, to give them legal recognition is just abominable. It defies any human sense of appropriateness. And then there's the disease aspect of all of it, AIDS and so forth."

The student who had documented the interaction of people in line raised his hand, and Dr. Carrol recognized him. "I say, live and let live. I've known several gay people, and though they didn't have someone permanent in their life, they knew friends who had been together some thirty-five years. If they aren't married, then who is? You have to ask, is this fair or what, that they are being treated differently, unfairly?"

The female art student raised her hand, and the professor acknowledged her. "Look, there are gay and lesbian people everywhere. I know several in my art classes, and I think one art professor is gay. You know, they live their lives like everybody else, pay taxes and what have you. I guess I never thought about all these things, about how they have been discriminated against, and how they could be fired for just being who they are. Now come on!"

"But it's against God's plan!" the skinny Baptist student shouted. "It's not natural."

The professor broke in, "Hold on. Back in the early seventies, the American Psychiatric Association removed homosexuality from its list of disorders and further emphasized that any negative psychological effects were caused by prejudice and discrimination. Let's try to keep our prejudices out of it. The paper and the talk here is about one social group which is in the majority, which would be heterosexuals, having tyranny over a minority, which would be gays and lesbians."

"That's right!" the Catholic girl shouted. Dr. Carrol pointed to her, acknowledging her right to speak. "My religion doesn't approve of homosexuality. I don't necessarily agree with that, but above everything else, after all, this is a country where you are supposed to be free and equal, protected by the Constitution, so in that case, you should have the freedom to be with anyone you choose and with equal rights."

Dr. Carrol quickly asked, "Does that include marriage?"

"Well, no," the girl responded. "Well, maybe civil unions or something equal."

The black student raised his hand, and Dr. Carrol acknowledged him. "I just want to say something. In the past, when people were talking about gay rights and equating it to civil rights and saying they were discriminated against, I just didn't see it, and most black people don't see it. In fact, they were offended that the gay people were trying to ride on the coattails of the black civil rights movement. Plus, most of them regarded it as a perversion because it was against their religious beliefs." Then he looked at Taylor and gestured toward him. "But you know, you presented a very valid argument, and it points out that discrimination is discrimination, no matter where it comes from, whether from the laws, religion, or just bias. So it's made me rethink this."

There was a pause in the discussion; then Dr. Carrol spoke up. "I wanted to add something to this topic. As I've mentioned before, I've studied and done extensive research on the native Fiji society. Historically, anthropologists have denied that homosexuality even existed on the islands. But during our research, further study revealed that, in fact, in many parts of the Pacific, homosexual activity had been authorized through ritual or a societal practice called *gender liminality*. It's really too much to examine here, but . . . but in essence it was culturally acceptable to have what they called a third sex. This third sex was usually a male who was very family oriented. They would traditionally follow the training of women's work and were never discouraged from doing otherwise and were perfectly accepted. They would usually have sex with other males, who were not of this third sex, and sometimes with females. And on other islands, homosexuality was even celebrated. But with the introduction of Christianity, and subsequent changes in their laws, most of that is looked on with hostility today."

The Baptist student shouted, "That's because this was a backward, primitive society that, at the time, wasn't given the opportunity to know Jesus! But now that they have, they've straightened up and know the way of God, and they condemn this sick activity."

Dr. Carrol looked at him and frowned. Then she looked at her wristwatch and said, "Well, enough of this topic. Who's next to give their report?"

A male student stood up and began talking about the interaction of his fraternity brothers and the responsibilities that each was assigned. When it was open for discussion, no one made any comments. The last talk was by a short male student who worked part-time at the student bookstore. He talked about his interactions with the full-time employees and the professors and students who bought books there.

The following week, exams began. Even though Taylor studied every moment he could, he would still meet Marcia at Lenoir Hall for dinner at six. On Friday morning, with most of the other exams behind him, he took his Sociology exam. Later that evening, when he met Marcia for dinner, he related to her what had happened after the exam.

"I had no problem with the test, breezed through it, and was the second to get up from my desk. I walked the exam to the front of the room and placed it on the desk where Dr. Carrol was sitting. She said, 'Mr. Hanes, can I talk to you for a minute?' This freaked me out. I sort of froze. I thought maybe she thought she saw me cheating or something. So we went outside. She closed the door and started talking to me softly." Marcia listened intently as she stirred sweetener into her coffee.

"She then explained that when she read my paper, she was really impressed with it because it was well researched, and she even checked on some of the references to see if they were accurate." Marcia nodded that she was following. "From there, she began talking about the research of one of her colleagues that has been going on about 1,300 American and Canadian

Indian tribes that have documented a third sex, which they're now calling *two-spirit* people. These people had been well-respected in their societies and usually didn't follow the traditional male or female roles, but they kind of took on different roles and often dressed in both male and female clothing. But their society considered them a higher spirit than everybody else because they encompassed the spirits of both men and women. Often they were shamans or medicine men. There were women too, who took on roles of warriors and even chiefs."

"So they were gays and lesbians?" Marcia asked.

"Evidently, and this dates way back. In fact, there is evidence that this third sex existed in the Siberian culture, like 15,000 years ago, which was the early man that crossed over the Bering Strait on a land bridge into Alaska. And this was the beginning of the population of North and South America."

"So why was she telling you all of this?"

"I don't know. Maybe she was trying to get me more interested in anthropology or sociology. But it also connected to what my paper was saying, which is that it was Christianity that influenced people to look down on homosexuality, and that it has been around since the beginning of time."

"Of course it has."

"But then she said she gave me a B minus because—"

"No," Marcia interrupted, "that paper was better than that. I read it and thought it was excellent."

"Wait; she said she *first* gave me a B minus, well, because it didn't fully conform to the original assignment, which was the interaction between two groups of people, and I—we must document it, so it had to be of a local nature. . . . Mine was more encompassing and sounded like a social commentary about gay rights. Then she said she reread it because she still liked the paper. Then, when I gave my talk, she said I really wasn't that far off the mark regarding the assignment, although it was a different approach. So, she reread it a third time and was so impressed with it this time, she moved my grade to guess what? An A!"

"Wow! Congratulations!" Marcia said.

"Yeah. Also, I've never considered myself a good speaker, and I always hated getting in front of the class, but I actually thought I did a pretty good job, and I guess this confirms that. But that's not everything," Taylor continued. "She then said I should submit it to *The Daily Tar Heel* as an article."

"You should!"

"I told her I didn't know. She said she knew someone on the editorial board, and if I didn't mind, she would submit it. So I told her okay."

"So, she thought they would publish it?"

"I don't know. In a way, there's a part of me that . . ." He grimaced and continued, "that doesn't want that to happen. My name would be on it, and everybody would recognize it."

"But wait a minute. Part of what your paper was saying was that changes don't happen unless people stand up against what is not right, you know, in the laws, in religion and in traditions."

"Yeah, yeah, you're right. And besides, I don't really know that many people on campus. You, Alex, Brad. Well, we'll see. It may not get very far. But I guess Dr. Carrol thought it was important."

Chapter 25

Stand by It

I don't know if my paper will get published in The Daily Tar Heel. *At first, I was hoping it wouldn't. I've seen so much hate against gay people in the paper already in the letters to the editor, and I know this would just generate more. But now my mind has changed. It was a good paper that I wrote, and I think it even made Dr. Carrol pause and think. I made people in the class look at it from a different perspective. You know, if you are right, you are right, and you can't let people's prejudiced feelings change what you believe. That would be caving. I'm proud of all the research I've done, all that I've learned, and proud of how I presented it. I'll stand by it.*

Chapter 26

Persistent and Engaging

On Wednesday, after going to the campus post office, Damien was excited. Knowing that because of a lack of funds, he wouldn't be coming home to New York for the holiday break, his mother had mailed him a stack of new records for his Christmas present, including one entitled "Varsity Drag." All of the 78s had arrived unbroken. She had written him a short letter saying that she hoped that he was doing well and noting that people at the club were now dancing the Black Bottom to this song. Damien had learned this dance from a female student who had traveled north over Thanksgiving. He couldn't wait to hear the "Varsity Drag" record, but he didn't have a phonograph. Bernard did, though.

Aware that Bernard usually had lunch at noon sharp, Damien caught up with him in the dining hall and asked if he could bring the records over to play. Bernard indicated he was committed to the books and a paper for the rest of the week, so he suggested

Friday afternoon. Bernard also noted that, during the week, most of the dorm fellows conscientiously avoided playing music out of consideration for anyone who might be studying. But on Fridays, many students played music with a radio, a phonograph, or—if they were capable of it—with their own instruments.

Friday evening was completely different from the weekdays. Many students would get together, pull out the hidden liquor, sit around, drink, smoke cigarettes, listen to music, and philosophize about anything that came to mind, including religion, politics, and women. Later in the evening, many who were unwilling to stop there would end up downtown at the speakeasy.

As soon as Damien had finished his last class on Friday, he rushed to his room, grabbed his records and a bottle of hooch, and headed for Bernard's dorm. But in his haste to get there, he had forgotten to urinate first. He knocked on Bernard's door, heard a "Come in," opened the door, rushed in, set down the records and hooch, and said, "I gotta piss; be right back."

Then he ran out the door and down the hall as Bernard laughed. "Good to see you, too."

Damien entered the bathroom. It was a typical large dorm bathroom with several urinals, toilet stalls, a line of showers, and a row of sinks. Two guys were in the shower stalls, one of average height and the other one a good six feet two and athletically built. Damien headed straight for the urinal and began to relieve himself. He stood there for several minutes, amazed at how badly he must have needed to urinate. He heard one of the showers being turned off and noticed through his peripheral vision that the tall fellow was now standing outside the shower, drying himself. Just as Damien was about to finish, he noticed the fellow, while continuing to dry himself, staring and approaching him from the side.

As Damien flushed and began to button up, he nervously looked at the fellow, who was standing, dripping wet, a head above him and about three feet away.

"You're that dancer, aren't you?" the fellow asked in a manner that seemed almost accusatory.

Damien didn't know how to take that; after a moment, he replied cautiously, "I do dance, and I'm studying the history of dance."

"I heard you were a great dancer." Smiling now, the guy was almost gushing.

"Oh! Must have been someone from last month's hop. Yeah, I like to dance."

"No, my girlfriend said you were a regular Oliver Twist and you must be a professional, that you knew all the latest moves."

Damien smiled. The university had one dance a month on average. Several were put on by the German club. Some were for formal slow dances, and more recently, others were a mixture of slow dances and the increasingly popular jazz dances. Damien had gone to last month's dance without a date and had asked several women to dance the Charleston and the Quick Step.

The fellow extended his hand. "I'm T. G. Howe." Damien extended his hand and shook it, noticing that the gentleman's hand seemed fifty percent larger than his and felt like it could reduce his digits to a pile of crumbled bone splints. "It's Thomas Gordon Howe, but most people call me T. G. for short."

"Good meeting you, T. G. I'm Damien Holdrich." Damien was feeling a bit uncomfortable with this naked guy looming over him, even though the fellow was casually holding his towel in front of him. Damien turned and started to leave the bathroom.

"Could you teach me some moves?" T. G. asked hurriedly as he followed Damien out the door.

Damien continued walking and answered, "I, uh, I suppose. What do you want to learn?"

"Tomorrow night, there's a hop. I think it's going to be strictly jazz music. I can do the basic Charleston, but I need some tips on some other moves. I want to impress my girlfriend."

As Damien continued down the hall with T. G. following him and still dripping, he noticed several other men heading for the showers in bathrobes or towels, apparently getting ready for a night out.

"Well, if you really want to impress your girlfriend, you need to learn the Black Bottom. The Charleston is passé."

"What's that?"

"Passé? Out of style. People are not dancing the Charleston as much. Well, they are here in the South."

By this time, T. G. had followed Damien into Bernard's room. Bernard had just poured two glasses of gin and looked up in astonishment, seeing the tall, muscular man standing in his room and patting himself dry.

"Bernard," Damien said as he waved in the air, "this is G. T., uh . . . something or other."

Bernard, his mouth open, reached out his hand. T. G. extended his, and they shook.

"It's *T. G.*, so do you think you could help me?"

Damien grabbed his glass, turned and looked at T. G., and took a sip. "Sure, more people should know how to dance." He turned to the phonograph and put on a record. While starting the turntable, he said, "Let's listen to this new recording. It's called the 'Varsity Drag.' It's turning into a big hit. Listen to the rhythm, and then we can try a few steps."

He placed the needle on the record, and it began to play. Then he picked it up and turned around and looked at T. G., still naked, his hair wet, and his towel still draped in front of him, and smiled. "Maybe you should go to your room and put some clothes on first. Or are you more comfortable that way?"

"Oh, I can dance better in shoes," T. G. replied, looking at their drinks. "You're going to have a party. I can't drink, because I'm in training. But I'll be right back." He headed out the door; then he turned and paused. "Well, maybe one drink. Technically, the season's over."

Once he was comfortably down the hall, Bernard broke out in laughter. Damien was laughing too as he said, "Yeah, look what followed me home."

"Do you know who that is?" Bernard asked, looking at Damien's expression, which suddenly changed from a smile into one of curiosity. "No, of course you don't. That b–baby grand is T. G. Howe, our star quarterback."

Damien was tilting his head as if he still didn't understand. Bernard continued, "Football! He's a b–big cheese. He's our star football p–player. Very good, I understand."

"Football! Oh, I see. He's certainly a big guy. You know they have to follow all those complicated plays. I bet he'll pick this up really easily. Sorry about all this."

"No, I guess I should be supportive of my fellow dorm mates . . . and the football team. So what's this your mother sent?"

"It's the 'Varsity Drag.' Great tune." He set the needle on the record, and it began to play.

Bernard immediately started shaking his head side-to-side and up and down to the beat. Suddenly, a young man dressed for an evening on the town peeked in.

"That's 'Varsity Drag.' I've heard about that!" Then another man pushed in, this one dressed casually and holding a drink and a cigarette, followed by another man smoking and drinking. The first one spoke as he swayed from side to side, "I love that!"

Then another tall guy wearing nothing but a towel came in and said, "T. G. said you were giving dance lessons. Can I get in on this?"

All the other guys were looking at each other; then one asked, "What dance?"

Damien spoke, "It's called the Black Bottom. It's what's popular in New York right now." As the last twenty seconds of the music played, Damien did a few steps to give them an example.

One enthused, "That's hip to the jive. Teach us all."

Bernard was amazed that all of this was going on in his dorm room, in which he probably had only one or two visitors throughout his entire freshman year. Damien started the record again.

All the guys began to introduce themselves to Damien. Some had never formally met Bernard and introduced themselves. They started discussing some of the records Damien had brought over, many unfamiliar to them. Then T. G. returned, fully dressed in pants, shoes, and a sport coat. Everyone moved aside because of his size and athletic status.

Damien got everyone's attention, but as more people came in, he realized that the room was too crowded for everyone to see him moving, so he directed everyone out into the hallway. All the guys were along one wall; Damien, his back to them, went through the steps of the Black Bottom several times without the music. Then he had them try it as they followed him. Bernard was standing in the doorway of his room, smiling with amusement at the whole event: a line of guys dancing in a row, some of them covered only with towels around their waists. Then Damien asked him to start the record, which he did, and suddenly everyone was doing, although not at all very well, the Black Bottom. When the record was finished, Damien instructed Bernard to play it again, and everyone practiced following Damien.

After the record ended this time, Damien, who had been hollering over the music, said, "Okay, next we'll try it with turns, but first I've got to get a shot." He went back into the room, took a swig and came back out. Several other guys went to their rooms and came back with drinks.

"Now you can use the same steps, but with your dance partner, you'll want to do some turns." Damien signaled Bernard to start the music again. As he stood in front of them, he held his arms up as if he had an imaginary dance partner and went through the steps. The others followed along, trying to copy his movements. Damien noticed that T. G. was having trouble incorporating the turns with the steps, so he reached out and took hold of T. G.'s right arm and put it around his shoulder and grabbed T. G.'s extended left hand with his right hand. They were now in the traditional dance hold position. "T. G., you are in the lead. But I will be guiding you." T. G. was not bothered by this in the least and was concentrating on what Damien was saying and doing.

Bernard saw that four other guys had paired up and were dancing together. Soon, the entire group of eight were all paired up dancing in the hall.

When the song ended, Damien got their attention and showed them some additional steps that they could intersperse with the basic steps to impress their dates. He explained that women were more attuned to dance moves, and if the men did them, their partners would easily pick them up by following along. After going through five moves, he asked Bernard to start the music, and everyone went through the moves in rhythm with the music. With one more play of the record, they all paired up again and practiced the dance, this time interspersed with the additional steps.

All the guys seemed really excited about their new skills, and one asked Damien to give them some new steps for the Charleston. He said he would be happy to, but he wanted a ten-minute break. No one complained, and they all went to their rooms for drinks with some taking a cigarette break.

When Damien was alone with Bernard in his room, Bernard said, "This may be your calling. You are a good teacher, too!"

"I've been dancing all my life. It's real easy for me to pick up new steps. And I guess I know how to simplify the process of learning."

"Damn! I'll be the only one in the dorm who won't be able to dance."

"Don't worry," he said as he took a sip of gin. "I'll give you private lessons."

Soon someone was at the door with a stack of records in hand, including the earlier hit, "The Charleston."

Damien went back into the hall and found the entire group waiting for him. T. G. came up to him and said, "I've got to meet June so I can't stay for this. But maybe, if you have time tomorrow, you can show me a few steps before the dance."

"Sure, T. G. It shouldn't take long. Have a good time." T. G. left, but everyone else who had been there before was lined up in the hall again. This time, even Bernard lined up, taking the space that T. G. had occupied.

First, Damien went through the basic Charleston step. Bernard had never danced in his life and was having great difficulty with it, but the liquor was relaxing him, and soon he was catching on. Damien went through three additional steps and had everyone pair up again. Damien paired up with Bernard, allowing Bernard to take the lead position as Damien guided him through the steps.

After the third playing of the record, even Bernard was dancing a reasonably good Charleston.

Then someone shouted, "Hey, is anyone still up for going into town?" Almost everyone said yes, and the crowd broke up. One of the fellows asked Damien and Bernard to join them, but they declined with thanks, asking if they could go some other time.

Damien and Bernard went back to Bernard's room and sat down for another drink.

"Wow," Bernard said. "That was the first time I've ever been asked to join them."

"I hope," Damien replied, "you didn't want to go."

"Oh, no. I was just surprised, that's all."

Damien looked through the records his mother had sent. One was by Bessie Smith, entitled "Me and My Gin." They laughed at that and put it on, and while they listened, they toasted Bessie Smith with their gin. Later Damien played "A Good Man Is Hard to Find" followed by "You Can't Keep a Good Man Down" by Mamie Smith.

They soon realized that the alcohol was getting the best of them and they had better get something to eat before Swain Hall, the cafeteria, closed for the evening. Bernard looked out the window and saw it was snowing. He noted that such weather was unusual for December in North Carolina. He changed into waterproof boots and put on a hat and scarf in addition to his usual overcoat. Before they left, he reached into the back of his top dresser drawer, pulled out a pint of Scotch, and put it in his overcoat.

Next, they stopped by Damien's dorm so that he could change into similar attire.

After they had eaten and left the dining hall, there was about two inches of snow on the ground. The campus looked beautiful, blanketed in white with large snowflakes still falling. At the same time, the snow was somehow muffling all the usual ambient noises. With all this and the alcohol still warming their bodies, it seemed like an especially pleasant environment to be in.

"Do you want to walk some?" Bernard asked.

"Perfectly good idea."

"There are some beautiful trails on the other side of the campus. Let's go there."

In ten minutes, they were on the edge of the campus where the trails began. The music from the recording "Varsity Drag" was still running through Damien's head, and he began to sing lines from the song.

Bernard smiled, took out the Scotch, opened it and offered it to Damien, who waved it away while continuing to sing. When Damien began the second verse, Bernard started to sing too.

Then Damien danced the Black Bottom as he sang, but he was slipping on the trail, which had iced over from a prior rainstorm. Seeing a large, fallen tree, he danced toward it, jumped on top and then jumped down toward Bernard, but he began to slip. He grabbed on to Bernard, and they both fell to the ground, laughing as they went. Once up again, they both took a swig and continued down the path, singing the first and second verses again.

After that, they walked for a few minutes without making any sound. Then Damien spoke up. "Bernard, you realize you have a really good voice?"

"You're drunk."

"No, no. Well, yes, I'm drunk, or at least a bit zozzled, but even so, I've got a good ear, and you have a wonderful baritone voice."

Bernard sang the lines again as if he were listening to himself for the first time.

"See!" Damien emphasized. "You really sound good. You've got to join the glee club next semester. Better yet, I'm trying to get a jazz revue going for next semester. You've got to join that! I will help. It would be easy, just popular songs!"

"Oh, I don't know about that. I could never do that. I could never perform in front of a live audience."

"Oh, come on. You will do it. I'll make you. You know I'm very persistent."

There was a long pause as Bernard looked at Damien's smiling, enthusiastic face. He finally returned the smile and said, "Well, you're partly correct. Yes, you are persistent . . . and engaging."

Chapter 27

And Still Going Strong

During Christmas break, Taylor went back to Tartan to see his mom and dad, and Marcia went to see her mom in Wichita. Of necessity, Taylor's mom had already moved into a continuing care center, and Taylor planned to visit her there every day during the thirteen days he would be in Tartan.

Most days, his mom didn't even recognize him, and when she did, she had no sense of where she was. This saddened Taylor; after discussing it with his dad, he headed back to Chapel Hill a few days early. He planned to get ready for the next semester, spend some time with Marcia, who was also returning early, and do some research on Bernard Pembroke and Damien Holdrich.

Once back at Carolina, Taylor immediately contacted Deedee, and they began searching through bound volumes of all local newspapers dating back to 1927 and looking for any other information they could find.

Taylor and Deedee were sitting opposite each other in the Castlewood library, hunched over large binders of newspapers, when Marcia entered, walking briskly and smiling.

"Hello, everyone, and Happy New Year. Figured I'd find you here," she said, and leaned over and kissed Taylor. Both Taylor and Deedee smiled and returned the New Year greeting.

"So how's your mom?" Taylor asked.

"As bitchy as ever!" Marcia growled.

"Marcia!" Deedee exclaimed. "This is your mother you're talking about. Show some respect."

"Sorry, but you don't know her. Aunt Zena and I went to visit Mom in Wichita, and she didn't show any respect to either one of us."

"What do you mean, dear?" Deedee asked.

"Well, we went through the whole explanation of how I am most likely a witch and have a witch's heritage from hundreds of years back, and she would not hear any of it. She badmouthed me and Aunt Zena, saying she was a bad influence on me. To be honest, it was terrible. I couldn't wait to get back."

"Oh, dear," Deedee said. "But you've got to agree that this whole witchcraft thing is a lot for people to take in. I didn't hold any beliefs until working here, and then the seance with Bernard Pembroke. Anyway, as far as your difficulty with your mother, I'm just sorry to hear that."

"Me too," Taylor added. "I hope you didn't sever your relationship with your mom."

"No, not completely, but it's definitely more uncomfortable. How's your dad and mom?"

"Dad's fine. Hanging in there. Mom's declined a lot. She often didn't even recognize me. That bothered Dad more than it did me. She's in a continuing care facility. She's going down fast. It was so hard to see her that way. Dad's working a lot. Mom's not communicating. Sometimes I wondered why I was even there."

"Dear me," Deedee added. "I'm also sorry to hear that. Alzheimer's can be devastating. And being so young."

Looking at Deedee, Marcia asked, "So, do you have a family that you were with over the holiday?"

"Yes, I have a much younger sister in Durham that I celebrated Christmas with, her and her husband and their children and grandchildren. I really had a nice time. I just stayed one night and came back home."

"What did you do the rest of the time?" Marcia asked. "Did you have to be at work here?"

"No, I didn't. I didn't do anything. Well, actually, that's not true. I did quite a bit. You remember you said that Bernard Pembroke had mentioned his friend's name was Damien. Well, I went through several class annuals from around the time they would've been in school. The university was considerably smaller at that time, with probably less than a thousand in each class, and Damien is not a common name. So I was able to find a freshman named Damien Holdrich. He was a freshman here in 1927. Pembroke was a sophomore. Apparently, Damien only stayed that one semester.

"Then I researched university records on Damien and Bernard to see if any other clues turned up. Since I've been working here so long and I have some contacts at University Records, I didn't have any trouble getting access to anything I wanted. It was a long, slow process, since most of this information had been transferred to microfiche, and if you've ever looked up anything on those machines, it takes a lot of time. Nevertheless, I was able to turn up Damien's hometown address and both Bernard's and Damien's declared majors and grades, and that's about it. Oh, it also lists the clubs and organizations that they belonged to." Deedee handed Marcia several sheets of paper.

Marcia perused them and said, "So, Damien had declared an A.B. major specializing in music and dance. And he was from someplace in New York City."

"And," Deedee chimed in, "we know that Bernard grew up in this house and graduated here at the university. And his major was . . . take a guess . . . business! Of course, back in 1927, it was called commerce."

"Then," Taylor said, "when I got here, we began looking more closely at the various club memberships in the annuals. And . . ." Taylor held this word as he began dragging out several annuals that he had marked with yellow sticky notes. Flipping one open and pointing, he continued, "and here, you can see Bernard Pembroke, president of the debating squad, here as president of the honor society, here in the fencing club, the Skimmers, the glee club, and the Players Theatre. This is all in his senior year. In fact, he was a real active guy; must have been extremely smart."

"Oh, he was!" Deedee added.

"Wait a minute," Marcia quickly interjected. "It seems to me . . . I don't know how you heard it, Taylor, but during the seance when Pembroke was speaking, it was like—like he stuttered or stammered."

Taylor said quickly, "That's the way I heard it, too."

"So," Marcia continued, "how could he be in the debating squad; president even?"

They looked at Deedee, who looked surprised and said, "I've never heard . . . Mr. Pembroke was an excellent speaker. He didn't stutter."

"Humph!" Marcia replied. "Maybe it has something to do with being in the Otherworld."

Taylor flipped open the 1930 annual to the senior photos. "Look at this write-up under his senior photo. He seemed to be very involved and well liked. I'll read it to you: 'Bernard Fitzpatrick Pembroke, Chapel Hill, N.C. Degree: B.S. Commerce. A stubbornness and determination characteristic of an intelligent fellow combined with conscientious thoroughness have been the fundamental basis for the enviable record he has compiled at the university, both as a scholar and as an activities man. What is a surprise to all is that Fitz, once of a quiet demeanor, has exploded in a blaze of pursuits in his last years. His even and likable disposition overcomes his innate elusiveness. All we know is that he is a man of searching and discovery. After building this university, expect him to rebuild the world, but we think even this world is too small for him. Fitz is a man looking for something.'"

"You know," Marcia said, "this tells us quite a bit about his personality. Especially that part about him being elusive and looking for something."

"Yeah," Taylor added, "so many of the other write-ups talk about making friendships and being a likable fellow. His calls him determined, elusive, and looking for something."

Deedee chuckled, "Well, that's pretty much the way I remember him. He never seemed to be close to anyone. Yet he was involved in a tremendous number of things . . . and knew a lot of people. Although it's my understanding he wasn't involved that much in Pembroke Construction. I did notice the reference to him building the university. It was his father, though, really, and his grandfather. I guess that was just a reference to his family's business."

"It is interesting," Taylor added, "that they pointed out that he was quiet in his first couple of years and his activities just exploded in the last two years. We noticed that when we looked through the annuals. In his sophomore year, he was in the Order of the Pantheon, which is a service organization still in existence, the rowing club, and the Political Awareness Club. And I think that's it. But by the time he was a senior, he was involved in a lot."

"Did he pledge a fraternity?" Marcia asked.

"No," Taylor replied. "He never pledged a fraternity. Now going over here to the rowing club, which they called the Skimmers, you have Bernard standing right behind Damien. Here they are identified by name."

"So that's him!" Marcia exclaimed. "That's got to be him."

"Definitely." Deedee added. "He was quite handsome, too."

"Yes, he was," Marcia added, squinting at the crewing club photo. "And look. They must've done quite well; he's holding several medals of some sort. Oh, he has one of those horns in his other hand. He must have been the guy—what do you call him—who shouts out the orders when to take a stroke."

"Hmm, I can't remember, but . . ." Taylor added, "now come take a look at this page with a picture from the musical that the Players Theatre put on, and who else is on stage in the chorus?

It's Pembroke! Although none of the people are identified, but standing right next to Bernard is Damien Holdrich."

"That's them," Marcia agreed; then she asked, "What musical?"

Taylor read the caption. "It says, '*Jazz It Up: A Musical Revue.*'"

"So now," Deedee continued, "we were looking through the local town paper and the university paper to see if there was any mention of Damien Holdrich, and we had just come up with something when you came in."

"What is it?" Marcia asked.

"Well," Taylor began, "Deedee had been looking through the town paper and found it first, and I was looking at the university paper and found some related articles. They both report the sudden disappearance of a student named Damien Holdrich. No leads or anything. We need to look further, but I don't think a body was found."

"What were the dates of those articles?"

"Both were late June. Classes would have ended. That would have been during the summer session. Now here is another possible connection. I found this article in the *Tar Heel*. It talks about this being the first year that the university has put on a musical. It's dated February 15. But it doesn't really say much, other than it would be a musical revue of contemporary music. However, Deedee found something in the local paper."

Deedee then spoke. "This was dated March 1, 1928. Listen to this! The headline reads 'Local Church Pickets University Production.' 'Approximately 15 members of the Church of the Holy Divinity picketed the opening night of the production of *Jazz It Up: A Musical Revue* outside the Players Theatre on the university campus. The picketers held signs reading "Jazz is the

Devil's Music." Other signs read, "Fornicators," "Sinners" and other condemnations. The leader of the church, Jesariah Jones, was quoted as saying . . .'" She stopped, staring into space. Then she added, "My God, could that be the same church and the same Jesariah Jones that's still in the news?"

"The Church of the Holy Divinity!" Taylor exclaimed. "Is that the same church that—that young preacher in the Courtyard comes from?"

"I believe it is," Deedee replied. "I know who you are talking about. Been in the news for years. He's always in the Courtyard. Or one of his members. Sometimes they are downtown in front of theaters or bars. They're really like a city institution."

"Yeah, I bet you're right!" Marcia exclaimed. "That wacko is out there all the time. He never gives up, even when people aren't listening."

Deedee continued, "I think he is a third- or fourth-generation preacher in the family. Let's see . . ." She grabbed a pencil and began writing numbers on a sheet of paper; then she stopped. "Quite possible. If Jesariah Jones was in his twenties back then, Jones would be in his late eighties or early nineties today. And I've gotten information from reliable sources who have been at this church. And I've seen some video clips of him on the news when their church was picketing funerals and other such nonsense. He's a very old man. So this is likely him. Jesariah Jones is still alive and still at his church. And still going strong."

Chapter 28

Memorial to Damien

We all came to the same conclusion: Bernard and Damien were most likely lovers. Also, Jesariah Jones and the Church of the Divinity must somehow be connected to Damien's disappearance. But now what? We are not investigators. We don't have any evidence. We'll need to do more research and hope something comes up.

It was interesting, though, that on Sunday morning, Marcia and I decided to go to the Athletic Club on campus. They have a nice brunch, and the food is probably the best anywhere on campus. The building, as well as most of its contents, is actually a memorial to all the athletic achievements throughout the history of the university. Several walls are filled with trophies. There are jerseys and banners hung high on the walls as well as autographed basketballs, soccer balls, footballs, baseball bats, hockey sticks, and what have you. From the ceiling hang several crew boats, all long retired but celebrated for some level of distinction.

One boat caught my eye because it was made of wood, whereas more modern ones are made of some composite material. So we were curious and *looked on the wall for some sort of identification. And soon we found the description of the boat, and it stated that in 1927, this boat had beat Duke and Wake Forest in the Intermediate categories, winning two gold medals. Then it listed the crew, with their first name followed by their nickname and then their last name. Bernard was listed as Bernard "Fitz" Pembroke, and Damien was recorded as the coxswain, with his name listed as Damien "Pluck" Holdrich. Pluck, evidently, was the nickname that the crew or other students had given him.*

Then I remembered when we were doing research on 1927 newspapers, I saw an article whose headline had the word "pluck," about a student riding on the wing of a biplane over the campus. I chuckled at it at the time, but after I had discussed all this with Marcia, we concluded it likely was Damien on the wing and Bernard Pembroke in the second cockpit. This could have prompted Pembroke's later interest in owning and piloting his own plane. I looked up the meaning of "pluck," and the dictionary said, "spirited and determined courage." Perfect. The fact that other students chose that name for him must say a lot about his character. And now it makes sense to me why Bernard Pembroke chose that name for his gay and lesbian equality scholarship. It both describes the inherent ideals of the scholarship and, at the same time, pays continuous homage to Damien.

The description of that boat also listed several other wins in 1928, 1934, and 1935. Then, at the bottom, we noticed that it was placed there as part of a donation by the Pembroke Foundation. Though obscure to all, probably even to the most astute campus historian, this was also done by Bernard Pembroke as yet another memorial to Damien.

Chapter 29

Do Some Investigation

Brad looked intently at Taylor as he lifted the pitcher of beer and poured some of it into his mug. "So you're telling me that you're seeing this ghost and that it just appears? And talks to you?"

Taylor looked over his shoulder and around the room as if conscious of anyone who might be listening. It was just the typical midweek crowd at Harry's, so about every other table was empty. Taylor laughed. "Yeah, yeah, I know. You don't know me very well and probably have every reason not to believe me, but yeah, I've been haunted, for lack of a better word, by this ghost."

Brad leaned back and smiled as he pondered the bubbles rising from the bottom of his mug. "Well, actually, who knows what's out there. I actually have—rather had—an aunt who claimed she was visited by my uncle from the grave. And there was quite a bit of evidence to support it. So who is this guy, and what does he want?"

Just then, Taylor raised his hand toward someone. It was Marcia, coming toward them. "Wait, I'll tell you. First, I want you to meet my . . . my friend, Marcia. Marcia, you remember Brad from the FAI meeting we went to."

Marcia smiled, said hello, and sat down next to Taylor. "Yeah, yeah, sure. That was an interesting talk."

"You want a mug?" Taylor asked.

"Sure, why not," Marcia sighed.

Taylor caught the eye of the server and signaled for another mug. "You sound down. What's the matter?"

"One of the main characters got mono, and the understudy is so unprepared and really is just awful anyway. We're less than two weeks away from the opening performance. She just shouldn't be in the play on any level."

"How'd she get the part? Oh, Brad, Marcia is a Dramatic Arts student and will be performing in *The Taming of The Shrew*."

"Oh," Brad responded, "that's Shakespeare's *Taming of the Shrew?*"

"Yeah," Marcia answered. "She got the part because nobody else signed up for it. There were other roles and activities that people went after. Realistically, hardly anyone gets on stage if they are only an understudy."

The waiter brought another mug, and Taylor poured a beer for Marcia. "Here, this will help."

"So," Brad said, "what character are you playing?"

"I'm the shrew, Kate."

"Yeah? That's like the lead part." Brad said. "I've seen a movie version with Elizabeth Taylor and that Burton guy."

Marcia smiled, shaking her head.

"So how's Alex doing?" Taylor asked. "He's another friend of ours who's in the play."

"Oh, he's great and loving every moment of it. Our scenes together are going to be great."

"Good. I'm looking forward to it. I was just telling Brad here about our encounter with Bernard Pembroke."

"Wait!" Brad said with surprise. "The ghost you are seeing is Bernard Pembroke?"

"Yeah! I was just about to explain."

"You're talking about *the* Bernard Pembroke, of . . . of university fame?"

"Yep. The same one."

Turning to Marcia, Brad asked, "Are you aware of this ghost that Taylor saw?"

"Aware! I saw him too! At least two times, anyway."

"So . . . what were you guys smoking?"

They all laughed, and Taylor said, "Nothing. We had a little beer—well, a lot. But not every time. That was just once."

"So did anyone else see the ghost with you?"

"Yeah!" both Taylor and Marcia replied. Taylor added, "The last time it was Marcia and me, Marcia's aunt, Alex, who lives in our dorm, and a lady who works at Castlewood."

Marcia quickly added, "It was a seance that was held at Castlewood."

"I had heard Castlewood was haunted," Brad said. "So give me all the details."

"Castlewood is haunted," Marcia added. "I'm convinced of that. Or at least Pembroke makes his presence there."

For the next fifteen minutes, Taylor filled Brad in on the details. When he got to the part of why Bernard Pembroke appeared angry at him, he was reluctant to tell Brad that he really wasn't gay and that Marcia was really his girlfriend. Nevertheless, Taylor told him everything. Brad immediately said that he sympathized with what Taylor had done and since Taylor was actually working to fulfill the requirements of the scholarship, he was okay with it. Brad was surprised to learn Pembroke was gay. He knew he had never married, but any biographical information just referred to him as having always been single and somewhat eccentric. In the course of relating this story, they realized that it was getting late, so they paid the bill and walked back toward campus as they continued talking. They reached the Courtyard, but before they split up to go to their respective dorms, Taylor related that they had seen a newspaper article from 1928 reporting that the Church of the Holy Divinity had picketed a musical in which Pembroke's lover, Damien Holdrich, was a lead. "And we believe this musical was performed not too long before he went missing. And the article mentioned the name of the preacher: Jesariah Jones."

"Wait!" Brad said. "Can that be the same Jesariah Jones— how many years ago was that—that is the leader of the church today?"

"We think so," Marcia replied. "He would be in his nineties. In fact, the woman who works at Castlewood, who is almost as old, says it's the same guy."

"That's amazing!" Brad said. "I knew he's been around a long, long time, but—"

Taylor interrupted. "What do you know about this guy who preaches in the Courtyard?"

Brad shrugged. "Not much, really. He has a really low IQ."

Taylor and Marcia both laughed. Taylor said, "No, really! He must be some kind of genius. He can quote any verse from the Bible."

"No, actually he does have a low IQ," Brad responded. "When I first got here, I would challenge some of the things he was saying. Sometimes it was like he didn't hear what I was saying and would just spout out something that didn't have anything to do with what I asked. And at other times, he would go back to the beginning of what he'd said ten minutes earlier and start again. So, one time I got into a conversation with a couple of Psych professors, and they both agreed he was an idiot savant."

"What is that?" Taylor asked.

"Did you ever see *Rain Man?*" Marcia asked.

"No."

"Well," Brad continued, "it's when people can't perform the most basic functions of life but they excel in one special, narrow area. Typical are people who are like human calculators and can work with numbers with amazing speed and accuracy or remember the telephone numbers of every person in an entire phone book."

"Or," Marcia added, "they can hear a musical piece, a complex musical piece played once, and then sit down at the piano and duplicate it."

"That's right," Brad continued, "so we concluded that he must be one. These people are called calendar, mathematical, or musical savants. We came up with the name "Biblical savant" since he can apparently quote all the passages from the Bible. I've watched him. He can't even get there by himself. There is some older woman, probably his mother or aunt, who drives him here, gets out of the car, and walks him to the Courtyard. At a specific time, around 5:30 or 5:45, she comes back and picks him up."

"Wow!" Taylor exclaimed. "So, he's like a robot that she just turns on spouting Biblical verses."

"Sort of. But he also talks garbage about things that aren't in the Bible. So I think he must have a photographic memory of all the sermons from his church, probably sermons given by the leader of the church."

"Jesariah Jones," both Marcia and Taylor said in unison.

"That's right," Brad said. "And you know, that newspaper clipping about the church picketing the musical revue has got me thinking. These people in this church really look at sin differently than the rest of the population. And they will do anything to make a point. Jazz and music in general, particularly back then in the twenties, were seen as the work of the devil."

Taylor quickly interjected, "That's what the old newspaper article said."

"Likely," Brad continued, "this Damien guy, since he was in that musical, could have been targeted by Jones. So maybe, like you implied, Jesariah Jones was somehow connected to the disappearance of this guy, Damien."

"That's kind of where we're heading," Marcia said.

"Yeah, yeah," Brad added as he pondered the whole situation. "We need to do some investigation."

Chapter 30

Being with Damien

Rowing practice had been canceled for Saturday, and Damien convinced Bernard to instead see *The Jazz Singer*, the first full-length feature film with sound, which was playing in Raleigh thirty-five miles away. Damien figured that they could take a bus that left at 8:50 in the morning and stopped in Morrisville and Cary before arriving at Raleigh shortly after 10:00 a.m. They could see the next show and take the 4:00 p.m. bus back to easily arrive on campus before dinner.

Bernard was barely awake when Damien came banging on his door shortly before eight in the morning. No one answered, so Damien rattled the doorknob several times. Bernard, bleary-eyed and in his underwear, unlocked the door and looked out.

"Ready to go? No, I see you're not." He nudged his way in and continued. "Shake a leg. We've got to hurry."

Bernard, without saying a word, got dressed and pushed his hair into place. "Is this g–good enough?"

"You look great. Let's go."

"What about breakfast?"

Damien looked down at the bag he was carrying. "I got some stuff here. You won't starve."

They rushed downtown, boarded the bus waiting at the gas station, and paid the driver. In minutes, the bus pulled away.

The bus was old even for 1928. It had torn seats and poor suspension and was very noisy, especially as the driver worked through several gears to full speed. The vehicle was about three-quarters full, with about half of the passengers being students going home for the weekend. The others were mostly older women, no doubt going to a bigger city for a day of shopping.

Once on the main road outside of town, the ride smoothed out a bit. Damien pulled out breakfast, consisting of cups of coffee, cold hard-boiled eggs, biscuits, and bananas, all of which he was able to get from the cafeteria just as it had opened.

"Not a bad breakfast," Bernard said. "What do I owe you?"

"Nothing. You can buy lunch."

A few minutes after they had finished eating, the paved roadway ended and turned to reddish hard-packed dirt. With the dips in elevation and turns of the steering wheel to avoid potholes, it became a challenge for the passengers to keep sitting upright. Damien and Bernard immediately gulped down all remaining coffee to avoid spilling it. The road was dusty; fortunately, the weather was cool, so the passengers all had their windows closed. No one spoke much because of the noise. The rough ride, including the two stops, lasted approximately an hour; then as they approached the outskirts of Raleigh, the paved roads returned.

Arriving at the downtown bus station, Bernard and Damien jumped off and asked an attendant for directions to the State Theatre. It was only a few blocks away, and within minutes, they were there. The marquee was emblazoned with TALKING AND SINGING: AL JOLSON, THE JAZZ SINGER. It was only a few minutes after ten, and already there were a few people lined up at the ticket window. Damien wanted to make sure he and Bernard would get tickets, so they stood in line. When they reached the ticket window, they learned that the feature played continuously all day long, with the next showing at 11:15. They decided to buy their tickets and waited for almost forty-five minutes until the crowd from the last show had left before they went in. Once inside, they got a seat at the end of the row about halfway down.

Minutes after some news clips, the movie started. There wasn't a man playing a piano in the theater as both Damien and Bernard had heard before. There wasn't a man playing an organ as Damien had heard in New York. There was the sound of a full orchestra, coming through speakers. And the audience was astonished, frozen in their seats as they took in every note.

For the first fifteen minutes, the movie was basically a silent film with a musical accompaniment. Then Jolson sang a song called "Dirty Hands, Dirty Face," perfectly synchronized to the moving picture. At the end of the song, Jolson turned to the cabaret crowd and piano player and said his famous line, "Wait a minute; wait a minute; you ain't seen nothing yet." Then he immediately went into "Toot, Toot, Tootsie," with which everyone was familiar from numerous earlier phonograph recordings. As it began, the audience laughed and clapped while Damien and Bernard briefly turned toward each other and smiled. In the course of the movie, Jolson sang a half-dozen more songs interspersed with scenes of synchronized dialogue. At the end of the movie, the audience broke into applause.

As the credits rolled and the crowd moved out, more people were walking into the theater to get good seats. Damien and Bernard looked at each other, and Damien said, "Let's stay for another show." Bernard was having a great time and immediately said yes. This time, the audience was made up of a younger crowd, apparently in their late teens through their late twenties. When the movie got to the part of Al Jolson singing "Toot, Toot, Tootsie," the whole audience chimed in. Damien was singing as loud as he could and looked at Bernard, who was singing too.

After the show, they walked down the street and found a diner to have lunch. Even after ordering, Damien was still softly singing lines from various songs.

"Thanks for dragging my ass out of bed," Bernard said. "I really enjoyed th–that, even if it means I won't complete my t–term paper and will fail the class and be k–kicked out of school."

Shocked, Damien stared at him, mouth agape. "Are you . . . did you . . ."

"Relax. I'm all c–caught up."

They both laughed; then Damien said, "I noticed you sure seemed to get involved with this music."

"Yeah, it was really n–nice."

"I heard you sing, and I noticed something."

There was a pause; then Bernard said, "That I wasn't s–stuttering." Damien smiled and nodded, and Bernard added, "I noticed that t–too."

"You've never sung before . . . other than when we were drinking?"

"No."

"Wow!" Damien exclaimed.

"You know, I've never seen much music p–performed, except in church. And that hop where I saw you d–dancing. Th–that was rather invigorating."

"What! Here at the university, there's all sorts of musical performances going on. There's the Friday Night Musicales; the university symphony performs regularly; there are dances with live bands. Even the football games have the band playing."

"I'm rather quiet. I k–keep my nose to the grindstone. I d–don't go to any of them. I've not had much exposure t–to c–classical music, so I don't g–go to those. And I d–don't do well with women, so I don't go to the d–dances. I d–don't like sports, especially football, so I don't attend the games."

"You are a hermit; that's what you are! I'm going to change that. I'll see to it. There is so much out there, so much going on. This Saturday, there's a symphony and chorus production of Mahler's Second Symphony. You're going to that . . . unless, of course, you already have plans."

"No, no, I'm free. Sounds g–good."

"Perfect! Well, you've also got to come to the Players production I'll be in. We've just started rehearsing. It'll be at the end of March. It's going to be the greatest production ever. You see, what I did is convince the Drama Department to put on a joint production with the School of Music. We have lots of talented actors and actresses and lots of talented singers. Some, like me, were taking classes in both departments. The music school was doing traditional music like cantatas, and the drama department was doing these boring, old fashion plays. And in the big cities like New York and Chicago, musicals are the big thing, with acting, singing, and dancing. So I suggested it, and all the students wanted to do it. The professors finally agreed, too. I even got some of the guys and gals from the School of Dance to participate, and we're doing a musical revue."

"What's that?"

"Well, we're just taking popular songs and stringing them together with a loose script of dialogue that just connects the songs and dances together."

"Sounds like fun."

"It is." There was a slight pause as if Damien were thinking of something. Then he spoke. "You know, I want you to come see us rehearse."

"Why?"

"Well, I think it's important for you to see the whole process, to fully appreciate what we are doing."

Bernard didn't say anything for a few seconds; then he replied, "We'll see, okay?"

"It's a deal," Damien replied. "That's swell."

Damien was persistent, and he and Bernard began spending more and more time together. He convinced Bernard to join him in a practice room in the music building, away from other dorm mates, to sing a new popular recording, "Side by Side." It had been recorded by a male duet. When Bernard and Damien tried it together, Bernard did not stutter and their voices seemed to blend well. Bernard was elated.

After practicing it a few times, Damien convinced Bernard to sing it in front of some of the other students who were putting on the show, to see if it could be included in the musical revue.

Everyone thought it was wonderful, and before Bernard even realized it, he had become part of the show. At first, he was only going to sing that one song with Damien. Then he was asked to sing along with the chorus in another song, and eventually, he was made part of the refrain section for three other songs. Despite his initial reluctance, he was enjoying doing something different, doing something in which he was not stuttering, meeting new friends, and being with Damien.

Chapter 31

Time to Celebrate

The Taming of the Shrew opened for a six-night run on Thursday, Friday, and Saturday for two consecutive weeks. It was viewed on opening night by a school reporter. He gave it an excellent review in the school paper on Saturday, highlighting Marcia and Alex's command of the Shakespearian repartee and their amazing physical feats. Taylor was busy with term papers for the first week, so he decided to postpone going until Saturday night, the final night of the production. There would be a cast party afterward, which Marcia said were always good. She also wanted to introduce the cast to Taylor. Taylor didn't want to see the play alone, so he decided to ask Brad if he would be interested, and he readily accepted.

In order to get good seats, Taylor and Brad agreed to meet early in front of the Players Theatre, a mid-nineteenth century Classical Revival building where the play was being performed. Taylor was the first to arrive, about an hour before the actual performance. Soon he saw Brad approach, and he waved to him. As Brad climbed the front stairs, he gazed up at the tall Corinthian columns on the front of the theater.

"This is a great building," Brad said. "It's like a mini Greek temple."

"You've never been here before?"

"I've walked by, but I've never been this close."

"It'll be the first time for me too. Even though it's okay to attend rehearsals, Marcia preferred I didn't, because it could ruin the spontaneity of seeing the full performance. Which makes sense, I guess."

They entered the small lobby of the building, grabbed programs off a table, and went into the theater. There were only about a half-dozen people seated at that time.

"Do you mind sitting close to the front?" Taylor asked.

"Anywhere. It doesn't matter to me."

Taylor and Brad walked down to the third row and sat in the two end seats of the center section. They removed their coats, draped them over the backs of their seats, and started looking through the programs. Soon their reading was interrupted by a great deal of animated talking behind the closed curtain. They frowned and smiled at each other and tried to listen. Suddenly, Marcia's head peeked through the curtain. When she caught Taylor's eye, she came out and waved them closer.

"Come here," she whispered loudly. She pointed to the steps along the side of the stage. "Come up here on the stage."

Taylor and Brad did as she requested and followed her to the other side of the curtain. They both paused for a moment as they were confronted with the medieval recreation of Padua, Italy, with people in costumes moving around the set.

Marcia brought them close and whispered, "He's here. Pembroke just appeared to one of the lead players. At least I think it was Pembroke." She waved them toward the back of the stage. Standing there was a young female student being held by an older woman who appeared to be a professor. The student was visibly disturbed and crying. Marcia said to them, "Janice, Dr. Patterson, this is my boyfriend, Taylor, and a friend, Brad." They both acknowledged them with slight nods.

Dr. Patterson said, "I was just trying to reassure Janice that seeing the ghost is a good thing." Patterson spoke with an overly theatrical voice, extending her vowels to an almost uncomfortable length. "When you see the Players Theatre ghost, it most assuredly means you will be a success, that great fortune will descend upon you as if by some divine intervention." Marcia was trying to interrupt, but Dr. Patterson continued. "It was proven with Allyson Sawyer, Amy Little, Paul Donavon, and others; they all went on to bigger and greater challenges." Marcia looked for a reaction from Taylor and Brad, neither of whom recognized any of these names.

Marcia finally broke in. "Dr. Patterson, we think . . . Taylor here has had direct contact with this ghost on several occasions. We think it might be the same ghost."

"Really!" Dr. Patterson replied, making the word three times longer than anybody else would speak it.

"Yes, we think it may be the ghost of Bernard Pembroke."

"Indeed!" Dr. Patterson again said in an overly dramatized voice. "Bernard Pembroke! In the past, I had heard people say it was probably him. It is good luck! It is to our favor. He was a great patron of the arts, particularly dramatic arts. But enough of this; the show must go on. We don't have much time." She quickly released Janice and walked away as if she had just remembered something that needed attending. Janice appeared more composed now, gently dabbing at her tears so as not to smear her makeup.

"Janice," Taylor said, "I want to ask you some questions about the ghost."

The girl just stood there staring at him; then Marcia spoke up. "Perhaps this is not the best time. Maybe at the cast party. You are going, Janice, aren't you?"

"Oh, yes. Sure."

"Okay, Janice," Taylor said. "See you then."

Taylor and Brad went back to their seats and sat down. The theater was now about half full.

"This is strange," Taylor commented. "Pembroke evidently makes occasional appearances at the theater."

"Well," Brad said, "according to what you guys dug up, Pembroke was involved in theater productions. He liked the arts. That professor said so, too. And she says it brings good luck. What that may really mean is if he approves of the production, he makes an appearance."

"I suppose that's as good a theory as any. But for what purpose?"

Once the play began, they mostly forgot about Pembroke. In act 2, scene 1, Petruchio exchanges witted barbs with Kate and physically tosses her around the stage. The entire audience, especially Taylor and Brad, sat entranced, carefully taking in every word and every motion. When the scene ended, the audience applauded and cheered and finally gave them a standing ovation. Alex and Marcia came back on stage briefly and took a bow.

The rest of the play, while very well executed, was much more tame. However, it held everyone's interest, and when the final curtain came down, the cast was generously applauded, with Marcia and Alex receiving further enthusiasm.

Marcia told Taylor and Brad to just go around the building into the basement where the party was, and she and Alex would be there after they had changed and removed their makeup.

By the time Taylor and Brad had gotten there, the room was filled with about a dozen people. They saw a large bucket filled with soft drinks; they went over, and each got one. The room was noisy with chatter about the play, and since neither Brad nor Taylor knew these people, they just stood and watched. Finally, Marcia and Alex entered, and the rest of the cast gave them a cheer and applause. Alex raised his arms while Marcia genuflected and raised her arms, both as if they had just finished an Olympic gymnastics routine. People laughed.

Taylor and Brad approached them.

"Marcia, Alex," Taylor enthused, "you were unbelievable."

"Thanks," Marcia replied. "It was a lot—a lot of work."

"It was," Alex added, "but we pulled it off. It was a lot of fun, too."

"I thought it was unbelievable," Brad added. "You were both wonderful. The whole play was great, but you guys were amazing."

"Thanks!" they both answered.

"Oh, Alex," Taylor said. "I don't think you've met Brad."

They shook hands, and Alex added, "No, we haven't met, but I remember you from that speech by the military guy who was kicked out of the military."

"Yeah," Taylor added. "Well, Brad has offered to help us analyze this Pembroke ghost thing."

"Great," Alex replied. "You know that was kind of weird—well, very weird that Pembroke showed up tonight. At least we think it was Pembroke."

"Oh, it was Pembroke, all right!" Marcia added.

"Yeah," Taylor said. "I wanted to talk to Janice and ask her about what she saw."

"She's not coming to the party," Marcia replied. "I talked to her in the dressing room, and she said with the ghost sighting and all, she was just exhausted, so she went back to her dorm to get to bed. I did get to ask her to describe the ghost, and she said, 'Flat-brimmed hat, leather vest and pants, middle-aged man.' It's Pembroke. Sorry you won't get to talk to her."

"That's okay," Taylor responded. "I only wanted to ask her what he looked like, and you got that answer. Did she say exactly where she saw him?"

"Yeah, there's a hallway in the back that leads to dressing and storage rooms, and he was there in the middle of the hallway. She saw him there, thinking it was someone in the wrong costume; then he just vanished, and she freaked. Oh, wait. She did say he was reaching out with his right hand and his mouth was open as if he wanted to communicate with her, but then he just disappeared."

Everyone pondered this for a moment; then Marcia spoke up. "I need a drink."

"Me too!" Alex added. They all headed over to the soft drink table.

"Is this all they got?" Marcia asked.

"Afraid so," replied Taylor.

"Okay," Marcia said, "I really need a drink. So, what do you all say we chat with these folks for a while and then head into town."

Everybody agreed. Then Taylor said, "Yeah, it's time to celebrate."

Chapter 32

Enjoying Myself

Damien and Bernard's relationship continued to develop as they were drawn closer to each other through their mutual interests. By February, they were at crew practice together every morning, eating almost every meal together, and often studying together. And now, with Bernard's involvement in the jazz revue, they were practicing together, several hours before dinner and sometimes after dinner too. In addition, most of their weekend entertainment involved each other's company.

While Bernard was enjoying being with Damien and practicing the songs in the musical revue, he still had much schoolwork that needed to be done, and one of the commerce courses was preying on his mind. For an assignment, he had written a business plan, and now he was required to give a talk about it in front of the class.

Damien sensed Bernard was upset about something. One evening, after a jazz revue rehearsal, he asked Bernard what was bothering him.

"I—I—I've got to g-give this t-ten minute speech in my c-commerce course, and—and I d-don't know how I'm going to get through this. I—I'm going to be so embarrassed."

"When?"

"T-two weeks."

"Have you started on it?"

"It's b-been done for q-quite a while. B-but I d-don't think I c-can give the speech. C-can you help?"

"Absolutely! I've been thinking about your stuttering. Look, you can speak when you're ossified, but naturally, you can't be drinking for class. You don't stutter when you're singing. I think we can work on that."

Damien scheduled one of the practice rooms in the music building for the next afternoon, and they met there at the appointed time.

"Look, my ideas are simple. You have to imagine when you are giving your speech that you are singing." As Damien was saying this, he gestured to his stomach with two pointed fingers and then let them flow up his chest and to his opened mouth. "So, when you start a word or a phrase, think about vocalizing it in the same way you would vocalize if you were to sing that word or phrase." He placed his two fingers in his opened mouth and added, "Keep your mouth wide open, making your sounds round as if you were singing. Okay?"

Bernard nodded.

Damien continued. "Do you want to try it? Where's your paper?"

"I–it's on the chair, b–but I've m–memorized it."

"Oh, very impressive. Okay," Damien said as he grabbed the paper off the chair. "I'll follow along as you recite. Now first, I want you to actually sing the words."

Bernard looked surprised; after thinking a moment, he asked, "T–to what t–tune?"

"Hmm," Damien said. Looking at the first sentence, he quickly mumbled some of the words to a tune. Then he added, "Well, maybe just try it monotone. Just sing one note for each word."

Bernard began vocalizing the first sentence. "A good business plan serves as a framework for starting, running and expanding your business." It was very monotone and flat—but without any stuttering.

Damien held up his hand for Bernard to stop. "Very good. A little high in the pitch. Lower the pitch a bit, and at the end of each . . . each natural phrase, try lowering your note a half-step and extending that syllable a bit." Then Damien demonstrated by vocalizing. "For instance, 'A good business plan' with 'plan' lowered and extended, 'serves as a framework' with 'work' lowered and extended, 'for starting' with 'ing' lowered, et cetera. Okay, you try it."

Bernard did exactly what Damien said, and after a few stumbles, he was vocalizing entire sentences without stuttering.

After a few minutes, Damien stopped him. "It's sounding better and better. I think we just need to speed it up and practice it."

For the next two hours, they practiced the entire speech several times. Bernard's business plan was about his father's business, with which he was quite familiar, having worked there for the last four summers. Whenever they came to a word over which Bernard seemed to stumble, either Damien would suggest a synonym or they would completely rewrite the sentence. After they had finished and were leaving, Bernard was smiling. "I think I can d–do this!"

Damien immediately replied, "I know you can. And I'll be there when you do it."

❀ ❀ ❀

When the time came for the speech, Damien skipped his regularly scheduled class and sat in the back of Bernard's commerce class, in a position that could be seen by anyone at the podium. After two other students had given their talks, Bernard was up next, and the professor said, "Do your best, Mr. Pembroke." Several students looked at each other and sniggered or repositioned themselves to get comfortable as if to indicate that this was going to be grueling.

Then Bernard began. "A g–good business p–plan . . ." He looked up and saw Damien pointing with two fingers to his wide-open mouth and then extending his arms as if singing a big note. Bernard continued, "serves as a framework for starting, running and expanding your business." It was controlled, not rushed but at a lively pace, with natural intonation and without any stuttering. He continued with his speech in a well-modulated voice at a good, even tempo, and before he knew it, he was at the end. When he finished, he looked first at the professor, who smiled and nodded, and then at Damien, who held two thumbs up.

A few days later, when Bernard met Damien at the cafeteria for dinner, Bernard announced his grade for the talk.

"I got a B," Bernard said.

"Oh. All right. Are you happy with that?"

Bernard smiled. "I'm ecstatic. True, I could have done better on the p–paper. He said that I lacked d–depth on the paper. B–but he said, as far as my presentation went, he felt it was top-notch, as g–good as anyone else's if not better. That alone makes me happy. Happy, happy! Very happy."

"That is absolutely wonderful!"

"And, once again, I have you to thank."

"Nope, you did it. You did all the hard work. I just guided you."

"No, I owe you one."

"Look, you are more than paying me back with your part in the jazz revue. By the way, people in the group think you are adding so much to the program."

"Well, I—I don't know about that. But I am enjoying myself."

Chapter 33

Do Some Planning

When Brad found out that Castlewood had an extensive library with copies of all the local newspapers that had ever existed, he asked Taylor if he could do research there, too. He wanted to help and felt he needed to find out more about Bernard Pembroke and Jesariah Jones. Taylor introduced Brad to Deedee, who not only gave Brad permission but also agreed to help him with his research. This was perfectly fine with Taylor and Marcia since both were quite busy writing papers and studying for tests.

On Thursday evening, Brad called Taylor and said that he had discovered some interesting information about Jesariah Jones and his family. Taylor was eager to find out what this was all about. He immediately went to Marcia, who suggested including Alex if he was available, and they all decided to meet on Friday night at Castlewood after it closed.

Around half past five on Friday, Marcia, Taylor, and Alex arrived at the front door of Castlewood. Upon entering, Deedee congratulated Marcia and Alex on the school paper's review of their excellent performance in *The Taming of the Shrew*. As they talked, they moved across the large room and into the elevator, and then toward the library.

"For some reason," Deedee said, "it is one of my favorite Shakespearean plays, and I must have seen it a half-dozen times, but it's been a while, and if I had known that you two were in it, I would certainly have gone to see it."

"Thanks," Marcia replied. "I should have mentioned it. We've gotten a lot of good comments from many people about it . . . from students and professors."

The conversation immediately halted as they entered the library and greeted Brad who was huddled over a table, but then it resumed.

"Yeah, great reviews," Alex said. "Did I tell you—no, of course I didn't—one of the professors of dance, Dr. Daniel, saw the performance and is going to recommend me for an audition for an internship with various ballet troupes around the country."

"No, what?" Marcia screamed. "You weren't even dancing!"

"Well," Alex replied with a smirk on his face, "all of life is a dance."

"Hey!" Taylor interrupted. "Isn't it, 'All of life is a stage?'"

"Very good, Taylor," Marcia said, "but not quite. It's 'All the world's a stage, and all the men and women merely players; they have their exits and their entrances, and one man in his time plays many parts, his acts being seven ages.' So, is this for real, an audition to become a member of their ballet troupes?"

"Not quite," Alex answered. "There's a long road from here. It's a group of representatives from various city ballet troupes who come to various universities to scope out the talent. They will see a local audition of seven or eight people. If they like anyone, they will ask them to intern for the summer. From there, if they were impressed with your learning ability and progress, they may encourage you to study with them or take classes on the outside and work with them. And I wouldn't go just anywhere. A big city is the only place I'd consider."

Brad asked, "Where are the representatives from?"

"Well, one's from Philadelphia, one's from Minneapolis, and one is from Seattle; then there are two I wouldn't even consider because of the states they're from."

"Which ones?" Marcia asked.

"Alabama and Mississippi. Need I say more?"

"Nope," Brad replied. "That's what I was thinking."

"Yeah," Alex added. "Not exactly the best states for a gay man to live in."

"Wait a minute, Alex," Marcia said. "I thought you wanted to do theater dance, like Broadway. You never, ever mentioned any interest in classical dance."

Alex shrugged and replied, "Well, I have taken some classical dance and did quite well with it, and I don't know, the prestige of working in a ballet troupe . . . Who knows? It kind of intrigues me, and maybe I have this talent that I wasn't even aware of. Instructors have said I was good, and even Dr. Daniel said I had potential."

"Well," Taylor added. "That's exciting. Can we come to the audition? You know, to cheer you on."

"Maybe. I guess. I'd have to check. Honestly, I'm really nervous about this. I'd be competing with ballet majors, although there aren't that many men . . . mostly women. But many of these people, especially the women, have been dancing since they were like nine years old. I didn't do any dancing at all until I was about sixteen; then I really was not doing that much ballet. But I can get by. They always want to see this fabulous grand jeté, and although I can do it, I've never been really good at that."

"What's that?" Brad asked.

"Oh, it's this huge flying leap. And with men and women, especially men, they expect you to be suspended—momentarily suspended in the air. I mean, I'm good at it, but not really, really good at it."

"You'll do fine," Marcia added. "You just need some confidence-building."

Looking directly at Marcia and speaking in a very serious tone, Alex asked, "Could you . . . work some sort of spell that would help me?"

Marcia looked at him incredulously, but smiled and slowly answered evasively, "I . . . suppose . . . it's possible."

"Okay," Brad said. "Let's get started. Let me show you what I've discovered." Brad waved them over to the large table, which had papers and diagrams laid out on top. Brad continued, "Well, since I had last seen you—"

"That would be at the play," Marcia quickly added.

"Yeah. Well, I've been doing a lot of research on Jesariah Jones. First, thank you, Deedee, for use of this library and all your research help." Brad smiled at Deedee, who smiled back. "I also pulled information from the main library and county records. And I came up with some interesting informa—"

"Wait," Alex interrupted. "Who's Jesariah Jones?"

"Oh, okay," Brad said. "We need to fill you in. Jesariah Jones is the ninety-year-old patriarch of the Church of the Holy Divinity."

"Yeah, I've heard of him," Alex responded. "Now I know who you're talking about. He's the guy who does all that offensive picketing, especially at weddings and funerals."

"That's him," Brad responded, "and that preacher guy who's almost always in the Courtyard is his great-grandson."

"Really!" Alex remarked. "Always condemning gays. I've never listened to him more than a minute; then I moved on. It was a waste of my time."

"Okay," Brad continued, "well, here's the interesting thing. We found out that Bernard Pembroke's lover, Damien, had produced the first musical on campus in 1928 and the same man, Jesariah Jones, had picketed in front of the Players Theatre back then!"

"Damn!" Alex reacted. "The same guy? He was picketing back then and still is. He just doesn't give up."

"The same guy. So, anyway, in some way, we think that Jesariah Jones was connected to Damien going missing. And that's why I was researching this."

"Sort of like a cold case revisited," Alex added.

"Exactly! Back then, the administration and the police didn't spend much time on it. Damien was gay, and society in general thought he was a degenerate libertine and that whatever happened to him, he probably had it coming."

"Yeah," Alex quipped, "my feelings of what would happen to me if I ended up in Alabama or Mississippi."

Everyone chuckled as Brad continued. "So, that's what we had known. So I began documenting the Jones family and the church and everything that I could find. I even got to know the sheriff in town and asked him about everything he knew about the church. It ends up that this church is pretty isolated by choice. They are like a cult. They marry secretly and don't register the marriages unless there proves to be some legal advantage to it. They have their babies born in the compound, unless they have some complications; then they go to the hospital. So it looks like a lot of the records are missing or at least incomplete."

"What about schooling for the kids and school records?" Marcia asked.

"Homeschooling wasn't as accepted back then, so the truant officer made them come to school, and consequently a lot of information was gathered by the school system. I also have lots of contacts at City Hall and the county courthouse, so what information I didn't get from the library, I got from them. Also, I know several retired sheriffs who were very cooperative with me. Everybody—and I mean everybody—has something against Jones and his church. Let me tell you, this is really a really weird family. And I don't know if it's genetic or what. So look at this."

Brad drew their attention to a large diagram. "This is the Jones family tree. I couldn't trace it any further back beyond Jesariah Jones's father here, who was named James Jesariah Jones. He lived in Crete, Indiana. There he had a son, who he named James Thurmond Jones, born in 1887. Later, he apparently abandoned his wife and son and moved here, remarried and had a son who we know as Jesariah Jones in 1905, 18 years later.

"So this guy James Jesariah Jones started two lines of weirdos. First in Crete, Indiana and then here. He was a preacher by trade. We can find evidence of this. His son in Crete, Indiana is believed to have been involved in the KKK. He had a son, and now this is interesting: His son is . . . was Jim Jones." Brad paused, waiting for a reaction from the group, but didn't get any.

Deedee spoke up. "They are all too young to remember any of this. Jim Jones, yet another preacher, was responsible for a huge mass suicide of his followers."

"That's right," Brad continued. "It is considered the single greatest loss of American civilian lives in a non-natural disaster."

"Yeah," Alex added. "I've seen a documentary on that."

"Me too," Taylor said.

"Was that the one," Marcia asked, "where those people all poisoned themselves—drank Kool-Aid or something?"

"Yes," Brad answered. "It was in Jonestown, named after him, in Guyana. Nine hundred and nine of his church's members were killed. Died! And several others were murdered who were not members. Now, none of this really means anything other than there could be a genetic link of insanity . . . and, of course, the connection to developing cult-like churches."

Taylor spoke up. "Let me get this straight: Jim Jones's father and Jesariah Jones, who still lives here, were half-brothers?"

"That's correct. So, that brings us to the other line here. We don't know what happened to the father after he moved here and had Jesariah. I wouldn't be surprised if Jesariah did him in. At the early age of twenty, Jesariah starts his church. We have the earliest report of him picketing outside of bars in town. Of course, there was this whole Prohibition movement going on, so in that light, it really wasn't that significant. Other organizations were picketing bars all across the country. Anyway, he had a son named Barnabas and a daughter named Jael. Jesariah's wife, Maisey, committed suicide in 1928. Apparently, she chose the gruesome way of walking in front of a train. As far as we know, Jesariah never remarried."

"He probably slept with his daughter." Alex interrupted. "These cult people often sleep with their relatives."

"You're probably right," Brad added. "I wouldn't be surprised if there was some inbreeding. But we don't have any actual evidence. So, Barnabas marries this woman named Wilma Mae Devins, a church member, in 1940. He is sixteen; she is twenty. From school records, we know her father's name, Gunther Evans, and her mother was Sarah. Sounds like an arranged marriage by the church. So Wilma Mae and Barnabas have a male child almost immediately, who they name Caleb. Wilma Mae goes bonkers or appears to and is picked up by the sheriff several times wandering the road. She is eventually arrested for setting several buildings on fire. She is sent to a state institution. Barnabas disappears. Barnabas's son, Caleb, marries sometime in the late sixties and commits suicide, but not before he has Ezekiel in 1974, who apparently is the guy we see in the Courtyard, the Biblical savant."

"Very wacky family," Marcia said. "And so many cases of insanity and suicides."

"And," Brad added, "that includes people that married into the family. But that, I guess, could be inbreeding."

Taylor spoke up. "Maybe living in that church was so bad, or they knew something that they couldn't live with."

Everybody was quiet for a few moments; then Marcia spoke. "So where do we go from here?"

"I'm not sure," Brad replied. "Any ideas?"

Taylor asked, "Can we infiltrate the church somehow?"

"They're very closed. It's a small church. They would be suspicious of any intruders."

"Yeah, I can see that," Taylor replied. "Deedee, you had told us you knew of someone who had actually gone to that church, didn't you?"

"I did know someone. That was several years ago, and the person was dying and was searching for some last hope and went to their church. But she came back disillusioned with it. Unfortunately, she eventually died."

"What about," Alex asked, "that girl that was committed. The mother of that—I guess, grandmother—of that guy who's in the Courtyard all the time. Is she still alive?"

"Wilma Mae . . . Wilma Mae Devins Jones," Brad replied, "I was thinking about that too. There is no record of her dying. She would be around seventy-five. The state hospital closed about ten years ago. Most of those people were put into group homes."

Marcia said, "We don't know what condition her mind would be in."

"Actually," Brad replied, "this may be a good approach. She's been away from Jesariah's influence for years. Maybe we can glean some information from her. I think if she's alive, I could track her down. It would take only a few days."

"Let's give it a try," Taylor said. "I've got some free time in the next two weeks."

"Me too," Marcia added.

Alex spoke up. "I'll be preparing for the audition."

"That's right," Marcia said. "If you need any help, I'll be available."

"Thanks," Alex responded. "I definitely could use something."

After further discussion had ended, it was still early in the evening. Alex suggested going out to dinner. Everyone agreed, except Deedee, who had already planned an evening of a light meal, television, and then bed, and Brad, who had to leave for a meeting.

As they were heading toward town, Taylor spoke. "You know, the more I think about it, this Wilma Mae might be our only hope for getting some answers. I hope Brad finds out she's around and she's lucid and we can get to her. Once we find that out, we'll have to do some planning."

Chapter 34

All Hail, Sodomites and Prostitutes!

By March, Damien was staying overnight in Bernard's room nearly every night. They were both in the Skimmers, and they were in the same musical production, which often rehearsed until after ten o'clock. Almost everyone in the dorm knew this. And because there was another bed in Bernard's room, other fellows in the dorm gave it little thought when they saw Damien in the shower or shaving in the bathroom early in the morning.

Most likely, there was talk among some of the men, but no one said anything publicly. This was partly because it was not the gentlemanly thing to do, partly because they all had roommates, partly because Damien was generous in lending the latest recordings his mother had sent, but mostly because Damien maintained a friendly relationship with T. G., the campus football star. He was basking in the stature and glow of a strong season, ending with wins against Davidson, Duke, and Virginia.

But this coming Thursday would be the opening night for *Jazz It Up: A Musical Revue*, with the show playing through the weekend. After that, what excuse could Damien and Bernard come up with to justify Damien staying in Bernard's room? Both Damien and Bernard were stressing over this and other recent events. Several people had dropped out of the show because of illness. Damien had needed to fill in for one of the male singers, requiring him to learn and rehearse two new songs with the band in a week's time.

Bernard was consistently being hounded by his father because he was well into his sophomore year and had yet to pledge a fraternity. Additionally, the student counselor, Dr. Pendlegraff, who was a friend of Bernard's dad, had dropped by and was inquiring about his activities. Bernard could only conclude that his father had spoken to Dr. Pendlegraff and now Pendlegraff was spying on him.

Bernard tried to reassure Dr. Pendlegraff that everything was going well, he was trying to be judicious with his time, and he was taking on new activities very carefully. However, he avoided mentioning his involvement with the jazz revue because he knew his father considered such activity as silly and a waste of time. This seemed to end the meeting with Dr. Pendlegraff, but Bernard had the distinct feeling that this wouldn't be the last of him. It was a relatively small university, and Pendlegraff had a reputation of being able to find out anything about anybody on campus. So this, along with stage fright about his first live performance and the demands of his regular schoolwork, all contributed to a high level of anxiety.

When opening night arrived, both Damien and especially Bernard were so high-strung they could barely talk. Backstage,

Damien tried dancing through some of the nervousness, which really did help. He knew the songs, he knew the dances, and he had performed on stage before. He kept telling himself that, and it did seem to help, so he turned his attention to Bernard.

"I c–can't do it. I c–can't do it," Bernard remarked.

"You can," Damien reassured him. "Look, I'll be with you the whole time. When you are in the chorus, don't worry. Even if you just move your lips and don't sing, nobody will know. The same with singing the refrains. And as far as our duet, we've practiced it many, many times. You know the song by heart. You've sung it numerous times in front of the other guys and gals. They love it. Now softly, sing the words to me."

Bernard sang the song softly, haltingly at first, to Damien, who mouthed the words as he sang. When he was done, Damien said, "See, you can do it. You can do anything. Just keep telling yourself that. You can do anything!"

Bernard felt more assured. In a few moments, the stage manager came by. "It's a full house . . . on a Thursday night. It'll be sold out for the rest of the weekend, and there's a line of people out there who maybe won't be able to get in. Oh yeah, there's a group of protesters, too!"

When Damien asked what that was all about, the manager said, "It's that Baptist church that you usually see picketing at the gin joints. They're objecting to us playing jazz and singing and dancing. The university tried to get them to leave, but they're on the street, so it's city property, not the university's."

Promptly at 8:00 p.m., the lights were dimmed. The master of ceremonies introduced the show, first with a verbal introduction and then with a song, both explaining that this was a story about Mary-Ellen West from Smithfield, North Carolina.

Then the curtain rose, revealing a street scene in her small Southern hometown. Mary-Ellen was played by a student named Connie, who was undoubtedly the strongest female singer and dancer in the group.

The story was just a series of popular songs strung together, interspersed with short skits and dance steps with dialogue about how Mary-Ellen longed to become a Broadway star. After the first scene where she expresses love for her hometown sweetheart, the son of a struggling tobacco farmer, she states that nevertheless, she must pursue her dream. She gets on a train, moves to New York City, auditions for shows, and works her way up to stardom.

Damien and Bernard were early in the revue and played two fellows on the train to New York, who were traveling all over the world together on an adventure. When they met Mary-Ellen, she asked what their final destination would be. They said they didn't know. Then they broke into their song, "Side by Side," with lyrics which expressed that even though they weren't rich, they could still enjoy traveling, being in each other's company and singing.

Bernard sang superbly, completely on the beat and in tune, and Bernard's baritone and Damien's tenor voice blended perfectly. The audience loved it, and for a moment, it seemed the audience was going to give them a standing ovation. But suddenly, the spotlight fell on Mary-Ellen, as she began to explain that she was heading to New York City to become a singing and dancing star, and right now, she had only a positive attitude. She then broke into the song "Blue Skies" with optimistic lyrics about bright sunny skies and all things in her life falling into place. Her enthusiasm helps convince the two men, played by Damien and Bernard, to come with her and pursue their future as actors on the stage.

The show lasted for approximately one-and-a-half hours, including intermission. It covered Mary-Ellen singing, dancing, and meeting characters who were producers, directors, and other performers, all of whom had their own story to tell with their own songs. As Mary-Ellen became a bigger star, she became more citified and looked more like a flapper, with heavy makeup and long, slinky dresses. But soon she realized she missed her hometown and her hometown sweetheart and pined for him by singing "Carolina in The Morning" to her sweetheart on the telephone. Toward the end, her sweetheart, who had struck it rich by buying tobacco futures in the stock market, moved to New York to be with Mary-Ellen. They were together now, and both were happy.

For the finale, Mary-Ellen and her boyfriend sang and danced "I'm Sitting on Top of the World" along with the full cast.

The show was lively with exciting music. The audience, composed mostly of students but also some faculty and townspeople, had longed to see live performances and were thrilled to see this show. At the final curtain, everyone applauded generously, and when Damien came out to take a bow, the audience gave him a standing ovation and then applauded even louder when Connie took her bow.

Damien, Bernard, Connie, another fellow named Barney, and a student named Babs had decided to head out immediately after the show to get drinks in town. To advertise the show, everyone had decided to go into town in their stage costumes, with the women in their long, beaded dresses and stage makeup.

Babs and Bernard both had flasks and passed them around to the others. They exited the back door of the theater, laughing and still heady with the success of the show, and moved toward the street. There they were immediately approached by people carrying signs, the same group of church protesters that the stage manager had mentioned before the show. Most of the audience had already left the property; evidently, these people had purposefully stuck around to confront some of the performers. One sign read JAZZ IS THE GROANING OF THE DEVIL. Another read SINGING NOT UNTO GOD IS VILE.

As the church group blocked them, the group of actors became silent as they tried to read the signs and assess the intent of the group. Connie, still holding the flask, read aloud the sign held by a middle-aged woman standing close to her. "'Harlots and Sodomites perform here!'" Then she turned to Damien and said loudly, "Damien, they've got us tagged correctly!"

The actors laughed; then a young man in his twenties with piercing blue eyes stepped toward the front of the group. He surveyed the women from head to toe with scorn on his face. "You painted women must repent, or you will burn in hell for the sins of the flesh!"

Damien stepped forward. "Wait a minute. What's your beef? I can't just let you insult these ladies like that!"

Bernard tugged on Damien's jacket and said quietly, "Let's go."

The blue-eyed man continued, "'And the woman was arrayed in purple and scarlet colour, and decked with gold and precious stones and pearls, having a golden cup in her hand full of abominations and filthiness of her fornication:' Revelation, seventeen, four."

Others in the protester group shouted "Amen!" and "Abominations!"

"Oh, now he's quoting from the Bible," Damien said. "Still don't make it right."

Bernard grabbed his arm and Damien went along, followed by the others. As they moved away, the man continued shouting after them, "'Turn from thy fierce wrath, and repent of this evil against thy people.' Exodus, thirty-two, twelve!"

After getting down the walkway, out of earshot of the protesters, Bernard spoke up. "You c-can't win with those p-people. J-just like Father. D-don't even bother." Everyone but Damien, who was angered, chuckled in agreement.

Damien grabbed the flask from Bernard and took a swig. He said, "Hey, let's forget that crap and have a good time. We're going to celebrate our opening."

"That's right!" Babs repeated.

Damien then held the flask high, turned to his friends and shouted, "All hail, sodomites and prostitutes!"

Chapter 35

Back to Her Childhood

In less than a week of searching, Brad had located Wilma Mae Devins Jones, the wife of Jesariah Jones's son, Barnabas Jones. She had been convicted of arson and sent to the state mental hospital in 1942; she was now residing in a group home in the nearby town of Durham, about twelve miles away.

Brad agreed to pick up Taylor and take him there. On the way, they planned how to gain access to Wilma Mae. The woman would be in her early seventies, and they didn't know her current mental state. They decided to approach whoever was the caretaker by pretending to be students in public health, doing research on the activities in a group home. They would say that they were familiar with Wilma Mae Jones and were wondering if they could talk with her for a while to view the group home from her perspective.

They parked in front of the home and gazed at the house, which dated from the thirties. It looked similar to most of the other houses on the street, except that it was one of the largest. Parked in the back, they could see a white van that was probably used to shuttle patients to and from the doctor or for other necessary outings.

"Well," Brad said, getting out of the car with clipboard in hand. "Here goes. Remember, act with confidence."

"Okay, I'll let you do all the talking. I'll just act like I'm taking notes."

They proceeded up the stoop and rang the doorbell. After a few minutes, they heard latches being pulled, and finally the door swung open. A short, middle-aged woman, apparently the caretaker, peeked out and spoke to them.

"Yeah, can I help you?" the woman said tersely. She squinted with one eye and had streaked gray hair pulled back in a bun, with wisps of hair hanging down from both sides.

Brad spoke, "Uh, good morning. Uh, can we come in?"

"Tell me what you want first."

"Is there a person living here by the name of Wilma Mae . . ." While he was wondering whether to use her maiden name Devins or her married name Jones, the woman fully opened the door and with a toss of her head, directed them in.

They walked into a large room that at one time had served as both a living room and dining room. At the far end was a large television showing a black-and-white Western movie. Two elderly women were positioned facing the screen. One was in a wheelchair, her head drooping, apparently asleep. The other one was in an overstuffed chair and just stared straight ahead. Immediately around them were several small tables with a few chairs scattered about, apparently used for games of some sort.

Before Brad or Taylor could speak, the caretaker said, "She's upstairs. Room eight."

Brad and Taylor were surprised by the lack of any questions about who they were. After a moment, Brad spoke. "We're just going to pay her a visit."

"I know. Students from the university."

The woman turned to a doorway that led to a hall and waved at them to follow. As they passed a staircase, she pointed up and said, "Holler if you need me."

Brad and Taylor said, "Thank you," and proceeded up the staircase.

The woman shouted after them, "Don't give her any matches or a lighter!"

Brad, amused, looked at Taylor for a similar reaction but noticed instead that he had a thoughtful, distant look.

"What's the matter?" he whispered.

"Nothing. It's—it's that this place reminds me of where my mom is right now. Nicer place than this, but some of the people look the same."

"Oh, I'm sorry. I understand."

"It's okay."

They reached the top of the staircase and saw room number 5 straight ahead, so they turned down the hall to the right.

The door to the next room was open, and inside they saw a woman dressed in a dark pantsuit, sitting in a motionless rocking chair and staring out the window. They slowly moved on to the next room, in which there was a woman sitting on top of her bed. She was waving her arms in a repetitious mechanical pattern as if she were performing some task on an assembly line.

"I've seen this before," Taylor said, "in Tartan. The woman probably worked in a textile mill. She's making the same motions you would make to run a loom." Brad cringed, and they moved on.

The next room was open also, with a metal number 8 on the door. They peeked in to see a woman sitting in a chair by the window with her head down, reading.

Brad knocked gently on the door and said, "Wilma Mae?"

The woman's head turned quickly and stared at them. She said in a strong Southern accent, "Who are you looking for?"

"Wilma Mae Devins Jones."

"Never heard of her." The woman pushed on the arms of the chair, stood up, and approached them.

Brad spoke, "Are you sure you are not Wilma Mae Jones?"

"No, I'm Amanda Billings."

"The woman downstairs said you were Wilma Mae." She just stared at Brad questioningly. He continued, "Do you remember growing up on a small farm run by a preacher named Jesariah Jones?"

The woman appeared to be getting annoyed. "That woman downstairs is crazy. I'm Amanda Billings, and I was born and grew up in the city of Boston. My family has been there for several hundred years." The woman reached for the doorknob and began to shut the door. "Now, if you'll excuse me, I've got things to do."

Brad and Taylor backed out of the room and, after a moment, quietly proceeded downstairs. At the foot of the stairs, they were met by the caretaker, holding a broom.

Brad spoke, "She claims she's not Wilma Mae Devins."

"Yeah, she's a different person every day," the woman replied with a twist of her mouth. "But she's really Wilma Mae Jones. Who'd she say she was?"

"Amanda Billings . . . from Boston."

The woman looked up at the ceiling as if in thought, and then she looked at them as she repeated the name. "Amanda Billings from Boston. That's a new one. And yes, she's always from someplace else. But she's Wilma Mae Jones, and she's from here."

Taylor spoke. "Does she ever have any visitors?"

"Never. I've been here eleven years, and the only ones who ever come to see her are the doctor and some mental health workers who do some sort of evaluation. A lot of people got nobody."

Brad asked, "So, is she always this feisty?"

"Heavens no. She is so many people. Sometimes she's real sweet. Try another day; you'll see. She's not the only one like that here. Sometimes she's Princess Something-or-other, and she'll speak with a British accent. Hard to manage her then. She wants the royal treatment!"

"Does she ever leave this place?"

"Nah, you can take her out for an outing if you like. None of our residents are violent or anything. Some can be pretty entertaining."

Brad looked at Taylor and then back at the woman. "Okay, we may do that." They moved toward the front of the home as the caretaker followed then Brad added, "It would probably be good for Wilma Mae to get out. Do we have to arrange it ahead of time?"

"Nah, just show up. I'm almost always here."

"Okay," Brad replied as he reached for the doorknob. It was locked and wouldn't open. The woman reached for a keypad and punched in a number. There was a click; then Brad pulled the door open.

"Security for our residents," the woman said. "Can't have them wandering unsupervised."

Once inside the car, they sat silently until they were driving down the street. Then Taylor spoke. "What do we do now? She's the only person we know that might have any information."

There was a long pause as Brad thought. Then he said, "Don't really know. Let's think about it for a while, and give it some time. But the good thing is that at least we've got an in with taking Wilma Mae out of that building."

"True," Taylor agreed. "She was only seven years old when Damien went missing. Maybe we could catch her when she's imagining she's seven."

"Yeah," Brad agreed, "or induce her to being seven years old."

"Yep, somehow, we need to get her back to her childhood."

Chapter 36

A Lot to Take

Taylor's mother died. All along, Taylor's dad had kept Taylor aware of her steady decline. For several weeks, she had had difficulty swallowing; then she stopped eating entirely and rapidly lost weight. She became weak and couldn't even sit up. Last week, his mom had been transferred from the nursing home to a hospice, and his dad had explained to him that this would be her final place before she would be gone.

Taylor knew that the opportunities to see his mother, or at least the living remnant of what used to be his mom, were dwindling. He had planned to come home this coming weekend. However, his father called him early Thursday morning with the news. Taylor happened to be in his dorm room because of a class cancellation. Taylor's dad related a long, detailed chronicle of his mother's last few days and last few hours of life. This was interspersed with long gaps during which Taylor and his dad both broke down in tears, unable to continue with the story.

Taylor expressed his deep regret for having not gotten home while she was still alive. His father did his best to reassure him that not only couldn't he have done anything but also that his mom wouldn't even have been aware that he was there. Yet Taylor still felt guilty.

Later, Marcia was able to help him focus on the good memories of his mom and forget about the details of the last few days of her life. The long talk with Marcia, extending late into the night, did make him feel much better.

Instead of trying to figure out a way home the following day, he decided to attend his classes on Friday, especially since there was an important Psychology test that he didn't want to postpone. The funeral was scheduled for Saturday, and Marcia said that she wanted to be there and would drive Taylor home in her car.

On Saturday morning, on the way to Tartan, they decided to pay a quick visit to Aunt Zena and tell her about Wilma Mae Devins and the difficulties they had faced in getting the truth out of her. They arrived at the front door and knocked, but there was no response.

Marcia opened the storm door and entered. She could hear the television playing in the background. She called for Aunt Zena, who came out dressed in her bathrobe.

"Marcia, honey!" Aunt Zena shouted with a big smile. "Taylor! What are you both doing here?"

Marcia looked at Taylor, who nodded for Marcia to explain.

"Well, Taylor's mom passed away, and we were on our way to Tartan for the funeral."

"Oh my gosh," Aunt Zena said as she approached Taylor and gave him a hug. "Why didn't you tell me? I'm so very sorry."

The three of them talked about the illness that had taken the life of his mom. Aunt Zena expressed sympathy for both Taylor and his dad. She added that if she had known, she would have gone to the funeral, but there wasn't enough time to cancel existing appointments for palm readings later in the day.

Taylor told her not to be concerned and quickly changed the subject to Wilma Mae Devins. They did not have much time before they would have to continue to the funeral, so Taylor gave her all the details as quickly and efficiently as he could.

Marcia chimed in and finished the explanation. "So you see, as far as we know, there is no person other than Jesariah Jones and his living daughter-in-law, Wilma Mae Devins Jones, who might have seen what happened to Damien Holdrich. So we were wondering. If we had a seance, could we bring back the spirits of some of these people who were early members of the church to ask them some questions?"

Aunt Zena stood frozen for a few seconds as if thinking; then she said, "Theoretically, yes. And if you could get Wilma Mae there, there might be a greater possibility of making contact with these souls since there is this familial connection. However, having said that, I'm not sure it would work. First, you said Wilma Mae is not all there, and I've never heard of people who have mental problems contacting the other side. And the other thing is that some of these people who we want to contact are culpable, and they would be like a hostile witness and might not want to cooperate."

Marcia and Taylor accepted this possibility but still wanted to pursue the seance, and Aunt Zena agreed to help. They decided to contact her about when and where the seance would happen, and then they got back on the road, heading to Taylor's hometown.

Marcia and Taylor arrived in front of his dad's house, but Taylor was surprised that his father's truck wasn't parked in the driveway.

"Dad said he would be here. Must have run out for something. I still have my key."

They got out of the car, carrying a garment bag and two small suitcases. Taylor put the key in the door, and it swung open. They entered and paused in the living room.

For a moment, Taylor took in the stillness of the room. The house looked as he remembered; his dad, always very neat at home, kept everything in place. "This is where I grew up." He looked around at the furniture and reminisced. "The same couch since forever. It's been recovered. That chair's from my grandmother. I made that magazine rack in wood shop. It sucks."

Marcia laughed. "It all looks pretty much like where I grew up."

Taylor headed toward the hall. "Come this way. I don't know if we should sleep together." Marcia looked at Taylor questioningly. "I think Dad would be pretty cool with it. In fact, maybe he would be relieved since he thinks I'm gay . . . or he would be confused." They reached the last room on the right and stopped. "Anyway, we'll put you in here, the guest room. Also, with Mom just having died, I . . ."

Marcia set her bag down and gave Taylor a quick kiss on the lips. "I understand. This will be perfectly fine. And there won't be any questions asked."

They both suddenly turned as they heard the front door unlatch, followed by the voice of Taylor's dad. "Taylor!"

"Back here, Dad," Taylor responded. Taylor's dad, wearing a dark suit, quickly approached down the hall, and he and Taylor embraced.

"Welcome home, son."

"Thanks. You remember Marcia?"

"Absolutely, and how are you?"

"I'm fine, Mr. Hanes, but I should ask you. How are you doing?"

"Please, just call me Ben. And I'm doing okay. You know, in some ways, it's a relief. I mean, we all knew it was just a matter of time, and thankfully, toward the end, she declined quickly."

There was a pause for a few seconds as everyone let this thought resonate; then Taylor spoke. "We put Marcia in here. Is that what you wanted?"

"Yes, that's fine. It's got clean sheets. Let me show you where the towels are."

Ben showed Marcia the linen closet and the bathroom while Taylor put his clothes in his bedroom. Then they all convened in the living room.

"Dad," Taylor asked, "is it going to be an open coffin?"

"Nah, I decided against it. They had done a great job. That's where I was just now. I went to deliver your mom's wedding band to have them put it back on her finger. They had taken it off when she went into the hospice. But she just didn't . . . . I personally prefer for people to remember her before she got sick."

"That's fine, Dad."

"Y'all better change. There'll be a limousine to pick us up in about thirty minutes."

"Oh, good. I thought maybe you'd want us to ride in your pickup, and I was going to ask Marcia to drive us all there."

"Hey, I know what you're thinking. But it's all cleaned up. No car parts in the bed or greasy tools in the cab. Thoroughly scrubbed inside and out. It looks great. But the limo will work better."

The funeral was held at the funeral home. When they arrived, the parking lot was already half full. They entered the lobby, where about fifteen people were standing around. Immediately, Taylor spotted Christine, his old girlfriend. Mr. Hanes moved off to talk to some people, and Christine approached and extended her hand. They shook hands as she softly said, "I'm so sorry."

"Thanks. Christine, this is Marcia Templeton." Christine looked at Marcia inquiringly as she smiled and said hello. Taylor then added, "My girlfriend." Christine looked surprised.

There was an awkward pause. Taylor was about to make some small talk with Christine when he noticed Trad quickly approaching him. He excused himself and approached Trad, with Marcia following. He and Trad hugged as Trad said, "So sorry, buddy. I know this is hard."

"Yeah, but how are you doing?"

"Really good," Trad responded.

"Oh, Trad. This is Marcia."

"Let me guess: edgy girl across the hall."

Marcia's mouth dropped; then Taylor said, "How did you know? Wait; I haven't spoken to you since I went to college that first day."

Trad laughed, "I just know you. When you said 'edgy,' I knew you were interested."

"Damn!" Taylor responded as he shook his head in wonderment. "I didn't realize I was that transparent. Marcia, Trad was my best friend in high school. We did everything together." Taylor looked into Trad's face. He was different in some way; maybe more mature or confident. At this moment, he was smiling, and he really looked impressive in a suit. "You know," Taylor continued, "you look really good. You look like a Wall Street businessman, decked out in that suit."

"I'm doing really good. You won't believe it. After you went off to college, I really started looking at my life, and I put myself into the culinary arts program at the community college. And I love it."

"Culinary arts!" Taylor responded. "I would have never guessed that. Well, that's great. What are you planning to do with that?"

"Well, I'm still working at my dad's bar, and he's real excited about my attending, so he's thinking that maybe later we can start a restaurant. You know, he owns that building next door that's attached, and it just sits there empty."

"Wow, Trad, that's exciting. You'll be competing with Hal's!"

"Yeah, but a little competition is good, right?"

Just then, Taylor noticed his dad waving them over and people moving into the auditorium to take their seats. Taylor and Trad quickly ended their conversation. After a few minutes Taylor, Marcia and Mr. Hanes were led to the chairs down in front. Taylor was surprised at the number of people there, but then he remembered that his parents had lived in Tartan for many years. By now, many people had known his mom from her job at the school and his dad from servicing their cars. Moreover, Tartan was a small town, and people somehow considered attending a funeral one of the few forms of entertainment that were available. It was a chance to see people they hadn't seen in a while and reconnect with them.

The service was conducted by Pastor Robbins of the Methodist Church. This was the same pastor who had leered at both Taylor and Alan at Hal's restaurant last summer, believing them to be gay, and then walked out. Taylor didn't like him for that and wished his father had selected someone else. To make matters worse, Taylor, Marcia, and his dad were all sitting in the front row, directly facing Pastor Robbins. The eulogy was obviously from some preaching book where you fill in the name of the deceased in a preprinted oration. It had no connection to his mother or who she was. The only factual statement that the preacher uttered was his admission that he did not personally know Kathryn Amanda Hanes. At least he was honest about that. But what made Taylor uncomfortable was that when referencing the family, the preacher would look directly at them. Then, at the very end of the eulogy, just before the final prayer, he looked directly at Taylor and leered at him just as he had before. Taylor leered back with aversion. The pastor must have noticed it, because he quickly looked down.

After the service, Taylor spoke to Jessie, who worked with his dad. He also spoke to Trad again and invited him to come over to their house for lunch, but Trad declined, saying he had an appointment. Christine had disappeared, and that was fine with Taylor. There was a brief graveside ceremony, and then the limo took them back home.

Several women had volunteered to stay at the house during the service in case anybody dropped by with food or to express their sympathies. When Taylor, Marcia, and his dad returned, there were huge amounts of food to choose from, ranging from meats and vegetables to breads and drinks. While they ate, Taylor carefully asked his dad how he was holding up, and he responded that he was doing fine. Taylor also asked him about the cost of the funeral and if that was going to be a burden on him. His father quickly answered that he had made arrangements with the funeral home to maintain their vehicles for a couple of years in exchange for the service. Taylor knew that his dad had incurred significant expenses during his mother's illness, so this news came as a relief.

They spent the rest of the afternoon talking to several groups of people, mostly friends of his dad, who had dropped by to express their sympathies. Dinner was a repeat of the earlier meal. A couple of hours after that, Marcia, Taylor and his dad said they were tired, and decided to go to bed.

Taylor hugged his father and asked, "Are you going to be all right?"

"I'll be fine, son. What about you?"

Taylor tried to answer that he was fine, but he began to choke up and released his grip on his dad. With tears in his eyes, he managed to say, "It's a lot to take."

Chapter 37

Happy and Sad

Tartan never changes. I can come back here after I graduate from college or even ten years after that, and it will be exactly the way I left it except maybe more rotting wood and peeling paint and fading signs. Nothing ever changes except for people dying. Now my mom is gone. My mom is gone, and I know it's a terrible thing to say, but I'm thankful since it has been so hard to see her decline. I can tell that Dad is relieved. I guess he just wants to get on with his life. Nevertheless, I loved my mom dearly. She was the best mom anyone could have. She gave me so much and taught me so much and cared for me so much. And I know Dad really loved her. But it was so very hard to watch her turn into something—very slowly turn into someone else that was not my mom. I'm sure Dad felt the same way. It must have been so much harder on him dealing with it every single day. It makes me love him even more.

I regret not returning home more last semester, but there was so much going on and going home took up such a big chunk of time. As soon as I got here and saw my mom and did a few things and went to bed and got up, it was almost time to go back. By that time, I was getting behind in what I needed to do. And I wanted to be with Marcia.

I don't miss anything about Tartan, and at the funeral, I knew I would never be back here again except to see Dad. I definitely miss Dad and think about him a lot.

It was good to see Trad and learn that he seemed happy and had some direction in his life, and it was good to see Jessie, who still worked at Dad's garage and who seemed to be happy with his life. He looked well. He told me that Alan had met a guy from Raleigh and had moved there and they were both going to open a florist shop and that he also seemed happy. I didn't miss Christine at all or the town or Pastor Robbins or any of the other people in town that looked down on me with their small, narrow minds. I am so happy I don't live here, yet I am so sad. Happy and sad.

Chapter 38

One Who Lied

Marcia and Taylor arrived back on campus on Sunday evening with just enough time to get in a few hours of studying. Taylor tried to read an assignment, but he kept getting distracted by thoughts of his mother and father. He needed to get his work done but didn't seem to be making any progress.

Around nine o'clock, Taylor picked up his phone to call his dad to check up on him and was alerted with a beep indicating someone had left him a message. He punched the code to retrieve the message. The electronic voice stated that the message was left on Friday, March 15 at 3:30 p.m. Then the message began, "Hello. Taylor, this is Jeff Black. I need to talk to you right away." This was followed by several seconds of silence as if Mr. Black were trying to figure out what to say; then the voice resumed. "Uh . . . anyway, call me as soon as you get this." And he hung up.

Taylor wondered what this was all about, but Mr. Black's office wouldn't be open until the following morning. Taylor had three classes in the morning, so the call would have to wait until tomorrow afternoon when he got back to his dorm. He continued with his call to his dad. Their conversation was brief, but Mr. Hanes assured Taylor that he was fine, and Taylor felt better hearing that. He hung up and started getting ready for bed.

On Monday, at 1:30, Taylor called Jeff Black. Marlene, his secretary, said Mr. Black wanted to see him in person. She set up an appointment for Taylor for the following day.

The next morning, after his first class, he was shown into Jeff's office. Jeff was sitting behind his desk and did not get up. Without even a greeting, Jeff pointed to the chair in front of his desk and said, "Close the door and have a seat." Taylor sat down and looked straight at him as Jeff reached for a file on the credenza behind his desk. "Taylor, some significant information has been brought to me that might impact your scholarship."

Taylor stiffened at this. Jeff's voice had a severe tone, unlike the friendly and casual tone he usually had. "We have learned that you spend most of your free time with a—one particular female student and, according to our sources, you spend the nights with her also." As he talked, he would glance down at the file and then up at Taylor. "And just so you know that we have some reason to believe this information, our source has provided numerous photographs of you and this student together. And from what I can tell, you are very . . . intimate with this person."

Taylor was shocked, unable to speak. Finally, he was able to eke out a word. "Photographs?"

"Yes, I'm sorry to say that it looks like someone was spying on you. I assure you, it was not us. We have treated you in good faith. However, it is my responsibility as the administrator of the trust and of this scholarship to monitor all recipients to make sure the requirements of the scholarship are . . . upheld."

Jeff looked up with a stern face and locked eyes with Taylor. Taylor wanted to shout that this was a lie, that he was doing well in school and he deserved to be here, that his mother had just died and he needed some sympathy. But he couldn't say anything, partly because he didn't know what to say.

After a few moments, Jeff flipped open the file, revealing a stack of photographs. He picked up the top one and positioned it on the desk in front of Taylor. It was a black-and-white shot of Taylor and Marcia, seated in an auditorium with their heads leaning against each other. Then he showed Taylor another photograph, this one of Taylor and Marcia giving each other a kiss in the Courtyard, apparently upon meeting there. This was followed by another photograph of them kissing while lying on a blanket on the lawn in the sun. Then he threw down several others of them in the cafeteria and several of them at local bars, in which Brad and Alex were included. Taylor's shock gave way to anger that someone was spying on them.

Then Jeff said, "Of course, this doesn't necessarily mean that you are not gay, but . . ."

After a few moments of seething silence, Taylor raised his hands in a relenting gesture. "All right!" Taylor began. "I'll tell you everything. I've . . . I've been feeling really guilty about this from the beginning, but I don't know, and there were several times I almost called you to tell you that it was a lie and that I'm not gay. But school was going so well, and it was everything that

I expected and more, and I met Marcia . . . that—that's her, . . . and we hit it off, and things were going well, . . . and . . . who—who took these photographs?"

"That doesn't matter, Taylor." There were a few moments of silence as Jeff collected the photographs and put them in the folder and back on his credenza. "Your tuition and board for this semester have been paid, but everything else from here on out on your scholarship is terminated. No reimbursement, no stipend, and this ends your scholarship from here on out. No scholarship for the rest of your time in school."

"Look, I've been fulfilling the requirements of the scholarship. I've learned so much about how gays have been discriminated against. I've done a lot of personal research, and I've been doing everything I can to help with the situation."

Jeff shook his head. "I'm sorry, Taylor, but from a legal standpoint, what you did is fraud. You were pretending to be somebody who you aren't."

After several awkward moments during which no one said anything, Jeff stood up and extended his hand. "Taylor, I wish you the best of luck."

❀ ❀ ❀

That night, Taylor met Marcia and Alex for dinner in the cafeteria. While occasionally glancing around the room looking for someone with a camera, he explained the whole situation of losing his scholarship. As soon as he mentioned the photographs, Marcia and Alex both exclaimed, "Dinah!"

"Dinah?" Taylor asked.

"Dinah Scott," Marcia answered. "She must have taken the photos."

"Yep!" Alex added, "Damn it!" Then he just stared ahead with his mouth open.

"Dinah Scott?" Taylor asked.

"Yeah," Marcia answered. "I've seen her with a long lens, and I've seen her with some sort of canister in the bathroom, developing some film. No question. I'm so sorry. I feel that this is my fault."

"Who's Dinah Scott?" Taylor asked.

Marcia answered, "She's that tightass bitch that was assigned as my roommate last semester. Oh God! She did this to get back at me. I feel so bad. I'm so sorry."

"No," Alex said, "it was my fault. She tricked me!"

"What do you mean?" Marcia asked.

Alex shook his head. "I can't believe this. Several months ago, I saw her in the hall with the camera, and I started kidding around with her, pretending to pose and stuff like that. And she started to flatter me and told me she needed a model for her photography class and wanted to know if I'd be interested. And I thought, sure, it'd be a good way to start my portfolio for when I need to apply for jobs, so we went to talk some in the TV room. And then I should have known. The talk, all of a sudden, turned to you guys. She was asking me all these questions about you two, and . . . and I guess I spilled the beans about your relationship, and I guess I even mentioned you were on the Pembroke gay scholarship. Then the bitch just kept putting me off, and eventually she said she couldn't do the photos. I'm so sorry, Taylor. I feel so stupid."

"Don't . . . no, no," Taylor said while waving away the thought.

"I need to get back at her," Marcia said. "Maybe a witch's spell."

"You wouldn't do that!" Taylor exclaimed.

"No, I wouldn't. So, what are you going to do? You can finish out this year, right? And maybe apply for some other funding."

"Yeah, I think I'll be all right this year. I've actually saved some money from the stipend, and there's only a month and half of school left, so I'll get by." Then he smiled and added, "You'll feed me."

She returned the smile and said, "Of course I'll feed you. Even if it will be beans every night, I will share. I'm so sorry. This is my fault."

"And," Alex added, "I'll do anything to help in any way I can. I feel so guilty. It's my vanity that got me in trouble."

"No, no. It was totally my doing," Taylor replied. "It's particularly tough at this point with losing Mom, but in some way, I feel better having come clean. After all, I was the one who lied."

Chapter 39

Mixed Emotions

The scholarship is gone. That's a given. In some strange way, like I told Marcia and Alex, I'm happy that I'm not living a lie anymore. In other ways, I'm sad. It's going to be tough financially, but I will not give up. I'm going to make it through Carolina one way or the other, even if I have to work my way through school or take semesters off to earn money. I'll make it happen.

I went to the Financial Aid Office to see about other programs or scholarships. The lady was nice, but as soon as she pulled up my record, she noticed the reason I had lost my scholarship . . . that I had lied when applying for the scholarship. That was on my permanent record. She said it would no doubt hinder my getting other scholarships, but I would also need to wait until the summer for other applications because presently they are processing incoming freshman scholarships for next fall. She pointed out that I could always take out a government loan, and, of course, I could go to school part-time and work my way through school.

Everyone is feeling for me. Marcia is encouraging. Alex too. Brad said he was sorry, but I also got the impression he was never happy I lied. And I very much respect his feelings. He offered to do everything he could to help me find another scholarship and said he would keep his ears open for any part-time jobs.

I haven't told Deedee. One thing: I want to keep using Castlewood and the library and continue looking for an answer about Damien. And another thing: I don't think she knows that I was on a gay scholarship. I think all she knows is that I'm on a scholarship funded by Pembroke. She knows I'm with Marcia all the time and never seems suspicious. She likes Alex and Brad. She wants to help Pembroke. She's a sweet lady who I would have, for some reason, difficulty telling that I lied. And in reality, she probably wouldn't care, or if she did, she would forgive me.

Another thing: I'll have to tell Dad. This certainly isn't a good time with all that he's gone through. He will be upset, but likely he'll be more upset that I lied than that I lost the scholarship. But maybe he'll be happy to know that I'm not gay. I guess most dads and moms would be happy about that. Overall, I guess he will be like I'm feeling now: filled with mixed emotions.

Chapter 40

End This Vileness

Carrying a pile of textbooks, Damien entered Bernard's dorm room, turning the knob while pushing the door open with his foot.

Bernard stood in front of the dresser without reacting as if he had been expecting him. He was looking in the mirror while putting on a tie. Damien placed his books on the desk with a sigh and said, "Hello. It's Friday, thank God!" He then slumped down on the bed.

Bernard didn't turn around, frustrated with the difficulty of getting a good knot in his tie, and started over.

"What's the matter?" Damien asked.

"Oh, it's Father. He's back from Atlanta and wants me to give a c-command performance at the dinner table."

At first, Damien was quiet and didn't respond. Then he said, "So our plans for tonight are canceled."

Finally having affixed the tie to his satisfaction, Bernard turned around and responded with a bit of anger. "Yes, damn it. This is the last thing I want to do, but the old man's b-been out of town traveling a lot, so I'll be a good son."

Damien looked disappointed. Bernard eyed him and pursed his lips in a kissing motion, adding, "Unfortunately, I may have to spend all day Saturday and Saturday dinner with him too. We'll see."

"Saturday too! Maybe this would be a good time for me to meet him?"

Bernard shook his head. "No, no, not yet."

"We don't have to tell him anything. Just introduce me as a friend. A good friend."

"Let's wait. I've g-got to judge his mood. I—I just d-don't know."

Damien was quiet for a moment as Bernard gathered a few toiletry items and clothing and put them in his briefcase. "So, what will you be d-doing? Maybe you could go out with some of the Players people."

"I don't know. I've got a literature paper. I'll get a head start on that. Maybe even complete it."

"That would be better. I don't want you to have too much fun. Especially since I will be so miserable. Damn, I'll miss you." There were a few moments of silence as Bernard reached into his dresser drawer and pulled out a square jewelry box and offered it to Damien. "Here, I've got you something."

Damien, surprised, took hold of the box and opened it. Inside was a gold watch. "What is this? For me?"

"I didn't want you to be sad, and I wanted t-to give you something."

"I've never had a wristwatch." Damien nervously took it out of the box and opened the leather band, ready to put it on.

"It's inscribed on the back. Read it first."

Damien turned it over and read it while squinting. "Yours is what you desired, loved, fought for. B.P." He sat for a moment, looking at it; then, in a stroke of recognition, he exclaimed, "Mahler's Second! Fifth movement!"

"Very good," Bernard responded. "I think it sums you up."

"It's beautiful! What a surprise," Damien said as he jumped up, ready to hug Bernard, but Bernard quickly held him back and glanced out the window. Bernard placed his finger to his lips to hush Damien and waved him over against the wall so they couldn't be seen from the outside. "Shh!" Bernard whispered. "Sounds carry down the hall."

"Oh, you are always so careful. All these guys like me. And you too! They're a friendly bunch."

"Damien, I don't think that is true. To your face, and my face too, they p–pretend to be friends, but behind our backs, they are something else."

"No, I don't—"

"Especially," Bernard interrupted, "in the South. My mother t–taught me that . . . and I believe she was right. We have to be c–careful!" He grabbed him by the shoulders and looked intently at him. "You p–probably can't imagine how you have changed me. Before I met you, I was like you said, a hermit t–trapped in this room. B–but you showed me that there's this whole other world out there that I would never have explored. That airplane flight, getting me to join the musical, and—and when we went to see the Mahler symphony a few months back. I would never have g–gone there or experienced such wonderful sounds. And when I sat there in the darkened auditorium with you by my side, experiencing new discoveries, I knew this was right and I . . . I don't want that to end."

"I don't either. I don't want it to ever end."

Bernard turned away and added, "But we'll have to be careful, and we'll just have to give my father more time. He would not accept this easily . . . if at all."

Bernard walked to his father's house, which took about fifteen minutes, and as he approached the front door, it opened. Standing there, holding the door, was Charles, a forty-year-old man who served not only as chauffeur of Bernard's father but also as his business assistant, butler, and caretaker of the house. Charles had been with the family for over twenty years, having been hired by Bernard's mother as their chauffeur and caretaker. After she died, Bernard's father expanded his duties to include helping with the business. Bernard genuinely liked Charles and respected him for his kind nature. The two of them also shared a common empathy. Charles had lost his wife nine years ago, within months of when Bernard's mother had died.

Setting the briefcase down, Bernard shook Charles's hand and patted him on the shoulder.

"How are you, Charles?" Bernard asked.

"Good, and you, sir?"

"Fine, and how is Father?"

Charles leaned over and softly whispered, "Not in the best of moods. He's in the dining room, waiting for you."

Bernard went directly to the dining room. The door was already open, so he walked in and could see his father's seated silhouette against the large, leaded glass window. His father was sitting at the end of the long dining table, reading a newspaper.

The sun was setting behind him, and the light filtering through the trees and glass almost created a mystical aura about him, a thought that Bernard at this moment found to be ironic. His father was not at all mystical but down-to-earth and realistic.

"Father," Bernard said while approaching and raising his hand to shake. His father looked up, shook his hand with a scowl, and leaned back in his chair.

"Is something the matter?" Bernard asked as he sat down in the first chair to the right of his father. His father didn't respond, so Bernard added, "Am I late?"

Finally, his father answered. "You're not late." Bernard could hear his father move his foot toward the call button underneath the table, followed by the muffled buzz in the next room, a signal that it was time to bring out dinner from the kitchen. Bernard spotted a crystal decanter with red wine sitting in front of them and an almost empty glass sitting in front of his father.

His father reached for the decanter and asked, "Wine?"

"Sure." Bernard knew his father was not opposed to drinking but found it unusual to see him have any except on special occasions such as Christmas or a wedding.

"So, what is all this? Why are we eating in the dining room instead of the kitchen?"

Bernard's father rotated the glass in his hands, causing specks of reflected window light from the cut facets to land on his father's face. He spoke slowly, almost solemnly. "I don't know. We have this big dining room, and we never use it anymore. The market has gone wild with my investments, the business is unbelievable, yet I never enjoy the benefits of all this wealth. It was different . . . when your mother was alive. She would always plan these large dinner parties. This table would be full. But now . . ."

At that moment, the door from the kitchen swung open. As Charles held the door open, a black woman, dressed in dark blue with a maid's apron and a maid's bonnet, entered carrying a large tray. It was Clara, who served as both the cook and maid.

"Hello, Clara," Bernard said. "How are you?"

"Fine, Master Pembroke. It's been a while." She uncovered the dishes and set them in front of Bernard and his father. She added, "And how has college been going? I've missed you."

"The food is not as good, Clara, so I've missed you, too."

Clara chuckled. "You do look mighty skinny."

"Clara, I prefer to call it lean and fit."

Clara turned toward Bernard's father and asked, "Will there be anything else?"

Bernard looked down at his plate, which consisted of nothing but a thick piece of round roast and a few potatoes. "Just meat and potatoes?"

Clara held her hand over her mouth in embarrassment. "Oh, I'm sorry! I was cooking for your father. Oh dear, I didn't buy any vegetables. We have some canned peas, but you know what they're like. . . . Wait a second. I just remembered I brought a big bag of lettuce from my garden. I could make you a salad. It's fresh out of the garden."

"No, Clara, I couldn't take your food."

"Well, lawsy me, I have bushels. It's coming off like manna from heaven."

"Well, all right, Clara, if you're sure."

Clara turned and rushed back to the kitchen, flicking the chandelier on as she went through the door.

Bernard turned back to his father. With the light on, he noticed his father looked older and heavier, yet it had only been three or four months since he had last seen him.

"Father, you should c-consider eating more greens. I know you say potatoes are vegetables, but you need some g-greens. It would be good for your health; not always m-meat and p-potatoes."

His father just grunted, took a gulp of wine, and began to cut his meat.

After a moment of silence, Bernard spoke again. "So, what do you think of this new legislation b-being submitted by some representative from Hoke County b-banning the teaching of evolution in p-public schools and, I guess, public universities?"

"Poole."

"What?"

"Poole," his father repeated. "Representative D. Scott Poole. I know him."

"Oh!"

"It's difficult for me," his father continued. "I can't get involved. On the one hand, I've got a contract to build a large Baptist church on the edge of Raleigh. On the other hand, I'm involved in putting up several buildings on campus here and at State. Harry Chase, the president of the university, spoke against it at the legislature the first time it reached them. This university is full of freethinkers."

That last comment, Bernard thought, was derisive. He knew his father wasn't religious, but that seemed like he was for the law banning the teaching of evolution.

After a moment of no conversation while cutting off a large piece of meat, his father added, "For business reasons, I have to stay connected to these legislators. They control the money." He plunged the meat into his mouth. While chewing, he looked at Bernard and added, "Speaking of connections, which fraternity did you pledge?"

"I haven't p–pledged a fraternity, Father."

"God damn it!" his father loudly growled. "You're almost through with your sophomore year! It's important for business purposes." He shook his head back and forth as Bernard squirmed in his chair. "I can see that when I die, Pembroke Construction will all just go down the toilet."

"F–Father, I just d–don't have any interest in fraternities and those p–people. They're all, well, . . . superficial people. Well, that's not fair. They are very social people, and I guess that's fine. Look, I've b–been making good grades in my c–commerce courses."

In a calmer voice, Bernard's father asked, "So, what else have you been doing? Still in the rowing club?"

"Yes, we're really having a good year. We topped Duke and State and Clemson."

"Wonderful; what else?"

"Well, the usual: c–classes, p–papers, lots of reading." Bernard didn't want to mention his involvement with the theater and decided he would try to change the direction of the conversation.

"So, Father, you mentioned some university c–contracts. Which ones are you working on?"

"We have some of the construction on the new library. The legislature has allocated $825,000, but I hear rumors that Governor McLean is going to pull $200,000 of that back, but still a sizable amount. We're competing for more of that money.

We've got some bids in on some dorms. And you know we did the field house for the new stadium and are still doing some details on that. I don't know if you know it, but the new stadium seats over thirty-three thousand people. Emerson only seated four thousand. This is bringing in a lot more money to the university and improving the prestige of our team. Many large schools had refused to compete with us before, because the gate receipts were so small."

"Wow! Thirty-three thousand. I knew it was b–big. I walked over to it several weeks ago."

"You didn't go to any of the home games?"

"Well, no. I've been very busy."

"Humph!" Bernard's father grunted.

Bernard continued, "Uh, speaking of football, the star quarterback, T. G. Howe, is in my dorm, four rooms down, and I've gotten to know him quite well."

"You?" Bernard's father reacted in surprise. "You're friends with a football player? You have no interest in football. Obviously."

"Well, T. G. and I have other interests in common." Bernard immediately regretted saying that because he knew his father would ask about those other interests, and he didn't want to explain that the common interests were popular dance steps. Fortunately, Clara came through the door with a large green salad and placed it at Bernard's place setting, interrupting the conversation.

"Clara," Bernard's father said, "the carafe is empty; we need more." She grabbed the carafe and went into the kitchen.

"So, where are you getting this bootlegged stuff?" Bernard asked.

"It's French. One of the senators smuggles it in."

"Really?"

"No doubt," Bernard's father continued, "this senator is running a highly profitable and illegal importing and distributing business."

"No doubt," Bernard agreed.

"I spoke to Dr. Pendlegraff the other day." There was a pause, and Bernard stiffened, wondering where this was heading. "And he said he noticed that you have been involved in, unbelievably, a music event. A musical revue or some other nonsense like that." Bernard sat quietly, clenching his teeth. He was angry and knew that if he spoke, he would just stutter. "What is this all about?" his father asked with apparent irritation in his voice.

"Nothing. It was c-called a jazz revue. And I s-s-sang s-some s-s-songs . . ."

"Damn it! Just spit it out!" Bernard's father shouted. "You sound like a snake. I spent suitcases of money for speech correction and—and sent you to this university, and you still have that problem. For God's sake, just spit it out. Just say it!"

Bernard was highly shaken and just barely able to swallow the last bit of greens he had just eaten.

"I also heard," his father continued, "that you're spending a lot of time with this fellow named Damien. Damien Holdrich."

Bernard, now furious, pushed his chair away from the table. "W-what is this? Am I b-being spied upon?"

Bernard's father clanged his knife down on the china, looked him straight in the eye, and replied, "Yes!" He added, "When your mother died, I thought you'd be more manly because she tended to baby you, but I was completely wrong." As his father continued, Bernard, astounded by what he was hearing, sat there incapable of replying. "I know this may be a university with a lot of liberal ideas, but beyond that, it is my home, and it's where I get a good portion of my business. It's also a small Southern town with lots of people with very narrow views. Why the hell didn't I send you to State?" After pausing a few seconds, his father continued. "Who is this Damien? Where is he from? A Yankee, right? Worse yet, from New York City!"

"Yes!" Bernard said, almost shouting.

"Who are his parents? What do they do?"

Bernard got to his feet and shouted, "For G-God's sakes, c-can't you l-like someone for who they are, n-not for who their p-parents are and w-what they d-do?"

His father stared straight ahead, grimaced and grabbed his chest as if in pain, and grunted out, "That's not the way the world works."

Noticing his father's discomfort, Bernard asked, "Are you all right?"

His father relaxed and let his hand reach for his wine glass. "Where is that wine? I'm fine."

"Good!" Bernard blurted out, and turned and walked out of the dining room just as Clara entered the room with a full carafe. As he approached the front door, Charles raced to open it for him.

"Nice seeing you, Charles."

"Same here, sir," Charles replied as Bernard exited.

Bernard's father poured himself another glass of wine and said to Clara, "Get Charles in here."

She left to get him but stopped when he entered the room. "Mr. Pembroke wants you."

Charles approached Bernard's father. "Yes sir."

"Charles, do you remember Benjamin Atkins, the private investigator we hired to do some investigation when we were being sued for that construction project?"

"That project in Atlanta?"

"Yes, that one. Would you set up a phone conversation between him and me. Call him sometime in the morning, and if he's available, I'll talk to him then."

"Yes sir. I'll call him right after breakfast."

"Good; maybe he'll be able to help me end this vileness."

Chapter 41

Maybe We'll Never Know

"Taylor, this is Deedee." It was half past three on Friday afternoon, and the telephone had just awakened Taylor from an hour-long nap.

"What?" Taylor slurred as he rubbed the side of his head.

"It's Deedee Delaney. I'm sorry, did I . . . did I wake you?"

"It's all right. I was just taking a nap. Rough week. Staying up late."

"Oh, I'm sorry I woke you."

"No, no. That's okay. I needed to get going. What's up?"

"Well, I . . . . I wasn't sure you'd be over here at the castle anytime soon, and anyway, I've discovered some letters and information regarding Damien Holdrich. I think they might help us learn what happened to him . . . . at least what was going on at that time."

"What kind of information?"

"Well, it's a report written by a private eye, hired by Bernard Pembroke Senior. It tells about the investigation of Damien's mother; then there's a newspaper clipping from New York City."

"Wait a minute. I just remembered Marcia and I and Alex were going to go out to a free movie on campus tonight, so maybe we could swing by there and take a look at all this. We could be there by around five. Would that be all right?"

"That would be perfect."

Taylor called Brad, who was available and offered to pick them up. Once they arrived, Deedee ushered Taylor, Marcia, Brad, and Alex into the upstairs library. As she began to speak, they sat down around a library table, and she laid out three yellowed typed letters, a newspaper clipping, and a large accounting ledger.

"You know, I have looked through every file that I could think of from Mr. Pembroke's file cabinets—and there are numerous files—searching for clues. I only found ancillary information that more or less reinforces what we already knew about Damien." As she aligned the documents side by side, everyone started to examine them. "But then I began thinking: Bernard Pembroke Senior was alive and well at the time that Damien went missing. Well, presumably he was well. He died several years later, but he was at the height of his business, so maybe he had something in his records relating to Damien's death. Also, at the time in the Twenties, being a homosexual was far less acceptable to society than it is today, even though it was the Roaring Twenties, when society's norms were a bit relaxed. It still wasn't something as tolerated as it is today."

They all sat there interested in what she was saying but wondering where this was going. Alex jumped in. "Hardly even open today. Here at a liberal university, somewhat more open, but you get outside of town and into the Bible Belt, and it's a whole different story."

"Absolutely," Deedee agreed. "Well, I thought maybe Mr. Pembroke Senior might not have approved of his son's leanings if in fact he even knew about them. So I thought it would be prudent to spend some time looking over his papers for something. Unfortunately, there was no diary or anything like that, at least that I'm aware of. But I did find three very interesting letters."

Deedee picked up one of the yellowed letters and then looked up. "First, here is a short letter addressed to one Dr. Pendlegraff from Bernard's father. I looked up any information I could find on Pendlegraff. He was a professor in the History Department but also served on a student counseling committee and must have been a friend of Bernard Senior. This is a typed carbon copy. Evidently, Mr. Pembroke Senior preferred to type all his letters, even his personal correspondence. Also, he must have typed this himself because there are several words where he made a mistake and he just x-ed it out. I doubt a secretary would have done this. It is dated February 1, 1928."

```
Dear Edward,

        I am writing this to solicit once
again a kind favor from you that will no doubt
impinge upon your valuable time.  But I have
not been able to find any alternative, so I'm
hoping that you will be able to comply.

        My son Bernard and I have grown
increasingly distant, and our failure to
communicate has become increasignngly more
apparent.  Part of this is because of the
```

nature of my very busy schedule and me being
out of town on business. However, whenever I
call him on his dormitory phone, it is always
reported to me that he is out of his room with
no knowledge of his whereabouts.

I have been very frustrated with him
in many ways, and as I've voiced to you in the
past, he doesn't seem to be progressing in the
right direction. For example, even with all
the ~~extneens~~ive coaching I've provided for his
speech problem, to this date, he seems to show
no improvement. I know you have offered in
the past to check in on him as a favor to me,
so I am asking you at this time to please do
so.

I am interested in knowing what his
activities are outside of class and the
fellows or ladies with whom he may be passing
his time.

I've attempted to call you to ask you
for this, but it seems your life is very busy
as is mine, and I didn't want to force you to
keep trying to return the call. So I thought
in the long run, a letter would be more
effice~~i~~ient.

Please give my kindest regards to your
lovely wife, Hilda.

> With highest regards,
> Bernard

"So," Deedee said as she laid the letter down, "what do you think of this?"

"Obviously," Marcia quickly jumped in, "Bernard's father was spying on him."

"And obviously," Taylor added, "Bernard wasn't very close to his dad."

"I agree," Deedee said. "Now let me get to the next one." She picked up the second letter and looked it over. "It would appear this is a typed letter from Bernard Pembroke Junior to Damien. It's not dated, so we'll have to guess when it was written. And strangely enough, like these other two, it was found in Mr. Pembroke Senior's file, labeled 'Bernard,' along with school records, information on Bernard when he was in high school and college, and several reports from speech therapists. And yes, evidently, Bernard Pembroke did have a severe speech problem when he was young. So, this is the letter purportedly written by Bernard."

```
Damien,

        What we had was great.  It was fun.
And after having spoken to my father and given
it much thought, I concluded that it was
simply that--fun.
        There really can be no future for us.
Society would not approve of our relationship,
and it would be too great a struggle on a day-
to-day basis.  In retrospect, I've felt you've
led me in a direction that is actually alien
to my nature and in a direction I should not
have gone.
        Additionally, my father has built a
highly successful and lucrative business.  I
want to be part of that ongoing progression
and share the benefits of that business, and I
can't see myself walking away from it.  I want
to be able to pass this legacy on to my
children and future generations.
        Consequently, take this letter as an
indication that I am completely and
permanently ending any relationship between
us.  At your convenience, remove all of your
personal possessions from my room and slip the
```

```
key under the door.  Please respect my
privacy, and I request that you avoid any
future contact with me.
     All the best to you.

                    Sincerely,
                    B. P.
```

"Wow!" Alex remarked.

"B.P.?" Taylor asked.

"Yes," Deedee said, "that's the way Bernard Junior always ended correspondence, at least with people he knew. His father was more formal and used the full Bernard Pembroke or just Bernard."

"Let me see that," Taylor said. Deedee handed it over to him. "This is a carbon copy, right?"

Deedee replied, "Back then, letters going out were usually typed using carbon paper, and then the carbon copy was filed away. However, the interesting thing, as I mentioned, was that this was in Mr. Pembroke Senior's file cabinet. So—"

"So," Marcia interrupted, finishing Deedee's sentence, "chances are Bernard Senior wrote the letter!"

"Yes," Brad added, "that makes sense. And probably had it delivered to Damien."

Taylor spoke up. "Both these letters were written on the same typewriter. I'm not an expert, but look at the way the capital P has kind of a crack in it. It appears in both letters. It's got to have been written by the old man."

"That," Deedee said, "is exactly the conclusion that I came to. After all, if you were writing a Dear John letter, would you type it and keep a carbon copy? Most likely, you would handwrite it. So I concluded that Bernard Senior must have

written this letter to try to get rid of Damien." Everyone in the
room was nodding in agreement.

Brad asked, "Could it be that Bernard Senior took it even
further?"

Alex added, "That's what crossed my mind. That maybe he
had him done away with."

"Wow!" Marcia said. "That's certainly possible."

Deedee continued, "Well, let me continue. Now we have to
believe that Damien must have been distraught to read this, but
that's not all. The third letter, which is the original." She lifted
up the typed letter. "It is written by a Mr. Benjamin Atkins to
Mr. Bernard Pembroke Senior. I looked up Atkins's name in the
accounting ledger and found that he had done some work for
Mr. Pembroke in 1925. Apparently, he was a private investigator
from Atlanta, hired to find out some information relating to a
lawsuit where Pembroke Construction was being sued.
Incidentally, his investigative information was instrumental in
getting the lawsuit dropped. And then there was another
accounting ledger item relating to this letter, dated April 7,
1927. Pembroke had written and mailed a check apparently days
after this letter. So let me read this to you." She began reading.

Dear Mr. Pembroke,

Per our telephone conversation of the morning
of March 10, 1927, I have been investigating
the background of a gentleman by the name of
Damien Holdrich, now attending the University
of North Carolina. The purpose of the
investigation, as requested, is to bring his
background to light.

In this investigation, I searched for his
previous and current employment, his family

```
members, pertinent social acquaintances and
any previous criminal activity that any of
them had been involved in.  I was able to
obtain a significant amount of information
through contact with coworkers, the assistance
of people in the local police borough and
various public records, as well as university
records.  Below are my findings.
```

Deedee set the letter down on the table and said, "So this is confirmation that Mr. Pembroke knew that Damien was involved in his son's life and was investigating his background."

"Oh, my God!" Marcia exclaimed.

"Go on," Taylor urged. "Keep reading." Deedee continued.

```
According to the university, Mr. Holdrich's
home address is 120 West 28th Street, New York
City.  I arrived there by train and then
summoned a cab.  For point of reference, this
is a neighborhood at the edge of a section
popularly called Tin Pan Alley.
```

"Tin Pan Alley!" Alex interrupted. "So much great music originated in Tin Pan Alley."

"Yes," Deedee agreed. "He even said as much." She continued reading.

```
Tin Pan Alley is the common name of the
section where there are a lot of musicians,
song writers and music publishers.  There are
also some illegal bars, speakeasies, and
gambling establishments.  Mrs. Holdrich's home
address is a third floor walkup in a
neighborhood that is populated by people
employed in some of these establishments, such
as singers, dancers, musicians, and card
dealers.  There are also a significant number
of women who are prostitutes, although their
```

pimps appear to live in wealthier
neighborhoods. Overall, the tenement
buildings in the area had an uncomfortable
feeling of squalor, occupied by immoral
degenerates, and not a single church was to be
seen anywhere nearby.

Marcia, Taylor, and Alex chuckled at this. Brad said, "Obviously, a little Southern religious prejudice was being injected into this report. But, nevertheless, this is filling in a lot of detail."

Deedee continued reading.

After inquiry with several sources, it was
determined that Damien's mother, Hannah
Holdrich, lived alone at the West 28th Street
address and apparently had raised Damien as an
unwed mother. Most sources said that Damien
was illegitimate and not even his mother knew
who his father was. When asked if Mrs.
Holdrich was a prostitute, one person replied,
"Aren't we all?"

Most sources said that Mrs. Holdrich was the
woman of a daddy, a man 25 years her senior,
named Allen Pitts, although they suggested he
rarely came to her place of work. Allen Pitts
was regarded as a man of means, having owned
several hardware stores and gas stations that
he has sold in the last ten years. Mrs.
Holdrich is known to have occasionally stayed
at his home, located on the Upper East Side.
This investigation did not determine his exact
address. Mr. Pitts apparently aided Hannah
financially. I later confirmed through the
University of North Carolina that Mr. Pitts
had paid Damien Holdrich's tuition for his
first year in school.

Hannah Holdrich worked at a speakeasy called
Thanks as a singing/dancing performer and

```
headlined with several other acts.  She billed
herself most recently as Hard Hearted Hannah
and used the popular song as part of her act.
In the course of my investigation, I was able
to see her performance.  She appeared to be
very young-looking to have been the mother of
a nineteen-year-old.  Also, she was blessed
with a nice chassis and a talent for singing
and dancing.
```

"Chassis!" Alex remarked.

"God, this guy," Taylor interjected.

Marcia added, "Yeah, he didn't even get the significance when the person responded, 'Well, aren't we all prostitutes.'"

Brad spoke. "Well, this guy was from the Bible Belt, and seeing New York City life, maybe for the first time, might have been a big shock to him."

"Okay," Deedee said, trying to get them to settle down and listen. "This is really the tragic part." She continued reading.

```
Once I had confirmation that the speakeasy at
which she was employed was an illegal
establishment patronized by local reprobates,
I felt it was my duty to report this to the
local police, which I did.  They graciously
accepted the information. After a week and a
half during which they did nothing to close
this place down, I spoke to the Chief of
Police myself.  I told him that the newspapers
would certainly make a lot of it if they knew
that the police were turning a blind eye to
all that was going on under their noses.  By
the evening of the following day, they had
made a raid on the bar.
```

"Most of these raids," Brad added, "were faked. The police were in on the deals and warned the proprietors that they were coming, and they would hide all the booze."

"Exactly," Deedee added. "Now listen to this."

```
In the course of the raid, apparently a member
of the mob started firing at the police, and
the police started firing back.  Several
people were killed, including Hannah Holdrich.
```

"Oh, no!" Marcia wailed.

"It was all this guy's fault," Taylor said.

"Yeah," Alex agreed. "He caused her death."

"He wasn't at all remorseful," Deedee said. "Listen." She continued reading.

```
I've included newspaper clippings about this
event.  This all proves that if you live a
life of decadence, you end up paying for it
one way or another.

Attached is an invoice for my services.  In
addition to my fee, it itemizes all my
expenses, including any money I paid to loosen
their tongues and the costs of transportation
and room and board.

With kind regards,
Benjamin Atkins
```

"Oh my God," Taylor said. "This must have devastated Damien. First, he thinks Bernard has given him the shaft, and then his mother is killed. Two big losses. Losing your mom is bad enough. I lost my mother. At least my dad is still around."

Marcia put her arm around Taylor and gently pulled him closer.

Brad asked, "Do you think Damien ever learned how it happened? Back then, communications were a lot slower and less reliable."

"Yeah," Marcia added. "I could just see Damien trying to call his mom and the phone just ringing in an empty apartment for days."

"You know," Deedee said, "this was about the time that Damien suddenly goes missing." She got up and pulled a file from a cabinet drawer. "Here. I copied a short article from the local paper dated, well, this is several months after the end of the semester. It mentions that a missing person report had been filed for Damien Holdrich, and that's all. He must have completed the semester because there are grades recorded for Damien. We can speculate that a neighbor or somebody informed the university that Damien's mother had been killed and asked them to contact Damien. There are no records of Damien after that."

Taylor spoke up. "At that point, Damien had no living relatives, presumably, and no connection with anyone other than Bernard and maybe his mother's sugar daddy. And the university probably had a history of students who just dropped out after their freshman year, for various reasons . . . couldn't take the pressure of school, money problems, girlfriend problems, family problems, . . . who knows, and they just never returned."

"Well," Deedee said, "this does say a police report was filed. Presumably, I guess it was Bernard who reported him missing."

"So," Brad interjected, "what we know now is that at some point after classes were over, Damien probably learns two things: one, that his mother has been killed, and two, that his lover Bernard is giving him the boot." Everyone was quiet as he continued. "So, logically, wouldn't you say Damien must have returned to New York? He probably wanted to make arrangements for his mother; school was over, and his personal relationship with Bernard had ended."

"Yeah," Taylor agreed. "I guess, then, he could have gone missing in New York or anywhere in between. Maybe we'll never know."

Chapter 42

Appeal to His Vanity

It was Thursday afternoon, the day of Alex's audition, and Marcia and Taylor found their way into the practice room where the representatives from the various dance troupes would be evaluating prospective interns. The room was a typical large dance studio with floor-to-ceiling mirrors and barres attached to three walls. There were several rows of metal folding chairs arranged in a small arc. Each chair in the first row was labeled RESERVED, obviously for the representatives.

Numerous students in tights, mostly female but also a few male, were positioned around the room, warming up and going through dance steps. There were also a half-dozen adults dressed in regular clothing. Taylor and Marcia immediately spotted Alex at the far end of the room; he easily stood out among all the others because he was tall and muscular. He was stretching against a barre and going through some steps. He saw them come in and acknowledged them with a thumbs-up. They sat down in the second row and waited for a few minutes.

"Look at Alex," Marcia said. "He makes all the others seem like the aliens from *Close Encounters*. They're all so petite."

Taylor chuckled. "Yeah, he's so much taller and heftier. Do you know what music he settled on? I know he was stressing out on that."

"Yeah, he's really stressing out about this whole thing. I don't know what he finally decided."

"So, what's all this about a spell? Did you cast a spell to help him do better?"

"God, he's asked me about four times. I've never seen him so worked up. But to answer you—no—for two reasons. I don't believe it's proper to use a spell for something like this. I mean where would it end? Next, it would be a spell to pick the right lottery number. A witch's power is not to be used for personal gain. And . . . the second reason is I didn't know of any spell that was appropriate for that. Aunt Zena always said that it is best to just give the person as much confidence as you can to let them know they can do it on their own."

For a few moments, Taylor considered this in silence. He finally said, "So, you led him to believe there was a spell."

"Well, . . . well, yes. From the way the conversation went, if I want to be truly honest, he thinks there is a spell in place."

It wasn't long before the first row began to fill with the representatives from the various troupes. A man directed all the contestants to stand in an area to the right of the judges and wait for their names to be called. He faced the small audience and welcomed everybody to this year's internship tryouts. He introduced himself as one of the dance professors in the school.

Then he introduced each person in the front row and asked him or her to stand up.

The first was a woman from the State of Mississippi dance troupe. Next was a woman from the Birmingham, Alabama dance troupe, followed by a gentleman from Seattle. Then there were a woman from Minneapolis and a man from Philadelphia. Several people at the end of the row were assistants to the representatives and were not introduced.

The professor called the name of the first contestant, a small young woman who stepped forward and handed an audio tape to an assistant to the professor. Each contestant was required to go through a prescribed set of steps using a movable barre that had been placed in front of the representatives, followed by a choreographed one-minute solo in the style of their choice. The young woman went through her prescribed steps. Then, after a brief pause, she signaled a person to start playing the tape, and she began her routine. The judges all scrutinized her every move. After she finished, they vigorously took notes.

Two other young women performed their auditions after her, followed by a young man. His routine was faster and more rigorous than the women's routines, circling the room with more leaps. Then, after two more women, Alex was up.

He moved through the standard prescribed set of steps and then signaled the assistant to start the music. The music started with clashing cymbals, followed by a quick, rapid-beat percussion that varied slightly in tempo. With this brisk rhythm, he moved through some classical ballet steps interspersed with a contemporary interpretation, with his body bending low to the floor from one side and then from the other. This was followed by several rolls on the floor, rising up to full height, several back bends supported by one arm, and then numerous spins on one leg. Following this were several traditional leaps interspersed with traditional footwork. As the pace of music quickened for about ten seconds, he went into the classic "turn and leap" several times in a wide arc around the room. From there, as the music volume built, he worked back toward the audience and rose in a soaring grand jeté, the large leap, in which he appeared to be momentarily suspended by some unseen force as the music seemed to hit seven beats while he was in the air. As the music ended, he finished with a scissor leap, landing in a one-knee position; then he rose to a full stance with one arm up.

Taylor and Marcia looked at each other with their mouths agape. The representatives, who had been thoroughly attentive to what they were viewing, immediately put their heads down to take notes. There was one more audition by a woman; then the professor asked the contestants to leave the room and invited the guests to partake of some refreshments set up on the side of the room. After a fifteen-minute break, the contestants would be called back into the room one by one for an interview session with the representatives.

Marcia decided to go to the table and get some water while Taylor went to the restroom. While Marcia was there, she heard bits of conversation between two women, one a representative of one troupe and the other apparently her assistant: ". . . true, but this is what people come for. He has all the physical attributes . . ." followed a little later by comments from the assistant that Marcia couldn't hear.

She edged closer to listen. "At his age, he may not get better," the representative said, followed by more comments from the assistant.

Then the representative said, "He seems to lack the rhythm, spatial awareness, and expressiveness, yet he has that physicality that will appeal to audiences."

Overhearing this bothered Marcia. Having studied some dance, she had also noticed that Alex wasn't as fluid as the other students. However, she felt he had more than made up for it with the variety within his one-minute solo and the strength and energy he had displayed.

When Taylor returned, Marcia told him what she had heard. Taylor exclaimed, "I think I heard a similar discussion with that man and woman over there when I was in the hall." He inconspicuously pointed out one of the male representatives and the woman he was talking to. "They were talking about awkward moves; then they said something about muscular build, so that must have been Alex. Then the man said something like 'I don't care if he's a klutz and a gelding; that's what people come to see.'" Marcia winced, and after a few seconds, Taylor asked, "What's a gelding?"

Marcia chuckled. "You certainly weren't raised on a farm. It's a castrated horse."

Taylor smiled and added, "That's what I was afraid of. So, are we going to tell Alex?"

Marcia thought; then she said, "Let's just wait and see if he gets any offers. There may be no point in saying anything. This pisses me off. It's just like the theater. No matter how good an actress you may be, they evaluate you on your looks first. It's just not fair."

"Hey, wait a minute; you're very nice-looking!"

"Thanks, but you know what I mean. The bubbly, cute blondes and all that."

"Yeah. Well, were you planning to stay for the interview?"

"No, they're open to only the representatives and the students, so let's go."

Later that night, while Marcia and Taylor were studying in her room, there was a knock on the door. It was Alex.

"Great job, Alex," Taylor said as he held the door and Alex walked in. "I was amazed."

"Good job," Marcia said. "When will you know something?"

Alex leaned against the wall, his head down. Then he smiled and said, "I already do. I got three offers."

Taylor's eyes met Marcia's. He said cautiously, "Three! Well, congratulations."

"Yeah," Marcia quickly added. "Congratulations."

"I guess your spell really worked," Alex replied. "Thank you!"

"Oh, Alex," Marcia said. "It was really you. You just needed that extra confidence boost. So, which offers did you get?"

"Alabama and Mississippi, neither of which I'll consider, and Philadelphia."

"So," Marcia responded, "you have options. That's great. Did they tell you right after the interview?"

"They asked everyone to stick around. Then they called several of us back for a short discussion with the representatives that were interested. They gave me a week to decide. The Philadelphia representative talked to me first, so when I met with the Alabama and Mississippi representatives, I told them no right off. They were taken aback for a moment, and I told them that their states were too deep in the Bible Belt and consequently weren't gay-friendly. When I told them that, they all looked disappointed and agreed and said they understood.

One did argue that I shouldn't punish the troupe because of the rest of the state. But that didn't swing with me."

Marcia looked directly at Alex, and in a serious tone, she asked, "Is this really what you want? To be a ballet dancer? I thought you were interested in musical theater."

Alex's face went blank. "Well, I . . . well, . . ."

Taylor and Marcia looked at each other. Then Alex continued, "I don't have to give them an answer for a week or so. So I can think about it."

"Good," Marcia replied. "You don't want to start down a road and find out it's not what you should be doing. So think hard about it."

After Alex left, Marcia whispered angrily to Taylor, "I knew they would do this. They just flattered him to get him to join their troupe."

"Yeah, I think you were right. It was all designed just to appeal to his vanity."

Chapter 43

Faith Does It

When I saw Alex seemingly floating in the air, it did seem almost magical. And I do believe he was able to do it simply because he believed Marcia had conjured up some sort of spell that allowed him to do it. Plus, he had the physical ability to pull it off. The reality was that he lacked the internal faith to believe in himself and do it on his own when he was perfectly capable of doing so. The power of faith. I guess faith healers exploit this all the time. People can really see or walk or do other things, but, for some reason, their faith or lack of faith prevents them. Then it takes the power of someone else to make them believe that they can see or walk.

Marcia and I have a dilemma: Should we tell him that the representatives from the dance troupes didn't think he had that much potential? That they want him on the stage only because he looks good and will draw a bigger audience? We don't want him to pursue a path that may not be right for him. Yet, I guess if he has the desire, he could become better, and maybe that is his path. And should we tell him that there definitely was no spell, he had it in him all along and he just lacked self-confidence? How's he going to take all this? Would all this just confuse him even more? I think it's better to let him figure it out for himself. But then again, should he have guidance from people he knows and trusts to help him along?

Pembroke stuttered, and even though he had numerous teachers working with him, he couldn't overcome this. Yet, somehow, in college, he did overcome this, maybe because of his lover Damien, and even got recognition in the speech club. Marcia also tells me that Aunt Zena helps many people who come to her with problems. Many of these problems are easily solved by Aunt Zena simply telling them they have the power and to just try. Just try! Faith does it.

Chapter 44

Let's Begin

It was another Friday night, and Brad, Taylor, Marcia, and Alex met at Harry's to have a few beers followed by supper. Taylor hadn't wanted to join them, because he was trying to save money, but Brad, Marcia, and Alex insisted and said they were buying since Taylor recently had a birthday. In addition to enjoying each other's friendship and winding down a busy week, they were also there to plan their strategy for finding out what had happened to Damien. As they sat in a booth, Brad spoke while pouring their first beers from a large pitcher.

"We know that Bernard's father didn't approve of Damien, and I guess there's this possibility that he could have had him killed. After all, people feel very strongly about homosexuality, and in their warped minds, they could justify it."

"Okay," Taylor responded. "Then there's that Jesariah Jones."

"Right," Brad continued. "There's Jones. And I look at it this way: Our only real connection to the past is Wilma Mae Devins."

"By 'real,'" Marcia quickly interjected, "you mean not supernatural."

"Correct," Brad conceded.

"But," Taylor added, "I know you mean she is the only one alive from that time period, but she is, you know, not completely there. That caretaker at the group home says that Wilma Mae is always somebody else, sometimes even part of the royal family."

"I know," Brad said, "but I was hoping that maybe with the proper hints or suggestions, she could—I don't know—maybe remember some of the things that happened."

Alex chimed in. "First of all, we don't know for sure that Jones guy was definitely connected to Damien being missing. And she was only seven or eight years old, so she may not remember anything or may not have even seen anything."

"But," Marcia quickly inserted, "getting back to that word 'real.' You see, I think that we can use the afterlife to help us get our answers. And I think that Wilma Mae might be what we need to spark the connection with the right spirits in the afterlife."

"Okay," Taylor said as he looked at Marcia. "I'm not sure how that would work."

"All right," Brad said. "I'm told I have a very open mind, but this may be going a little—"

"Well," Marcia interrupted, "it's like this. I'm not sure I can explain. But it's a shot in the dark anyway. What I was thinking is that we can call for some of Wilma Mae's relatives—you know, her father or mother—and ask them questions. They might present themselves if she is there. And another thing: From my viewpoint—and I'm not a psychologist—Wilma Mae seems like someone who is very troubled herself because she might possibly have seen something. And—"

"And maybe," Alex interrupted, finishing her sentence, "that's why her mind makes her into someone else, because she can't tolerate her being herself."

"Exactly," Marcia agreed.

"She saw something," Brad mused, "that, subconsciously, her mind could not deal with. I can see that."

Taylor nodded in agreement as he sipped his beer; then he said, "So, we need to get to Wilma Mae again."

Their pizzas arrived and interrupted their conversation, but after a few bites, they resumed plotting their strategy. They would get Wilma Mae next Saturday, take her to Castlewood, and have another seance there.

❈ ❈ ❈

It was a demanding week for Marcia. In addition to her usual coursework, she had taken on the task of arranging the whole scheme of getting Wilma Mae out of the group home. In spite of her busy schedule, she was able to borrow some costume accessories from the Dramatic Arts warehouse and put together some details of their plan.

It was late Saturday afternoon, and Marcia, Taylor, Brad, and Alex were all in her car, heading to the group home where Wilma Mae lived. Marcia let Taylor drive because she wanted to tell everyone about a discussion she'd had with Aunt Zena.

"I think most of you have gotten some information from books and movies about why ghosts exist. You know, there's some incomplete business on this earth that they still need to deal with. I discussed this extensively with Aunt Zena. She said that, for various reasons, these souls become stuck between the earthly life and the Otherworld and they are unable or unwilling to fully cross over. Most often, it is due to confusion at the time of death, sometimes resulting from a sudden or traumatic death. Other times, it is because the person is determined to stay and accomplish a particular goal, like watching over a loved one. They don't know that they may be more effective at this if they cross over. Some fear that they have done something wrong and are afraid of punishment in the afterlife, whether they actually deserve it or not, and can be led to believe this because of religious instructions during life. Finally, there are cases where souls are very harmful and evil and they are not permitted to cross over. But even these, Aunt Zena said, can cross over but require the intercession of higher, stronger spirits that can give them guidance to the light. We both agreed that this is most likely not the case in this situation."

"Good," Taylor said. "I certainly don't want to deal with some super evil force. Pembroke was bad enough."

"I agree," Alex said.

Brad, finding this discussion rather bizarre, just sat there silently but absorbed all that was being said.

"So," Marcia continued, "Aunt Zena and I concluded that Pembroke is stuck and hasn't gone over because he has unfinished business. Maybe he's angry because he was gay and society didn't accept him. He did devote a lot of money to helping gays and lesbians with the scholarship program and other things. But we really think his unfinished business was that the love of his life, Damien, was missing on Earth. And then when he started to cross over to the Otherworld, Damien was not waiting on the other side either, so he resisted crossing over."

Everyone was quiet for a few moments. Then Taylor said, "So, this seance we are going to do . . . will we try to find this out?"

"Yeah, hopefully," Marcia answered, "and maybe, with Wilma Mae's help, we'll get some clues about what happened to Damien."

Brad finally spoke up. "You do realize, don't you, that posing as a medical doctor is a serious crime, and all this could not only get us expelled but also jail time."

"Relax," Marcia said. "We'll just have to be careful not to lie to anyone, and we'll be okay."

"I think I've heard that several times before," Taylor joked.

"Look," Brad said, "the caretaker said we could take her on an outing. Why are we doing all this?"

"Well," Marcia answered, "she probably meant an outing during the day, like for lunch. This is in the evening. And besides, I've never played a doctor before, so I thought this would be fun."

After parking in front of the group home, Marcia led the contingent to the front door. She was dressed in a dark blue business suit with low heels. Her hair was pulled back tightly and pinned. She wore dark-rimmed glasses and a stethoscope dangling from her neck, items she had managed to borrow from the Dramatic Arts warehouse. In effect, she was dressed to portray herself as a medical doctor or psychiatrist. Alex was to act as her assistant. To give him a tough-guy look, he wore short-sleeved green medical scrubs, which showed off his biceps, and a tattoo transfer. Taylor and Brad appeared as they had before, as students, but Taylor was carrying a large paper bag.

Marcia rang the doorbell and waited for the locks to unlock. The same woman as the last time appeared and asked, "Yeah, may I help you?"

"Hello, I'm Marcia Templeton. We're here to pick up Wilma Mae Devins for some research and tests."

The woman seemed surprised; nevertheless, she held the door further open and waved them in. "Tests? This late? Nobody contacted me about taking Wilma Mae out."

"What?" Marcia said, feigning surprise. "Didn't someone call you? And I apologize for being so late, but we had numerous patients in this test, and we got significantly behind."

"Nah, no one called, but it's fine; it's fine," the woman responded as she waved them in farther. Upon recognizing Brad and Taylor, she said, "Oh, you guys are part of this research." Brad and Taylor nodded and smiled. Then she noticed Alex standing tall beside her and asked, "And who is this?"

Marcia answered, "Oh, that's Alex, you know, in case we have any problems restraining the patients."

"Wilma Mae is very docile," the woman responded. "You won't have any problem with her. I leave in an hour and a half. When will you have her back? The patients will be eating in about a half hour."

"Oh," Marcia calmly answered, "we will feed her. It's part of the experiment. And we should have her back around nine o'clock."

"Nine o'clock?" the woman replied. "Well, I guess that will be okay. We have a night security guard. Comes in just before I leave. I'll just tell him to expect you to return her then."

The woman then brushed by them and went to the kitchen. Taylor and Brad both smiled and pointed upstairs. Marcia proceeded upstairs, followed by the others. Upon reaching Wilma Mae's room, she removed her stethoscope and handed it to Taylor. He put it into the bag and retrieved a large tiara, which he handed to Marcia. Marcia knocked on the door and proceeded in.

Marcia saw Wilma Mae seated on her bed and said, "Princess Wilma." The woman turned and looked at her inquiringly. "It's time for your chauffeur to drive you to the palace for your state dinner."

The woman just stared at Marcia and the other strangers standing near the doorway. Then Marcia approached her, held out the tiara, and said, "It's quite a formal affair, so you will want to wear your tiara."

"Yes, I think so," the woman calmly responded as she eyed the sparkling tiara and allowed Marcia to place it on her head.

"What about your royal cape, Your Highness?" Marcia asked.

For a moment, the woman looked confused; then she said, "Yes, probably."

Taylor reached into the bag and pulled out a large purple cape fringed with fur. This had been used in many Shakespearian productions, among other plays. The woman stood and turned her back so that Marcia could place it over her shoulders.

"Do you have to potty or anything, Your Highness, before we go?"

Wilma Mae turned around abruptly and said, "I'm a princess. I just went, and I know when to go."

"Yes, Your Highness," Marcia replied while securing the cords of the cape in front. "Well, then," she continued, "your entourage is ready."

Marcia waved Taylor, Alex, and Brad out the door, and they slowly walked down the stairs as if in a procession. Wilma Mae followed, and then Marcia.

As they reached the bottom step, they saw the caretaker looking at them and smirking. "So, a royal night out," she said as she moved toward the keypad to unlock the door.

"Yes," Marcia answered. "Princess Wilma Mae will be attending a royal state dinner."

"Great, Your Highness!" the woman replied mockingly. "I won't wait up for yah."

As they approached the street, Marcia suddenly became concerned that Wilma Mae would react negatively when she saw that the car, rather than being a royal carriage or a limousine, was a beat-up Lumina. But Taylor opened the door, and the woman got in regally, with Marcia taking care to keep the robe from getting caught in the door. Marcia got in on the same side, and Alex went around to the other side and got in. Taylor got in the driver's seat, and Brad got in the front passenger seat. Wilma Mae looked around the crowded car; she turned her head to Alex and then to Marcia and seemed disturbed. "Why is it that you both are riding here, crowding me?" she asked.

There was a moment of silence as everyone looked at each other for an answer; then Taylor spoke up. "Your Highness. It is for security. If anyone tried to assassinate you, these people would block their bullet and protect you."

Marcia stared at Taylor, who was looking at her through the rearview mirror; then she added, "Yes, Your Highness, we would take the bullet."

"Oh, I see," Wilma Mae responded. "Yes. The plot to wipe out the monarchy!"

"You will be safe with us, Your Highness," Alex added.

During the first fifteen minutes of the ride to Castlewood, everyone sat in silence, mulling over how to proceed. Then Marcia said, "Your Highness, I need to go over your agenda tonight."

Wilma Mae just stared at her as Marcia continued. "We will be going to the castle of Lord Bernard Pembroke."

"Lord Pembroke," Wilma Mae repeated as if she recognized him. "Is my crown on straight?"

"It's perfect, Your Highness," Marcia reassured. "Now, before dinner, there will be a large state meeting where you will be introduced to—well, in a very formal way, you will be introduced to some of your family members, more of the royal family."

"I see," Wilma Mae responded. "Royal protocol."

"Yes, royal protocol. These will be relatives that you haven't seen in quite some time."

"Who will be there?" Wilma Mae asked.

"Many will be . . . many are invited, but we are not sure who will show up. Unfortunately, we just don't know."

"The king and the queen?" Wilma Mae asked.

Marcia paused; then she said, "That's a possibility."

Wilma Mae placed her hand on her face as if checking her makeup. She then remained silent for the remainder of the trip.

As they entered the gates of Castlewood, Wilma Mae began to crane her neck to get a better view. The sun was beginning to set, but the sight of the huge, dimly-lit edifice was impressive enough to put a smile on Wilma Mae's face. Taylor drove the car under the porte-cochere and came to a stop. Brad got out and opened the rear door. Marcia slipped out and extended her hand to Wilma Mae. Wilma Mae eased over and slowly exited the vehicle. Alex hurried to the large front door, opened it, and held it open. As Marcia guided her, Wilma Mae slowly proceeded through the doorway, followed by the rest. Inside, standing at attention, were Deedee and Aunt Zena, both smiling broadly.

Marcia rushed toward them and immediately said, "Ladies, please let me introduce you to Princess Wilma Mae Devins."

Deedee and Aunt Zena eyed each other with curious looks; then they both grinned and curtsied.

"Is everything prepared?" Marcia asked.

"Yes," Aunt Zena replied. "Everything is set up in the library."

"Good," Marcia answered. "The princess and I will first take a look at Lord Pembroke's exquisite grand hall. Then we will take the elevator and meet everyone else upstairs." Marcia took Wilma Mae farther into the large room and pointed out the various decorative details and wall hangings as the others proceeded upstairs.

Wilma Mae looked around for a few moments, then shrugged and said, "Nice, but not much furniture."

"Yes, Your Highness. I believe it's now time to go to the royal state meeting."

In the library, Deedee had placed two large library tables side by side, making one large square table. When Marcia and Wilma Mae entered the library, everyone else was already seated around the square table. Alex announced, "Princess Wilma Mae," and everyone stood up.

Marcia seated Wilma Mae with her back to the door. Taylor sat to the right of Wilma Mae, and Marcia sat to her left. To the left of Marcia were Aunt Zena and then Alex. To the right of Taylor were Brad and then Deedee.

Alex lit candles around the room. Taylor got up and turned off the chandeliers so that the room was illuminated only by the candlelight and the soft glow of twilight from the large library window.

When Alex began to place lighted candles on the table, Wilma Mae got excited. "Fire, oh fire! I'm not allowed to play with fire!"

Zena got up, grabbed the candles, and said, "There is no need to have candles on the table." She placed them on a table at the edge of the room.

Wilma Mae was still eyeing the candles and asked, "Why are we in the dark for this meeting?"

"Your Highness," Marcia replied, "this is a very solemn affair, and it must be calm and quiet while we await the arrival of our other guests. The dim light helps set the proper mood for their arrival."

Wilma Mae nodded as if she understood.

Marcia looked around the table; everyone seemed ready. Then she said, "Let's begin."

Chapter 45

A New Light

Marcia softly spoke. "Now everyone join hands." Marcia and Taylor both reached out and took hold of Wilma Mae's hands. "Everyone, relax and close your eyes. Remove any negative feelings you may have. Once we reach spirits in the Otherworld, you may release your grip on the person next to you and open your eyes and ask questions as you wish."

They all closed their eyes and were silent for a few minutes. Then Marcia spoke in a slow, controlled manner. "Everyone, please relax and let your mind go blank. Let your mind be free from all thoughts. Concentrate on a blank void. Open up your mind and be welcoming to spirits from the Otherworld." There was a long pause as everyone took the time to remove any thoughts from their minds. Then she spoke again, even slower and more softly. "We are here to reach spirits in the Otherworld. We are looking for the parents of this woman who is with us, Wilma Mae Devins. Please come to this table and speak to us."

Immediately, all felt a stirring in the air and a change in temperature. Brad was particularly startled, having never been in a seance before. He quickly opened his eyes but saw only the stirring of the drapes. As Marcia continued with her incantations, Brad closed his eyes once again and tried to concentrate on letting his mind go blank.

Marcia continued. "Gunther Devins, the father of Wilma Mae Devins, are you here?"

Marcia waited for an answer, but there was no response. After a few seconds, she tried again. "Spirits of the Otherworld, we are here with Wilma Mae Devins and are seeking to contact her father, Gunther Devins. Gunther Devins, father of Wilma Mae Devins, are you here?"

"I am here," a soft, deep voice said. "And I am here," a female voice said.

Marcia softly said, "Everyone, you may now open your eyes and release your hands." They did, and all gazed at the window. There, floating in front of the window, were two apparitions, one of a man in loose-fitting farm clothes and the other of a woman in a homespun gingham dress with an apron. Darts of light slowly flicked by the images and all around the room in a gentle, irregular fashion.

Taylor, who was sitting next to Brad, could hear him whisper, "Oh my God!"

When Wilma Mae saw the images, she spoke. "Mommy, Daddy?"

"Wilma Mae," the woman answered, "we are here, your mother and your father."

"I miss you," Wilma Mae gently said. "You left me all alone."

The man and woman didn't reply but slowly turned to look at each other and smiled.

Marcia said, "You are Wilma Mae's parents, Gunther and . . . and what is your name?"

"I am Sarah Devins, Wilma Mae's mother," the woman answered.

"Sarah, Gunther, we have called for you because we are seeking answers about events that happened many years ago. Wilma Mae was perhaps seven years old. There was a young man who might somehow have become involved with your church, and . . . and he ended up missing."

Gunther and Sarah looked at each other. Marcia continued. "Do you know anything about this young man? His name was Damien Holdrich."

There was a long pause as Gunther and Sarah looked at each other; then they bowed their heads. Gunther said slowly, "Reverend Jones had long been disturbed by the sins he saw at the college and in town. He had gathered us to picket the saloon in town to speak the word of God to the sinners inside. Our womenfolk were busy pickin' peas in the field. The other men were either workin' or sick. So it ended up bein' just him and me."

As Gunther continued to speak, all present at the table began to see images and voices of what had happened that day in 1928. The images started with Gunther and Jesariah, holding picket signs, standing outside of a building on the main street of town. Jesariah was a thin, wiry man of average height in his twenties, dressed in faded coveralls. Suddenly, the door of the building swung open, and a large man holding Damien by the back of his jacket shoved him out the door and discarded him facedown on the sidewalk. Damien was deliriously drunk.

Gunther and Jesariah studied the crumpled body of Damien. Then Jesariah said, "Drinking is a sin against God and your own body. Look at this vile, pitiful creature." Jesariah pushed Damien with his boot, rolling him over on his back. "Well, lookie here!" Jesariah exclaimed in a high-pitched voice. "This is that college boy we saw at that theater with the painted ladies. He and his friends are on a fast train to the damnation of hell. Brother Gunther, what do you think we can do for this college boy to make him see the light?"

Gunther thought for a moment; then he said, "Reverend, I don't know, Reverend. Pray for him, maybe?"

"He needs more than prayer. Let's take him to the church so we can straighten his soul."

They gathered him up, threw him in the back of the pickup, and drove to the church. Sarah and Wilma Mae heard the truck approach the church from their nearby house. They left their pea shelling near the sink and rushed to the opened door and watched.

Wilma Mae at the table spoke up. "I remember seeing Daddy and Reverend Jones drag this fella out of the pickup and carry him into the church. He was very inebriated."

Once inside the church, Gunther and the Reverend tossed Damien onto the floor. "Put him in this chair," Jesariah commanded, pointing to an armless straight back chair. They grabbed Damien, but Damien struggled even though he was almost unconscious. "Tie him to the chair," Jesariah ordered. Gunther went outside and came back with rope, which he wrapped around Damien, securing his arms and legs to the legs of the chair with multiple knots.

The Reverend went up to him and started slapping Damien on the cheeks. "All right, college boy. They teach you nothing but falsehoods and the life of depravity. They spit on God's words. Can you hear me, college boy?" Damien's head began to roll as he awakened. Staring menacingly at Damien, Jesariah repeated louder, "Can you hear me, college boy? You rich boys are taught that money, power, and pleasure are what life is about. Well, it ain't, and I'm gonna show you the way to salvation." Jesariah abruptly turned to Gunther. "Gather the others; there's going to be a sermon tonight, an important sermon." "Everybody!" he shouted. "Everybody; women and children!"

Jesariah went to the pulpit and grabbed the Bible as Gunther went out the front. For several minutes, Jesariah flipped through the Bible, softly mumbling various verses as people from the church filtered in from their nearby homes.

Within minutes, Gunther was back with Sarah and Wilma Mae, then a little girl. Another couple came in with their preteen boys, followed by an older couple with gray hair. And finally, a couple in their mid-forties entered. He was using a crutch and walked with all his weight on one leg. They all sat in the pews as their eyes darted between Damien, who sat in front of them slumped in the chair, and Jesariah, who stood to the side of the pulpit.

Jesariah looked over his congregation with his piercing blue-eyed stare and began to speak. "My Brothers and Sisters, I called you here tonight to learn a lesson." There was a long pause as Jesariah crossed behind Damien and raised the Bible he was holding above Damien's head. Then he spoke, shouting and lengthening certain words, "The Bible says the drunkards of Nineveh will be DESTROYED by God and 'they shall be DEVOURED as stubble.'" His tone softened when he quoted the chapter and verse. "Nahum, one, ten." He then continued shouting. "'Let us walk honestly, as in the day; NOT in rioting and DRUNKENNESS.' Romans, thirteen, thirteen. "'they which do such things shall NOT inherit the KINGDOM of God.' Galatians, five, twenty-one."

One man responded, "Amen, brother!"

Jesariah moved a few steps away from Damien; then he paused as he turned and directed everyone with a wave of his arm to Damien. "Here you have, my loving and kind people, my dear brothers and sisters, an example of what our great UNIVERSITY is producing. This BASTION of knowledge, this RECEPTACLE of wisdom that is in our nearby town of Chapel Hill." There was a momentary pause as if he were thinking; then he continued. "Chapel Hill, Chapel Hill; . . . what chapel were they thinking of? There's no chapel for God to reside in or for his word to be spoken. We know how they WARP God's law, TWIST his words for their own pleasure, and even deny his very existence. Why, even today, these so-called denizens of wisdom are working hard to deny the word of God and to bring laws into our schools preventing the teaching of God's love to us. They want to deny the Bible, God's VERY words that state that Man was created in the image of God by God, and say that instead, MAN, through some mystical fantasy, EVOLVED from monkeys!" Jesariah shuffled forward, bent over with one arm arched over his head, mimicking the stance of a monkey. Then he turned and stared at the congregation. "Yes, my friends. MONKEYS!"

Several people laughed, causing Damien to awake with a start, frightened by all the people staring at him.

"But enough of monkeys," Jesariah continued as he moved closer to Damien. "Let's turn to this disgusting rag of a man. Ah . . ." Jesariah gestured again to Damien. "Awake, ye drunkards, to see God's judgment."

"Amen!" the older woman shouted.

Damien, groaning, looked up with reddened eyes at Jesariah.

Jesariah looked down and stared at him with his piercing blue eyes and said, "Look at him. What is this? 'Who hath babbling? who hath wounds without cause? who hath redness of eyes?' Proverbs, twenty-three, twenty-nine." Jesariah turned around, and his eyes suddenly darted toward his small congregation. As he looked from one to the other, he shouted to them, "Is THIS what you want to happen to YOU? You know the Bible says, 'Look not thou upon the wine when it is red, when it giveth his colour in the cup, when it moveth itself aright. At the last it BITETH like a SERPENT, and STINGETH like an adder.'" As his eyes locked on Wilma Mae's, she made a weak attempt at hiding behind the folds of her mother's dress. "You young people, see what this fermented fruit has done." His eyes darted between the two boys and Wilma Mae. "See how this drink of the devil has defiled one of God's creations! You don't want this to happen to you, do you?" Everyone just stared at Jesariah, unmoving. Then, he repeated loudly, "DO YOU?" Everyone shook their heads and quietly said, "No."

Then Jesariah turned his attention back to Damien. Looking at him, he asked, "What is your name?"

Damien rolled his head and mumbled, "Damien."

"WHAT?" Jesariah shouted. "WE CAN'T HEAR YOU!"

"Da–Damien," he repeated more clearly. Then he struggled under the ropes. "Wha . . . what are you . . . why am I tied up?"

"Damien, Damien," Jesariah spouted. He moved in front of Damien, leaned down, and stared directly at him. "You are here, by the grace of God, so that we can help you."

"How—how did I get here? I—I don't feel good."

"We found you thrown in the street. Thrown out of a SALOON. Why, even THEY did not want you." Jesariah shifted his eyes from Damien to his congregation and then back to Damien. "What were you partaking of? The wine of the devil? The demon rum? Is that what you were drinking?"

"No, no," Damien mumbled. "It's—it's just hooch."

"HOOCH!" Jesariah screamed as he walked in a small circle in front of Damien. "Hooch; ah, yes, the evil, vile Devil's liquor you were drinking when I saw you at the theater." He turned to the rest and continued talking while pointing at Damien. "When I first saw Damien, this wretched excuse of a man, he was coming out of their temple of sin, the same temple where they were playing the devil's music, those barbaric and immoral sounds that corrupt our youth, what they call JAZZ, and he was drinking HOOCH! He and his friends and the PAINTED LADIES, all made up in feathers and shiny silks and baubles. As GOD has said, WOMEN should 'adorn themselves in modest apparel with shamefacedness and sobriety; not with braided hair, or gold, or pearls, or costly array; But (which becometh women professing godliness) with good works.' One Timothy, two, verses nine and ten."

He continued talking as he moved around the room, "No doubt, after the demon rum and the devil music, they all fornicated in the lust of their bodies. These ungodly souls corrupted themselves in FORNICATION!" Approaching Damien and staring down at him, he shouted, "IS THAT RIGHT, DAMIEN?"

Not responding, Damien's eyes closed, and his head tilted. Jesariah continued, "'For from within, out of the heart of men, proceed evil thoughts, adulteries, fornications, murders, Thefts, covetousness, wickedness, deceit, lasciviousness, an evil eye, blasphemy, pride, foolishness: All these evil things come from within, and defile the man.' Mark, seven, twenty-one through twenty-three."

"Amen!" one woman replied.

"Please," Damien mumbled, "what do you want?"

"I want you to repent!"

"Repent?" Damien slurred. "What's that?"

"I want you to say you're sorry for all the evil that you have done."

Damien bowed his head. "I'm sorry. I'm sorry for everything. I've done everything wrong. I have."

"Say you're sorry for your drunkenness."

"I'm sorry. Sorry for being drunk."

"Say you're sorry for not living a Godly life."

"I'm sorry."

"Say you're sorry for fornicating with those women."

Damien shook his head. "No. I haven't fornicated with any women."

"You have. Say you HAVE."

"No, I have not. No. I like men."

"WHAT?" Jesariah screamed as he stared intently at Damien. "You LIE with men?"

Jesariah turned to the congregation and locked eyes with each one of them as he said, "He LIES with men." Some of the women were holding their hands over their mouths, shocked by what they had heard. The men sneered as if repulsed.

As he continued looking at the congregation, Jesariah intoned, "The Lord said, 'Thou shalt not lie with mankind as with womankind: it is . . .'" Turning swiftly to Damien, he shouted, "'ABOMINATION'!"

Several people shouted, "Amen!" Another shouted, "ABOMINATION!"

Jesariah swiftly turned to the congregation and commanded, "Sisters, take the children to your houses and order them to remain there and come back to the field of worship."

The mother of the two boys quickly ushered them out the door, followed by Sarah and Wilma Mae.

Once they were outside, Jesariah swung his clenched fist into Damien's chin with all his might, and Damien blacked out. Jesariah turned toward Gunther and shouted, "Brother Gunther, help me carry this filth to the field of worship." Gunther grabbed the front legs of the chair, and Jesariah grabbed the back of the chair, lifting Damien up. They carried him outside to the field adjacent to the church, placing him on a spot that had remnants of charred wood from previous bonfires. The rest of the adult congregation, which included the elderly couple, the lame man and his wife, and the father of the two boys, followed them to the field.

Jesariah shouted to his congregation, "Gather firewood and kindling and place them around this demonic reprobate!"

Gunther immediately went to the woodpile behind the church, but the others stood there, aghast at what they had just heard.

The elderly man approached Jesariah and asked, "What are you doing?"

Jesariah turned to him in anger. "O Brother Elias, do you have doubt in my spiritual leadership? Have I not been ordained to be the shepherd of your souls? Have faith, Brother Elias, for I speak the word of Christ and the Father Almighty."

The man stood there, not knowing how to react. While staring into the man's eyes, Jesariah added, "And remember, as the Bible commands: 'Obey them that have the rule over you, and submit yourselves: for they watch for your souls, as they that must give account, that they may do it with joy, and not with grief: for that is unprofitable for you.' Hebrews, thirteen, seventeen." Continuing his unblinking stare, he added, his voice seething, "Brother Elias, I am one with God!"

The man drew back and turned to his wife. A few minutes later, Gunther returned with a wheelbarrow loaded with split pine. He and the father of the two boys began placing them around the base of Damien's chair.

Damien remained unconscious as they continued following orders and stacked more firewood and kindling around Damien, leaning the materials against him up to his chest. Then the men covered them with branches and dried leaves.

Soon the women returned, and the entire adult congregation stood looking at Damien encircled in wood, kindling, and leaves.

At the table, Wilma Mae spoke up. "I did not listen to my mother. I wanted to know what was happening. I slowly opened the front door and walked toward the field of worship. There I hid behind the water barrel at the back of the church and watched as my father laid wood and leaves around the man tied to the chair."

Jesariah looked into everyone's eyes, one by one, as he slowly said, "The Bible teaches us in Romans, six, twenty-three, 'for the wages of sin is death; but the gift of God is eternal life through Jesus Christ our Lord.' In one Corinthians six, the Bible says, 'Know ye not that the unrighteous shall not inherit the kingdom of God? Be not deceived: neither fornicators, nor idolaters, nor adulterers, . . .'" Gesturing toward Damien, he continued, "'nor effeminate, nor abusers of themselves with mankind, Nor thieves, nor covetous, nor drunkards, nor revilers, nor extortioners, shall inherit the kingdom of God.' I dare say, my good people, this man—no, not even a man—this reprobate, this immoral degenerate, this vile essence of a human, has debauched himself with all these sins!"

Then Jesariah grabbed a box of matches, struck one and looked at the flame. As the flickering fire reflected in his crazed eyes, he said in a muted voice, "How fitting that they call these matches 'lucifers.'"

The flame from that match grew large in Wilma Mae's mind. She watched as Jesariah threw the match on the edge of the dry leaves, which quickly began to burn. He lit another match, walked around Damien, and dropped it on the leaves. Then he lit another and dropped it as he slowly intoned, "God teaches in Leviticus, eighteen, twenty-two, 'Thou shalt not lie with mankind, as with womankind: it is abomination.'"

As the flames began to reach higher, Damien started to come to, but still drunk and unfocused, he did not know what was going on. "I'm sorry," he mumbled. "I deserve to die."

As he struck the last match, Jesariah intoned, "As a vessel of God, I do as he commands: 'If a man also lie with mankind, as he lieth with a woman, both of them have committed an abomination: they shall surely be put to death; their blood shall be upon them.'" With that, he threw down the last match, which seemed to make the flames leap higher.

Now Damien was feeling the intensity of the fire and began to scream. "Stop, no, stop, get me out of here. Help!"

Jesariah turned away from Damien, pushed through his congregation, and abruptly shouted, "Come!"

Unable to endure watching, they followed as he led them back into the church. The older woman cried and buried her head in her husband's shoulder. Jesariah moved to the front of the pulpit. Grabbing a hymnal and holding it high, he shouted over Damien's screams, "We will sing praises to the Lord Almighty. Gunther, play the organ." Gunther immediately sat down at the pump organ and began to pump the pedals as Jesariah yelled out a hymn number. Gunther nervously began to play "Rock of Ages." Sarah's eyes darted from Gunther to Jesariah and then to the stained glass window through which glowed the flickering light from the fire.

Jesariah shouted, "Sing, my beloved ones, sing!" They all began to sing, but Damien's screams could still be heard over the voices and the woman who was now crying louder.

Jesariah rushed over to Gunther at the organ. "Louder. Play louder!" Then turning to the congregation, he shouted, "LOUDER! Sing LOUDER! God can't hear you! LOUDER!" They all complied, and now Sarah and the other woman and her husband were crying. Through the stained glass windows, the flickering light seemed to glow even brighter as Damien's screams intensified. And then Damien was quiet.

Wilma Mae, seeing all of this for the second time, sat there frozen and horrified.

After a few minutes, Jesariah waved at everyone to stop. He stared at the congregation and said angrily through gritted teeth, "'And they shall no more offer their sacrifices unto devils, after whom they have gone a whoring. This shall be a statute for ever unto them throughout their generations.'" He hurried down the aisle and out the front door.

Wilma Mae at the table was crying and placed her head in her hands.

"Stop!" a loud, deep voice rang out through the library. All the images disappeared, and there, standing by the window, was the apparition of Bernard Pembroke with tears in his eyes.

"What madness," he sobbed. "My Damien . . . tortured and killed."

Everyone was quiet for a few moments as they recovered from what they had just witnessed. Then Marcia, with tears streaming down her face, spoke up softly. "We are all sorry for your tragic loss and understand that it must be heart-rending. For my part, my own heritage, having lost many ancestors in such a way, makes me empathize even more with your suffering."

Brad spoke up. "Ask him when . . . when was the last time he saw Damien alive."

Pembroke started to answer before Marcia could open her mouth. "The semester was over. With great struggle, I had decided not to continue hiding from my father my relationship with Damien and who I was. Damien and I had agreed that we would remain together even if my father disowned me. If that should happen, we would go first to New York and then on to Paris where society was more open and accepting.

"But then Damien learned that his mother had been killed. From there, everything seemed to happen so quickly. We agreed he would take the first train to New York, and I would talk to my father; then I would take a later train and meet him there.

"When I told my father everything, he went insane and said he never wanted to see me again. I left the house and went to the bank to withdraw money for the trip, but my father had closed my accounts, and I had no money. It was several days before I could scrape together enough money from various sources to pay for the train ticket.

"When I got to New York, Damien was not there. His mother's friend had decided not to wait any longer and had the funeral for Damien's mother.

"Damien never did arrive. I waited in New York for a week and told his mother's friend that I needed to get back to look for Damien. That gentleman helped me financially to get through this period.

"I later found out Damien had purchased the ticket to New York but had never used it. From that moment on, I used every resource available to find him but turned up nothing.

"Charles, my father's assistant, later disclosed to me that he was the last one to see Damien alive when he delivered a letter to him from my father. Because of your research, I now know what the letter said and what my father did, something for which I will have great difficulty ever forgiving him.

"With all my resources, I searched for him in the earthly world, and I searched the spiritual world, and Damien was nowhere to be found. Until now, I didn't know what had happened to Damien."

Marcia, still with tears streaming down her face, glanced at Zena, who tilted her head in response, then at Taylor, who nodded, and then back at Pembroke. She said, "Perhaps we can, in some way, summon the spirit of Damien and try to find out where he is."

Pembroke did not answer but simply lowered his head and disappeared.

Marcia began, "O Spirits of the Otherworld, those who lead us and guide us, grant us some guidance tonight."

After a few moments of silence, Zena leaned toward Marcia and whispered, "Ask for Ariel. She helped us before."

Marcia nodded and spoke. "O Ariel, who have guided us in the past, please come to us. Help us this night."

After a few moments, Marcia added, "Ariel, Ariel, are you—"

"I am here," a frail, unsteady voice interrupted. "And what do you wish of me?"

"Ariel, thank you for responding. Ariel, you have helped us find spirits who have left this earthly world but have not continued to the Otherworld. That may be the case with a spirit we are seeking tonight."

"Whom are you seeking?"

"His name is Damien Holdrich, son of . . ."

Marcia groped for the name of Damien's mother, and Deedee prompted, "Hannah."

"Yes, his name," Marcia repeated, "is Damien Holdrich, son of Hannah Holdrich and the love of Bernard Pembroke."

"Yes, I know of Damien Holdrich. He is a sad, broken soul."

"Could we contact him? We wish to speak to him."

There were a few moments of silence; then Ariel spoke. "I've communicated with Damien, and he will not come forth and will not speak. He seeks to maintain his distance from all spirits."

Marcia looked at Zena, then at Taylor, then at Brad. All were expressionless, not knowing what to do. Then Taylor spoke up. "Pembroke hasn't gone over because he had unfinished business. Ask Ariel to ask Damien why he hasn't gone over."

Marcia smiled and nodded at Taylor. "Ariel, please go to Damien. Ask him why he has not crossed over to the other side. What is keeping him in his spiritual state?"

"I will ask," Ariel replied.

In a few moments, Ariel spoke. "Damien said he wishes to be left alone."

Taylor leaned over to Marcia and whispered, "Tell her to tell Damien that the letter he received from Bernard while in the earthly world was not written by Bernard."

Marcia looked back at Taylor and then glanced at Aunt Zena, who whispered, "It's worth a try."

"Ariel," Marcia said, "please tell Damien that if he received a letter from Bernard in the earthly world stating that he wanted to end the relationship, it was not from Bernard. It was written by his father to break them up. Tell him that Bernard has been searching for him for decades and . . . and loves him."

Ariel responded. "I am here to help spirits cross over. I will do as you ask."

In a few moments, a darkened entity appeared before the group. Its shape was unlike a human form, irregular and grayish in color.

A voice spoke from the form. "After I learned of my mother's death, I bought a ticket for a train leaving that afternoon for New

York City. While I waited at the station, the platform was packed with students who had completed the school year, all catching the train home. They were happy, laughing with friends. Many of the fellas were saying goodbye to their girlfriends. Everyone was lighthearted. They were hugging and kissing each other, knowing that they would see each other again soon when the summer break was over. As I sat there, thinking of my mother, with tears running down my face, someone approached me and handed me a letter. It was from Bernard. He was breaking off our relationship. I could not believe it and went to a phone booth to call him. His phone rang and rang, and no one answered. I lost sight of where I was. It was like I was nonexistent. The train left without me. In my oblivion, I wandered across the street into a speakeasy and began to drink. The afternoon turned into evening. I remember that later there were people who were trying to make me realize what a bad life I had lived. They said that I didn't deserve to cross over, and if I did, I might be punished for eternity."

"Ariel," Marcia said, "Bring us Bernard Pembroke."

"I will summon him," Ariel responded.

"Damien," Marcia continued. "First, you are a good person, and those people you met at the end of your earthly life were doing evil deeds to you. They abused you and killed you, for which their souls will have to account. You did nothing wrong."

Just then, Bernard appeared, but he was not the middle-aged man they had seen before. This time, he had the appearance of Bernard when he had been in college.

Damien asked, "The letter I received on the last day of my earthly life was not written by Bernard?"

Upon hearing Damien speak, Bernard brightened and said, "Damien, is that you?"

There was no response. Then Bernard added, "I did not write any letter to you. Please, please let me see you."

At that moment, Damien appeared but seemed to convey a sense of profound melancholy.

"Damien!" Bernard said with excitement. "I looked for you ever since we had parted. I looked for you in New York and the rest of the world. And you were not to be found."

Damien looked at him, and after a moment, he said, "I wanted to disappear. I had hurt you, and I had lost everything, and I had sinned against the universe. The life I had lived had caused me to be damned."

"No, Damien," Bernard replied. "You never, ever lost me. And you never, ever hurt me or did anything wrong. I want to be with you!"

Damien replied, "Bernard!"

Bernard extended his hand and said, "Come, we've lost some time, but we've found each other again."

At that moment, both their images began to glow brighter and slowly moved toward each other. As the images met, they merged into an even more brilliant light that rose up slightly and then disappeared.

Ariel spoke. "They have crossed over. The spirit world wishes to thank all of you."

"And," Marcia replied, crying again, "Ariel, we thank you for your help."

Alex immediately got up and turned on the lights.

Marcia, with tears running down her face, looked around the room and gave a big sigh while smiling at everyone. Then she turned to Wilma Mae and asked, "And how are you doing?"

Wilma Mae, still with tears in her eyes, thought for a moment before answering. "Fine. Fine. You know, I haven't felt this good in a long time. A long, long, time. I can . . . see everything in a new light."

Chapter 46

Hand of the Enemy

Marcia was still very agitated and drained after the seance, so Zena took control of the situation. "Everyone, everyone, please! Please give me your attention." They all looked at her as she continued speaking. "It's important that we record what we have just seen. So, Deedee, if you could supply us with pen and paper, I want each of you, as concisely as possible, to jot down what you have just observed."

"Good idea," Brad said. "We should write it down before we discuss any of this." Deedee went to a desk, pulled out a pad of paper and a handful of pens, and began to distribute them.

Zena continued, "Don't say anything to each other at this point. When we have all finished, we can talk freely about it."

Everyone, including Wilma Mae, began to write on their individual papers. After several minutes, when everyone seemed to be finished, Zena asked them to sign their notes, which they did. Then Zena gave them permission to speak. As they were beginning to share their images, Brad went around and collected their papers. When he reached Wilma Mae's, he stopped, took it and said, "Hold it, everyone. Wilma Mae has summed it all up." He held up her paper, which had large scrawls on it, and read it aloud. "'I saw Preacher Jones kill a man with fire. Signed, Wilma Mae Devins.'" Everyone was silent as they stared at Wilma Mae, who sat there staring straight ahead with tears in her eyes.

Brad continued, "I know Sheriff McCullen. I was concerned about going to him with information that we got from a seance. But with this . . ." he said, shaking Wilma Mae's writings, "and all your statements, I may be able to convince him to get a search warrant for some investigation at the church."

Nearly everyone had recorded on paper virtually identical accounts of what they had seen. The one exception was Marcia. Besides seeing what everybody else had seen, she had seen a historical montage of every one of her witch ancestors who had been burned. In a flash, she saw and understood the history leading up to the accusations, the details of each trial if there had been one, and the execution by burning. Brad, however, asked her to write an account without reference to witches, which Marcia reluctantly did.

As soon as he could make an appointment, Brad was in the sheriff's office with these accounts and carefully explained what they had seen. As it turned out, the sheriff had worked on a missing person case ten years before that involved the use of a psychic to supply evidence. That evidence eventually led to the capture of a man who had abducted and killed a twelve-year-old boy.

Brad also had the sheriff speak to Wilma Mae, who was now exceptionally lucid and able to detail where Damien's remains had been buried. The sheriff was very familiar with Jesariah Jones and his church since Jones and his congregation had repeatedly picketed theaters, concerts, abortion clinics, bars, and even funerals. The sheriff didn't have much respect for him and had no reservations about searching his property if he could get a search warrant from the judge. Fortunately, the judge was the same one involved in the conviction of the man who had abducted and killed the boy and was willing to give some credence to information derived from the seance. But the real clincher was the testimony of Wilma Mae.

Two days later, Sheriff McCullen, with a search warrant, two deputies, and two workers arrived at the church, followed by Brad, Taylor, and Marcia in her car.

When the sheriff got out of his car, Jesariah Jones came out of the church, followed by his great-grandson, whom Brad, Taylor, and Marcia all recognized as the man who preached in the Courtyard. The sheriff showed Jones the search warrant, and Jones didn't say a word. Based on information from Wilma Mae, the sheriff and his crew proceeded to an area next to the church and began to use probes and metal detectors. Then they started to dig.

Jesariah and his great-grandson watched them silently. After an hour and a half, one of the sheriff's deputies found something metallic and solid a few feet below the surface of the ground. It was a gold wristwatch with a broken crystal and an engraving on the back with the initials "B. P." Then they discovered human bones too.

Upon seeing this, Jesariah Jones and his great-grandson turned and went back into the church and sat down on chairs near the pulpit. After a few minutes, Sheriff McCullen and a deputy followed them inside, arrested Jesariah Jones on suspicion of murder, and began to read him his Miranda rights.

Jesariah seemed shocked when the sheriff put him in handcuffs. "Why this?" Jesariah asked. "I'm a ninety-two-year-old man of the cloth!" When the sheriff did not reply, Jesariah said, "'Not for any injustice in mine hands: also my prayer is pure.' Job, sixteen, seventeen." As he was led down the aisle to the door, he turned to his great-grandson and said, "'Their enemies also oppressed them, and they were brought into subjection under their hand.' Psalm, one hundred six, forty-two."

Jesariah was escorted to the sheriff's car, where Taylor, Marcia, and Brad were standing nearby. As a deputy opened the rear door, the sheriff placed his hand on top of Jesariah's head to guide him into the back seat. But just as he sat down, Jesariah turned directly to Taylor, Marcia, Brad, and the sheriff. Staring up at them with his piercing blue eyes, he said, "'And I will bring a sword upon you, that shall avenge the quarrel of my covenant: and when ye are gathered together within your cities, I will send the pestilence among you; and you shall be delivered into the hand of the enemy.'"

Chapter 47

Very Busy Next Year

Last week, I had a very interesting meeting with Matthew Sheffield, one of the principals of the law office of Sheffield and Sheffield, which administers the Pembroke scholarship. The paper that I wrote for Sociology class was submitted by Dr. Carrol to The Daily Tar Heel *and was published in early March. It generated a lot of responses, both good and bad, particularly the part about legalizing same-sex marriage. But, as a result, people from other organizations started planning gay rights rallies and scheduling debates. It became a topic of discussion among students, and I see that as a good thing. I was asked to join one of the debates myself, which was a new experience for me. I found that the more involved I got with these issues, the more I felt they were important and the more I wanted to help. But the best thing was that Matthew Sheffield, who had been traveling, finally got to see the article in* The Daily Tar Heel *and recognized my name. He remembered that I had received and then lost the scholarship. After reading my article, he brought to everyone's attention that they should rethink the policy of giving the scholarship only to gay students and also consider anyone who fought for equality for gays and lesbians. Jeff Black pointed out to him that the directive of the trust was specifically written to allow only gays and lesbians. Mr. Sheffield told Jeff that, back in the '60s, he had written the directive for Bernard Pembroke, who was a personal friend and for whom he had done other work. He knew what Mr. Pembroke's intentions were and that someone like me was doing what the directive intended. His reasoning was that he had written the directive and there was no reason he couldn't rewrite it. He also mentioned that it needed to be rewritten to include support for bisexual and transgendered people, which was not thought of when the trust was originally set up.*

So, as a result, I got the scholarship back for the next three years, as long as I keep up my activities in support of gay rights. Furthermore, it turns out that Mr. Sheffield's sister, who lives in Ohio, is a lesbian and a very involved activist. Mr. Sheffield said he hadn't understood what she was always ranting about until he read my article, and then it became clear. And for the first time in his life, he began to empathize with her. Now, he wanted to get involved, too, and since he was practically retired, he volunteered to be counsel to FAI and any other organization that supported gay rights and needed legal advice.

There was already going to be a gay awareness week in October. And now Mr. Sheffield suggested additional programs for this event, including guest speakers, particularly civil rights leaders, movies on civil rights, and in-depth debates on legalizing gay marriage. Of course, he wanted me to be very involved in all the planning of these events. It'll be a lot of work, but I actually look forward to it.

Oh, he also suggested I consider planning for law school, since he thought I had a good legal mind. It has got me thinking about it.

Now that I have the scholarship back, I can afford to go to summer school and get ahead with some of my classes and be with Marcia. She's attending summer school, too, and plans to go to graduate school, so I'm happy that we'll be together for at least three more years. And after that, who knows?

I was reluctant to leave Dad alone in Tartan, but he's been quite busy. He joined an organization for people who have lost spouses, has taken night classes at the community college, and has joined a group that gets involved in outdoor recreational activities. I've even heard him mention a woman in one of his classes, something that has never happened before.

Deedee is doing very well. And wouldn't you know it, I inadvertently fixed her up with a new boyfriend, and their relationship seems to be very strong. Edgar, the older lawyer from Tartan that I got to know at the diner during the summer, wanted to revisit Carolina, where he had done undergraduate work and law school. It had been forty years since he was last here, and he wondered if I would show him around. It was before summer school started, and I had plenty of time, so he came up one day, and I gave him the grand tour. In the process, I took him to Castlewood since it was such an important part of my life as well as part of the history of the university, and we ran into Deedee there. This chance meeting spawned a long-distance relationship, and now both Deedee and Edgar are on the road a lot visiting each other.

Alex has graduated. He didn't take any of the internships with the ballet companies. He said he finally realized that his heart wasn't in ballet and he felt he needed to put more trust in himself and not in what other people told him. So he was looking more at musical theater, which he always loved. He moved to New York, is rooming with a friend, and has already gotten some callbacks for some shows. So who knows, maybe we'll be seeing him hoofing on stage on Broadway.

Brad is also going to grad school and will remain involved with FAI. He also wants me to get more involved with the organization, and I'm sure I will.

So, in the fall when the school year begins, I'll be spending a lot of time with Marcia, working a lot with Matthew Sheffield, and working with Brad and FAI. And, oh yeah, there will be schoolwork, too. Phew, I can see that I will be very busy next year.

The End

O believe, my heart, O believe:
Nothing to you is lost!
Yours is, yes yours, is what you desired
Yours, what you have loved
What you have fought for!

O believe,
You were not born for nothing!
Have not for nothing, lived, suffered!

—Gustav Mahler
Symphony No. 2

Everything About This Novel

Acknowledgements

I wish to thank my beta readers Rhonda Black, Shari Wernow, Robert Lee Scott, Rich Roberts, Jeff Nethery, Julie Walther, Sherry and Errol Bos, Jenny and West Wingate, Terry West and particularly Lori Hammer because of her enthusiasm and encouragement. Great appreciation is extended to Brian Zargham for reading, helping edit, making legal suggestions involving copyright issues and giving feedback on the novel. Also, thanks to his wife, Mallory, for reading the novel and giving feedback. Great thanks goes to Cheryl Lilly and Joel Schnitzer, who were part of my small writing group which allowed me to begin writing this novel. Many thanks to Elliot Engel, Ph.D. who critiqued the novel and suggested changes. Thanks to Amy Cuomo, Ph.D. for her valuable critique. Great appreciation is extended to Brian Karli for all his detailed help on the Jenny aircraft and its operation. It is his plane which the artist used as a model for the cover. Brian has finished restoring this Curtiss JN-4 and regularly flies it. Thanks to Aaron Stark for giving me permission to use his photo of the plane as a basis for the cover. Thanks also to Skip Frostenson for all the valuable information he provided regarding rowing teams in college. And thank you to Matt Hendrick, a University of North Carolina graduate, who advised me on college life during the period the protagonist was in school. Special thanks to Steven D. Litvintchouk, my editor, who made this a much better book. Very, very special thanks to the William Faulkner Literary Awards committee for presenting *Finding Pluck* with the first prize for novel.

Fact or Fiction

Several of my beta readers asked me if all the historical and background information in *Finding Pluck* was true. Here is my answer.

The town of Tartan in North Carolina does not exist, but is based on textile towns that I have known in the state. I did take liberties with the layout of the campus of the University of North Carolina at Chapel Hill where most of the novel takes place. Readers who went to school there will no doubt wonder where the lake and river were when they attended college. Also, they will wonder why they never passed by Emerson Hall which in the book was the old football stadium that had been converted into a dorm. I simply added these things for the purpose of dramatic narration.

All the information regarding the treatment of gays and lesbians in the military and all the examples cited were based on actual occurrences. All the references about laws that discriminated or criminalized homosexuals are factual. Laws cited that discriminated against African Americans or women were fact-based. Examples cited in the book about homosexuality in Fiji society and examples of two-spirited people in American and Canadian Indian tribes are factual. Reference to gays and lesbians in Siberian culture dating back 15,000 years is based on actual research. Practically the only thing that was not true is the existence of ghosts and the Otherworld. But, really, who knows?

Peter Difatta